"All right then. Remember, all you have to say is stop." He moved his hands up, his fingers threading through her hair.

He dipped his head and pressed his mouth to her throat, his heated dew coating her skin there. Her eyes closed. She sighed. His tongue created a lazy circle while his fingers returned to her hair. She heard the ping of hairpins hitting the floor and felt the shifting of weight as he began liberating her bound-up strands. Then the tresses were falling around her shoulders and he was groaning. "Glorious."

Running his tongue along her collarbones, dipping it in the hollow between, before trailing his mouth up her throat to her ear, outlining the delicate shell, and nibbling on her lobe.

With a low moan, she dug her fingers into his shoulders. At an angle, his chest pressed against hers.

"I want to do something terribly wicked to you," he rasped near her ear.

"What?" The word came out on a rushed breath, her back arching slightly, her hips turning toward him as though she needed to be closer to him, absorbed by him.

"Just say yes."

By Lorraine Heath

LORRAINE HEATH

In Want of a Viscount

The Chessmen: Masters of Seduction

AVON

An Imprint of HarperCollinsPublishers

IN WANT OF A VISCOUNT. Copyright © 2024 by Jan Nowasky. All rights reserved. Printed in the United States of America. No part of this book may be used or reproduced in any manner whatsoever without written permission except in the case of brief quotations embodied in critical articles and reviews. For information, address HarperCollins Publishers, 195 Broadway, New York, NY 10007.

First Avon Books mass market printing: February 2024

Print Edition ISBN: 978-0-06-311471-5
Digital Edition ISBN: 978-0-06-311472-2

Cover design by Amy Halperin
Cover illustration by Victor Gadino

Avon, Avon & logo, and Avon Books & logo are registered trademarks of HarperCollins Publishers in the United States of America and other countries.

HarperCollins is a registered trademark of HarperCollins Publishers in the United States of America and other countries.

FIRST EDITION

24 25 26 27 28 BVGM 10 9 8 7 6 5 4 3 2 1

To the Keepers of My Heart,
Dr. Marc Shalek and Dr. Lee Hafen,
as well as the nurses, technicians, staff, and
cardio therapists at
Baylor Scott and White Heart Hospital,
Plano, TX
for their dedication to healing.

And for Nathan,
who has held my heart
for nearly half a century now.
Further adventures await, babe.

In Want of a Viscount

CHAPTER 1

London
July 1875

JOHN Castleton, Viscount Wyeth, more commonly known among his intimates as Rook, pulled the brim of his beaver hat down lower to shade his face as the sentinel standing watch outside the Elysium, a private club for ladies, shoved open the heavy door and allowed him to enter the foyer without any bother. A few years earlier, the club had been a secret, its existence whispered about as one did the existence of elves and fairies—with a great deal of skepticism.

But secrets had a tendency to eventually come into the light. Most certainly his father's had. As a result, he knew a great deal more about the club than most of the men of his acquaintance. He'd been given a private tour of the establishment. After all, his brother—one of his sire's bastards—owned it.

Seeing no ladies wandering about in the entryway, he relaxed somewhat and removed his hat. While the club itself was no longer clandestine, the identity of its members was protected, and he hadn't wanted to recognize anyone he might know or cause any lady of his acquaintance embarrassment. What went on within these walls was considered wicked and could ruin a good woman's reputation if it became known that she frequented this domain of sin, debauchery, and the forbidden.

Obviously recognizing him from other visits he'd made recently, the young female standing behind a counter gave a small bob of a curtsy. "My lord."

"I need to have a word with Mr. Trewlove. Where might I find him?" The guard outside had confirmed that he was in this evening.

"He's making the rounds. I'll send someone to fetch him, shall I, if you'd like to go on up?"

"That would be most appreciated. Thank you."

A short distance from the counter, between the two walls encasing a narrow set of stairs, dangled a red braided rope with a sign hanging from it announcing, *Private. Enter at your own risk.* After slipping one end of the barrier off its corresponding peg, Rook walked through and then secured the flimsy barricade that he knew no one would dare violate. Aiden Trewlove had a reputation for protecting everything he considered his. His dangerous repute more than any bit of woven cord kept people from overstepping the mark.

The stairs were dark but a light at the top served as a beacon. Most of Rook's childhood had been like climbing this stairwell, gloomy and solitary, light and knowledge just beyond reach. While attending Eton, he'd begun to hear about his father's exploits, the Earl of Elverton's ravenous lust, his countless mistresses, and his numerous bastards, the latter two groups spread far and wide over London, and beyond to the farthest corners of England. But the most vicious rumor of all, the most hurtful, the one he'd furiously hated and bloodied several noses over—and had his own bloodied a time or two—was that his mother—the present Countess of Elverton—had been the naughtiest, most lascivious, and most favored paramour of his father before he'd taken her to wife.

Eventually the truth had won out, and Rook now knew that she'd given birth to three of the earl's illegitimate sons. His father had delivered each to a baby farmer, with the hope that they would die as a result of the woman's lack of attention. Many foundlings did. However, Aiden had been given to Ettie Trewlove, a widow who had raised him as though she'd given birth to him herself.

A few years earlier, Rook had met Aiden when the man had saved their mother from being murdered . . . by her very own husband. Rook had never been particularly fond of his sire, but he certainly hadn't envisioned that the fellow responsible for his existence was capable of such a vile act. The earl's brutal encounter with Aiden had resulted in their father barely surviving an apoplectic fit that had left him incapacitated and bedridden.

Rook reached the top of the stairs and stepped onto the landing. Farther down, the corridor had a half wall that allowed one to look out over the main gaming floor, but here draperies provided a hidden alcove. To his right was another set of carpeted stairs that led up to the rooms Aiden had inhabited before he married. Rook knew he sometimes still used them when responsibilities kept him working late, but he'd purchased a small residence where he lived with his wife and son. However, he had his heart set on acquiring a larger estate.

Rather than go up those stairs, Rook leaned against the wall, awaiting Aiden's arrival. He supposed he should be tempted to peer between the part in the draperies to possibly discover who might be visiting this evening, but he believed people were entitled to their secrets. Certainly he had his.

He heard the echo of footsteps as someone dashed up the stairs. In short order, Aiden emerged from the darkness into the light. Even after all this time, Rook was still taken aback by their similarities in appearance: dark hair, dark eyes, strong jaw. Their father's jaw. Aiden was slightly taller and a bit broader, his body having adjusted to the physical labors demanded of him when he was younger. He grinned. "How are you, brother?"

That address also always took Rook a little off guard. He had no legitimate siblings. Before this man had come into his life, he'd known none of his father's leavings. Now he also knew Finn, another of his father's by-blows, given to Ettie Trewlove six weeks after Aiden. Apparently, the earl had possessed an insatiable appetite for bedding women, never content with enjoying one at a time. He'd been unfaithful not only to his wife but to his lovers. "I'm well, but bring upsetting news."

Aiden took a step forward, his brow creasing deeply. "About Mother?"

"No, Father."

"I don't give a bloody damn about that degenerate. He can go straight to the devil as far as I'm concerned."

"It appears he'll be making that journey soon enough. He's taken a turn for the worse."

"Glad to hear it. At least Mother won't be hovering over him and caring for him any longer."

Rook knew it stuck in his brother's craw that their

mother had spent the past three years seemingly devoted to tending to her husband, although Rook suspected she was also tormenting him in subtle ways. He'd overheard her telling the earl tales about her paramour—even though she had no lover. She no doubt wanted him to suffer as she had during all the years that they'd been together when he hadn't been faithful or discreet regarding his numerous affairs. Not that Rook held it against her for wanting a bit of revenge. After all, the earl had set about poisoning her when a younger lady had caught his attention. "Speaking of Mother, she's mentioned that on occasion she's enjoyed some time at your club."

Aiden shrugged. "One of my gents has spoiled her. A foot rub in the Goddess Parlor. A waltz in the ballroom."

"I don't require details."

A small smirk from Aiden followed that comment. No doubt he considered Rook something of a prude because he always directed the conversation away from exactly what pleasures women had the opportunity to experience within these walls. Then tipping his head to the side, Aiden leveled an assessing stare at him. "Since you're here, perhaps you could do me a favor."

"Depends on the favor."

"I'm short a couple of gents tonight. One sent word he was ill. The other, who the deuce knows. However, I have a lady in want of a kiss. She's been waiting for gone on half an hour now, but all my other fellows are occupied. Perhaps you'd be kind enough to oblige her."

Rook had learned early on to hide his thoughts or feelings. Still, it took every ounce of control he possessed not to gape at the ludicrous request. "You mean kiss her?"

"You sound horrified, like I've just asked you to murder her. Yes, kiss her."

"You kiss her."

"I'm married, madly in love with Selena. I no longer give the ladies anything other than a smile or a wink." He jutted out a chin that very much resembled Rook's own. "You're not a novice to kissing, surely."

"Of course not, but I don't give them out willy-nilly. Besides, the majority of your members are of the nobility. She's likely to be someone I know, which could prove rather awkward." He was not in the habit of secreting ladies of the *ton* into hidden corners for stolen kisses.

"Actually, she's American, only recently arrived. What are the odds you've met?"

"Probably none." The couple of American women he knew were either married to peers or being courted by those with ranks above his own. It was highly unlikely the women would risk censure by visiting this establishment where the mothers or sisters of their suitors might catch a glimpse of them engaged in questionable behavior. "Still, it doesn't sit right with me, old chum."

"Look, Johnny . . ." His mother referred to him with that moniker. It was more personal, created a stronger bond. Rook suspected Aiden understood it was better suited to cajoling. "She's a spinster, never been kissed. She's waiting in a private room, her nerves no doubt beginning to fray as the minutes tick by. All you have to do is go in, take her in your arms, lean her back a bit, press your lips to hers, and sigh as though you've never been so entranced. Would that truly be such a hardship?"

It had been a considerable length of time since he'd been with a woman, so while it might not be a hardship, it could remind him of what he was missing and send him in search of pleasure—which he never did hastily because he had certain requirements he insisted be met. On the other hand, delivering only a kiss seemed innocent enough. "What's her name?"

"Haven't a clue. I don't recall ever seeing her here before. Possibly it's her first time to visit. You're dressed finely enough that she's bound to assume you're an employee. You can make up a name for yourself. Be whomever you like. Embrace the fantasy."

"What fantasy?"

"Of being a woman's dream."

"What makes you think I'm not already?"

"If you are, she's a secret. Your exploits certainly don't make the gossip rags."

"You read gossip?"

"It's the best way to know how to keep the elite satisfied. So will you do it?"

Unlike his father, Rook didn't give anything of himself—not even his kisses—to a woman lightly. He possessed a sterling reputation for treating ladies with the utmost respect. He never exhibited any untoward behavior. Never wanting to be likened to his sire, he was above reproach. He never engaged in shenanigans. This request seemed very much like something he ought not do.

Yet, in the farthest darkest regions of his mind, a seductive voice was temptingly whispering, *Where's the harm in being a bit wicked for a few minutes? It's only a kiss.*

"No one will know of this?"

"Absolutely not. Everything that happens within these walls stays within these walls."

"All right then. This once. But don't make a habit of asking me for favors such as this."

"Who knows? With any luck, it could very well turn out to be a favor to you."

WHAT IN THE blue blazes was I thinking?

Leonora Garrison decided that she was stark, raving mad. Or drunk. More likely drunk. She was relatively certain the absinthe was responsible. She'd never before indulged in the green fairy—as some affectionally referred to it—nor heard of it until tonight. However, the name sounded innocent enough, but then the green spirit had cast its spell over her, and she'd had another. Then a third, and with the final glass came the courage to request a kiss.

Hence, she now was sprawled on the chaise longue in this private chamber awaiting the arrival of a gentleman to grant her wish. A maid at the hotel in which she was staying had told her about the Elysium Club and its reputation for fulfilling women's fantasies.

Leonora considered leaving at this very moment to return to that very hotel, but her legs didn't seem to remember how to work. Her bravery was beginning to waver. Especially as she'd been here for some time now. After twenty minutes, she'd stopped glancing at the pocket watch she always kept near at hand. Tonight it was in her reticule. She didn't want to know precisely how long it took them to find a gentleman willing to press his mouth to hers.

At twenty-seven, she'd never been kissed. She

wasn't hideous by any means, but neither was she the delicate flower most men seemed to prefer. Having come from pioneer stock, she was nearly as tall as many fellows she knew, and they seemed intimidated by her forthright approach to life. She didn't mince words, nor did she engage in trifling conversation. She never had fanciful thoughts or partook in fanciful actions. Which was the reason that tonight's indulgence in the green fairy was so baffling. She preferred whiskey. Her father had always treated her as more of a son than a daughter. Perhaps because his son, four years her junior, preferred play to work while she preferred work to play. Which might have also contributed to her lack of suitors.

A light rap caught her attention. She shoved herself up onto her elbows to squarely face what was to come. Slowly, silently the door opened.

A man walked in. She shouldn't have been surprised. After all, she'd been expecting him. Still, he was different than she'd anticipated. More polished, more refined. In spite of the fact that he was wearing ordinary day clothes as opposed to the evening attire in which the other gentlemen here had been dressed, he gave the impression he would be perfectly comfortable dining with royalty. No, it was more than that. Royalty would gladly invite him to do so.

"Hello," he said tentatively, his hand still on the latch, the door ajar, as though he couldn't quite decide if, having seen her, he should bolt back out. "My name—"

"No names," she stated briskly. "No false flattery. As little speaking as possible, if you please."

His eyes widened slightly. They were a dark rich

brown like the chocolate she so favored. He gave a
curt nod. "As you wish."

And closed the door. Apparently, he had decided to
stay, and her heart kicked into a frantic rhythm.

"I was told you're in want of a kiss."

She liked his voice. Deep, a little gravelly, perfect
for whispering naughty things in her ear. Perhaps she
should have started her journey toward sexual discovery with that request rather than going straight to
the intimacy of a kiss. She tried not to blush with the
reminder that she'd had to ask for this, that it wasn't
being given freely. She nodded.

"Did you want it in any particular place?"

She had options? On her hand, she supposed. But
she'd had kisses there. Since she'd been wearing
gloves, she didn't think they really counted. Once,
she'd turned a corner into a hallway and come un-
expectedly upon a footman pressing his lips to a
maid's neck, both of them making little mewling
sounds, unaware of the intrusion. But that wasn't
what she wanted. "On the mouth."

He grinned. He had a devastatingly alluring grin
that assured pleasure would be delivered. She imagined he had women here—everywhere—falling at his
feet. He was no doubt requested by many, which was
probably the reason it had taken him a while to get to
her. "I meant . . . did you wish to move elsewhere? Or
be in a different position. Sitting perhaps or standing?"

Oh, Lord. He probably thought she was a ninny in
addition to being unwanted. Of course that's what he'd
been asking. How could she be so incredibly daft? It
was the fog that had entered her mind along with the
liquor.

"Here." She didn't want to explain that she'd forgotten how to stand. She also realized she'd not sat up as much as she'd thought. Her position was more of a recline.

"All right." He tugged off his gloves. They were dark brown leather, the kind men wore about town, not in a ballroom. His large hands appeared strong and capable. She wondered what sort of experiences he provided, if he fulfilled the fantasies of those who wanted someone a bit more down-to-earth, relatable . . . or rough. Unrefined. Since a good many of the women here were of the nobility, perhaps while at their various societal affairs, they had their fill of all the men they could want in evening attire, and so they sought something different. He set the gloves on a table near the door.

"I see a sideboard with decanters. Would you care for something to drink?"

"Just get on with it." *Before I lose my nerve.*

He studied her for a heartbeat, two, before giving a little nod. "As you wish."

His strides were long, confident. He obviously had no misgivings about doing this. Which was good, even if it wasn't desire that had brought him to her. But his job, his occupation. How she wished that wasn't so.

Odd time to realize it was not only a kiss she craved, but a man looking at her with desire swimming within his eyes, a man touching her because he couldn't *not*.

When he reached her, he lowered himself to one knee. His lips were full, the bottom one a bit plumper than the upper. Beautiful really. Or maybe that was the opinion of the green fairy. The absinthe certainly made him appealing. And he smelled good. A lemony orange if such a thing existed. His eyes held a kind-ness. "Don't be nervous."

"I'm not." She was. "How many women have you kissed tonight?"

"You'll be the first."

"Don't you like kissing?"

"I enjoy it very much, probably a bit too much, but whether or not I kiss a woman depends entirely upon what she wants."

Why wouldn't a woman want a kiss from him? Why wouldn't she want to explore those lips that obvi-ously had been created specifically for sinning? Why wouldn't she want to hold his head in place and simply take? "Are you not any good at it?"

He grinned again, a smile that held the promise of passion and so much more. "You tell me."

Cupping her cheek with one hand, he tilted up her face slightly and lowered that intriguing mouth to hers. It was softer than she'd expected, a pillow that welcomed, tenderly molding itself against her lips as if the fates had designed them as a perfect match to his. Then the tip of his tongue slowly outlined those very lips before following a path along the seam, urg-ing it to slacken and separate as he went. Without fur-ther ado, she did as he bade and opened herself up to him. His low growl, almost feral in nature, should have frightened her. Instead, it only served to make her want more.

He tasted dark and dangerous. She recognized a hint of the flavor. Whiskey. Had he enjoyed a glass before coming to her or had he been in the company of another just prior to being sent to her? She didn't like the spark of jealousy that speculation instigated. Even if he hadn't kissed the girl, he'd been gifting her with his attentions. Selfishly, she wanted him all to herself, realized she wished he wasn't someone who so easily shared his favors with others.

But she shoved aside all those intruding thoughts, which were ruining the experience, to better concentrate on the present. He was hers for only a few minutes, for only as long as this kiss lasted. But already she didn't want it to end anytime soon. How long had they given him? How many minutes could he stay with her before he would have to leave to see to another's request and need?

She didn't know how it came about, but her fingers were suddenly entangled in his thick, silky hair. Strange sounds were coming from her. Sighs. Squeals. Moans. She wanted to tell him that it wasn't her making them. It was the green fairy. But she didn't want to separate her mouth from his in order to utter a word. All she wanted was more of his lips plying their talent over hers.

They were so very skilled at taunting and teasing, applying pressure and backing off. His tongue was master of its domain, parrying with hers, plundering the recesses of her mouth as though he'd stumbled upon unexpected treasure and wanted to thoroughly analyze each find.

His arm came around her, drawing her up and nearer so her breasts were flattened against his firm broad chest. And her fingers, the dastardly things, began exploring the breadth of his shoulders. She wanted to undo all his buttons and take a journey over the skin their release would reveal. How far would he let her go before objecting? How far would she dare?

What were the rules? What was allowed?

She'd always assumed a kiss was a relatively passive act that involved only the mouth, but his encompassed the whole of her, down to her curling toes. Her entire body seemed to spark and tingle. As his hold on her tightened, she felt herself melting into him, like candle wax heated by a solitary flame. He was incredibly warm and comforting. His ministrations lured her nearer until she wondered if they'd ever part. She hoped not. She dearly hoped not.

He comprised her entire world. He dominated her awareness until nothing existed beyond him. He was all that mattered, all that was of substance. And yet . . .

Everything started to have a dreamlike quality to it. She could no longer tell where she ended and he began. They were absorbing each other, and a haze began to settle in.

Green. Murky. Distant.

The green fairy was wreaking havoc now, wanted him all for herself, the little witch. Leonora was clutching him, striving to hold onto him.

But in the end, he floated away.

Rook felt the woman go limp in his arms only a heartbeat before her mouth released its hold on his. Easing back, he looked down on her. She appeared thoroughly contented.

She was also bloody well asleep!

Damnation! He'd never had a woman react in that manner when he'd been kissing her. If anything, they always became more animated. Had he bored her? She certainly hadn't responded as if uninterested.

She'd clutched, grabbed, and held him as though she was being tossed about by a tempest at sea and he was the raft that would safely deliver her to shore.

And dear God, the sounds she'd made. The whimpers, the sighs, the moans. They'd made every aspect of him tighten with need and want. They'd urged him to push himself into her and fuck her completely and thoroughly, and it had taken every ounce of self-control he possessed not to follow that path.

Then it had all come to an unsatisfying conclusion as though it had meant nothing at all.

His masculine pride wanted to dump her right there and then. But his mother, blast her, had raised him to be a gentleman of the first water and so he lowered the lady gently to the fainting couch as he might set down the finest of delicate porcelain.

Fainting couch? Perhaps she wasn't asleep but had fainted. Maybe his ministrations had overwhelmed her. Had taken her by storm. Perhaps he'd been too vigorous in his attentions, leaving the novice overcome with sensations. Lightly he nudged her shoulder. "Miss? Madam?"

A little mewling escaped from those slightly parted lips that he wanted to take possession of once again. She shifted onto her side, tucked a hand beneath her pink-tinged cheek, mumbled something about a fairy, and then emitted an endearing snuffling snore. Asleep then. Bloody hell. What was he supposed to do with her now?

Leave her to it, he supposed. Yet, he couldn't quite force himself to his feet. Instead, he lowered his backside to the floor and studied her. Her face sported a maze of faded freckles. Did she not wear a bonnet when she went outside? Her exquisite dark pink gown indicated she could certainly afford a hat. As did the pearl combs adorning her red-tinted hair, and the diamonds at her ears and throat. Anyone who frequented this club had money to spare. She was no exception.

She was also quite damned dictatorial. He'd rather liked it. No names indeed. He did regret he hadn't insisted on that at least, not that he'd have provided his true name. A corner of his mouth quirked up. He doubted she would have either.

She'd been intent on keeping matters between them as impersonal as possible. He wondered if he'd demonstrated the futility of that endeavor. Skin touching skin always created a bond. Whether it was a pleasant thing to be remembered was something else entirely. He wasn't quite certain he'd ever forget the time spent with her. The Lady of Sighs. That was how he'd remember her.

He considered striving to awaken her, but decided it was simply best to leave. She was safe here. All women within Aiden's domain were. His brother's desire to protect women—the manner in which he'd protected their mother—was one of the reasons Rook admired him and they got along so well.

After shoving himself to his feet, he bent over and pressed a kiss to her forehead and then for good measure, brushed his lips over hers. "Farewell, lovely lady. I hope it was all you imagined."

He grabbed a velveteen blanket that was folded on a nearby chair and draped it over her. Then he walked to the door, turned back, took one last look, and left.

LEONORA STIRRED TO someone whispering softly in her ear. "Miss? Miss?"

Slowly, carefully, her head feeling as though workers were building a factory within it, she eased her way out of the rapidly distancing lethargic haven—grimacing as the pounding hammers battered her skull more forcefully—and opened her eyes.

A young maid gave her a blindingly bright smile before straightening. "It's morning, miss."

"Morning?" Squinting, she gingerly glanced around, taking care not to move her head too quickly. "This isn't my hotel room."

And this young girl wasn't her maid, the one who helped her dress, the one she'd sworn to secrecy when she'd slipped out of the hotel last night after her mother had gone to bed. She'd been bored and had decided to go in search of adventure.

"No, miss. You're in the kissing chamber at the Elysium Club."

Ah, yes, *that* club where women's fantasies were supposed to be adhered to. She'd gambled a bit, enjoyed a few drinks . . . and then apparently come here for a nap. In spite of the discomfort rampaging through her head and her roiling stomach, she moaned and stretched, unable to recall the last time she'd slept so deeply. "I had such a lovely dream. Must have been the absinthe."

"It has been known to release inhibitions. Some say it even causes hallucinations."

It certainly had done that. "The most handsome man appeared. He didn't talk much but still he was quite charming. And he—wait. What?" She sat up ramrod straight, slammed the heels of her hands against her protesting head, and groaned low. "The kissing chamber?"

"Yes, miss. It's where ladies are sent if they want only a kiss."

"The man was real."

The girl laughed lightly. "I should think so, miss."

Dear Lord, what had she done? She touched her lips, surprised to find they weren't swollen from all the attention he'd given them. However, when she ran her tongue over them, she could still taste him. Dark and dangerous. And oh, so very alluring. "Where is he?"

"Probably gone home. We're doing the tidying up now. Didn't really expect to find anyone in here."

"Who was he?"

"Don't know, miss. Don't know who they sent to you. Maybe Michael? He's ever so good at delivering what the ladies want. Or so I've heard."

"What shade is his hair?"

"Blond."

"No, it wasn't him. This man's hair was a dark brown, sable." She had a gossamer memory of running her fingers through the silky-soft strands. Had she been that bold?

"Julian, mayhap? Or another? Any of 'em really. They all do the kissing."

Pressing the tips of her fingers to her forehead, she stroked and rubbed, trying to ease the ache that was throbbing unmercifully if left alone. "What else do they do?"

"Anything a lady wants."

She peered through her splayed fingers. "But only if she asks."

"Oh, yes, miss. You're done up all nice and tight. I suspect he only kissed you."

"Yes, yes of course." Slightly disappointed, she cast aside the blanket, briefly wondering where it had come from. She had no memory of it. Or the man leaving. Or the kiss stopping. It had seemed to go on into eternity, into her dreams.

She'd have to commend Mr. Trewlove on the men he hired. The one he'd sent to her had made her feel wanted, beloved. Unfortunately, he'd left her yearning for more. Even if it had all been an act, he'd been damned good at performing.

Suddenly the kiss lost its shine because it hadn't been born of desire but bought by what she'd paid to gain entry. A fee. Like purchasing a thoroughbred horse. On one hand, her coins had certainly not gone to waste. He'd earned every farthing. On the other hand, she'd been a task completed so those coins would land on his palm. He'd merely gone through the motions, but oh, what lovely motions they'd been.

CHAPTER 2

$\mathcal{S}$ITTING in the library of the Twin Dragons with his three closest friends, Rook very much wished he was at another club: the Elysium. It had been three nights since he'd kissed the Lady of Sighs, and he couldn't stop thinking about her. He'd even returned last night, gone up the stairs, stood in that hidden alcove, and peered through a part in the draperies, hoping to catch sight of her. But after only a few seconds, he'd turned away, feeling very much like some sort of depraved soul—tawdry and unworthy of her—spying as he was.

Aiden had found him there, battling with his conscience. Rook had greeted his brother with "Has she returned?"

"Who?"

Rook couldn't believe that was a serious question. How could Aiden have forgotten? "The woman you insisted I kiss."

"Did I insist?" He crossed his arms over his chest. "Thought I merely asked."

Rook decided it was a good thing they'd not grown up in the same household as he suspected they might have often come to blows. "Has. She. Returned?"

Aiden grinned. The bugger had known precisely

whom Rook was asking about and thought it amusing to pretend otherwise. Or perhaps he simply found it humorous to torment his brother. "Not to my knowledge."

"Then I can assume she's not here this evening?"

"Not that I've seen."

Had his kiss been a disappointment? If she'd enjoyed it, wouldn't she have come back for another? Only she didn't know his name. If she tried to describe him, no one would be able to identify him because he didn't work there. Those who had seen him before certainly wouldn't expect that he would engage in such inappropriate behavior. Another bloke would be sent to her, would kiss her—and that scenario had an unfamiliar tightness squeezing his chest because he didn't want someone else fulfilling her fantasies. He wanted to fuel her desires.

Those wayward thoughts continued to plague him, even now when his friends were chattering about an investment opportunity they'd been pursuing of late. He couldn't seem to latch onto their words because he was wondering how he might have kissed her differently. Had he gone too fast, too slow? Had he been too aggressive? Not aggressive enough? Had she tasted the scotch he'd tossed back before going to her, and as a result, labeled him a drunkard? Or perhaps she'd not liked the flavor. She, on the other hand, had tasted delicious. Addictingly so. Sweet, yet earthy. He wanted to taste her again, damn it.

He wondered if he could convince Aiden to share whatever information he knew as a result of her arrival at his club. Was she visiting or did she live here permanently? Would he know precisely where she resided? And what then? Send her flowers? Might she consider him a danger if he were to go about seeking her out when she was in truth virtually a stranger?

"Are you listening?"

Not a stranger. Not after what they'd shared. Not after the way her hands had clutched at him. He imagined how she might respond to attentions beyond a kiss, to intimate touches that followed a path from her neck down to her toes.

"Rook?" King's harsh tone had him jerking his attention back to the matter at hand.

"Apologies. I was thinking . . . about something else." Someone else. Another time. Another place. Where he would much rather be.

"It's not like you to drift off. You're normally quite focused."

He'd certainly been when it came to that kiss. For those few minutes, all else had floated away: troubles, worries, the past, and a legacy he was striving to escape. All that had mattered was her and being with her.

"Is it your father?" Knight asked.

It should be. All of his thoughts should be on his sire . . . and his mother. How to make the upcoming transition into widowhood easier for her. Although he suspected she'd adapt rather effortlessly. It wasn't as though she'd been the center of the Earl of Elverton's life, nor he the center of hers. "It's any number of things. What were you saying?"

"I received word from Sam Garrison that he has arrived in London and would like to meet with us in person to discuss our interest in possibly investing in his munitions factory. Apparently, he brought his husband-hunting sister with him."

As soon as King uttered the words, Rook felt three pairs of eyes land on him like a physical punch. With an eyebrow arched, he glanced around at his fellow Chessmen, a moniker they'd acquired while at Oxford, because of their ruthless strategy when it came to investing. "Why are you staring at me?"

"You're the only one amongst us not yet married," Knight said.

"How precisely does that signify?"

"Rumors are that he has several parties interested in investing in his enterprise. Your flirting with the sister might give us an edge when it comes to partnering with this Garrison fellow, should we decide in favor of his business."

"Flirting. That seems rather underhanded to me."

"Wouldn't be the first time we've gone to great lengths to achieve what we wanted," Bishop reminded him.

"But we've never used an innocent to do it." Or taken advantage of an untried heart. He knew how vulnerable that sort of heart could be. In his youth, his had certainly been open to battering and bruising. But now it was like a fortress of stone. Nothing could get past its defenses. "Besides, I doubt we need the leverage."

He glanced around the library of the Twin Dragons, a club open to men and women where all sorts of deals sometimes transpired. "The money we can provide will no doubt be sufficient. If we decide the investment will pay off. Garrison has been so astoundingly secretive about what he's offering that I'm finding it difficult to assess the value of giving him our coins. Or to trust him, truth be told."

"I quite agree," King said. "However, I thought to

give him the opportunity to present his case in person. Dinner tomorrow night, my residence. Wives included, of course, to ensure Miss Garrison doesn't feel out of place."

Which would ensure that Rook did, since it would obviously be expected that he would give the woman some attention. Perhaps he should beg off and go to the Elysium. But he had no reason to believe the Lady of Sighs would return tomorrow. In all likelihood, he'd never see her again.

THE FOLLOWING EVENING, as his carriage rumbled through the streets on its way to King's, Rook knew he'd made a mistake in stopping by his parents' residence first. His father was withering away, unable to communicate except by blinking. Rook suspected his sire's mind remained agile but imprisoned, like his frail body. Yet, he couldn't help but wonder if it was a just punishment for a man who had murdered his first wife and attempted to kill his second. And now there were those who spoke in whispers wondering if he'd also been responsible for the death of his older brother—in order to inherit the titles that rightfully would have gone to the elder.

Rook was grateful he and his father had never been close. Still, his deterioration was difficult to witness.

However, his mother sat by the bed, serenely reading aloud *My Secret Desires*. That the book had been written by Knight's wife and detailed their love affair from years before didn't seem to bother the countess, but Rook had never been able to bring himself to read of his friend's exploits. Certainly, he had no one who was going to write of his affairs. The few lovers he'd had were known for their discretion. He showered them with enough coins and baubles to ensure they remained so.

But after spending time being reminded of the sort of man who'd sired him, he wasn't in the mood to attend a dinner, to be among friends, or to discuss business. He wanted—needed—a heady distraction. A kiss that melted his bones. Delicate hands with long, slender fingers plowing through his hair before curling over his shoulders in an attempt to hold onto him forever.

He wanted to be held forever.

With a curse at the unfamiliar yearning, he glanced out the window. Fearing he'd be as insatiable as his father, he'd learned to tamp down his desires and never allow them full rein over him.

But ever since that night at the Elysium, since the Lady of Sighs, he'd been unable to think of much else except for the glorious manner in which her mouth had moved over his. The way in which she'd welcomed him.

For someone who had claimed to have never been kissed, she was certainly a fast learner. A natural. A siren. A vixen. He wanted to taste her again. But that was unlikely to happen. She could be on a ship back to America. Would he ever find anyone her equal? Anyone who might possibly have the power to break through the barriers he'd erected and stir such unyielding passion within him?

His carriage pulled into the drive that circled in front of King's residence. Judging by the number of vehicles queued up, he was the last to arrive. His coachman brought the team of horses to a halt. A footman opened the door and Rook stepped out. It was a lovely summer's evening and the thought of spending it with friends, in spite of his earlier reservations, perked him up considerably. Even if a bit of business was involved. He welcomed the distraction from his morose musings.

He bounded up the steps, not surprised when the door immediately opened, and King's butler allowed him entrance with a brisk nod. "M'lord."

"Keating."

"They're waiting for you in the grand drawing room. If you'll be so kind as to follow me."

Rook had known the servant for ages, but the man remained as formal as ever—and was well aware that Rook knew exactly where to find the grand drawing room. Still, he responded, "Lead the way."

A few steps in, he added, "I assume everyone's here."

"Yes, m'lord."

"Including the Americans?"

"Yes, sir."

"What's your impression of them?"

"I have none, sir."

"Come now, Keating, you must have formed some opinion. Brash? Arrogant? Boastful?"

Keating stopped to face him. "The gent reminds me of a puppy, sir, full of boundless energy and eager to please."

Eager to get his hands on their money. "And the young woman?"

"Watchful. I don't think she quite trusts us."

"The British in general or the Chessmen in particular?"

"I'm not entirely sure."

He'd have thought she'd have been zealous about pleasing as well if she wished to court success regarding her hunt for a husband. "Well, I'm certain the wives will put her at ease and reassure her that she has nothing to fear."

"I expect you're correct, sir."

"I usually am."

With a slight shift in his lips that almost passed for a smile, Keating continued his trek down the wide hallway, and Rook dutifully followed. King, being the Duke of Kingsland, usually handled such affairs with a great deal of formality and aplomb, as befit his title. Rook respected rituals and had nothing against adhering to them.

The butler preceded him into the drawing room, and Rook had only a second to notice that everyone within was gathered together talking. King without his wife, Penelope, who was no doubt off ensuring something or other was being correctly done. Knight and Regina. Bishop and Marguerite. A tall, hefty fellow with reddish-blond hair. The American no doubt. A petite woman with auburn hair salted with a few strands of silver. His sister.

Keating cleared his throat. "Your Grace, Lord Wyeth has arrived." He then discreetly departed as everyone turned to give Rook their attention.

The husband hunter was somewhat older than he'd expected, experience in those eyes that assessed him. Based on the creases along her brow, he'd have thought she'd have long ago married and would have had several children by now. Obviously, she'd had no luck snagging a man. Her straight firm mouth that expressed disapproval might have played a role in her spinsterhood. The judgment in her blue eyes made him want to squirm. "My apologies for my tardiness."

"Nothing to worry over," King said, stepping forward. "We've been discussing the weather. Allow me the honor of introducing—"

His words came to an abrupt halt as light but brisk footfalls sounded, echoing along the hallway and growing louder until they filled the parlor and came to a sudden halt.

"Forgive the delay," Penelope announced.

Rook turned to greet King's lovely and efficient wife, but the words that tumbled through his mind refused to be uttered.

Because standing beside King's duchess was the Lady of Sighs.

CHAPTER 3

𝒢ᴏᴏᴅ Lord. It was *him*. The man from the Elysium. Only it couldn't be because the Duchess of Kingsland was introducing him as John Castleton, Viscount Wyeth. Certainly, a lord wouldn't work at a place that engaged in fulfilling a woman's fantasies. Wouldn't work at all from what she understood. They considered themselves a privileged lot and avoided any sort of occupation.

Did he have a twin? A twin who looked exactly like him but wouldn't inherit, who wasn't given an allowance, who had to earn his own coin, make his way in the world?

Or perhaps it was simply that every now and then, nature forgot when it created someone and it created them again, in another time and place. A duplicate. She'd read about them in German folklore. Doppelgangers.

But if he was either a twin or a replica, if they'd never met, then why had his eyes briefly widened with recognition? His nostrils had flared, like he'd remembered her scent, was possibly trying to draw more of her fragrance into his lungs. Only he couldn't be the man who had knelt beside her and carried her so skillfully into the realm of pleasure.

She had to be mistaken. Although she'd believed she'd never forget what the gent had looked like, she had to admit to some murkiness around the edges of her memories, thanks to the influence of too much absinthe. So perhaps he only reminded her of the fellow, because of his dark hair and eyes, along with the intensity with which he seemed to be taking her in.

He gave a little bow. "A pleasure to make your acquaintance, Miss Garrison."

That voice. Deep, silky, rich. Low and intimate. *Don't be nervous. You tell me.*

She swallowed hard, striving to get her lungs to work. She couldn't return his sentiment, couldn't claim pleasure because she feared the word would come out as a strangled croak. Since that night at the Elysium, she'd thought of that man, possibly *this* man, a hundred times at least, regretted not allowing him to give his name because if she returned to the club, how could she ask for him in order to ensure that he was the one who came to her?

She gave a shallow curtsy. "My lord."

Her voice was a strangled croak anyway, and she cursed her traitorous body for showing any indication she was struggling with this unexpected development.

"I was giving Miss Garrison a tour of the library. She loves books," the duchess said.

"Reading makes for a wonderful pastime," he said. "Are you enjoying England?"

"It has its moments."

When a corner of his mouth lifted ever so slightly and his brown eyes warmed, she knew he was no twin or doppelganger. He *was* the one they'd sent to her. How he had come to be that man was another matter entirely. Did he lead a clandestine life? Did the Elysium allow him to fulfill his own fantasies of pleasuring the innocent? Did he use the various encounters for blackmail? Her mind was rife with questions, none of them flattering toward him. And none that she could ask outright at the moment without giving away her own sinful behavior.

"If you'll excuse me—" Needing to put distance between them, she stepped around him in order to move nearer to her family, not that they were wont to provide a modicum of protection. "You should have come with us, Mama. You'd have been impressed with all the tomes."

"Unlike you, my girl, I prefer to live life within the world, not between the pages of a book."

Her father had adored Leonora. His death nearly a year ago had come as a blow, even though she'd been expecting it. The doctors knew little about the illness that had caused his muscles to atrophy and his body to fade away, and thus there had been nothing they could do to stop its progress. She dearly missed him and wished he was here now to share in and be part of her endeavors.

Her mother had never approved of her, which was no doubt one of the reasons Leonora hadn't stayed on the ship in order to travel back to New York once it became clear that her mother had tagged along with a definite agenda in mind: to see her daughter married to a lord, believing it would lift her own esteem.

But Leonora had no wish to marry. Instead, she had her own dreams that could be accomplished by not remaining on the vessel. So here she was, striving to prove herself of value and worthy of her family's kind regard, while also hoping to obtain that which she longed for: to be recognized for her talents and acknowledged as a true partner in the business.

She took the sherry her brother had been holding for her and forced a delicate sip when she would have preferred downing all the contents. Between her mother's designs, her brother's tendency to take nothing seriously—even their dire straits—and the arrival of a man with the power to distract her, possibly to destroy her, she was teetering on the edge of a precipice, and a single misstep could cause her to lose everything for which she'd worked so hard and devoted years hoping to acquire. All done surreptitiously. All done with the knowledge of only a few.

Glancing over at Wyeth, who'd joined his friends, she could hope only that her encounter with him would also remain confidential.

LEONORA KNEW THAT among the aristocracy, rules existed regarding the order as to how one was seated around the dining table. Precedence, she believed it was called. She thought aristocratic ladies were required to memorize some tome in order to learn where to properly place people so as to not insult anyone. She couldn't imagine giving a fig as to which chair had been designated for her backside.

Still, she wasn't altogether certain that the duchess had adhered to the proper sitting order. She and her husband were at opposite ends of the table. The three other Chessmen were lined up to the duke's right, her brother to their host's left. They'd seated her beside Sam, which put her across from the viscount. Her mother was beside her, the other two wives on either side of the duchess.

She was rather certain that Sam had asked for her to be placed beside him—out of brotherly love and because she wasn't comfortable around strangers, he would have told them. But the truth was that he worried business might come up and he would need to be rescued. Because unlike him, she'd always hung on to every word their father had uttered as if it had come from God. Because that's what he'd always been to her: a deity.

He'd known everything, had commanded men and been a mover of industry. He'd built railroads, been instrumental in discovering ways to make factories run more efficiently. But his passion had been weaponry. The evolution of it had fascinated him, and she suspected, like her, he would have spent considerable time examining the armor that had been on display near the library as though a knight still stood in it. Her taking long minutes to study it had delayed her and the duchess returning to the drawing room. Perhaps she wouldn't have been so surprised by Wyeth's presence if she'd been there when he entered the chamber.

Maybe she could have thought of something witty to say as he escorted her—at the urging of the duchess—to the dining table. The duke had offered his arm to her mother, who had preened as if being gifted with the Crown jewels while Sam had accompanied the duchess. Instead, Leonora had not even been able to look at the viscount, to meet his gaze.

Because the few times she'd glanced over at him before the butler announced that dinner was ready to be served, she'd found it difficult to breathe and wasn't certain it was entirely due to his being privy to her embarrassing secret. She feared it might have something to do with how remarkably handsome he was, with a patrician nose, bold cheekbones that would offer a resting place for his thick eyelashes, and a jaw that had quite possibly been chiseled from stone. And those lips. Those damn plump lips that had been sculpted to provide a cushion for a woman's mouth.

She realized, sitting at the table now, that she was staring at them, remembering the softness moving provocatively over her own, urging her to part them and allow him entry. She'd so blithely obliged and unleashed her inhibitions because she'd never expected to see him again. She'd thought he was a commoner, someone of the streets. Not a damned noble, not someone her brother was striving to entice into investing. Not someone with the power to prevent her from achieving her dreams.

When she lifted her attention from his lips, she discovered his eyes, speculative and curious, homed in on her face with such intensity that he might as well have been skimming his fingers over her skin. His look was so thoroughly assessing, so profound, so incredibly penetrating. She suspected if he dipped his smoldering gaze, he'd set her clothing alight.

With heat flaming her cheeks, she jerked her attention back to the soup that had been placed before her. She had no idea what kind it was. It had no flavor—or if it did, her senses were so overwhelmed by the memory of his taste that it dominated all else.

She supposed she was expected to speak with him about mundane matters, topics she'd learned at the boring finishing school to which her mother had sent her because they were the nouveau riche and the woman who'd given birth to her in a small house on the outskirts of Chicago had wanted to erase any evidence of their origins. While Leonora thought their rise out of poverty was the most interesting thing about her family.

But she didn't want to discuss mundane matters with him. She wanted to know why a man who was supposedly as rich as Croesus—according to her brother, all the Chessmen were—was working in a questionable establishment. And worse, she wanted to know if he'd enjoyed kissing her . . . at all. If she'd done it correctly. If he ever pondered doing it again.

ROOK COULDN'T STOP thinking about kissing her— what it had been like and how much he wanted to do it again. Only longer, slower. He wanted to stretch it out into eternity.

Not that she seemed to have any interest in kissing him. Every now and then she darted a quick glance at him. Once her gaze had lingered—on his mouth if he was forced to guess—but she appeared to be discomfited by his presence. And thus far, he'd noticed her blushing half a dozen times. He wondered if she was striving to forget what had happened and was discombobulated to find herself sitting across from the reminder in the flesh. That might explain the tension radiating from her when he'd escorted her to the table. He supposed it was also possible she didn't recognize him. He was fairly certain she'd been rather sauced that night. Which might account for the way, upon first being formally introduced to him, she'd looked at him with confusion as if he was a stranger, someone she'd never before encountered.

Penelope had seated all the gents at one end of the table, so they could discuss gentlemanly things like cheroots, Kentucky bourbon, and the increasing migration of settlers across America. Rook hadn't been paying a great deal of attention or contributed to the discourse. Instead, he'd watched Miss Garrison lift her wineglass and carry it to her lips. He'd been mesmerized by the gentle movements of her throat as she'd swallowed. And he noticed the tiniest drop of wine that clung to the corner of her perfect mouth. He wanted to dip his tongue into that shallow alcove in order to taste the wine and her. Trace his tongue along that seam and urge her, once again, to open herself to him. Only he wanted her to open more than her mouth. He wanted her to open all of herself.

Although he suspected she'd require he reveal himself entirely as well, and *that* he wouldn't do.

He didn't know why it hadn't occurred to him that the American at the Elysium would be the husband-hunting sister King had mentioned Garrison had brought with him. Perhaps because several deuced American husband-hunting women were racing about of late, with their enormous dowries and their bold ways. They wanted titles, to be addressed as *my lady* or *Your Grace*. They yearned for the instant respectability that came with landing a lord.

They believed marrying into the nobility would offer them a life of ease. They had little understanding of precisely what it was they were gaining. Therefore, Rook had no patience for their machinations. Not that any of it affected him because marriage was not a path he intended to traverse.

It would be selfish on his part to subject any woman to the legacy he would inherit along with the title. If that meant he never obtained an heir, he wasn't altogether certain it would be much of a loss. Better to bring an end to this branch of the family tree rather than let it flourish. He had a cousin who was next in line, a cousin whose father was known for his philanthropic nature.

Not one who was abhorred for his libertine ways. Rook had once thought his father could embarrass him no more than he already had. He'd believed, unlike all the other children his father had played a role in bringing into the world, that he—as the Earl of Elverton's legitimate son and heir—had been loved by his sire. But his father held no more affection or respect for him than he did the others. Providing an heir was an obligation he had met—and he'd sought to take advantage of his son, as he did every other person in his life. No one had been safe from his sire's need to dominate and destroy, to cause harm.

"Are you striving to cook the partridge a bit more with that heated glare?"

Rook swung his attention to Mrs. Garrison, who'd been rude enough to put him on the spot. Her eyebrows, thicker and heavier than her daughter's, were arched in query. "My apologies. I was distracted with thoughts of my father. He is unwell."

"Oh?" Now a speculative gleam shined from those blue eyes, a shade that matched her daughter's, and yet were not nearly as lovely or pleasant to gaze into. Windows into the soul, indeed. This woman cared only for herself and her own interests. "What rank is he, pray tell?"

"He is an earl, madam. The Earl of Elverton."

"Which you will become when he dies." As if incredibly pleased by that discovery, she lifted her wineglass with a victorious smile, and he was surprised she didn't make a toast to his father's ill health and speedy demise.

"Mama," Miss Garrison chastised.

"Don't take that disapproving tone with me. It's important to know which men will be elevated within Society and which are where they shall remain. If you'd pay more attention, I wouldn't have to."

Miss Garrison looked on the verge of growling, and he'd have growled right along with her. He didn't know if he'd ever met a more unpleasant soul, one who took no pains whatsoever to disguise her disagreeable nature.

Her facial features suddenly going serene, as though the lessons of a lifetime had taught her how to survive the harsh demands of her mother, Miss Garrison directed her attention to him, sincerity and true concern reflected in her blue eyes. "I do hope his health improves."

It's quite unlikely rested on the tip of his tongue. Instead, he said, "Thank you. I'll convey your good wishes."

Someone had once told him, "Meet the mother and you'll know the daughter." The man had been striving to make the point that the daughter would be a replication of the mother in later years, but Rook was left with the impression that wasn't the case here. Miss Garrison wasn't at all as uncouth as her mother. She possessed a refinement and graciousness that the older woman lacked. He wondered how she might have persevered to develop those qualities when the harpy who'd raised her offered no example to emulate.

He found himself more curious about the young lady than he'd been that night at the Elysium. But now was not the time or place to satisfy his curiosity, so he glanced around the table. "Do carry on. I believe Bishop has yet to explain how he was once suspected of committing murder."

With a grin and a wink, Bishop tipped his wineglass in a salute toward the area where the ladies sat. "Until my wife came to my rescue."

Rook had the odd desire to rescue the husband-hunting Miss Garrison, although he also suspected she was perfectly capable of rescuing herself. Which made her all the more intriguing.

CHAPTER 4

Eight courses. Leonora suffered through eight excruciating courses. When dessert was finally devoured, she was more than ready for the moment when the men went off for a cigar and scotch while the women adjourned to the parlor for tea.

Except that wasn't what happened. Everyone went to the library for a refreshment of their choice. Unfortunately, absinthe wasn't available. She would have liked to chug back an entire bottle of the stuff simply to forget this horrendous night and the number of times her mother had surreptitiously pinched her arm in an attempt to convey that she needed to carry on a conversation with the only eligible gentleman at the table. Her prodding had served merely to incite Leonora's obstinacy and ensure she didn't speak to the gent.

Not that she could think of anything polite to say to him anyway. Everything she'd considered had seemed grossly impolite and had more to do with how far beyond kissing his services went. At the moment, however, she did manage a polite thank-you after he strode over and handed her a snifter of brandy.

"My pleasure," he responded, and the heat coursed

through her at the manner in which he managed to make *pleasure* sound anything except innocent.

Why did he have to use that particular word when it carried such potency? Was he intentionally seeking to remind her of the wondrous sensations that had swept endlessly through her like waves crashing upon a shore? Not that she was having any success in not thinking about how her body had responded to his kiss. It was as though having experienced it, every aspect of her was constantly on alert, ready to jump into the fray in order to enjoy the pleasure again. She was striving to think of something appropriate to say. *You have such powerful hands. Your lips are exquisite. Your mouth is far too skilled at delivering what a woman craves.*

A loud clearing of a throat nearly had her jumping out of her skin. Had her thoughts somehow communicated themselves to the others in the room? Her mother often used a throat-clearing to indicate she was none too pleased with something Leonora had done or said.

But it was only the Duke of Kingsland, seeking everyone's attention as he lifted his glass. "To the success of all future ventures in which any of us might engage."

"Hear! Hear!" echoed throughout the room.

In an unladylike manner, Leonora gulped some brandy, relishing the burn, hoping it might distract her from more pleasant musings and help her focus on the reason they were here.

"Now, Mr. Garrison," the duke began, in a tone indicating he would brook no argument and was accustomed to being obeyed, "we're most anxious to hear the details of this investment opportunity you're keen on offering to us."

"You're going to discuss business with ladies about?" Mama asked, clearly horrified by the possibility, but Leonora thought it wonderful to be included in a conversation that usually excluded women. She'd never liked being ushered out of the room when the discussion drifted to what were usually considered only manly pursuits.

"My wife is extremely skilled at investing," Kingsland said. "She charitably has a consortium of women she regularly advises regarding how a lady can increase her yearly income through investments. The other wives here aren't shy about sharing their opinion on matters. Their perspective often offers insights we'd not considered. Hence, we find their input invaluable. Therefore, enlighten us, if you please. What makes your munitions factory different? What sort of weapon are you offering that will ensure we make a profit?"

Sam downed what remained of his scotch and glanced toward the sideboard as though in desperate need of another. He was usually verbose except when it came to discussing the business. "At the moment we're holding it secret, but we will be giving a demonstration to interested parties very soon. Until then, you'll need to be patient."

"Except it's not a weapon," Leonora interjected, believing it important that they be a bit more forthcoming with these men in order to earn their trust.

"But it could be . . . in the right hands," Sam said with a bit of ire in his tone and a glare that conveyed she shouldn't say anything else. Too bad she was known for not being skilled at reading expressions.

She gave a caustic laugh. "No, it couldn't. It's a writing machine. No threat at all." Except possibly to the pen-producing and inkwell industries.

She was very much aware that for the span of a few seconds, Wyeth's gaze left her to communicate something with his comrades. She wondered exactly what Sam had told them in his letters. Then the viscount was looking at her again, his gaze steady and assessing, as if he'd just discovered a trinket he'd taken for granted was actually valuable. "Does it work like a printing press?"

"No, it's more like a piano. Only what I refer to as keys are small and round and each represents a letter. When you hit a key, an arm with that letter on it swings up, and strikes ink, then paper that's been situated into the machine."

"Your correspondence indicated your expertise is weaponry," Bishop said, sounding none too pleased, as though the evening had been a waste of their time. She needed to convince them it hadn't.

"It was," she assured them, "but we can't compete with Colt or Remington, so we want to go in a different direction."

"With a writing machine," the Earl of Knightly said, with a skeptical tone he might have used had she suggested they manufacture and sell fairy wings. "We have a means for writing, Miss Garrison. Pen, inkwell, paper."

His pens no doubt had gold nibs. "But it's a slow process, my lord, what with constantly having to collect ink on the nib and drawing the letters. In addition, not everyone has legible penmanship."

"She's obviously familiar with your atrocious handwriting, Knight," Wyeth said, and Knight's lips twitched. She wasn't exactly certain what he found humorous, but he didn't seem offended by his friend's comment. "Perhaps we should wait until we've had a chance to examine the contraption ourselves before judging."

She was terribly grateful for his stepping in and didn't waste any time in adding, "It *is* more impressive when you can observe it at work."

"And not nearly as boring as talking about it," Mama said tersely, no doubt upset that Leonora had stolen Sam's thunder. "Surely tonight was an opportunity for us to get to know one another. But you'll need to trust Sam's instincts regarding the forthcoming demonstration. We don't want to ruin the astonishment surrounding the revelation." She held up her empty snifter. "May I have more brandy, please?"

Leonora wasn't at all surprised that Mama would side with Sam, would strive to protect him. Taking their mother's glass, Sam began walking toward the sideboard, asking as he went, "So what does one do for amusement over here?"

She could have sworn she felt Wyeth studying her. Possibly because she was blushing, if the heat rushing to her face was any indication, having discovered on her own what one did for a diversion. What she had done for fun with him. What she feared she might not be averse to experiencing again. How many kisses did it take to make a woman a wanton?

If the group was disappointed with the way the

evening had gone regarding the gathering of information about an investment, Kingsland, Knightly, and Blackwood didn't show it but simply began politely offering Sam advice on where to go for entertainment. Intent on learning what sort of investments interested the duchess and her consortium, Leonora had taken a single step toward the gathering of wives when her mother spoke. "How many bastards have you, Lord Wyeth?"

Leonora cringed. Honestly, the woman truly was taking matters too far. It occurred to her that perhaps it was her mother's coarse manner more than her new money that kept her out of the New York ballrooms.

"None, madam," he answered curtly.

"Have you been married before?"

"No."

"No children whatsoever then."

"No."

Leonora returned to Mama's side and strove for a low, discreet tone. "Mother, can you cease with the inquisition about matters that are entirely none of our business?"

Mama gave her a slow, assessing perusal that made her want to shrink into nothing. Her tone, unfortunately, was far too caustic and loud to be missed by Wyeth since he was standing so near. "I want to ensure that it is your son, and not one from a previous marriage, who inherits. In addition, you're twenty-seven, no spring chicken. Quite on the shelf I think is how they refer to it here. You have but a few fertile years left to you. I want to be satisfied any potential suitor is capable of getting you with babe."

She was surprised her head didn't actually explode.

So many things there for her to respond to, but she went with only one. "What in God's name makes you think he's a potential suitor?"

"I've never considered you a great beauty, but he could scarcely take his eyes off you during dinner. And still he seems interested, even if you are ignoring him. These Brits are fascinated by Americans. Why do you think Sam insisted on bringing you?"

She knew exactly why her brother had brought her and it had nothing at all to do with matrimony. She looked at Wyeth. No, Rook. His friends had referred to him as such and the moniker seemed to fit him better. He certainly appeared more comfortable with it. Perhaps he didn't fancy being reminded he was a lord. "Please forgive her impertinence. I assure you that I have no interest whatsoever in you as a potential suitor. If you'll be kind enough to excuse me, I need a bit of fresh air."

As well as solitude in order to regain her composure. She hadn't planned to discuss the writing machine tonight. She knew she was far too protective of it, but it was important to her for reasons other than financial. And she certainly hadn't planned to discuss matrimony.

Because she'd been given a tour earlier, she knew which hallway to traverse in order to reach the door that would lead her onto the terrace and beyond it into the gardens. As she made her way to it, she decided she would run screaming through the flora until she reached its end. Would climb over the wall and race through the streets until they swallowed her up.

But once she was outside, she went only as far as the low wall at the terrace's edge, grateful to discover she still held her snifter of brandy and it wasn't yet empty. She'd been so mortified by the earlier exchange with her mother that she hadn't even realized she'd clung to the glass. It was a wonder with her tight grip that she hadn't shattered it. She couldn't excuse Mama's rudeness or convince herself that the woman's interest in seeing her daughter married stemmed from the goodness of her heart. She might prefer a duke for her daughter, but she'd accept a viscount. It was the *lord* part in which she was most interested. She wanted only to be able to announce that she had a grandson who would one day be the bearer of a title, sit in the House of Lords, and might even dine with the Queen.

Leonora was fighting the prospect of marrying for a title like a recalcitrant child kicking and screaming because she was being hauled off to do a chore when she'd rather play with her dolls. Although she was far removed from playing with dolls and most of her life had been a chore.

Not that she'd resented what was expected of her while her father had been alive. Before she could even read, he'd sat her on his lap and shared the wonder of ledgers, as though he was reading her a fairy tale. There were villains—those who didn't pay or sought to undermine him—and he was always the hero. Sometimes, he'd even mentioned the damsel, her mother, when she'd helped him secure an endorsement or someone's favor. And, of course, there was the witch—another side to her mother—who was never pleased with any progress made, who always wanted more.

To live in New York where she considered Society to be of the highest caliber, until she discovered the old guard would not allow her into their elite circle. In spite of the palace her husband had built for her, and the latest Parisian fashions she wore, and the elaborate balls she hosted that were largely ignored by those who mattered.

She'd spent a fortune—her husband's fortune—striving to prove they had more money than God. Until they had hardly any left. Leonora knew her mother wasn't entirely to blame. Her father had made a few hasty, almost desperate investments, striving to keep the coffers flush. Perhaps because his wife was indulging her whims, he had decided to indulge his and begin his munitions company. Never mind that Colt and Winchester and Remington were known and respected throughout the country and abroad. He'd believed he could offer something better. Until she'd finally convinced him to offer something else. Of course, by then—due to his failing health—it was too late for him to achieve the additional success he craved, and he'd passed the obligation of seeing him remembered on to her. Not intentionally, of course. But she'd felt the weight of a boulder slip from him to her as though he'd been Zeus and she Sisyphus. And she'd spend the remainder of her life rolling that boulder up the hill only to discover she could never place it at the summit. Except she was determined not to give up until she'd succeeded, and her father was again recognized as the genius and capitalist he'd once been.

Having a goal and being occupied with something momentous had served as a distraction from the ravaging done by his illness, and she'd been more than willing to support his endeavors, to help him secure whatever peace he could. While the burden might rest heavy now, when her father was alive she'd appreciated every moment, every achievement, every success their working together had brought them.

Sam had been only twenty-two when Papa had passed, hardly ready to take on the responsibilities of managing a company that had yet to get its legs beneath it. She was the one who had scoured through the books, determined their solvency. She was the one who recognized that they needed an influx of cash if they were to have any hope at all of building upon what Papa had begun. He'd intended to grace them with a life of ease. Instead, with his death, providing for her young brother and aging mother had fallen to her.

She didn't begrudge her brother his lack of business acumen. But the challenge was to ensure they were well cared for while not betraying her own desires—which meant not choosing the easier path of marriage to a man of wealth and benefiting from his accomplishments rather than her own. Leonora's last words to her father had been a vow: she would see his factory and final vision for the writing machine succeed.

Hearing the soft footfalls, she glanced over, for some reason not at all surprised when Rook came to stand beside her. Having drained her brandy, she looked longingly at his glass of what she assumed was scotch. "I don't suppose I could have a sip."

Without hesitation, he relieved her of the snifter and gave her the crystal tumbler. "I suspect you need it more than I do."

Leonora took a swallow, grateful the excellent scotch warmed her throughout. The night wasn't too chilly, and yet, she might as well have been encased in ice, she was so cold. She couldn't look at him but focused instead on all the shadows moving about the garden with the slight breeze. "Thank you for . . . your role in bringing the conversation regarding the writing machine to an end. It is easier to explain when it's on display."

"I didn't mind doing so at Knight's expense. His handwriting is atrocious."

She almost laughed, but was very much aware of his watching her, could almost feel him outlining her profile. But she couldn't stop the quick quirking up of the corners of her lips. "You like to tease your friend."

"We like to tease each other."

"So you've been friends for a while."

"Since our Oxford days, gone over a decade now."

She couldn't imagine it. She had acquaintances and women with whom she spoke but no one she would josh around with or insult slightly as a way to show she cared about them.

"You're quite passionate about this new machine of yours," he said, and she heard a bit of admiration in his tone.

"I believe it has the potential to make a difference in how things are done. That it has a significant role to play in the future."

"Which you'll share during your demonstration."

It wasn't a question, but still she answered, "Yes."

Then they both went silent. She could hear the chirping of insects. In this large city was this small garden that reminded her of the lawn they'd had outside of Chicago. She'd been happiest there, had never felt entirely comfortable in New York. She suspected she might not be comfortable here. It was far too busy and contained too many things to take apart and examine. It contained the man standing next to her. "You're *him*, aren't you?"

Embarrassed her voice had come out all rough and ragged, she thought about blaming it on the scotch, but instead she held quiet, very much aware of his perusal. She didn't think she needed to clarify. If he was whom she believed him to be, he would know what she was asking. Seconds ticked by. Then minutes. Then hours. Days. Weeks. She lived a lifetime as she waited.

"I am," he finally said quietly.

She'd thought knowing for certain would have given her the confidence to face him. Instead, she kept her gaze homed in on the distance as she took another sip of the scotch. For bravery. For escape. "Why do you work there? To fulfill your fantasy of rescuing damsels in distress?"

"I don't work there."

She jerked her head around. The breeze lifted strands of his hair, moving them about like it would tall grass. Her fingers ached to comb through the long lengths. "But you . . . you came to me."

He nodded. "The owner, Aiden Trewlove, is my brother. I'd gone to the club to deliver a message about a matter, and he was short a couple of workers that evening and he asked me to see to your needs."

Her *needs*. Brought on by her stupid stupor.

She turned her attention back to the gardens because it was too painful to look at a man who knew she'd had to prod someone into kissing her.

"You didn't return to the club."

"No, I—" She stopped. Blinked. Considered, then faced him. "How did you know?"

"Because I did."

"Why?"

"I was hoping to make things up to you, to give you a kiss that wasn't so boring it put you to *sleep*."

A sharp edge cut through the last word, and she realized he'd been insulted by her drifting off. She would have felt the same. She smiled wryly. "You didn't. It was the absinthe. I drank too much, gathering up my courage to request the kiss."

She had the sense that he was acutely studying her, striving to determine how much he could pry. After all, most couples knew a great deal about each other before they kissed, while she and he were doing it all backward. Arse over tit she'd recently heard someone say, and it seemed to apply here because she felt as though she was tumbling down a narrow tunnel, not knowing what was waiting on the other side.

"She was wrong, your mother, regarding you not being a great beauty."

"You don't have to flatter me just because of the . . . time we spent together."

"It's not in my nature to render false flattery. Your passion, Miss Garrison, that night as well as when you were just discussing your writing machine caused you to fairly glow, brighter than any streetlamp. Beauty that comes from within is always preferable to that which comes from without."

She'd never had anyone, other than her father, offer her a compliment. While she attempted to take it in stride, she suspected she was glowing not like a streetlamp fighting off the darkness but the sun bringing light to the world.

"The night we met, I was·impressed with how you

knew what you wanted and asked for it. I know too many women who weigh their words carefully, afraid they'll be judged or found lacking."

"I wasn't trying to impress. Honestly, I didn't care what your opinion of me was as long as you delivered."

He grinned. "I failed there, didn't I? You nodded off."

"As I said, that had little to do with you."

"Do you remember our time together then?"

Oh, she most certainly remembered it. "Some of it is a green haze."

But she didn't want to rehash it, was slightly disappointed that he hadn't returned because he'd *wanted* to kiss her again, that his return had been instigated by his conviction that he owed her or his need to demonstrate he could keep her engaged to the point she'd stay awake. "I apologize for my mother's earlier inquisition and impertinence. She can be quite forceful when she sets her mind to it."

"I could say the same of you. I recall you issued a few orders."

"I wanted to ensure my expectations were met."

"Were they?"

Rook inwardly cursed himself for the asking, cursed again when she averted her gaze. She obviously wasn't quite comfortable discussing what had transpired between them. And yet it was almost a physical presence. "You don't have to answer."

"If you must know, you exceeded them. I suppose you've kissed a lot of women."

"Not as many as you might think. I'm quite particular." He was a man. He had needs, but he kept them on a tight leash as much as possible, determined to never leave any bastards in his wake.

"Except when it came to me," she said. "You knew nothing at all about me."

"I knew enough. You were eager, unafraid, daring, bold."

Her soft laughter arrowed straight into his soul. "That was the green fairy. She dominated."

The light from the library window cast a halo around her, although he couldn't envision her as an angel. An angel wouldn't kiss with the enthusiasm and wild abandon that she had. He didn't think her fervor had been the result of the absinthe. Liquor might, on occasion, serve to unleash one's inhibitions, but it certainly didn't alter the very fabric of a person, wouldn't cause them to do something that wasn't in their nature. It couldn't change a leopard's spots. But if she needed to blame what happened on the liquor, he wouldn't argue, although he was damned tempted to show her at this very minute that it wasn't spirits that had guided her.

"I'm sorry about your father."

Her response took him by surprise, but he quickly determined she was striving to direct his attention away from pursuing a discourse on their more intimate encounter. She didn't seem entirely comfortable with it. Because he wasn't a worker as she'd thought? Because their paths were bound to cross again under very different circumstances? "Don't be. He has made far too many people miserable."

"Like your brother? Mr. Trewlove? I assume he was born on the wrong side of the blanket since he doesn't carry your surname."

"He was. I only recently discovered he existed, but we've become close in a rather short period of time."

"Is it wrong of me to assume your father was unfaithful to your mother?"

"He was a right bastard to be honest, but I'd rather not discuss him."

"Perhaps at this moment, you could use this more than I." She offered him his glass.

Not much remained, but enough. He tossed back the scotch, aware of her watching him. While he knew it was impossible, he could have sworn that in that final swallow, he tasted her.

He glanced over his shoulder. No one stood at the library window, but he was fairly certain the inhabitants inside could see her silhouette and his. Her mother no doubt was mentally gauging the distance between them. Too close and she'd probably be screeching for a wedding. He wondered if it was the mother more than the daughter who was in search of a match.

He looked back at her. "Before you, I've never had a woman fall asleep on me while we were intimately engaged. Afterward, yes, but not during. I was rather disappointed we didn't get to finish that kiss."

Her eyes widened slightly. "Well, we did. It came to an end."

He smiled. "Did it, Miss Garrison? Or is it simply waiting to be continued?"

CHAPTER 5

❧

$\mathcal{H}$ E'D left her then, taken both empty glasses with him, and rejoined his friends in the library. While she'd been too stunned to do much of anything except wander along the green between the edge of the garden and the terrace until her mother had finally come to her in order to announce they were to depart.

If the gentlemen had spoken more of business, Sam would have expressed his ire once they were in the carriage. Instead, he'd remained silent throughout the journey to the Trewlove Hotel where they had a suite of rooms on the top floor. She suspected its owner, Mick Trewlove, had once lived within these very walls, but a maid who came in to clean each day had revealed that he'd moved his family to a posh house.

The maid had also whispered that all the Trewloves were by-blows. Leonora had been surprised to learn that Rook communicated with his brother, more astonished by the affection in his voice when he mentioned him. Most were intolerant of those born outside the boundaries of marriage. That Rook wasn't said much about his character, shed it in a favorable light as far as she was concerned.

Sitting in a plush chair by the low fire in her bedchamber, sketch pad in hand but pencil unmoving, Leonora contemplated all this, her thoughts continually drifting back to Rook. Had he issued his parting words because he knew she took that kiss to bed with her every night, examining it from various angles as she drifted off to sleep, and sometimes being fortunate enough to relive it in her dreams? Could it really have been as all-encompassing, as all-powerful, as she remembered?

Tonight, on that terrace, a few times he had looked like he might lean toward her and press his lips to hers. She'd not have stopped him. She'd have welcomed him—

Then she would have married him because her mother would have insisted.

She was beginning to understand the true beauty of the Elysium. It offered the chance to explore without suffering consequences, especially as the men who worked there wouldn't be wandering around the aristocracy. Rather unfortunate that Aiden Trewlove had imagined she wouldn't either when he'd sent his brother to her.

With a growl of frustration because she might never escape reminders of that infamous club if the Chessmen did indeed invest, she turned her attention to her sketchbook and began drawing lines, circles, swoops, and intricate designs. She'd always found solace in the way the pencil sketched what she envisioned in her mind.

During her journey across the Atlantic, she'd felt swallowed up by the vastness of the sea—the blueness of it, the beauty of it. Staring out at something that offered no distractions, she'd come up with an idea for another sort of machine. She'd drafted what she envisioned for the outside easily enough, but the inner workings were a bit more complicated, and she was certain once she figured them out that the outside of the contraption would no doubt need to be altered somewhat.

Her father had always encouraged her to start with the first cog and go from there, but she preferred to begin with how it would look when completed, so it served as a beacon for her imagination, gave it a focus. She knew her mind would take wrong turns and travel along paths that led nowhere but that was all part of the journey. None of the hours she devoted to exploration were wasted because even the aspects that didn't work contributed to her discovering what did.

Therefore, she'd sat in a chair on the deck of the ship and spent hours filling up pages with notions and potential solutions. And all the possibilities waited patiently for her when she needed a diversion from her wandering musings that now included a kiss that had not yet been completed.

The rap on the door startled her, and she was rather certain she was blushing with guilt because of the direction in which her rambling thoughts had been traveling at a breakneck speed only a minute ago. She had to swallow and clear her throat before she could call out, "Come."

The door opened but a crack, just enough for her brother to peer in. "May I?"

Although her maid had assisted her in preparing for bed, she was wearing a wrapper and was adequately covered. Besides, it was difficult to look at her baby brother and see him as a grown man. "Of course."

Attired only in shirtsleeves and trousers, he wandered in, closing the door behind him, and joined her by the fire, leaning his shoulder against the mantel. "Mama was in fine form this evening, wasn't she?"

"You're fortunate no unmarried ladies were in attendance, or she'd have had you betrothed by night's end," she told him, with a wry quirk of her lips.

"If the lady had a substantial dowry, it could solve our problem."

"And create others. Money makes for a lonely alliance."

He shrugged. "Rook seemed to take an interest in you. When you were on the terrace with him, did you use the opportunity to sell him on the idea of that machine of yours?"

She'd had other matters to parse out. "No. After we indicated a demonstration was needed to fully appreciate it, further explanation seemed pointless."

Running his thumb along the edge of the mantel, he studied it as though it was the most fascinating movement he'd ever seen. "If you were to entice him into marriage, we wouldn't need any investors at all, would we? Certainly, he has the means to ensure our family's business doesn't go under. If Mama is correct, and he has an interest in you—"

"He doesn't."

"Then why did he join you on the terrace?"

"To reassure me that he didn't hold me accountable for Mama's obnoxious behavior. She was loud, rude, and embarrassingly inappropriate." Setting her sketch pad aside, she shoved herself out of the chair and began to pace. "I don't appeal to Lord Wyeth."

If she did, wouldn't he have tried to arrange an assignation? Or at least hinted at one? Although he had indicated the kiss had not yet come to an end. So when and how would it? Had she not been struck dumb, perhaps she would have asked.

"You don't have to appeal to him. You just have to get him alone and be discovered."

She brought her pacing to an abrupt halt and glared at him. "I don't want to acquire a husband by subterfuge. It would result in the most unpleasant of marriages."

"Sacrifices must be made. For Father. In his memory. He began this business and had high hopes for it. You don't want him to be seen as a failure. For that to be his legacy."

All of that was true, but still—

"Why did you tell them they'd be investing in a weapon?"

"To pique their interest. And they know what weapons are. To try to describe your writing machine . . . well, you saw how that went. They weren't too keen on the notion."

"I'm rather certain it had more to do with the sense of being swindled. You promised them one thing when we're trying to sell them on something else. These are not men to be trifled with. We convince them to invest on the merits of the company and our plans for its diversification. If you're not in agreement, then I might as well hop on the next ship home and find another way to keep things running."

He stepped away from the fireplace. "I need you here, Nora. I haven't your confidence regarding the potential for this plan of yours to change our direction, and I certainly don't understand all the inner workings of that machine. I'm depending on you to help me convince others that the risk is minimal, and the gains will be great."

"No more talk of doing it through marriage."

"You have my word."

"We may have lost our edge with the Chessmen tonight." She didn't blame them if they no longer were interested in handing over their money. She feared her brother was playing a game when he didn't fully comprehend the rules. "We need to approach other potential investors if we are to have any hope at all of securing the funding we need."

He gave her a shy, but wily smile. "I know you think I'm useless, but I may have mentioned our need for investors to a few additional nobles when I visited a club or two. And who knows? Perhaps you'll meet someone you fancy if we're here long enough and other lords show an interest in you."

She sighed with frustration. So much for giving her his word. "Sam, I am not the product. The writing machine is. Although I'm thinking we might want to change the name of the company." It had once been Garrison Munitions. Then they'd discussed changing it to Garrison Writing Machines. "I thought we might want to go with Garrison Machine Works. Then we're not limited to what we can create." She held her breath, striving to decide how much to tell him, but he was her brother. The company was his. "I have an idea for another machine."

He glanced over at the pad resting on the table. "I thought you'd been spending an inordinate amount of time sketching. I considered that you were striving to avoid Mama tossing eligible men your way while we were on the ship." He dropped down into a chair opposite the one in which she'd been sitting and crossed his legs. "So tell me about it."

She eased into her chair and fought not to bounce with her excitement. "For now you're to tell no one about it because I've yet to work out all the particulars and that could take months if not years. But presently, I'm calling it the sales tallying machine."

SITTING IN KING'S library, slowly sipping his scotch while his friends and their wives also lounged about in the seating area, Rook felt as though something was missing. He didn't really want to give a name to it but if forced, he would have had to admit it was Miss Garrison's presence.

Even when she'd remained on the terrace after he'd returned to this room, he'd enjoyed looking through the window at her silhouette and found comfort in it. She'd been more relaxed out there, without her mother badgering her. He'd noticed the occasional discreet pinch and had decided if he saw one more headed her way, he was going to intercept it. He didn't understand the older woman's actions. Even his father, for all the pain he'd caused, had never physically harmed him.

"I believe we all owe you an apology, Rook," King began, "for even suggesting you might want to court the girl, much less marry her. The behavior of the mother was appalling."

Rook certainly couldn't take exception to that last statement. "I have the impression that Miss Garrison isn't husband hunting. Rather Mrs. Garrison is son-in-law hunting."

"I don't think she's going to have much luck with achieving that end if she comes across as forcefully in the future as she did here tonight."

"It hardly seems fair to Miss Garrison," Penelope said. "I rather liked her. When I was giving her a tour, nothing escaped her notice. She examined a few things quite closely, which resulted in our delay in returning to the parlor."

"She did leave me with the notion that she is curious by nature." Naturally, Rook wasn't going to divulge that he'd met her previously. As Aiden had said, what happened within the walls of the Elysium stayed within those walls.

"I feel as though we've been deceived," Knight uttered. "We were supposed to be investing in a munitions factory. That's what Sam Garrison proposed to us."

"I know we were exploring our options," Rook said, "but in the end, we'd have not invested. Miss Garrison has the right of it. There are too many established firearms companies. Not only in America but here. The Gun Quarter in Birmingham alone must have close to a hundred gun manufacturers. They supply our military, as do the Americans. We can't expect to make much profit selling only to the occasional sports hunter."

"Then why entertain the notion of investing with him?"

"He wrote that he had something new to offer," King reminded him.

"And they do," Penelope said. "As a former secretary, I know it can become quite bothersome when an abundance of correspondence is needed. I'm intrigued by the notion of a machine that would do the writing for me. I want to see it at work."

"A writing machine," Knight repeated before glaring at Rook. "My handwriting, by the by, is not atrocious."

"It's awful," Bishop muttered.

Rook grinned. In fact, Knight's skill with forming letters was only a little worse than his own, and while it had not been his intention to embarrass his friend—and Knight's confidence was such that it would take a great deal more to knock him off his high horse—he'd felt a need to offer Miss Garrison some support when it was obvious she was so extraordinarily passionate about this contraption in which she wanted them to invest.

"She knew a good deal more about what they are offering than her brother," King said. "Once she started speaking, he fairly faded into the shadows."

"You gentlemen can't be surprised by an informed woman in your midst when three of you have intelligent wives who either presently or in the past have managed successful careers that saw them in good stead," Penelope said.

The grin King gave his wife was filled with pride and affection. "Not at all. Simply making an observation."

"Mr. Garrison," Rook began, "reminds me of a barker at a carnival who is constantly calling out for people to come over. But then he leads them to someone else who is the true talent."

"Are you implying that you fancy Miss Garrison?" Knight asked, his smile all too knowing.

"Simply pointing out that she shouldn't be overlooked. After all, you three misjudged your wives and had to do a bit of groveling as I recall."

CHAPTER 6

‿‿⁀‿⁀‿

$\mathcal{T}$HE hard rain had fallen all afternoon, which made it the perfect day for sitting near a window, listening to the constant patter of raindrops hitting glass, and striving to determine and map out the inner workings needed for her tallying machine.

The weather, however, was not so conducive to traveling to a ball. Yet here they were, dressed up to the nines, in a carriage the hotel had provided for them, rambling along through the water-slogged streets.

Three days earlier, Sam had been beside himself with glee when he walked into their suites at the Trewlove Hotel and tossed the invitation to the ball on her lap. "We're being courted," he'd announced.

Leonora had barely picked it up and read the first line before her mother had snatched it from her fingers. "Another duke," she'd gushed.

"Another married duke, I believe." Since it was the Duke and Duchess of Wolfford requesting the honor of their presence.

Mama had given her a quelling glare. "Perhaps he has a younger brother who could inherit the title should the present holder perish."

Leonora had felt ill with the realization that her

own flesh and blood would wish ill on someone for personal gain. There was ambition, but then there was greed, and she feared her mother was hovering on the precipice of avarice.

"I suppose the Chessmen will be in attendance," she said casually now, even though her gloved fingers had knotted tightly together, and she longed for her sketch pad to help settle her nerves. She'd never been comfortable at the few balls she'd attended in New York. According to her mother, they were *practice* balls to prepare them for the moment they would enter the elite ballrooms, but Leonora had spent more time warming the seat of a chair than gliding over the dance floor.

"I should think so. I get the impression they're well-liked," Sam said. "And I don't think they're the sort who would appreciate being snubbed."

She had no plans to snub them, although she was of a mind to avoid John Castleton, Viscount Wyeth, during the upcoming days. Because she feared he might be correct. Their kiss was simply waiting to be continued. She wasn't entirely certain she was prepared for the journey upon which its completion might take her.

SHORTLY AFTER ARRIVING at the Wolfford residence, where footmen holding umbrellas aloft had assisted them out of their carriage and ensured they made their way inside without getting drenched, Leonora learned that the duke did indeed have a younger brother—Lord Griffith Stanwick—because her family was being introduced to him . . . and his wife. Wicked girl that she was, she took a great deal of pleasure in knowing that her mother's hopes for the duke's early demise were thwarted. The duke also had a sister, Althea. She was married to a man who would one day be a duke as well, a man everyone referred to as Beast.

"What do you think of England thus far, Miss Garrison?" the unavailable Lord Griffith Stanwick asked.

That it is a place for wicked indulgences. "I haven't had the opportunity to experience a great deal of it yet."

"Perhaps you could direct us toward some unmarried lords," Mama said, and Leonora hoped no one heard her back teeth crashing together as she fought not to reveal her irritation with the woman's inability to be discreet.

"Are you hoping to remarry, Mrs. Garrison?" Lady Kathryn, Lord Griffith Stanwick's wife, asked.

"What? No. Absolutely not. My daughter, however . . ." She let her voice trail off, all that was needed to make her point that her daughter was desperate. Leonora wanted to shout that she had no wish to marry but didn't want to engage in an argument in front of these people she'd only just met.

"Actually, my husband has a club for the unmarried," Lady Kathryn said. "The Fair and Spare. You should pay it a visit. I think you'd enjoy all the various entertainments."

"Spare? That's what you call second sons, isn't it?" Sam asked.

"Indeed. I'm a spare," Lord Griffith said. "No firstborn sons who will inherit a title are allowed inside the doors."

"Well, that won't do her a damn bit of good, will it?" Mama asked succinctly. "We'll not settle for less than a titled gent."

"Mama," she ground out.

"Well, I won't have it. We've traveled all this way, and you finally have the opportunity to make something of yourself if you'd put more effort into the endeavor."

She wondered why a hole couldn't open up beneath her feet and swallow her up, allow her to escape from this maddening discourse and Mama's obsession with her marital status and her desire to use it to *her own* advantage rather than striving to ensure it was to her daughter's. Leonora felt rather like those young princesses who had been forced to marry aging kings in order to prevent wars: sacrificial, unappreciated for herself and any contributions she could personally make.

She turned to the other women in the group. "Would you be kind enough to direct me to the ladies' retiring room? I have a pebble in my slipper that's becoming rather annoying, and I should like to eliminate its existence before the dancing begins." She'd already had several gents ask her for a dance, and she was planning to take advantage of the opportunity to entice them into possibly investing.

As though they were the firmest of friends, Lady Althea slipped her arm around Leonora's. "Here, I'll take you."

The soft smile she gave her husband promised a swift return. Then she was guiding Leonora through the throng of guests. "Mothers can sometimes be troublesome," Lady Althea whispered in sympathy.

"Was yours?"

She laughed lightly, sadly. "No. 'Twas my father who caused the trouble, but thankfully my older brother managed to put matters to right."

Leonora had no older brother to do the same for

her family. Not that she felt she needed one. She enjoyed managing the business, wanted to keep doing so. Which was the problem. Marriage, particularly to a noble, would rob her of that opportunity. She couldn't imagine an aristocratic husband allowing her to work, to do as she pleased. Sam, eventually, would have the confidence to take over their company, and she should be striving to assist him in achieving that goal. But what was she if not the overseer of the family business? What would be her place within the family then?

She'd never really had a position outside of it. It was a bit frightening to consider not having the security of what she'd always known.

"It's not much farther," Lady Althea said, drawing Leonora's eyes toward her. "You look to be in considerable pain."

"No, I just . . . when I embarked on this journey, I hadn't realized my mother and brother viewed this as a husband-hunting expedition. I thought we were looking only for investors. And to that end, I don't suppose you could point me in the direction of any men of means—not necessarily lords—who might be willing to take a risk on a new and exciting venture."

"I suspect I could introduce you to a couple of gentlemen who might be interested in what you are offering."

At the very least, Leonora could ensure they received an invitation to the demonstration they'd be holding. She'd managed to get permission to use the hotel ballroom for their purposes in a few days.

She and her escort walked through the doorway, and Leonora stuttered to a stop as she encountered a brick wall, one that reached out and wrapped a large hand around her upper arm to steady her.

"Ah, and here's serendipity stepping in to provide you with just what you were looking for," Lady Althea said. "Rook, allow me to introduce—"

"We've met," he said quietly, his hold on her loosening, his white-gloved fingers grazing over the inside of her upper arm before retreating. She'd felt the warmth of the glide as though nothing separated his skin from hers. Heat coursed through her as she recalled what he had touched with bare fingers: her cheeks, her throat.

"Oh, I'm not all surprised. The Chessmen always seem to know about investment opportunities before anyone else."

His gaze stayed on Leonora. "Staying alert and informed gives us an advantage."

"As though any of you need it. If you'll be kind enough to excuse us, we're on our way to the ladies' retiring room. Miss Garrison has a pebble in her slipper."

"We can't have that, can we?"

Before she even realized what was happening, he had hold of her arm again, led her to a chair, and managed to put her in it without shoving or forcing her. She'd been mesmerized by the teasing warmth in his eyes and thought she might follow him anywhere.

Then he gracefully went down on one knee. Her breath backed up into her lungs and her mind raced from a fantastical image of him asking her to marry him to the memory of him posed like that just before he'd kissed her. Whichever he intended now was unconscionable, and yet she seemed powerless to speak, to move, to do anything other than study the planes of his face in this lighted foyer. Every line was strong, designed by a deft hand, so that each flowed into the other. He was all angles: sharp cheekbones, pointed chin. This close, with a nearby lamp providing light, she could see that his eyes weren't as dark as she'd originally surmised, but more the brown of a fawn she'd once watched in the woods.

But his lips were exactly as she remembered. Every detail of them. The plump lower one that even now she wanted to run her tongue over, the upper that she wanted to nibble, and the seam begging for her attentions. The choices were too many. The skin at his throat, above his knotted neckcloth, called to her to taste, to explore.

"Which one?"

She jerked her gaze up to his eyes, hoping he hadn't been able to detect precisely where she'd been looking, trusting hunger had not been written all over her face. That he had not in fact been asking if she wanted to taste or explore. "I beg your pardon?"

"Which slipper has the pebble?"

As he waited, his hands were near her feet, ready to attend to the task. The pebble had been a lie, simply a means to escape the odious conversation with her mother. Now, she was trapped by her own deception. "I believe it worked its way free."

"It's best to be sure, don't you think? You're certain to be dancing much of the night. Right or left?"

Lady Althea leaned down slightly. "Do you really think this is appropriate?"

"It's merely a slipper. I shan't have to even expose her ankle."

Leonora was aware that several ladies and a couple of gentlemen had stopped to gawk or take a gander out of curiosity. She wanted to jump up and run. On the other hand . . . "Right."

He wound one hand around the ankle that remained hidden beneath her skirt, his fingers dancing lightly over her stocking as his other hand removed her shoe and extended it up to her for an inspection so she could find the errant pebble. While she carried on with the pretense and searched, his palms explored the arch of her foot, her heel, her toes, slowly, so slowly, kneading gently as though she'd truly been hurt and required his tender ministrations to ease any bruising caused by the troublesome piece of stone.

She'd always considered her feet too large, but at that moment, she wished the slipper was three times its size so examining it would take longer and thus his investigation could continue. But their audience was growing, and whispers were beginning to echo around them. "It's as I thought. It's gone."

"Jolly good." He took the slipper from her and carefully slid it back onto her foot. She didn't want to consider how many women for whom he might have performed the same service after they'd visited his bed. He was entirely too adept at removing the satin shoe and putting it back into place. She suspected he was equally skilled when it came to various aspects of a woman's clothing.

In one fluid motion, he unfolded his body and stood. Offering his hand, he helped her to her feet.

"Thank you, my lord."

"I wouldn't want you limping about when we dance."

"Are we going to dance, my lord?"

"If your card is not already full."

She wished it was. He made her feel light-headed,

as if she'd just enjoyed several glasses of absinthe. Instead, she held up her wrist, the card dangling from it serving as an invitation. She watched as he used the attached tiny pencil to scrawl his name next to a waltz. Then he gave a curt bow. "Until later, Miss Garrison."

His walking off seemed to signal that everyone else should scurry away.

"Hmm," Lady Althea hummed. "Rook usually spends more time in the cardroom than on the dance floor."

"He's giving me attention only because he has a possible interest in investing in our company. He wants an advantage."

"I'm not really sure he needs one. Your brother won't turn away an investor, surely."

Were they coming across as desperate? It would put them at a disadvantage. They needed people clamoring to invest. "No, I suppose he won't."

"Shall we return to the ballroom now that your . . . pebble has been seen to?"

"What he did was rather scandalous, wasn't it?"

Lady Althea smiled. "Not so scandalous that you'll be forced to marry, but I'm quite certain it'll warrant a mention in the gossip sheets on the morrow."

Leonora had never been the object of gossip. Unfortunately, she suspected it was going to thrill Mama no end should it come about.

"I'VE NEVER KNOWN you to take much interest in watching the dancing," Knight said, sotto voce, as he and Rook stood at the edge of the ballroom. "You're usually off playing cards by now."

Rook was tempted to tell him to mind his own business. Instead, he confessed, "I signed a dance card."

"Miss Garrison's, I presume."

"Why would you think that?"

Knight's grin was irritatingly confident. "Regina claims to have detected a spark between the two of you during dinner the other night."

"Your wife wrote a novel about a woman in love with a scoundrel." Although it was extremely biographical in nature. "She no doubt imagines sparks everywhere."

Knight gave a little nod while lifting a single shoulder in a shrug. "Perhaps. So with whom are you dancing?"

Rook had no reason not to say. After all, Knight would soon be witnessing him waltzing around the grand parlor with her.

"Miss Garrison," he finally growled.

In all honesty, Rook wasn't quite certain why he'd requested a dance of the American. Perhaps because now he knew that her ankle, arch, and toes were as perfect as her lips. And having kneaded that slender foot, he'd wanted to touch her once more before the night was done. Best to do it in a safe spot where witnesses would ensure he remained a perfect gentleman and on his best behavior. Not that he was prone to exhibiting any sort of misbehavior. Upon further reflection, however, he should probably ask a couple of other ladies to dance so no one else drew the conclusion Knight had: that Miss Garrison was somehow special.

Although he could claim to be striving to determine more about the investment opportunity.

"The way you've been watching her, I'd venture to guess that you're going to seek more than a dance."

He didn't want to admit that he felt rather possessive about her. He'd seen her give cautious smiles to numerous dance partners, and he wanted one for himself. One that was more fully formed, not timid or shy. One that was as forceful as she'd been that first night. "Unlike you in your youth, Knight, I've never lured ladies into darkened corners for kisses."

"Then I'd say it's about time you did. You've always been far too proper. The right lady can make you want to be extremely improper."

"And you have experience with that."

"I don't regret a single moment of it. Well, except for the part where I left her at the altar. Thank God, she forgave me."

"Rest assured, I have no intention of following your ludicrous example of doing what I ought not. Or King's or Bishop's."

And he'd certainly never leave anyone at the altar because he had no plans to ever make a trip to the altar to begin with. "Devil take you, we're only going to dance. But if I did have more in mind"—he was no doubt going to regret asking—"since the rain doesn't seem in favor of stopping anytime soon, and even if it does, the gardens will be too wet and muddy, where might I find a bit of privacy in this mausoleum?"

Because he had decided England could begin sinking into the sea, and he wasn't going to retreat until he'd drawn the last bit of pleasure from that mouth that haunted him whether he was awake or asleep.

"You seem to have recovered well from the damage caused by the errant pebble in your slipper."

They were only a few steps into their waltz, but already he wished he'd asked for a second, while he'd had a chance. He'd caught a glimpse of her card and every dance had been claimed.

Her cheeks flushed pink, and he wanted to lay his fingers against her skin and have the heat travel from her into him. "It was a tiny pebble, hardly caused any discomfort, but still irritating."

He arched a brow and lifted one corner of his mouth ruefully. "Strange how it left no marks at all. I was unable to feel even the tiniest of dents where it had been."

She pursed her luscious lips and glared at him hotly. "Very well. There was no pebble. I lied so I'd have an excuse to get away from my mother, who was doing her damnedest to mortify me."

Pleased that she'd confessed the truth, he offered a sympathetic smile. "I assumed as much."

"I suppose you never lie."

"I don't, because I know the secret of lies."

A small pleat appeared between her brows, and he wanted to ease it away with a press of his thumb, just as he'd explored her arch. Her foot had responded by curling over his hand. What other reactions awaited his sensual stroking of her flesh?

"What secret?" she asked.

"That when you lie, your eyes turn purple."

She gawked. "What are you talking about? That's not true."

"Of course it is. My mother explained it all to me when I was a lad. Therefore, whenever I lied, I closed my eyes so she wouldn't see that they'd turned purple."

She laughed. Dear Lord, it had been a mistake to try to ease that sound from her because he was left to decide whether he wanted her to be the Lady of Sighs or the Lady of Laughter. The echo of her glee was intoxicating. But then so were her sighs. Was he greedy to want a mixture of both?

And why from her? Other intriguing women had crossed his path through the years, but the infatuation had been short-lived. He couldn't imagine her becoming less interesting. What made her so different? So addictive?

"Surely, you didn't," she said.

"I did. But in my defense, I was only four or so. My experiences at the time were somewhat limited, so I was a bit naive."

She was smiling and it transformed her face into the loveliest he'd ever seen. "Ironic. Your mother lying about lies."

"Indeed. I often tease her about it."

"You get along with her then?"

He hoped his answer wouldn't cause her any sadness because his mother was very different from hers. "I do. We've always been close. I think . . ." He shook his head.

"You think what?"

Why did he want to tell her the deep, dark facts regarding his parents, their pasts, and how they'd influenced him? Because if her mother believed he was the sort she should marry, Miss Garrison needed to know the truth regarding his scandalous family? How they'd shaped him into the man he was? But they were not the sort of words that should be uttered in a ballroom where the light from the massive crystal chandeliers glinted off strands of her hair as they circled the floor. Therefore, a change of topic was warranted.

"You never did share with me if I was any good at kissing."

Her eyes warmed slightly, and a corner of that luscious mouth hitched up. "I was rather foxed that night. I might not have been in the best state to judge. After all, I thought we'd finished, and you claim we didn't."

"Then I'd say it's high time we got on with it and brought it to its rightful conclusion."

CHAPTER 7

Leonora very much wished that they had finished their dance, the orchestra had finished playing, and the ball had finished completely. The last thing she wanted was to bring that kiss to an end because she wasn't certain what waited on the other side of it. Based on the manner in which his gaze captured and held hers, the way the brown of his eyes darkened, and the intensity with which he studied her, she suspected the kiss was merely a prelude to something far more enjoyable . . . and wicked. More alluring than the green fairy, more prone to leaving devastation and quite possibly regret in its wake.

Something illicit. Something a proper lady avoided. Something that tested the boundaries of propriety.

Because in his study of her, she also read a challenge and a vow. *Dare to follow me and I'll take you on a journey where you'll learn the perils of pleasure. For which you'll thank me afterward. Facing those dangers can be addictive and you'll gain a stronger desire to experience them again.*

She swallowed, licked the top center of her upper lip. He watched her movements with eyes that began to smolder, and she was hit with the wild and heady awareness that she held some power over him.

"I noticed you conversing with a few ladies. I didn't think to ask the other night if you were courting someone." She didn't know why the words caused a sharp pain in her chest.

"If I was, I would have never kissed you or suggested I do so again."

"You're loyal then."

"Extremely."

Unlike his father who had numerous bastards. She was grateful to know in that regard he would not be like his sire. Not that it truly mattered. Once their kiss was completed, they'd be done with each other. She didn't know why the thought saddened her.

"I've been deliberating returning to the Elysium," she admitted.

"As I've told you, I don't work there."

"Perhaps . . . you could arrange something with your brother so the kissing room was available, and you could meet me there."

"That's too involved and delays matters. I had something else in mind. Here. Now. Tonight."

Her eyes flared slightly. "This moment? While we're dancing?"

His smile was devastatingly beautiful and filled with compassion at her naivety. He might even be inwardly chuckling as he appeared somewhat amused. "Hardly. Such a display would lead us both to the altar."

So he wasn't considering her for marriage. That was good to know as she had no wish to wed. Or so she told herself. She never had before. It was all Mama's harping planting seeds of . . . possibilities . . . in her mind.

"In the hallway where I tended to your foot"—her face warmed at the reminder—"if you carry on to your right, you'll reach a fork. Take the corridor to the left. At its end, you'll spot a recess where a statue of a snarling wolf sits on a tall pedestal. If you ease around it, you'll find yourself in a tiny alcove of shadows. I'll be waiting for you there."

"My dance card is full."

"Then I suppose someone will be disappointed."

The cocky grin he gave her indicated he knew it wouldn't be him.

He brought them to a halt. She'd been so entranced with his deep voice laying out his proposition, she'd failed to notice the tune drifting to a close. Without another word, he escorted her to the edge of the dance floor and bestowed upon her a nod filled with such confidence and arrogance—as though he comprehended that she'd be unable to resist him—that she decided she absolutely would not follow the directions he'd so meticulously laid out. The kiss would definitely go unfinished.

IN THE END, she disappointed herself . . . and Lord Lawrence Brinsley-Norton, younger brother to the Duke of Kingsland. As she hurried down the corridor, she was certain that since only the remaining portion of a kiss needed to be addressed, it could be done in the space of a single dance, perhaps two, but she would disappoint no more than a couple of lords—if she disappointed them at all.

She suspected a good many of her dance partners were whisking her around the ballroom in an attempt to gain favor with her brother or mother. For business reasons or matrimonial, thinking that neither was dependent on her opinion. Time with her was an obligation, not a desire.

Except when it came to Rook. He wasn't driven by desire, of that she was fairly confident. But in him, she sensed a competitive streak to prove his kiss was well done enough to lure her away from other gentlemen. She was giving him a victory, which she'd not intended; yet she couldn't help but feel she'd be winning as well.

If she could ever reach that blasted alcove.

It was a goodly distance away from the chair in which she'd sat while he'd slowly stroked her foot as if it was a new discovery to be thoroughly examined—just as she explored anything unknown she ran across. Which meant their meeting place was far from the ballroom and by the time she'd reached the fork he'd mentioned, she was quite isolated from any other guests wandering about. It occurred to her that continuing on might be an unwise idea, but then another kiss might prove that the wondrousness of the first was a result of her foxed state rather than his skill, and the warmth that invaded her body with the memories of it might dissipate so she could more easily sleep without feeling like she was suffocating in her own skin and he was the only one with the means to free her.

At long last, she reached the statue for which she'd been searching. On one side of the hallway was a closed door that probably led into a library or drawing room. On the other, the alcove. Peering over the wolf's back, she saw only darkness beyond. No chandelier provided light within this corridor. Only a lamp on a table farther down.

To know of this tucked-away spot, he must have kissed dozens of women here. Hence, she was one of many, which was all to the good because that meant he knew what he was about. Still, once in her life, she would like to be made to feel special. She almost had that night at the Elysium, except her dulled mind hadn't been able to forget that they'd had to send someone to her—that she'd had to *ask*.

Only tonight, he'd done the asking. Or at least the demanding. In such a commanding voice, it was impossible to ignore, like a general giving orders to his troops.

If he was doing as he'd promised and was hidden away in there, he was observing her hesitancy. Watching, waiting. Waiting for her to be sure of herself. It was only when it came to men that she lacked complete confidence. They always seemed to find her interests a bit odd. She'd been able to share them with her father—it had pleased him when she had. But other men had always looked at her strangely, caused her unease.

If she left now, Rook would know her to be a coward.

Although perhaps he wasn't there. After all, she'd danced with another gentleman after Rook had left her, the entire time her thoughts focused on what—who— was awaiting her arrival. He may have lost patience and abandoned this spot. He may have never shown. But if he had and if he was still there—

Her heart was pounding with such force, she was surprised it didn't knock the wolf right off its pedestal as she flattened herself as much as possible and eased by its snarling mouth and into the blackened abyss.

Where she was greeted by an arm coming unerringly around her waist and drawing her up against a solid wall of firm muscle and sinew hidden beneath evening attire. It seemed appropriate somehow that he was the castle of his little group of friends, the fortification that offered protection. He made her feel safe. Here, secreted away from all the other guests, secluded, she should have felt some trepidation. Who was to hear if he took advantage?

Yet, she found herself relaxing in his arms as though she'd just downed a large glass of absinthe, her inhibitions and doubts floating away.

Pressed up against him as she was, he had to be aware of her going lax. She suspected it was what he'd been anticipating because suddenly one hand was cradling her face, tipping her head back slightly, his thumb stroking down to touch the corner of her mouth so his lips blanketed hers with a precision she admired, a precision needed for anything mechanical to work properly, for anything that moved to do so smoothly. She had a collection of windup toys her father had given her over the years, that she had taken apart and put back together in order to understand the magic of them. They had fascinated her, but not as much as this kiss.

While precise, it was not mechanical in any way. Although she suspected the wait may have served to wind him up. She might have smiled at the thought had she not begun getting lost in the wondrous sensations his incredible mouth was eliciting.

Since this kiss was a continuation of the one before, he hadn't bothered with any slow seduction to ease her into opening her mouth to him. She'd instinctually parted her lips to give him access, and he'd come in conquering, plundering. Yet she experienced the thrill of victory.

He groaned low and the vibrations from the rumbling of his chest danced over her breasts, smashed as they were against him. He still tasted dark and dangerous. Had probably indulged in a bit of scotch before coming here to wait for her. She liked the flavor of him. Liked the way his tongue parried with hers, explored the confines as though they had all the time in the world.

Suddenly she felt as though they did, and she wanted all those moments, hours, and eons to occur within this nook. She feared at least three gentlemen would be disappointed because she was certain to miss three dances if not four. She did hope she wasn't disappointing Rook, but if he wasn't enjoying the kiss, would his mouth still be clinging to hers? Would his hand roam over her backside, tenderly squeeze, and then press her even more firmly against his hardness? Would his body even react to such a magnificent degree if he wasn't as entranced as she?

Tonight it was all her. And all him. No green fairy to intrude. It was far more powerful than she'd remembered. There was hunger. Need. Want. Desire.

It was everything. She wished for it to never end.

ROOK HAD NEVER so desperately wanted a kiss *not* to end. She was deliciously sweet, even though tonight no absinthe flavored her tongue. And the sounds she made, the soft mewling, a kitten being stroked with the gentlest of hands. His Lady of Sighs.

He did take care to be tender, not to ravish as his own needs dictated. She pulled at the animalistic cravings that raged within him, cravings he feared he'd inherited from his father, that were in his blood to be passed down through the generations. Cravings he'd chained within the dungeon of the fortification he'd become—to protect himself and those who would suffer if he unleashed the full force of his appetites. Yearnings once set free that he might be unable to control.

Yet control them he had, for years now.

Oh, but he'd never wanted as he wanted now. This woman who seemed both innocent and worldly. Who gave as much as she took. Who didn't hold back her passions. Who wasn't coy. Who'd asked for what she wanted and then let him have his way with her mouth.

Their tongues tangled and explored. He dared to skim his fingers over the bared portions of her shoulders. Her gown was slightly fancier than the one she'd worn to the Elysium, but the same rich shade of pink, as if she understood how it complemented her complexion. He envisioned her spread out on sheets of the same color, matching the vibrancy she would bring to sex.

He wanted to go down on his knees, lift her skirts, and taste with as much enthusiasm as he was delivering to her mouth. But she'd asked for only a kiss. It was all he'd deliver.

But he'd make certain it was one she'd never forget, one that would spoil her for any other man. With a rough groan, he bent her back slightly and deepened the kiss.

SHE'D BEEN RIGHT not to have gotten up from the chaise longue when he'd delivered the beginning of this kiss because her legs could barely support her now and were in danger of melting away completely. However, based on the tight hold he had on her, she'd probably remain upright—as long as his lips stayed on hers. She clung to him as though he was her salvation.

How was it possible for something so simple to be so breathtaking?

She had to believe that he was drawing out the kiss because he found it as rewarding. Low groans emanated from him, and each was music to her ears, that she had the ability to entice such glorious sounds from him. She wasn't quite certain she'd find the strength to return to the ballroom when all she craved was to remain here and enjoy all the sensations he brought to life within her. She'd never imagined something without coils and springs could be so complex and complicated. Could fascinate her in so many various ways. That *he* could fascinate her so. She had the fanciful thought that she could stay here with him forever.

But, of course, she couldn't, and he seemed to be drawing the kiss to a close because he went quiet and cupped her face before easing away from her.

"We've come to the end, haven't we?" she asked. She was nothing if not inquisitive, needing to know all the answers. And the certainty of them.

"Yes." He traced his thumb over her lower lip, and she wondered how he'd managed to unerringly find it within this blackened abyss. "How is it that you'd never been kissed? You're certainly adventurous enough, going to the Elysium as you did, meeting me here in this alcove."

Adventurous? She supposed worse descriptions could apply to her behavior: scandalous, naughty, sinful. Mama would toss all of those at her if she ever learned what Leonora had done. But Rook was no doubt striving to be tactful, just in case they became partners in the enterprise. "Not to mention that I'm an old maid with years to have done it?"

"You're hardly old. But surely you had suitors."

"No, I wasn't really interested in any of the men in my life. Mother focused all her efforts on Sam, believed he'd be her entry into proper Society. He's handsome, charming, certain to catch some lady's eye. I, on the other hand, am too stubborn, not nearly obedient enough, too inquisitive about the wrong sort of things—"

"Like kissing?"

She laughed lightly, finding it difficult to believe that her curiosity about kissing was wrong. Truly where was the harm in what she'd done? No scarlet *K* marred her bodice. She wouldn't get with child. She'd given away nothing of import. "I don't care one whit about all the different embroidery stitches and how they can be used to create beautiful samplers. I care about mechanical things."

She stopped, aware of the heat rushing to her cheeks because she was blathering on, found him so easy to blather to. She'd never shared with any other man the things she enjoyed.

"Such as," he prodded.

"I'm on the cusp of boring you to tears."

"I'm curious. Tell me."

She knew what it was to be curious, to be constantly searching for the answers. She took a deep, fortifying breath. "When I was eight, I took my father's pocket watch apart. Mama was furious when she discovered all the pieces laid out on the table. Sent me to bed without my supper. My father's punishment was so much worse. The disappointment in his eyes nearly cleaved me in two. The next day he sat me in front of that table and simply said, 'Put it back together so that it works.' I remembered where each spring, gear, and wheel went. When I had completed the task, not only did it work but I understood how."

"I haven't a bloody clue."

"I could explain it, but it's not very titillating conversation without a demonstration of all the parts involved. Besides, taking a watch apart once in my life was more than enough." In his will, her father had left the timepiece to her, not to Sam. That, too, had upset her mother. "Afterward, if I wanted to know how something worked, my father would take me to someone who could show me with diagrams or to a factory where I could observe the item being assembled. Trains, music boxes, anything with a part that moved. And if it was something he could purchase for me, I was allowed to take it apart. It all fascinated me. I found it so exciting. But . . . when a gentleman gives you attention, is dancing with you or taking you on a walk about the park, his eyes tend to glaze over when you're explaining the various types of levers and how effectively they can be used. I suspect yours have glazed over by now but it's too dark for me to see."

"I promise you they haven't. But you've yet to fully explain how it is that you avoided being kissed. Do continue."

Avoided, as if it had been her choice. Although she suspected in a way it had been. "Over time, I developed a reputation for being a bit . . . strange. I once overheard—"

She stopped abruptly. She'd indulged in a glass of champagne earlier. It was loosening her tongue. Or maybe it was the intoxication of the kiss. Or perhaps it was merely the keen interest of the lord before her.

"What did you overhear?"

She shook her head. "It was nothing really."

"If it was truly nothing, I don't think you would have stopped. Whatever you overheard must have had a profound effect. You can trust me with your secrets."

He already knew one of them: her visit to the Elysium. And she'd trusted him with her mouth. "It's silly and I probably give it too much credence, but I heard a gentleman tell a group of his friends that I would probably explain the force behind a . . ."—she cleared her throat, giving herself a few seconds to find the courage to repeat exactly what he'd said or to find the proper metaphor that would convey the ugliness of it—"force behind a . . . a thrust . . . on my wedding night."

Her cheeks scalding with embarrassment, she rushed on. "I'll never forget how quickly the gentlemen agreed, even as they were laughing. I stopped going to balls, spent more time with my father because he didn't seem to mind my curiosity. Now you know my whole life story."

And she could scarcely believe she'd shared all that with a stranger who wasn't truly a stranger. Or perhaps he was only partially a stranger. There was so much she didn't know about him; wished he could be taken apart so she could understand every aspect of him. Because what she did know rather fascinated her.

"I very much doubt you've shared your entire life. You're too complicated for such a simple story. And those other blokes were right fools. I consider myself fortunate to have provided your first kiss. I hope only that I haven't set unrealistic expectations for any other gents who might come your way."

She understood that he was hoping for the exact opposite. This man certainly didn't lack confidence. He'd also gone unerringly still as if he'd been taken by surprise and was holding his breath in anticipation of something wondrous arriving. She wished for light with the same depth of greed that she wished for investors. She wanted to see his eyes, his face clearly, so she could determine what he was thinking because she had the sense that the teasing and ease with which he'd joked about unrealistic expectations was no longer with him. That something far more serious had taken hold of him. His thumb continued to slowly stroke her lip, and the sensations he was evoking were almost as erotic as those he'd brought to the fore with his kiss.

"If you're absent from the ballroom much longer, you'll be missed . . . if you haven't been already. Should anyone ask, you can claim to have needed some time in the ladies' retiring room. Just don't close your eyes when you lie."

She released the smallest of laughs.

Abruptly stepping away from her completely, he cautiously leaned forward and glanced down the hallway before ducking back inside and cupping her chin in his palm. "I'll go first in case any wandering and errant guests need to be shepherded out of your path."

Like a border collie guiding sheep. She suspected he'd be quite good at it, and she didn't want to consider how often he might have performed this service to protect the reputation of other women with whom he'd engaged in a clandestine assignation. Yet neither could she tamp down the small thrill that she could add this daring encounter to her list of adventures she'd never expected to experience.

He released his hold on her, moved to the statue, stopped, and glanced back. "I'm glad I'm not the one you disappointed tonight."

Then he was gone.

CHAPTER 8

$\mathcal{H}$E didn't know how many kisses he might have experienced in his lifetime. They offered harmless release. They didn't beget any children, although they often led to the action that caused the begetting of children. Still, if a man was able to control his urges, they provided a modicum of safety.

Except hers didn't feel at all safe.

Especially in that tiny, shallow alcove where her body had been forced to squash up against his in order to fit within the restricting confines. He'd wanted to trail his lips from her mouth to those enticing swells that offered temptation just above her bodice, to move the cloth out of the way and suck on her nipples. He'd yearned to reach down, drag up her skirts, and skim his fingers over her foot that had so fascinated him, and then explore the silky skin of her calf, the back of her knee, her satiny thigh. Although in truth, he wasn't certain he could have stopped there. Her soft sighs were a siren's song beckoning him into dangerous waters.

But what she and he were doing had been a continuation of what they'd begun at the Elysium and her request there had been for only a kiss on the mouth.

Therefore, he'd restrained himself and taken merely what she'd been offering.

When he'd left her, he'd ensured her path to the ballroom was clear before he'd taken his leave from the ball. He'd been unable to force himself to remain, because something inside him balked at the notion of watching her dance with additional men. He couldn't recall ever experiencing jealousy before. However, he was relatively certain that this haunting feeling wasn't that. He barely knew her and certainly hadn't had enough time to develop any affection for her. Yet he couldn't seem to shake off the odd sensation that her lush mouth belonged to him.

Which was probably the reason that he used his fist rather than the knocker to bang on the door he'd finally reached. Or perhaps he was simply irritated with the rain that somehow slashed at him sideways, making an umbrella of little use.

The door finally opened. The butler gave a quick nod of acquiescence and stepped back, giving Rook room to slip into the foyer. "My lord."

"Is Mr. Trewlove about?" He'd already checked at both of Aiden's clubs and discovered his brother was at neither.

"Yes, sir. In the library. If you'll be so good as to follow—"

"I know where it is. I'll escort myself." After dragging off his coat, which had managed to protect most of him from the pelting raindrops, he handed it and his hat to the servant. He wasn't of a mind to follow the stately butler who would no doubt move at a snail's pace. He wasn't quite certain what sort of mood he was in, but he did know it required liquor.

His steps were long and brisk. He entered the library to find Aiden sitting behind his desk. He glanced up. "He's dead," he uttered without emotion.

"No. Our father still breathes." Or at least as far as he knew he did. "I was in need of a drink and wondered if you'd like to accompany me to the Mermaid and Unicorn. My carriage awaits."

"In this downpour?" Aiden got up and moved toward a sideboard. "I've some excellent scotch here that should suffice. You appear to have been battling the rain. Get yourself to the fire."

Rook sat on the edge of a plush chair, giving the flames the opportunity to dry what the rain had soaked—the lower portion of his trouser legs. When Aiden offered him the tumbler, he lifted it in a quick salute before swallowing a good portion of it, welcoming the heat that burned straight down to the marrow of his bones. The rain had chilled him. He waited until Aiden had settled into the chair across from him before stating, "You weren't at the Wolfford ball."

His brother shrugged. "Because many of the gents and ladies of the upper crust frequent my establishments, I tend to make them uncomfortable at their merrymakings. Thus, with rare exception, I limit my appearances to those affairs hosted by family."

"Your wife"—daughter of an earl, widow of a duke—"doesn't mind missing out on the revelry?"

Aiden grinned roguishly. "The revelry I offer her in the bedchamber more than makes up for it."

Rook didn't know why Aiden always made his sexual innuendoes. Coming here was probably a mistake because he suddenly had a vision of making revelry with Miss Garrison. A quick change in topic was warranted. He nodded toward the desk. "Why don't you hire a man of business to see to your affairs?"

"Because I don't want anyone else knowing exactly how many coins fill my coffers to overflowing. Vice can be extremely lucrative, but I prefer the details to remain between me and the devil." His brother's grin faded away. "So what's troubling you?"

"Nothing." He lifted his glass. "I merely wanted some good scotch."

"As though you don't have good scotch in your residence. I'd wager there is more to your coming here than that, and I never lose a wager."

Rook took a smaller sampling of the amber liquid. "The woman you had me kiss . . . she's moving about in our circle."

"*Our?* You mean yours, the nobility?"

"What other circle do you imagine I inhabit?"

"Oh, probably some you've yet to acknowledge. However, regarding the woman—I'd have not thought she'd suit the nobility."

He was suddenly incensed on her behalf. "Whyever the bloody hell not?"

Those words came out harsh, causing Aiden's eyebrows to rise with his surprise at their cutting delivery. "Nothing specific springs to mind. She simply had the air about her of being common."

"Common? She's anything except common."

Aiden settled back more comfortably as one might when expecting to be entertained by a bard. "How so?"

She kissed like a fallen angel, a mixture of innocence and wickedness. From his place in the small cubbyhole, he'd watched her battle her conscience—debating whether to step into the breach or withdraw.

She'd bravely taken the risk and joined him. For which he'd known he'd be eternally grateful when his mouth landed on hers. "She's curious, inquisitive."

"That much was evident by her request at my club. There's more, surely."

"She's here with her brother and termagant of a mother to find investors for their business. She's quite animated about the equipment they want to produce. A writing machine. They're preparing to give a demonstration in the near future apparently. Perhaps I can secure you an invitation."

"How does that make her uncommon?"

"She takes things apart, studies them, reassembles them." That was too simple a description when there were so many different aspects to her. Like a multifaceted diamond, light reflected differently depending upon how one held it. "She's simply unlike most women of my acquaintance."

"Was she at Wolfford's ball?"

"Yes."

"Ah."

"What the deuce does that little condescending sound signify?"

"It wasn't condescending, merely an acknowledgment of enlightenment. I'd wager you danced with her. Did you also kiss her?"

Rook glared at the dancing flames and wondered how Aiden might feel about being tossed into them. He didn't fancy being so easy to read when he'd never been before.

"You did," his brother said quietly, reflectively.

Shifting his gaze over to his host, Rook wondered why the devil he'd bothered coming here. "She's adventuresome."

"Again, something that was evident by her request at my club. Therefore, it appears that my sending you to her did turn out to be a favor to you."

What it had turned out to be was a maelstrom of confusion. When she'd shared her tale of what she'd overheard about the force of a *thrust*, and her hesitation to say that particular word in the context where it was associated with sex, he'd wanted to board a ship, sail to America, and bash a few heads together in order to teach some blighters manners. "It was merely a kiss."

"That's what I thought the first time I kissed Selena." Who was now his wife. "She'd come to my club as well. Strange, how we—two brothers—were both initially unnerved by a woman we'd kissed at my club."

"I'm not unnerved. I was in want of a drink and some company. As the other Chessmen are at the ball—that left you to humor me. At which you're failing miserably, by the way."

"But I do have excellent scotch."

Rook couldn't help himself as he chuckled low. He did enjoy visiting with his brother. "Indeed you do." He tossed back what remained of his. "It's late. I should head home so you can enjoy some revelry with your wife."

"I did so earlier in the evening, but yes, I'm planning to do so later as well. Seems I can never get enough revelry."

"I don't need the details," he grumbled as they both stood. "Thank you for the scotch and for the . . . company."

"My pleasure. Let me know how things progress with the uncommon woman."

"She and I are done."

"I thought the same thing after I kissed Selena. Thank God, I was wrong."

But it was different for Rook.

The apple doesn't fall far from the tree he'd once overheard someone from Eton saying about him. Everyone equated him with his father. Didn't sons long to follow in their fathers' footsteps?

He'd had a time of it making friends at Eton and had spent much of his years there alone and lonely. It was only when he'd first entered Oxford and met three young men who had been there for a while but despised their fathers as much as he did his that he finally found friendship.

And eventually wealth but neither was enough to wash off the stench of the earl, to no longer be judged by his father's reputation but by his own. That had taken adhering to the strictest of proper conduct. While his friends had developed reputations as scoundrels, he'd been viewed as a saint. He never took advantage of women. Never stole a kiss, never snuck a young lady into a darkened corner for a bit of exploring. Daughters and sisters were safe from his advances because he never did what he ought not.

Until tonight. Until Miss Garrison had entered his life. In that alcove, kissing her, he'd yearned for so much more, had been tempted to break the vow he'd long ago made to never risk bringing an illegitimate child into this world. Miss Garrison could prove to be a danger to his vow and his sanity because he'd never wanted anyone with the intensity that he yearned for her.

If he was wise, he'd avoid her in the future. She made him want to be wicked, wicked as he'd never been. No, it was more than that. She made him crave wickedness.

Was that how it had been for his father? This yearning to possess that blocked out all reason, that made it difficult to think of anything other than the intimacy he might share with her? How he yearned to see her unveiled. How he longed to touch all that no other man had ever skimmed fingers along, had ever kissed.

Even now he burned with a need to return to that alcove and lift her up until her legs were wrapped around his waist and her cries of pleasure were echoing around him.

Christ, what the hell was wrong with him? He wanted her with a hunger he'd never before known, one that was terrifying.

Best then to keep his distance. But even as he had the thought, he feared he didn't possess the strength to resist her.

MAKING HER WAY to the ballroom, slowly and cautiously, without being spotted was easier than she'd expected. Rook had been masterful at clearing the way for her and she rather imagined he'd done so with the efficiency of those who swept the streets clear of horse dung.

The unexpected challenge she encountered, however, was that her legs remained weakened from the blistering kiss he had delivered. She made her entrance as unobtrusively as possible and settled near a mirrored wall where several ladies stood. She didn't know how many dances she might have missed and didn't recognize the tune presently playing, but surely before the next dance began, her partner would find her. She would move to a more visible spot once her breathing returned to normal and her legs were steadier.

Taking a quick but intense glance around the ballroom, she had no luck in sighting Rook. Maybe he'd gone to the cardroom or was filling a plate from the food-laden tables in the refreshment room. Or was off searching for something stronger than champagne. She'd welcome a glass of whiskey, herself.

She fought off the sorrow at possibly never seeing him again—at least not until the demonstration next week. She would ensure he received an invitation. Tomorrow she would visit a stationer to have them printed. Although she should probably use the writing machine to create them. Yes, that was what she should do. Shouldn't take more than a day or two. Mama wouldn't help, of course, and Sam would use the excuse that he needed to be out moving about London in order to interest various parties in the notion of investing.

But she drew comfort from the clack of the keys as they did their work. To her the sound was as beautiful as a rhapsody played by the finest of orchestras. She'd taught her fingers to know precisely where each key was, so she no longer needed to even look at them to create words on paper. She suspected others might find satisfaction in conquering the keys in the same manner. Perhaps she should create a book to help toward the endeavor in much the same way one mastered piano keys.

"Miss Garrison."

Jerking her head around, she smiled at Lord Chidding, a viscount to whom Lady Knightly had introduced her earlier in the evening. "My lord."

He held out his hand. "The next waltz is ours."

"Of course. I'm looking forward to it." She slipped her hand in his and went with him to the edge of the dance floor.

His timing was perfect. The music went silent for several beats and then another tune began to float out from the orchestra, and she found herself moving over the dance floor with Viscount Chidding. She fought to keep her focus on him and not to begin searching the passing couples to see if Rook had returned to the ballroom and with whom he might be dancing.

"You seemed to be lost in thought before I approached," Chidding said kindly.

"I was contemplating our writing machine, a device we've created to make it easier and faster to produce correspondence. Finding investors who also believe in its potential is one of the main reasons"—main? It was the *only* reason they were here, even if she had gotten sidetracked by a luscious pair of lips—"that we made the journey to your lovely country."

"Ah, yes, Knightly mentioned something about it."

She was gratified to know it was being talked about. "Favorably, I hope."

"He did indicate it was an interesting, if somewhat . . ." His voice trailed off as though he'd suddenly realized he was talking of things that were boring to ladies or maybe he feared hurting her feelings with whatever followed *somewhat*.

"Interesting but somewhat?" she prodded because encounters with other men and hearsay over the years had taught her to buffer herself against the hurtful until it could do little more damage to her pride than the sting of a bee to her flesh.

"An interesting if somewhat confusing prospect. He's confounded regarding the reason we need a machine to write."

"I've heard his handwriting is difficult to read."

Chidding grinned, a warm, kind grin and she found herself liking the man immensely. "He recently wrote out some investment opportunities I should look into. Fortunately, he also told me about them. I don't know how long it might have taken me to decipher what he'd written, otherwise."

Her heart gave a little jump of excitement. "You invest?"

He seemed embarrassed, his cheeks burnishing pink. "I'm a novice, only recently dipping my toe into the waters, so to speak."

"I could share the costs and possible profits of our company with you, if you've an interest."

His cheeks darkened from pink into a fiery red. "To be honest, Miss Garrison, I haven't the means to invest in anything at the moment. Not until the others pay off."

She felt at once bad for humiliating him by forcing him to make such a confession and for mortifying herself with her eagerness to get him to take an interest in their enterprise. She might have saved them both some blushing and shame if instead she'd opted to discuss wedding night thrusts.

"Still, I do hope you'll attend our demonstration next week. You never know when fortune might smile on you, and you'll find yourself with money to burn."

He laughed lightly. "I doubt fortune will ever give me a grin as wide as all that, but, yes, I'd very much like to see this machine of yours."

She had a strong urge to describe it, to entice him with the mechanics of it, because she wanted him to have an interest in it. But she didn't want word to spread that she was a bore, so no one would dance with her. Therefore, instead, she reached back into her memory for all the topics that a proper lady was supposed to discuss with a gentleman and snagged the first one she found. "Lovely weather we're having."

Thunder chose that moment to boom so loudly it fairly shook the foundation beneath her feet. She dearly hoped it wasn't a portent that their journey over here was going to end in disaster.

CHAPTER 9

MATRIMONY IN THE AIR?

The ladies of the ton *released a collective gasp heard throughout London when Lord Wyeth was spied going down on bended knee before the American heiress Miss Leonora Garrison. A bit of trouble with her slipper seemed to be the cause for his grand gesture and his granting her his attention. Still, his positioning sent hearts aflutter and raised the ire of some who had hoped the viscount would kneel before them. Later, he was seen dancing with the newcomer. The elusive lord is not known for showering his affections on the ladies. His preference, while at balls, for engaging in cards or billiards is more widely known. However, one can't help but wonder what game he might be playing with the American.*

At the breakfast table, Leonora sat stunned as Mama read aloud, with an air of triumph, from the gossip page. Even Sam, damn him, appeared far too pleased by the wording, his eyes glittering with victory.

Mama set aside the newspaper and leveled a hard-edged glare at her. "He'd best be playing the courtship game."

"You're making too much of this. He was simply helping me with that damn"—nonexistent—"pebble. Then we danced. And that was it."

"You didn't sneak off for a rendezvous?" Sam asked.

Leonora hoped that her cheeks, her entire face, didn't flame red, but based upon the heat that had come upon her, she feared she was close to igniting. "Absolutely not."

His features shifted into a frown of disappointment. "Pity. It would have moved things along."

"Things?"

"Acquiring an investor."

"I would have thought, judging by the number of guests, that we could well be on the verge of getting an investor."

"It's my understanding that the abundance of guests had little to do with us and more to do with curiosity regarding the Duke of Wolfford. Apparently, a tremendous scandal recently involved that family. However, in spite of that, you warranted a mention"—Mama flattened her palm on the newspaper—"and I would say that bodes well for us. You mustn't be shy about encouraging him should your paths cross again."

"Based on the words in that article you just read, he isn't looking for a wife."

"Few men are until they've been caught."

"They're not trout, for goodness' sakes."

Her mother angled her head thoughtfully. "With the right bait, all men are."

She wasn't going to manipulate him in order to gain an investor. They should be able to secure an infusion of funds based solely on the company's merits.

"Maybe the fishing will be better when we attend the Rosemont affair," Sam said laconically.

"Rosemont?" Leonora asked. She hated that the nobility went by so many names. First names, last names, titles, pet names. It was all so deuced confusing.

"He's an earl, married into the Trewlove family. While they're commoners, their spouses aren't, so they must have some money to them and, apparently, they are looking for an investment opportunity."

"Why can't we simply meet with them? Present them with an invitation to our demonstration?" She'd get right on creating the invitations following breakfast. "Why must we attend another ball?"

"Because that's how it is done over here," Mama snapped. "I daresay there are matrons in New York who would give their souls to receive an invitation to a ball hosted by someone of the nobility. They shall read about each one we attend, because I shall ensure an announcement appears in the *New York Times* alerting the snobbish elite that we are being so honored." She shoved back her chair and stood. "They shall rue the day they snubbed me."

With her fists clenched, she strode from the dining room, and Leonora suspected Mama wished she could punch each of the matrons who had failed to ever request her presence.

"The invitations make her happy," Sam said quietly.

"Oh, yes, I could tell by all the joy emanating from her as she marched out."

He leaned forward. "I understand one of the wives has a brother you might like. A Lord Camberley. An earl."

"Sam, I'm truly not looking to marry."

"I'm not asking you to. Just be nice to him. Be nice to them all. We want them to like us."

"Business decisions aren't made on personalities."

"But they are made on character. They have to trust us in order to give us money."

She was impressed Sam had finally worked that out for himself. "I'm well aware, which is the reason I'm so opposed to Mama's strategy of encouraging men to believe I might give them my hand. It's deceptive."

"It needn't be. You don't have to go so far as to imply you're looking for a husband, but it would help tremendously if you'd simply be . . . likable."

BEING LIKABLE APPARENTLY included a late-afternoon stroll through Hyde Park at the fashionable hour. Leonora didn't know why they had to come to this particular park when a small pleasant one was not far from their hotel. But it seemed her mother had spent her time at the ball ferreting out all the ways a girl could throw herself into the path of a lord.

So here they were, she and her mother strolling along the green. Sam had made his excuses, deciding to go to a club to meet with some men who might be enticed into investing. Leonora simply hoped it didn't involve attending another ball. She considered claiming a megrim because she found balls to be incredibly taxing on her nerves. All the people, the din of conversations, and always being on show exhausted her. But she was nothing if not a dutiful daughter and whenever she hesitated, she was reminded that she was doing this for her father's memory.

"Look more interesting, dear," Mama muttered, and Leonora wondered exactly how she was supposed to do that.

She'd brought her sketchbook, hoping to find a few minutes to sit beneath a tree and work, but she was rather certain that particular activity would not make her appear more interesting. Perhaps she should skip as she had when she was a child or twirl about or lie on the ground and make out the shapes of various things in the clouds.

As a couple of ladies walked by, they glared at her as if she was strutting about nude. She wondered if their attitude had anything at all to do with that morning's gossip rags. If they saw her as a threat, in danger of stealing away one of their precious lords. Perhaps she should use the writing machine to compose a letter to a newspaper editor announcing she was not on the hunt for a husband but rather an investor and she had no plans to remain in this country, so marriage was quite out of the question.

But then she'd be harangued by Mama and receive further lecturing from Sam.

She caught sight of a man riding a chestnut mare, and his path seemed to be in a direction that would lead him to her. It took her a moment to recognize him, having only met him once—when he signed her dance card. Lord Lawrence Brinsley-Norton. One of the men she'd disappointed. She'd not crossed paths with him after she'd returned to the ballroom and had welcomed the reprieve, but it seemed now she'd have to pay the piper his due.

He drew his horse to a halt near her and quickly

dismounted. Swiping his hat from his head, he smiled. "Mrs. Garrison, Miss Garrison. What a pleasure to see you enjoying our park."

"We'd heard that everyone who mattered would be here at this hour," Mama said.

"Are you searching for anyone in particular?" he asked.

"No," Leonora answered quickly, before Mama could say she was searching for someone for her daughter to marry. Although in truth Leonora had been glancing around wondering if she might see Rook. "Just enjoying the lovely weather that greeted us after last night's rain."

"We must make the best of the sunshine while we can." He slid his gaze from her to Mama. "Mrs. Garrison, have I your permission to walk ahead with your daughter?"

Mama hesitated, no doubt because he was a lord who wouldn't inherit a title. It had gone to his brother, the Duke of Kingsland. "I can see no harm in giving her your attention for a few minutes."

Lord Lawrence offered his arm. She took it. As they walked along with Mama several steps behind, she focused on a polite way to apologize for missing their dance. She knew the slight couldn't go unrecognized. "I'm sorry to have missed our waltz. I'm not accustomed to so much dancing, was feeling quite light-headed, and needed some time in the ladies' retiring room. Unfortunately, I drifted off for a spell." She'd given the same excuse to the other gentlemen with whom she was supposed to have danced. She wasn't particularly happy with how easily the falsehood rolled off her tongue. It seemed since arriving in this country she was engaged in quite a bit of fibbing and sneaking around. She'd always been so upstanding before.

"No need to apologize. While I was naturally disheartened not to have found you, when I couldn't, I went to the cardroom where my fortunes changed for the better and I ended up staying there for the remainder of the night and making a tidy sum."

She considered suggesting he invest that unexpected tidy sum in their enterprise, but she didn't want to come across as too desperate. She also suspected that should his older brother invest, he would as well. And if his brother didn't, Lord Lawrence would be unconvinced that it would turn out to be a profitable endeavor. "Surely, I'm not the only one with whom you were going to dance."

"No, I do like to take a few ladies about the floor before heading toward wagering."

She suspected he was simply trying to make her feel less guilty. "Well then, I'm glad you had such a good streak of luck last night."

He shrugged. "I also know that I can't compete with Rook."

Breathing became suddenly difficult. "What do you mean?"

"I didn't intend to make you go as white as a ghost. It's just that gossip abounds that you have captured his attention."

"He assisted me with a pebble in my slipper. That's all. Nothing untoward has happened between us."

"Pity. I've always found him to be far too straitlaced. I thought perhaps knowing you might loosen him up a bit."

"Why would you think that?"

"Americans, at least the few ladies I know, don't seem to be as inhibited as many of my fellow countrywomen."

"I assure you that I always behave properly." *Except when I don't.*

"I meant no insult."

"None taken."

"Then perhaps you'll honor me with a dance at the next ball we both attend."

"I would be delighted to do so."

"Splendid. I shall take my leave now." He leaned nearer and lowered his voice. "From what I understand your mother doesn't like you wasting time with gents who won't inherit a title."

She might run mad with all the gossip and the reputation Mama was giving them with her constant queries about eligible lords. But Leonora also knew what it was to be considered lacking. "I personally have nothing against them and have found the ones I've met quite charming."

"How very kind of you to say so, Miss Garrison. I look forward to our next dance." He slipped his arm out from hers and tipped his hat toward her mother. "Good day, Mrs. Garrison."

He mounted his horse and trotted away. Her mother was instantly at her side. "He will not do."

"I don't think he was trying *to do*."

"Here is a much better prospect."

She didn't have to look long or far before she spotted Rook astride a black steed.

Rook had spied her walking with Lawrence, and it had taken every ounce of self-control he possessed not to gallop over, scoop an arm around her waist, lift her onto the saddle, and race away. The gossips would love that.

He had the errant thought that he would as well. He'd set her precariously between his spread thighs and the pommel. She would wrap her arms around his waist or neck to ensure she didn't topple. Then she'd offer that gorgeous mouth of hers for the taking.

But he wasn't one to lose his head over a woman, to lose his head at all. He always remained in control of his emotions and his actions. Therefore, he tightened his fingers on the reins and urged his horse to casually trot over to her. He brought his mount to a halt, slid from the saddle, and swept his hat from his head. "Good afternoon, Mrs. Garrison. I'm hoping you'll give me leave to stroll toward the serpentine with your daughter." *While you languish behind us, your daughter out of reach of your pinching fingers.*

"As long as you'll keep a respectable distance between you. I'll not give the gossips any more fodder."

Fairly envisioning her eyes turning purple, he suspected her words were a lie, that she'd very much like to give the tongue-waggers a good many more reasons to spread rumors. "I shall be on my best behavior," he assured her. He wouldn't have had to say that to an English mother because they all knew his behavior was exemplary. Except of late. He hardly recognized the man he'd become in that little nook, when all of his senses had been filled with Miss Garrison.

"I assume you saw the bit of gossip about you and my daughter."

"I did. I hope it didn't bring you too much embarrassment."

"Are you often written up in the gossip sheets?"

"This morning was a first." And had irritated the devil out of him. "It shan't happen again."

Looking more disappointed than satisfied, she pursed her lips and nodded.

He didn't offer Miss Garrison his arm because if she touched him, he wasn't certain he'd possess the wherewithal not to embrace her. Her dress was a pale pink, the shade of her lips, not the dark hue of the one she'd worn the night they'd met. It was buttoned nearly to her chin and at her wrists and he considered the pleasure he'd take from granting all those buttons their freedom, and in doing so, give the same pleasure to her. Holding the reins, he clasped both hands behind his back and began walking, grateful she joined him and her mother followed a few steps behind.

"What's the horse's name?" she asked.

So they were going to converse about unimportant matters. He wondered if she'd done the same with Lawrence. "Well-mannered."

"What sort of name is that for a horse?" She sounded truly horrified.

"What would you name him?"

"I don't know. Onyx. Shadow. Night."

"I preferred a name that would remind me how I should behave when riding him—should behave at all times, actually. I'm sorry if the gossip caused you any undue trouble."

She glanced over her shoulder before turning her beautiful blue eyes on him. "She may be complaining but she was thrilled. My name has never appeared in newsprint before. We have that in common, you and I. This morning's mention was a first for both of us. I'm considering clipping it out and saving it as a souvenir of my time in your country."

"A souvenir is usually something that brings about a good memory. Am I to deduce that you want to remember our time together?" He kept his voice low, hushed so it wouldn't reach the ears of her mother.

Miss Garrison was wearing a wide-brimmed hat that kept the sun from her face. Still her cheeks flushed pink, and he didn't think it was from the warm day.

"It was enlightening," she finally muttered.

For him as well, although he wasn't going to admit that. He'd never known a woman who brought as much enthusiasm to something as simple as a kiss. Or at least all the kisses before hers had seemed simple enough. Hers, however, were complicated. They made him yearn for something intangible, something he couldn't quite identify.

"I returned to the ballroom without encountering any trouble," she said, dropping into sotto voce with just a tinge of guilt along the edge of her words.

"I know. I didn't leave until I saw you enter, apparently without being accosted on your journey there." There had been the slightest spark of triumph in her expression, and he'd felt a measure of pride at her success.

"I didn't see you."

"I'm quite adept at blending in." He'd learned the skill at a young age in order to avoid his father's notice.

"I did manage to locate the gents I should have been dancing with and apologized with the lie you suggested.

Except for Lord Lawrence. I couldn't find him until just a few minutes ago. He was most understanding."

Strangely he felt a measure of satisfaction in knowing she'd chosen himself—or at least his kiss—over Lawrence, or at a minimum a waltz with him. It didn't lessen his irritation that the man had approached her here, had strolled along beside her, her arm snugly held in the crook of his elbow. Whereas Rook was denying himself that pleasure because he found it so damned difficult to resist her.

"Is it wise to be seen walking together like this? Will we be written up in the gossip sheets again, do you think?" she asked quietly.

He released a frustrated sigh. "I should hope not." Then he looked over at her, and found her studying him, and he had the odd sensation that perhaps she was striving to take *him* apart. He offered a recalcitrant grin. "But if so, you'll have another souvenir."

Her smile was the sort for which men launched ships. Soft and teasing, warm and heady. He couldn't recall ever having such a beatific expression cast his way. It was rather addicting.

"The ladies of New York will scarcely believe I made the gossip rags."

Perhaps that was the reason she was considering cutting it out and saving it. He experienced a surge of anger because across the Atlantic she'd not been appreciated. She wasn't odd and he didn't give a tinker's curse if she knew the force behind a thrust. He was more interested in the fact that her curiosity knew no bounds—that because of that curiosity he knew the perfection of her mouth moving over his and her taste. If he wasn't so concerned with keeping his own reputation pristine, he might accommodate her by ensuring she was mentioned every day in the gossip sheets. "I don't know that I'd like the ladies of New York."

"They would most certainly like you."

Do you like me? Where the devil had that thought come from? It was disconcerting. Didn't matter if she liked him or not. Physically they were compatible. The kiss proved that. What more was needed for a quick liaison?

"Do you always take strolls with your sketchbook in hand?" he asked and was treated to her cheeks again going awash in pink. He didn't know if he'd ever known anyone who blushed as much as she did.

"I was hoping to sit beneath a tree and do a bit of drawing, but apparently, according to Mama, doing so wouldn't make me appear interesting."

Devil take her mother. Although he suspected she'd consider her daughter interesting if she had a lord nearby fawning over her. He glanced back. "Mrs. Garrison, we're going to take a respite by this nearby tree. We've a thousand chaperones wandering around if you'd prefer to continue to stroll about."

Turning back to the lady, whose blue eyes were suddenly wide with wonder, he offered his arm because her wants far exceeded his. Still, when her gloved fingers landed on his forearm as lightly as a butterfly settling onto a petal, he felt as though she'd gifted him with the world.

When they reached the tree, she released her hold and he let go of the reins. His horse was well-behaved enough not to gallop off. Rook shrugged off his coat and began to spread it beneath the shade provided by the massive leaf-heavy branches.

"What are you doing?" she asked.

"The ground is no doubt still somewhat damp from yesterday's rains."

"Oh, I hadn't even considered that. Sitting on the grass was a silly idea."

"You won't be sitting on the grass. You'll be sitting on my coat." He held out his hand in order to assist her in lowering herself.

"I can't. It'll get all dirty."

"My valet enjoys nothing better than the challenge of determining how best to make a well-soiled garment look as though it's never been worn. Don't deny him his fun."

She laughed, a joyous sound. He found it remarkable that she could be so lighthearted when her mother's censure had to weigh her down.

"I don't believe you," she said.

LEONORA HAD NEVER heard anything more ridiculous in her life. His eyes were twinkling with merriment, his hand, steady and sure, waiting for hers.

"'Tis true," he responded with such earnestness. "And you should know it to be true because I didn't close my eyes."

She nearly laughed again. Instead, she placed her hand in his, ignoring the sense that it was returning home. She acknowledged the strength in him as he slowly lowered her to the ground, not that the power of his muscles came as a surprise. She'd felt them beneath her fingertips each time they came together.

Once she was situated, he crouched before her, balancing himself on the balls of his feet.

"I suppose your valet also likes the challenge of polishing your boots until they shine," she teased.

"He is fastidious about my boots."

She smiled at him before looking past him to where Mama stood on the path conversing with an elderly woman, whose clothing and bearing indicated she was someone of import. "Mama is speaking with a lady I don't recognize."

Rook twisted around slightly. "King's mother, the Dowager Duchess of Kingsland."

She sighed. "She'll be asking for advice on marriageable lords. Wealthy marriageable lords."

He returned his attention to Leonora. "Ignore her for now and enjoy the opportunity to draw your . . . machines."

Her breath caught. "How did you know?"

"You don't strike me as the sort to spend her time filling pages striving to draw perfect flowers or courting couples strolling about. Will you show me if I have the right of it?"

"It's an idea I had for a new sort of machine, but I haven't worked out all the particulars."

"I should think that's usually when it's the most interesting . . . in the beginning . . . when it's merely the spark of an idea . . . and so much potential for what it could be is waiting to be tapped into."

He'd described so well how she felt at the moment regarding what she'd designed thus far. It was like unwrapping a gift, loosening the bow, peeling back the paper, seeing only a part of the item, slowly revealing the whole of it. She'd always taken her time opening presents, drawing out the anticipation. "Is that how you feel about investing? That it has an unknown quality to it and you're waiting to see how it all plays out?"

He seemed to be giving her question some thought. She liked that he was taking her questions seriously and giving them due consideration. "I suppose so, yes. I experience an excitement as I wait to discover if what I've invested in will soar or fall."

"Our company will soar," she couldn't help but assure him.

As though admiring her spunk for not letting an opportunity pass to try to sell him on their enterprise, he grinned and nodded toward the sketchbook in her lap. "End the suspense. Allow me the honor of confirming if I did indeed guess correctly. That it's not a rose, or tree, or a couple engaged in mischief."

Her heart was thundering because she never shared the details of her drawings until she'd worked everything out, until it all came together to make sense in her mind. She might *tell* Sam about it, but she didn't show him anything until she'd taken the idea and given it form. Yet there was something exciting about Rook taking an interest. Inhaling a deep, shuddering breath, she dared to lift the cover of her sketchbook to reveal what she thought might be the final product. She turned it toward him.

He studied it as though it was a masterpiece in a museum. He reached for the paper, halted. "May I?"

She nodded and watched as he slowly turned the page back to reveal the next that was the skeleton of the thing. Another flip of parchment, more details. "What is it going to be?"

"A tallying machine."

He lifted his gaze to hers. She saw no mockery

reflected in his eyes, only interest. "What does it tally?"

"Throughout the day, it will keep a running total of sales so when a shopkeeper closes up, he can count the money in his till, and it should match the amount the machine indicates."

"If it doesn't match, it'll let him know sticky fingers are withdrawing money from his till."

"In a manner, yes, although mostly it will save him from having to take the time to add up all his sales. He'll be able to get home to his family sooner."

"How your mind must work to even imagine such a thing."

"Boringly," she said lightly.

"On the contrary. Brilliantly."

She brought her pad back to her lap. "Well, I haven't figured out exactly how to make it all work."

"But you will."

His confidence in her was both unsettling and comforting. Only her father had ever held such belief in her, and during the past year she'd felt his absence as though sunlight had been taken away. "I shall endeavor to persevere."

Their gazes locked, and she couldn't seem to find the strength to look away.

"I believe you've taken up enough of my daughter's time," a harsh voice suddenly announced. "We need to carry on with our stroll as it's important to be seen."

Rook held Leonora's gaze. "I couldn't agree more that it's important to be *seen*."

She was left with the impression that he was indicating something very different from what her mother was.

He unfolded his body, offered his hand, and pulled her to her feet. Then he snatched up his coat, and in spite of it being slightly damp, wrinkled, and a little worse for wear, he drew it on because he was after all a gentleman, and those in polite society didn't wander about in shirtsleeves and a waistcoat only. He grinned and winked at her. "My valet will be overjoyed with the challenge that awaits him. Good day, Miss Garrison."

"Good day, my lord."

He turned briskly toward her mother. "Good day, madam."

Then he mounted his horse and trotted away, leaving Leonora feeling as though the burdens she carried weren't quite so heavy.

CHAPTER 10

That evening, at the request of their hosts—the Earl and Countess of Rosemont—Leonora, Mama, and Sam arrived early in order to have the opportunity to meet the six Trewlove siblings and their spouses before the other invited guests arrived. Yet even before introductions were made, she recognized Aiden Trewlove, in spite of her hazy mind when she'd made her request of him. She could more easily see the resemblance between him and Rook now.

Aiden gave nothing away, and she was left with the conviction that he didn't remember her. Which was all to the good. It would make the evening less awkward.

To her surprise, within the group was Althea and her husband, Beast, who apparently had been raised within the Trewlove household. With a sly smile, Althea greeted her warmly and took her hands. "I hope you're pebble-free this evening."

She laughed lightly and said quietly, "Thus far. However, I reserve the right to discover one at any minute."

Sherry was passed around to all and Mick Trewlove, the owner of the hotel in which they were staying and who it appeared was the elder of the family, made a toast. "To the pursuit of new ventures. May we all find them worthwhile."

"Hear, hear!" followed just before everyone took a sip.

Her mother began explaining to the earl's wife, Fancy, that she was hoping Fancy would assist by introducing Leonora to eligible gentlemen this evening. Not wanting to get dragged into the conversation or an argument with Mama, she took several discreet steps away. Before she could escape completely, however, Aiden Trewlove was standing before her.

He reminded her so much of Rook, with his dark hair and eyes, but there was a roughness to him that she suspected had been honed by the streets. His gaze direct, he studied her openly and with a frankness that indicated he wasn't one to play games. Finally, he lowered his head slightly and said softly, "I should forewarn you that someone you met recently at my club will be in attendance this evening."

Rook. Naturally, he would be here. She should have realized. Strange how the tension that had been building as she worried about what her mother or brother might say to bring her embarrassment began to ease. "Thank you for letting me know."

"He'll be pleased. I daresay something more than a pressing of lips happened that night."

"No, it didn't." Would it have if she hadn't fallen asleep?

He grinned, a wicked, teasing grin, and she realized that in spite of the hardships he'd experienced growing up on the streets, he was more relaxed and at ease than Rook. She was convinced that somehow the viscount had endured a much harsher and more challenging upbringing. "Methinks the lady does protest too much."

"You can think anything you like—"

"Leonora," Mama interrupted tartly and rudely. "I'd like to introduce you to Lord Camberley. He's an earl. Brother-by-marriage to Mr. Trewlove here."

He was as fair as Rook and Aiden were dark. Taking her gloved hand, he pressed a light kiss to her fingers. "I do hope you'll honor me with a dance."

"Of course." She offered him the card that she'd yet to secure to her wrist. After he'd signed his name, he handed it back to her.

"I look forward to our waltz." Appearing slightly uncomfortable, he nodded at Aiden. "I'll speak with you later."

After he walked off, Mama pinched her arm. "You could have been a bit more enthusiastic. He's in want of a wife."

"But I'm not in want of a husband." She turned to Aiden. "Do forgive our petty squabble held in front of you. It's so very unbecoming."

"I suspect, Miss Garrison, that any gentleman would forgive anything of you. If you ladies will excuse me, I've been too long gone from my wife." With a dip of his head, he also departed, leaving her within easy reach of another pinch, which came quickly and with a bit more force.

"That man is going to let Camberley know that you don't want marriage, undoing all of my hard work."

Which, no doubt, had simply involved talking with a gentleman and leading him like a horse to water, only in this instance the water didn't wish to be drunk. "Mama, perhaps you could be a bit more subtle with your goals."

"That won't work when you're not doing anything to help me reach them. Besides, Sam has been open about why he is here, what he wants to accomplish, and tonight we are guests of honor. We could have men lining up to ask for your hand."

"Once we get investors, I'll return to New York to assist Sam with all the changes required at the factory and the challenges that will arise. What husband—especially one from the nobility who has to remain here because he sits in the House of Lords—is going to be happy about that?"

Mama rolled her eyes. "It would be more helpful for you to assist Sam by marrying so funding for the continuation of the factory will be a foregone conclusion. Sam's business will flourish, and he'll achieve success."

Sam's business. Because in his will, their father had left it to his son. It wasn't fair when Leonora had worked beside her father for so many years, when she knew the ins and outs of the business, when she found satisfaction in ensuring all ran smoothly.

"Why can't Sam marry? A woman comes with a dowry."

"Because no matter whom Sam marries, unless it's one of Queen Victoria's daughters, who could see that her mother bestowed upon him at least a knighthood, she isn't going to get me into the Astor ballroom. It has to be you. I'm depending upon you to elevate my standing."

With as little effort as possible. "But at what cost, Mama?"

"At a cost you should be willing to pay."

"Shouldn't we marry for love?"

"We marry for survival. In a good marriage you depend upon each other for that very survival."

They weren't talking about her survival, however. They were discussing the survival of a company. She would find a way to make that happen without getting married.

Rook had considered not attending the Rosemont ball, but then word had filtered through his club that the Garrisons would be in attendance, and those who had yet to make their acquaintance were hoping to. Although some were skeptical but taking an interest in learning more about what was being offered. After all, if the Chessmen hadn't already jumped on it, then a bit of caution was no doubt warranted.

It was well-known that the Chessmen seldom invested in an enterprise that didn't pay off. While they never outright stated with whom they were investing, male gossips being what they were—decidedly worse than women—often someone in need of additional financial backing might let it be known they had the Chessmen's support.

He hadn't arrived early, but it appeared most had, no doubt hoping something new or exciting about the investment opportunity might be revealed before too many were about to hear. Yet, in spite of the crowd, still he spotted her, waltzing with the Earl of Camberley of all people. He was surprised by the jolt of seething temper that rushed through him with the power of a lightning bolt. He wondered how Aiden might take it if Rook murdered his wife's brother. Then he wondered how Miss Garrison would react because she certainly hadn't come here expecting to sit in the corner like a wallflower. In spite of what she'd revealed about the gents she'd encountered in New York, he couldn't imagine her experiencing the same here, of being ignored or a fellow walking by her without extending his hand in invitation to dance or take a turn about the garden.

"I was beginning to think you weren't coming."

At the familiar voice, he curled up a corner of his mouth, turned, and faced his brother. "I didn't want to appear overly eager to hear what Sam Garrison might have to say this evening. Best not to show too much interest until you've gained the upper hand in negotiations."

"Maybe I should have you give Camberley lessons in investing. I'm striving to help him get his estate in order and profitable again, but it's slow going. An infusion of capital would be nice, and your expertise appreciated. Although based on the hard set of your features only a few minutes ago, I suspect you'd rather murder him than help. He's dancing with your woman."

Rook was aware of a muscle in his jaw ticking. "Have I ever mentioned how damned irritating you are?"

Aiden had the audacity to laugh. "On many an occasion, but then all my brothers do."

"How many do you know?"

His broad smile diminished. "I was referring to my Trewlove brothers, not the ones our father sired."

Rook nodded. While he certainly didn't wish to carry the burden of being born out of wedlock, he did envy Aiden the close bond he had with the siblings of his heart, even if they weren't all of his blood. In his youth, Rook had often wished for someone with whom to share his troubles. Still, better late than never. "And she's not my woman."

"That's not the impression I got when you visited."

Why was he even bothering to argue with this man? Aiden had the ability to sense what people truly wanted at their very core. It was one of the reasons he presently had two very profitable businesses.

The music ceased playing. He looked toward the dance floor. Miss Garrison and Camberley were standing in its center talking. Why wasn't he escorting her to the edge of the dance area or to her mother? Or to some chairs? Or to a wall?

A polka began, and the blighter took Miss Garrison back into his arms. Two dances in a row simply weren't done, not without creating gossip and speculation regarding a gent's intentions. Camberley might not live through the evening. "What game is he playing at?"

"I'm not sure. Her mother said he was looking for a wife. First time I've heard of it, although when he's had too much to drink, he'll mumble on about finding a girl with a large dowry. But as the Americans are here seeking investors, I can't imagine she'd be a good choice, that her dowry would provide him with the means he seeks."

"Perhaps he believes the business will, eventually."

"Will it?"

He experienced an unexpected flash of surprise with the realization that Aiden trusted him to know the answer, and his word could mean the difference in his brother investing his hard-earned coins. The answer was not something to be taken lightly. "I'm not yet sure. But if you'll excuse me, I have a matter to attend to."

LEONORA LIKED THE Earl of Camberley. He was charming, easy to talk with, and had numerous times made fun of himself, his propensity for wagering, his reliance on Aiden to get his affairs in order, and the man's role in helping him to marry off two of his sisters—if he didn't count the one Aiden had married himself. Then it was three. Only one left, but Lady Alice had little interest in marriage, preferring independence. Leonora wished her family was as supportive concerning her marriage preferences.

"Perhaps you should ask Mr. Trewlove to assist you in finding a wife," she told him now as they moved speedily over the floor. He'd daringly signed his name beside two dances. She'd never had anyone dance more than once with her. She was quite flattered.

He laughed. "I'm not sure he'd have my best interests at heart or even understand what it is I want in a wife."

She refrained from asking what that was because she feared his response might be *you*. And then what was she to say? "I suppose when it comes to a partner for life it is best if we make our own decisions."

"Indeed. Do you seek love, Miss Garrison?"

"I seek happiness." Whether or not that included love was another matter.

"What would make you happy?"

Investors. "As you like to wager, why not make a bet on the success of our business rather than on a hand of cards?" She wished she possessed the sort of flirtation skills where she could bat her eyelashes without looking as though she was merely striving to rid herself of flecks of dust that had landed in her eyes. "In both cases, at their very core, fate is doing the dealing."

He seemed intrigued by the notion, then slowly shook his head. "My club will extend me credit. I assume you won't."

She almost suggested he seek a loan from a bank, but she certainly didn't want to encourage him to go into debt for her. "It would rather defeat the purpose, I suppose."

He smiled warmly. "However, it does make me wish I had all my affairs in order, so I could fulfill your wishes, as I do believe there would be nothing more satis—"

A large, white-gloved hand suddenly landed on his shoulder, forcing him to stagger to a stop. She nearly tripped over him, might have fallen if a second hand—no, it was an entire arm—hadn't come around her back to steady her.

"I believe this dance is mine," Rook said with such utter conviction and arrogance that she wouldn't have been surprised to look at her card and discover that somehow his name had indeed replaced Camberley's.

"But I claimed it," the earl insisted.

With heads whipping around and necks craning, curious couples glided past the immobile trio.

"Let me sweep her around the floor once, and I'll bring her back to you. And pay off your debt at the Dragons."

Camberley opened his mouth, closed it, and made a hasty retreat to the edge of the dance floor. Before she could object, speak, or even catch her breath, she was once again on the move but this time with Rook.

"That was rather rude," she finally managed to mutter.

"Rude would have been punching him." An icy chill accompanied his words, and she was surprised frost didn't form on the air between them.

"Why would you have done that? He seemed nice

enough, and he is related by marriage to your brother, which I suppose in some manner makes him related to you."

That strong, rock-hard jaw of his seemed to grow even harder, his eyes more formidable, a man laying claim to what he owned, to what belonged to him. A small thrill went through her with the realization that he might actually be jealous. She couldn't recall a man ever being upset because another was giving her attention, but then so few had.

"He's not a bad fellow," he finally ground out. "It's just that I have every intention of kissing you again tonight. I shouldn't like the taste of his mouth on yours, and I wouldn't think you'd want the flavor of another woman's on mine."

She felt a bit barbaric, better understanding his need to punch Camberley. She could easily see herself yanking on some lady's hair if she was granting him favors. *Mine*, she wanted to claim when he wasn't that at all. Serendipity had brought him to her, and it could just as easily take him away. He wasn't committed to her. He was a man determined not to be bested in any action he undertook. His resolve was the reason behind his success.

"And if I have no intention of being kissed by you?" she asked, putting a bit of steel in her tone to indicate she wasn't going to rely on only him to grant her wishes, and also perhaps to make him a little envious, if he wasn't already.

"Why would you deny yourself what you so obviously enjoy?"

Because she was in danger of becoming addicted to that mouth. "Could Camberley deliver what I so obviously enjoy, do you think?" She wasn't certain it was wise to taunt him. He looked quite capable of committing murder at that moment.

"No." The word came out like a bullet fired from one of her family's pistols, with an accuracy designed not to miss its mark. It slammed into her doubts and shattered them. He was the only one with the ability to give her what she wanted. Anyone else would fail miserably at the attempt.

"You're quite sure of your prowess."

A corner of his mouth curled up, a touch of arrogance sparkling in his eyes. "Aren't you by now?"

Oh, yes. Not that she was going to admit it.

They'd almost completed their circle.

"At your earliest convenience, make your way into the garden. I'll find you."

His low, sensual delivery had anticipation arcing through her like the electricity in a demonstration her father had once taken her to. She found it difficult to breathe, and she sounded slightly winded as she spoke. "My dance card is once again full."

"Then once again someone is bound to be disappointed. I sincerely hope it isn't you."

Without missing a step, he smoothly handed her off to Camberley and disappeared into the crowd of onlookers. She wanted to follow him now, this minute. Instead, she offered a weak smile to her dance partner. "I feel I should apologize for his atrocious behavior and interrupting our dance."

He laughed. "Don't. I'm relieved to have my debt at the Dragons paid off. It's a shocking amount, so I'll have a bit of revenge when he goes to pay it."

"What is the Dragons?"

"It's a gaming hell, and its membership includes women as well as men. I've seen your brother there."

"Oh, have you?" Maybe that was where Sam was spreading the word about his need for investors. Or perhaps he was following Camberley's example and working up a debt. Sam did enjoy his entertainments.

The final strains from the music began drifting away, and they came to a stop.

"Thank you for the dances, my lord."

"Entirely my pleasure, Miss Garrison."

After he escorted her to the chalked edge of the floor, she didn't bother to look at her dance card to see who she was going to disappoint. She knew only that she wasn't going to disappoint Rook . . . or herself.

SHE HAD NO idea how Rook would do as he'd promised. How he would find her. The garden was massive. And dark. So very dark away from the torches that burned along the path. But she hadn't wanted to remain in the light and risk being seen sneaking about among the lush greenery.

But just when she thought she was on a fool's errand, she became aware of a presence stepping out of the shadows at her back. She recognized the fragrance, the faint lemony-orange scent that was his, the one she'd been searching for, the one she'd wanted to find.

Without saying a word, he placed his hand, fingers splayed, on the small of her back and directed her toward thicker bushes. They carried on in silence for several minutes. She hadn't known that various shades of darkness existed, but the farther they walked, the more inky the shadows became until she began to wonder if they would be able to see each other at all.

Then she spotted a narrow beam of light filtering through the abundant trees and the heavy foliage. It was only a tiny sliver, but it was enough. He led her to it, pressed her back to the brick wall that waited there, and took her mouth as though he were a starving man finally offered a bit of sustenance.

No gentle persuasion this time. Only hunger, only need. The hunger hers as much as his. She had the insane thought that she wanted to devour him. She wanted to taste every inch of him. That mouths and lips and tongues were not enough. She needed more. She needed all of him.

He eased her a fraction away from the wall. His powerful hands stroked her back, climbed up to her nape where he kneaded the tight, light muscles for a moment before gliding down, around to the curve of her backside, squeezing. It was heavenly. To sense how badly he wanted her. Unlike their journey here, he wasn't quiet. He was growls, groans, and moans.

She dragged her hands down his chest, inside his jacket until she reached the waistband of his trousers. Daringly she tugged on his shirt, pulling the hem free of its confines, and slipped her hands beneath the fabric to touch the warm skin of his belly. She was aware of him going still a heartbeat before he broke away from the kiss to press his lips against the soft, sensitive spot beneath her ear. "Good girl. Carry on," he urged before bringing his lips back to hers.

While he plundered her mouth as though it might be stolen away from him before he had his fill, she leisurely moved her fingers up over his taut stomach and then along his ribs one by one until she felt the outline of his nipples. Slowly she circled her thumbs around the silky skin, surprised to find the hardened peaks. He groaned low and deep, like she was using a medieval torture device on him. It shouldn't have made her feel so happy. She considered asking if she was hurting him, but he was no shy creature. He would stop her if he didn't like what she was doing. Thus, she continued to taunt and tease, wishing he wore no shirt or waistcoat so she could run her tongue over one of the stiff pearls.

She had never felt so powerful.

She slid her hands around to his back where the muscles bunched and flexed with his movements as he explored her mouth and deepened the kiss. His hands came up and cradled her face. The frantic need wavered and his ministrations gentled. He drew back. Then he leaned in and kissed one corner of her mouth and next the other.

Her breaths coming in little pants, she kept her hands where they were because she wasn't ready to disconnect from him completely. Lightly he traced his thumb back and forth over her lower lip.

"The curve of your neck," he rasped, "your shoulder, your breast . . . your nipple."

Her eyes widened at his brazen words. "What are you talking about?"

"That night at the Elysium, all the places you could have asked to be kissed, and you chose your mouth. A thousand times since, I've wished you'd said everywhere. Every place you dare. Every place you want. Every hill, every valley. Every inch."

"You claimed to be asking about a location within the room."

"I was. But you weren't. What spots came to mind? Which ones did you almost ask for?"

If he wasn't cupping her chin in the palm of his hand and his thumb wasn't still caressing her lip, she might have ducked her head or better yet pressed it against his comforting chest. Instead, she barely shook it.

"Tell me. I'll lock it away and no one will ever know."

She squeezed her eyes shut and whispered, "My hand."

She expected he might laugh, mock her at the simplicity and dullness of her answer, especially when he was bold enough to speak out loud incredibly intimate parts of her person. But no sound came. His thumb stilled at the corner of her mouth. Slowly she opened her eyes to find him studying her with a mixture of interest and revelation.

"I haven't much of an imagination, I'm afraid," she confessed. "I have to be able to take things apart in order to understand them, to see the possibilities in them."

"Is that the reason you asked for a kiss? So you could take it apart and examine it?"

She gave the tiniest of nods. "I wanted to understand the mechanics of it. Only it wasn't mechanical. It was . . . sublime."

Wherever the light was coming from, it allowed her to see his flash of a smile. "They're never the same, you know. Kisses. So many factors come into play. The couple. The moment. Desire. Want. Need. How long it's been. Sometimes it's all hunger. Other times it's comfort. And once in a while it's farewell. And that's the hardest kiss of all."

Her heart felt as though it had been pierced, and her chest ached. Her fingers pressed into his skin as much as they could, which was little because of the firmness of his muscles. "Have you ever given one of those—the farewell kind?"

"Eventually everyone does. You might not think it is at the time, but it doesn't make it any less painful once you realize it was."

While he hadn't exactly answered her question, she couldn't help but feel that he was speaking from experience, and she very much wished he wasn't, that he hadn't gone through something so agonizingly unpleasant.

"Was this a farewell kiss then?" She didn't know why she sounded as though it was something she was dreading. They'd hardly had a hello kiss. She barely knew the man.

His thumb that had been tucked into the corner of her mouth stroked the curve of her cheek. "No. I knew only that I wanted to kiss you again, that the last one left me yearning for more."

The answer was overwhelming and unsettling.

"You gave no hint of that at the park today."

"You have no idea how difficult that was, to remain civilized. Even now, I want to engage in deliciously wicked actions with you."

"But you haven't."

"I wouldn't without permission."

Suddenly she realized her hands were still beneath his shirt, her fingers drawing lazy circles over his skin. She eased them out from beneath the fabric. "Before things get out of hand here, I should probably return to the ballroom."

"Aren't you at all curious regarding what happens following a kiss?"

Was that an invitation or a dare? Either way, she did hope not enough light shone on her that he could see she was dreadfully, wantonly curious. But she did know enough to comprehend that what followed was for the wedding bed, not a moonlit garden.

She shook her head. "I couldn't. I—" If she ever were to marry, how would she explain to her husband that she'd once given herself to a man out of curiosity? It seemed so very wrong to join her body with that of a man she didn't love. More importantly, one who didn't love her. "I may have been brazen enough to request a kiss, but my virtue . . . I can't take it that far . . . outside the boundaries of marriage."

The slightest furrow appeared across his brow, and his eyes seemed to bore into her as if he were mining her soul. Far too late, she realized her words might have given him reason to believe she was suggesting *he* marry her.

"No, I . . . I didn't mean that . . . you . . . that we . . . I simply meant that if there's any chance in the world that I might change my mind and someday marry . . . my husband should be the first to . . . plow, so to speak." Or so her mother had told her countless times. *A man isn't going to purchase the cow if he can get the milk for free.* Such a flattering way to make her point, to ensure her daughter felt like livestock.

"A couple can fuck without actually fucking." His low voice hinted at secrets that he was willing to share. "To be honest, I have considerable experience at proving that true. You need only grant me permission . . ."

His voice trailed off, leaving much unspoken but far too much communicated. She had little doubt that *when you're ready* was implied, a foregone conclusion he'd reached, thinking her unable to resist his allure. But she would resist because if she'd learned anything tonight, it was that he held far too much power, could turn her into a wanton with little more than the darkening of his eyes promising a kiss.

"My mother is no doubt frantically searching for me."

He bestowed upon her a broad smile that practically shouted, "Coward!"

Stepping back, he began to straighten his disheveled state, tucking the ends of his shirt into the waistband of his trousers. She could hardly believe she'd been unabashed enough to practically undress him. And yet she couldn't seem to regret knowing exactly how warm his skin was.

"I'll escort you to the path," he said evenly, "but from there it would be best if you carried on alone. We don't want to be seen together."

"Don't like being written up in the gossip sheets?"

"Worse than that would await, I'm afraid, judging by the eagerness of your mother to see you married to a titled gent."

Was he implying that he considered marriage to her to be a horrible fate? Well, she needed to set him straight regarding her own feelings on the matter. "She may be eager for it, but I'm not. I think a husband could prove . . . stifling."

He canted his head and studied her. "Not if he's the right husband."

"How does one determine that when courtship, for the most part, involves sitting around and drinking tea?"

"What is it that you'd prefer to marriage?"

"Managing the business."

"Do you not have a competent man to oversee it?"

She reeled with disappointment. A short while ago, his mouth was doing wonderfully delicious and

wicked things to hers. And now it was spouting obnoxious advice on a matter that was truly none of his
concern. "Women are competent."

His eyes widened at her sharp tone. "I didn't say
they weren't."

"You implied it."

He seemed at a loss, or perhaps he wasn't accustomed
to arguing with women. Or having one challenge his as-
sumptions. "I didn't mean to give offense. I've simply
never known a woman to oversee a large, complicated
enterprise."

"You don't think managing a household is complicated?"

"I've never really given it any thought."

"Most men don't. They think everything happens
magically or is seen to by fairies during the night."

His gaze was once more homed in on her with an
intensity she couldn't read. "I shall hope you get your
investors, Miss Garrison."

To see her succeed? To see her fail? She dared not
ask. Nor did she want to know his opinion on investing with them. Didn't want to learn that the kiss might
influence him one way or the other, to discover she
had no womanly wiles with which to entice. But if
she did, she didn't want them to be the reason for his
endorsement. She wanted the business to stand on its
own as she'd never been allowed to do. "We should
go," she said instead, coward that she was.

"By all means." He offered his arm, but if she
touched him again, she might ask—beg—for another
kiss, even if it was a farewell one. But she'd been begging all along, hadn't she?

Still, she wrapped her fingers around the crook of

his elbow and welcomed his leading her toward the path. "Did your valet appreciate your filthy coat being handed over to him?"

"He was giddy with excitement."

She liked having that special moment shared with him, a few minutes that were hers to own. Unwisely, she yearned for more of them. "There seem to be a lot of places in this city where women can get into mischief," she said.

"Indeed."

"Have you ever been to this Fair and Spare?"

"Firstborn sons who will inherit are not admitted."

"Ah, now I recall something about that rule. Why is it the case?"

"The owner, a second son, believes spares aren't appreciated and receive less attention at affairs such as this. Like your mother, ladies want the titled gent."

She was relieved that he'd referred to her mother and not herself. "And the Twin Dragons?"

"Not so biased. I do have a membership to that club. I can be found there most evenings, to be honest. If not at the tables, then in the library, usually discussing business ventures. Do you gamble, Miss Garrison?"

"Shifting our manufacturing focus is a gamble, one with very high stakes."

"But you think it will succeed?"

"With every fiber of my being."

He stopped and waved his hand forward. "The path is just past that hedge."

Unfurling her fingers, she faced him. "Consider investing, my lord," she said quickly before darting to the path—because that was the reason they were here, after all, to find the means to expand their business.

Not to learn about the intricacies of sexual gratification that occurred between adults.

WATCHING HER GO, Rook knotted his hands into fists to stop himself from reaching for her. The parting should have been easy. Instead, he'd wanted to secrete her away.

He wondered why he'd blathered on about the various types of kisses. Naturally, she'd have inquired about the farewell one. If he'd ever given one. He'd almost told her, had fairly longed to tell her the truth.

But speaking of it would have left a bitter taste in his mouth when he was still savoring the flavor of her.

Then she'd asked if he had bestowed upon her a farewell kiss. He should have claimed he had, so they'd both know that they were done. Yet he'd been unable to bring himself to do it. As it was, he felt as though the business between them was decidedly unfinished. She made him yearn to be wicked, to do what he'd never done before.

He'd thought about asking her to come to his residence. He lived alone, save for the servants. While it was a luxurious spacious townhome, too many neighbors were about, most upper crust, and she might be spied arriving or leaving. Although late at night, with the hood of a pelisse covering her head—

But he suspected his residence would eventually become the dower house and his mother would live there, and so he'd refrained from enjoying any debauchery within it. And he had the odd suspicion that Miss Garrison would leave her mark as indelibly as if her face had been painted on the walls. That her jasmine fragrance would remain and that somehow his mother would know that the American heiress had visited there and engaged in an intimate encounter with him. Or several, because he couldn't help but believe that like the kiss, any sort of brazen familiarity would serve only to have him yearning for more.

Whatever was wrong with him? He never took this much interest in women, took them as they came, left when their encounter was done. He rarely sought them out. They joined him, of their own accord. Just as she had tonight in the garden, and before that in the nook. But he'd gone to her first, and somehow that made her different.

He wondered if she might ask Camberley for a kiss, if she might in fact decide to do some comparing. He could well envision her doing so, going after anything she wanted with all the means at her disposal. She'd daringly met each of his requests for a tryst, bravely overcoming any hesitancy she might have experienced.

He'd never played the clandestine game of being involved with someone who flitted about in his social circle. It was a dangerous way to go. One slip, and a man might find himself at the altar with a woman he liked but with whom he was not entirely compatible. It was not a risk he'd ever taken . . . until her.

However, he wasn't going to take the risk again. He knew that for a fact.

No matter how enticing she was. Regardless of how much he'd liked having her in his arms.

She called to a savage part of him that wanted to possess and conquer. She made him yearn to toss his well-regarded reputation aside as if it mattered not at all, as though he hadn't spent years cultivating it. She made him want to embrace wickedness.

But he was determined to carry on with his steadfast vow to always be above reproach. Strange how the thought brought with it a measure of sorrow, along with the realization that the kiss they'd just shared had in fact *been* a farewell.

CHAPTER 11

It had been two nights since that kiss in the garden, two days since that stroll in the park. Strangely, it was their time together in the park that haunted him. Her hesitancy to share her drawings as though she'd scandalously etched out nude men. The doubt reflected in her eyes when she'd finally revealed rods, levers, and knobs. She was going to eventually arrange them in order to make them all work together—

When he couldn't even seem to sort his cards properly, so they made any sense. Lady Fortune was not smiling on him tonight. Thus far he'd lost every hand of brag dealt.

Feeling restless, he'd come to the Twin Dragons to be entertained. Tonight no balls, dinners, recitals, or soirees were happening—at least none to which he'd been invited, which meant probably none. He was a bachelor, a wealthy bachelor with a sterling reputation, a bachelor few mamas left off their guest list. Especially if they had unmarried daughters.

While he'd made a point of dashing hopes by admitting he had no plans to wed, he supposed there would be mothers hoping to marry off their daughters to him, long after his hair had gone silver, his shoulders stooped, and he required a cane to remain erect.

His fellow Chessmen were spending the evening with their wives, doing one thing or another, leaving him the odd man out. He didn't envy them their marital bliss, but he firmly believed it wasn't for him. Aiden might not mind passing his blood on to the next generation, but then he'd been spared being raised under the influence of the Earl of Elverton. While Rook wasn't naive enough to believe Aiden's had been an easy existence, he'd at least escaped the daily encounters with the horrendous man and the shame of being known and acknowledged as his son.

"So, Rook, what do you think of Sam Garrison's investment opportunity?"

Lord Kipwick had asked offhandedly, as though merely making conversation, but when Rook looked across the table at him, he saw an earnestness to his expression that made Rook wish no one turned to him for advice. Investing was always a risk, and there had been a couple of times, in the beginning, when he'd guessed wrong. One could minimize the risk with thorough research and a study of what was happening in the world, applying common sense, but it couldn't be eliminated completely. "I'll know more once I attend the demonstration."

"I received an invitation to it today."

He had as well. Uniform letters, but obviously it had not come from a stationer. Nothing embossed, nothing decorative. Nothing fanciful. Nothing distracting. It struck him as exactly the sort of invitation Miss Garrison would prefer. Straight to the point.

However, it also indicated that a ball would follow

the demonstration, and he was rather certain that was the mother's doing, a continued attempt to land herself a son-by-marriage.

The other three gentlemen at the table nodded and murmured, confirming they, also, had been solicited. Like him, they were all unattached. Like him, they were all lords. While they couldn't hold a candle to him when it came to coins in the coffers, they were comfortably well off. He didn't particularly like the notion of them fulfilling Miss Garrison's desire for investors or imagining the brightness and gratitude that would sparkle within her eyes with their commitment to her enterprise. She would no doubt view them as heroes of the tale, saving her family's business from doom.

Perhaps when next they met, he'd agree to provide the needed funds. To hell with her having to rely upon anyone else. Only he didn't want her grateful to him for his money—he didn't want any financial transaction to be responsible for her looking at him as if he'd hung the moon. He wanted her not to care about his wealth, not to yearn for it. But instead to yearn for him.

He didn't want to buy his way into her heart.

Into her heart? What the devil was he even on about here? He wasn't the type to give his heart away, not any longer. And he certainly didn't want to own her heart, to have her gift him with it. A gentleman did not toy with a woman's affections if he had no plans to ever place a ring on her finger.

"Sam Garrison seems almost as anxious to marry off his sister as he is to find investors," Lord Langdon said.

"She's a bit of a strange bird, though," Lord Falstone uttered, his attention on his cards.

"In what manner precisely?" Rook asked, not

bothering to disguise the menace slithering through his voice.

Falstone must have noted it, because with eyes as wide as saucers, he jerked up his head to stare at him. "Are the rumors true, Rook? Are you courting her?"

"I merely don't think any lady needs to be disparaged, especially one who has committed no offense, and I'm truly curious regarding what caused you to make your statement."

"Well, uh, our discourse when I danced with her."

Rook glared and arched a brow. "By all means, do go on."

Falstone cleared his throat. "Well, uh, you see, ah"—another throat clearing—"she mentioned how much more practical it would be to have a small *mechanized* pencil attached to a dance card rather than one that required sharpening to expose more . . . graphite, I believe is the term she used . . . and then went on to explain how the mechanized pencil worked"—no doubt in response to Falstone's perplexed expression, but then looking somewhat befuddled tended to be his usual state—"and told me the first patent for such an instrument went to two Englishmen, a little over fifty years ago."

Before Victoria sat on the throne. Fascinating. He imagined that Miss Garrison had intimately explored at least one mechanized pencil. "You didn't find that at all interesting?"

"It's a writing instrument, old chap."

"Most gents would have appreciated a discourse that went beyond the usual weather, fashion, and flowers."

"But her enthusiasm for the details and how the blasted thing worked . . . a lady should care nothing for that."

Rook was tempted to say that a lady should care nothing for *Falstone*. Not to recognize or value Miss Garrison and her clever mind proved the idiocy of the man was beyond the pale.

Kipwick gave a low laugh. "Then you'd best avoid her, Falstone, when the next opportunity arrives for dancing with her. She'll no doubt explain precisely how the roulette wheel works."

"What gives you the impression that would be her next topic of conversation?" Rook asked, truly curious as to how the man had drawn that conclusion.

"She's been staring at the one over there for nigh on ten minutes now." He nodded toward an area behind Rook.

Rook twisted around. Because there were tables between here and the roulette wheel where she was standing, he was able to spot her easily enough. She seemed mesmerized by the spinning wheel, and he could well imagine that she was indeed striving to determine exactly how the contraption operated. Because that was what her inquisitive mind craved, an understanding of how things worked. Turning to those at his table, he tossed down his cards. "If you gents will excuse me, I'm going to seek my entertainments elsewhere."

In the days following the Trewlove ball, when she'd finally had a chance to have a moment alone with Sam, she'd asked him if he'd visited the gaming hell that Lord Camberley had mentioned. Indeed, just as she'd suspected, he had been frequenting the club to meet gentlemen and use the opportunity to sell them on the notion of their business. Or so he'd claimed that to be his endeavor.

But they'd barely walked through the door when he was standing behind those sitting at the roulette table and placing his bets. And Leonora had found herself intrigued by the spinning wheel. Surely it couldn't be as simple as she envisioned. The wheel spun one way, the tiny ball traveling in the opposite direction circled the bowl until it lost its momentum and dropped into a slot. Shouts of joy mingled with groans of despair then filled the air. Slaps on backs occurred, whether a person won or lost. A gaming hell that included men was much noisier than the Elysium, whose clientele was all female.

It was so crowded, mostly ladies sitting while gentlemen standing behind them reached over and between to set tokens on numbers or squares on either side of the table. The racket was nearly deafening. The *clack, clack, clack* of the ball bouncing as it hit barriers until it settled into place. She watched as the croupier used an L-shaped stick to gather up the losing bets—Sam's included.

More bets placed, another spin of the wheel, a hurling of the ball—

She knew she needed to move on to address her purpose in coming here. When Sam had confessed where he was spending his time, she'd decided to join him tonight in order to pass out the invitations to their demonstration to anyone who might have an interest. Surely if they had a membership here, they had a modicum of wealth—unless they were all like Lord Camberley and in debt to the gaming hell. But she'd spent most of her day typing—she'd decided that was how to describe the action taken on the writing machine because in a small way it resembled typesetting—out the invitations. Two dozen were weighing down her reticule.

Unfortunately, etiquette demanded that she not approach any gentlemen who had not been introduced to her. Sam, however, could speak with anyone he wanted. But he was otherwise occupied, at least until he lost all his tokens. Therefore, she'd have to wait until he was available.

Meanwhile, the spinning wheel fascinated her. She wondered if she could build one without ever having seen the inner workings. She wished she had the funds to purchase one so she could peer inside.

"Miss Garrison."

At the soft, silky voice near her ear and the speed with which her heart pistoned, Leonora had to face the truth that she hadn't really come here to hand out invitations. Rather she'd been hoping to cross paths with Rook. Knowing he spent many a night here, she'd planned to wander about, surreptitiously searching for him, but she'd gotten distracted. She turned slightly. "My lord."

"You don't seem to be wagering."

"I don't think one should unless one can afford to lose the coins."

"Your brother doesn't seem to hold with that philosophy."

She glanced over at Sam's dwindling stack of tokens. "It appears he doesn't."

"I was wondering if I might steal you away for a bit."

Her gaze dropped to his talented lips, and she was fairly certain he had kissing in mind, for surely there were clandestine corners here where a couple could find privacy for a few minutes.

"Let me tell Sam so he doesn't worry." But her

brother merely distractedly waved a hand and said, "Have fun."

She almost told him that she was on the verge of being ravished, but she wasn't certain even those scandalous words would be enough to turn his attention away from the table, and anyone who overheard them might believe she was speaking true. While she'd been talking to him, a few more people had gathered around, and she was hemmed in. Her "excuse me, let me pass" was being ignored, no doubt because the din of conversation and gaming made it impossible for anyone to hear her, and she most certainly wasn't going to lean toward strangers in order to speak in their ears, nor was she going to shout in an unladylike manner.

Then similar to the seas parting, a path opened up and Rook was holding out his hand to her. Dear Lord, but the man did have a commanding presence. She slipped her hand into his, grateful when he effortlessly led them through the crowd of people clustered around the table. Then he smoothly shifted her hand to the crook of his elbow.

"I assume this is your first visit to the club," he said, "unless you came between the ball and now."

"I've never been before. It's quite energetic."

He chuckled low. "That's one way to describe it."

"People throw away their money with such haste." She shook her head as they wended their way around games of dice or cards. "I don't understand why they are so opposed to wagering on something—like our family's business—that has fewer risks."

"Investing requires patience, and as you're no doubt aware, the payoff can take a while. Whereas here, it's instant gratification—if one wins. Otherwise, disappointment rules. But I'm of a mind experiencing the disenchantment only serves to heighten the joy of winning."

"Were you playing?"

"A game of brag. Wasn't winning. Although, with you now on my arm, I feel my luck has changed."

She couldn't help herself. She laughed. "That's a ridiculous attempt at flirtation." Horrified at how quickly and easily that had come out, she stopped walking, causing him to do the same. "I apologize. I didn't mean to imply you were flirting."

"I was and you're correct. My words were ridiculous. Perhaps this will serve me better." Like a magician wishing to bring attention to something he'd conjured, Rook waved a hand to direct her attention away from him.

They'd crossed the gaming floor to a distant corner where an isolated roulette table seemed to be waiting patiently to welcome those willing to place bets. Ropes surrounded it in a manner similar to those she'd once seen at a boxing match.

"Is this going to be a private game?" She had the random thought that perhaps they'd wager kisses instead of tokens. In which case every bet would result in a win one way or another.

"No." His eyes sparkling with mischief, his grin triumphant, he lowered his head slightly in order to hold her gaze. "You're going to take it apart."

THE DELIGHT WASHING over her features was like the sun breaking through storm clouds. She looked at the table, gazed back at him. "You're not serious."

"I am. I noticed the way you were studying the

roulette wheel over there. Was I mistaken regarding what you were striving to decipher: how it worked?" Assuming he had the right of it, he'd spoken to the club owner with whom he had a friendship and learned it was easy enough to disassemble and re-assemble, so uncomplicated in fact that Rook could even do it. And it just so happened that there were no plans to use this table tonight.

And so it was that Rook was now standing beside a woman whose face was aglow with anticipation.

"I don't have tools," she said.

"Apparently none are needed." He untied the rope from one of the stanchions standing guard and indi-cated she should precede him into the inner sanctum. She inhaled deeply, reminding him of his reaction the first time he'd taken a journey in a hot air balloon. The unknown of it had been a bit frightening, but at its core it had been thrilling. He couldn't help but believe that for her the discovery of how something worked held the same monumental exhilaration. He did hope she wasn't going to be disappointed.

Once they were inside their private arena, he refas-tened the rope to its pole because he wanted no one intruding, even as he was aware of people wandering over out of curiosity.

"What's happening here, Lord Wyeth?" a gentle-man asked.

"Miss Garrison has been granted permission to ex-plore the inner workings of a roulette wheel."

"You don't say. I've always wondered . . ." His voice trailed off as he shuffled closer to the rope. A few oth-ers were gathering around.

"Fortunate for you then, Miss Garrison always satisfies her curiosity." If he hadn't assisted her with this endeavor, he was relatively certain she'd have eventually found a way to get to the insides of the device.

"I suppose you asked for instructions regarding how to take it apart," she said, so focused on the mechanism that he doubted she was aware they had an audience.

"I did. Would you like a clue?"

"No, I . . . I think the key is probably the spindle."

As a gentleman he'd felt it was only polite to offer her the quick solution, but he'd suspected she'd want to figure it out for herself. It was exhilarating and a bit unsettling to realize he knew her so well. "I believe they call it a turret."

She canted her head to the side. "Yes, I can see how it resembles one."

She wrapped her hands around the slender, protruding part of the wheel, and tried to turn it. But the thing didn't budge.

"Might be easier without your gloves. Allow me to remove them for you." He watched the delicate muscles at her throat work as she swallowed.

"I can do it." She whipped them off and shoved them into her reticule. He wondered if she'd known that he would have taken his time, would have made it a sensual experience for them both.

Unfortunately, the absence of gloves didn't help at all in getting the turret to budge. He moved his hands until they were hovering so near to hers that he could sense their warmth. "May I assist?" he asked.

"It would be rather like losing, letting the machine win, if I can't do it myself."

"There's no shame in having a partner, Miss Garrison.

You must understand that or you wouldn't be seeking investors."

She nodded, although he couldn't help but believe that she felt as though she was falling. "Yes, of course, I welcome your assistance."

Half covering her hands, tightening his hold on the spindle, he suspected she'd done most of her exploring of gadgetry alone, except for the moments when her father was with her. But he was gone now, and Rook wondered with whom she might now share the discoveries. Certainly not her mother and probably not her brother.

It would be rather like reading a book and then finding no one else who had read it, so he had no one with whom to discuss what he'd liked and what he hadn't. The Chessmen tended to share the same reading tastes, so it wasn't unusual for them to get into spirited debates regarding a story and that prolonged their reading gratification.

But her interests were more isolated, and he found himself resenting anyone who discouraged her enjoyment of them or failed to recognize their value—like Falstone, for instance. Daft man.

He could feel her slender hands beneath his, the softness of them. The silkiness of them, and he recalled the pleasure of her fingers slipping beneath his shirt in the garden, exploring him, curious about him, discovering him.

Now working together, they caused the turret, a fancy screw to be honest, to finally budge and begin to turn. He immediately pulled his hands away, giving her the triumph of finally disconnecting it. She set it aside and went to work removing the parts associated with the turret until the wheel head with its numbered pockets was ready for extracting.

Clasping her hands tightly, she turned her attention to him. "Shall we do it together?"

He didn't think he'd have felt greater gratification if she'd said, "Shall we go romp about in your bed?"

Slowly he shook his head. "Enjoy your victory, Miss Garrison."

Carefully she lifted out the wheel head and clutched it to her chest as she looked down into what she'd uncovered. "It's as I surmised," she said quietly, a tinge of disappointment in her voice. "It's only a bowl with a top and a decorative screw holding it all in place."

"I'm sorry it wasn't more."

She looked up at him, earnestness mirrored in her lovely blue eyes. "Don't be. The simplest of machines can provide inspiration for something more complicated. No discovery is a waste. Besides, with a few adjustments, I think it could be modified so the croupier could affect where the ball lands, increasing the odds of winning for the house."

He laughed. "Why, Miss Garrison, you're not suggesting that a gaming hell cheat, surely?"

"I'm advising that one should be aware that it very easily could."

He thought it might take a thousand horses to drag him away from staring at her teasing smile that practically lit up the room. Instead, it took a solitary shout.

"Lord Wyeth, tip the table over so we can see inside the blasted thing."

Rather than do that, he untied the rope and let the dozen or so people who'd gathered take a look at what she'd uncovered. After the curious had their fill and wandered off, he helped Miss Garrison put it all back together. When everything was as it originally had been, he asked, "I don't suppose you'd join me in the library for a libation?"

LEONORA HAD NEVER been so grateful for an invitation in her life. With books lining shelves, newspapers on tables, and thickly padded leather chairs for comfort, the library was just the sort of room she appreciated. Much quieter than the gaming floor. Two seconds after they'd settled into their seats opposite each other, a liveried young man was standing nearby.

Rook held up a finger and waved it toward her. "Brandy?"

"Actually, I'd prefer whiskey."

He looked up at their attendant. "Scotch, Peter, for the lady and myself, your best bottle."

"Yes, m'lord." And off the lad went.

"You know his name."

"I don't believe in taking those who serve me for granted."

The servant returned straightaway and set a crystal tumbler in front of each of them. Rook flipped him a coin which he readily caught. "Appreciate it, m'lord."

It seemed Rook believed in being generous as well.

He lifted his glass. "To new discoveries."

As all the discoveries he'd shared with her flashed through her mind, she feared her smile looked somewhat timid or abashed. Still, she nodded, took a sip, and welcomed the burn of the excellent scotch. While the taste might have reminded her of time spent with her father, nothing about Rook reminded her of him in the least. Although he was immensely relaxed, his presence dominated their corner, making it seem that he took up far more space than he did. She imagined other men approaching him, a king holding court, to discuss business.

"So what brought you to the Dragons tonight?" he asked, true interest reflected in his tone.

You. A desire to cross paths with you. Two days without speaking with him had seemed an eternity. No one else made her feel as though the words she spouted were important, and yet she thought if she spoke of something as simple as the shape of a cloud, his intense gaze would never waver or wander from her, seeking something more fascinating. "Sam and I wanted to pass out invitations to those we might have missed." She retrieved one from her reticule as evidence regarding the truth of her words. "But we both got distracted."

"How many are there?"

"Two dozen or so."

"May I have a look at them?"

A strange request when she knew one had been delivered to him just that afternoon. Perhaps he hadn't had a chance to read it yet. She handed it over.

"All of them?"

She dug them out and gave them to him, watched him peruse the first one, lightly and slowly tracing a finger over the numerous inked indentions where the raised letters on her machine had struck paper. She'd never expected to be envious of a slip of parchment, but she found herself wishing for him to map out all her various dips, hollows, valleys, and peaks in a similar fashion. Fighting the urge to squirm, she took another sip of the scotch and worked to give the impression that she was unaffected by his sensual out-lining of words.

"You created all these yourself?"

Her throat felt tight, and she had to clear it before she could answer. "It seemed I should if I'm going to tout the merits of the writing machine. An example, if you will, of only one of its many uses."

"Do you anticipate it'll put stationers out of business?"

"No, not at all. I doubt anyone else will have the patience for creating an abundance of duplicates. They might generate one as an example . . ." She lifted her shoulder in a hapless shrug. Most would see the machine as a tool, whereas she saw it as a friend. It never made her feel unappreciated. It brought her calm in an odd sort of way. On rare occasions, she even spoke to it. While the conversations were one-sided, she'd found that voicing concerns often gave her a new perspective.

"Would you be opposed to my asking Peter to hand them out for you?"

She should place them in waiting hands herself but knew if she started talking about the machine with potential investors, she would carry on until their eyes went glassy. Besides, she was much more comfortable speaking with Rook than with strangers. And as it had occurred to her earlier, she couldn't very well hand them out to men she'd not yet been introduced to. She considered asking Rook to accompany her—for surely he knew just about everyone—but it wasn't his prod-uct to sell. Besides, she wanted a little time to simply sit here with him. They'd had so few moments when they weren't giving in to passion. "I'd appreciate it."

He raised an arm and snapped his fingers. Almost immediately, Peter was back at their side.

"Be a good lad and distribute these among the members for Miss Garrison, if you please. Inquire as to whether they already received one, and if so, carry on to someone else."

"I'd be honored, m'lord."

A few more coins landed on the lad's palm along with her invitations. After the servant dashed off, Rook leaned back, stretched out his legs, and crossed them at the ankles. He reminded her of a large cat settling in to watch the mousehole.

"I suppose your brother is carrying a handful of invitations inside his coat pocket to dispense as well."

He spoke with the apathy of someone asking if she'd like milk with her tea. It was a tone she'd heard numerous times, and truthfully it stung a little coming from him, and yet she also detected the barest hint of displeasure dancing along the edge of his words. "No, he isn't. But together we were going to distribute the ones I brought. I needed him to make the introductions. That's Sam's skill. Talking to people. He has a knack for catching their attention and holding onto it."

"I've spoken with him a couple of times since the dinner at King's. He's not wont for discussing your business. To be honest, the impression I had that first night was that he has very little knowledge when it comes to your enterprise. That you're the one managing things. Have I the right of it?"

She had a momentary tightening of her gut at the thought of being unfaithful to Sam, but this man deserved the truth if he was considering investing. "He was so young when Father died. Two and twenty. Only recently graduated from the university. Unprepared for the responsibility."

"He was older than I was when my father challenged me to begin looking after the family estate. Which I succeeded at while finding a way to get out from under his thumb. Are you too kind to say your brother is lazy?"

It seemed cruel to label him as that. "He just never had a chance to spend time learning the family business before it was handed to him."

Rook tipped his head slightly. "You don't have primogeniture in America. Was the company divided between you and your brother?"

"Why all the questions? Why does any of it matter?"

"If I'm going to invest—which I've not yet decided to do—I want to ensure someone capable is at the helm. I want to understand the structure of the company. I need to have confidence that it will turn a profit."

"It will. It may take a little time but I've no doubt that lawyers, exporters, importers, and others will see the advantage of being able to produce a list or correspondence that can be easily read."

"And you might be a bit biased if half the business is yours."

Why was he harping on about this?

"Well, it's not. It all went to Sam."

The smallest spark of triumph lit his eyes, as if he'd suspected all along that was the case and merely wanted confirmation.

"What went to you?" he asked solemnly. "A dowry?"

"No. Father's pocket watch. I carry it in my reticule, because it is far more valuable to me than the business." Although truth be told, she'd have liked a share of the company as well, even if it was only a small share.

"May I see it?" he asked.

It was so personal, and yet she had a strong urge to

share it with him. Removing it from her reticule, she extended it toward him.

Leaning forward, he took it, placed his elbows on his thighs, and studied the golden timepiece and its thickly chained fob with the intensity that only a few minutes ago he'd been studying her. Turning it over, looking at it from every angle. He held it near his ear, listening to its consistent ticking.

"Is this the timepiece you took apart?" he asked quietly, reverently, as if he'd been handed a treasure that awed him with its magnificence.

"Yes."

He lifted his gaze to hers. "It's of a good quality. Speaks volumes of his faith in your abilities that he trusted you to reassemble it rather than taking it to a watchmaker."

Once he returned it to her care, she noted how it had absorbed some of his warmth, and she closed her fingers more securely around it.

"No doubt one of the reasons the management of matters has fallen to you," he continued. "It does rest on your shoulders, doesn't it?"

This man seemed not to miss much. "We don't advertise that fact because . . . well, because not everyone would be as accepting of a woman holding the reins when losing money is at risk."

"However, you don't intend to lose money."

"No, I do not."

A silence followed. It wasn't uncomfortable, and she didn't feel a need to fill it with words. A good deal of peace was found in simply sitting here with him.

"You're likely to get your second souvenir tomorrow," he said quietly. "I'm not known for sitting with women in the library of this club."

She wondered if he'd somehow managed to read her mind—or if perhaps he was experiencing the same contentment. "Where do you sit with them?"

He grinned. "No place a lady should visit."

Her cheeks warmed, and she took another sip of the scotch, wishing she hadn't asked because she didn't want to envision him with other women.

"I'm curious, Miss Garrison—"

"Curiosity is a good thing. I don't believe it ever killed a cat but rather lack of."

He chuckled, his eyes crinkling. She liked when he laughed. "I'm curious as to why it is that your mother allows you to roam about without benefit of a chaperone."

"I have a chaperone. Sam."

"And a damned good one he is. I could have waltzed you right out the front door and he'd have not noticed."

He was correct about Sam. But she could hardly blame her brother for his lack of attention when he never before had been responsible for her. She'd always taken care of him, as well as herself. Another reason she wasn't keen on marrying. She suspected a husband would be prone to stifling her independence.

"He certainly didn't escort you to the Elysium," he continued.

"No. He'd already left for the evening, so I waited until Mama had retired. But tonight, as we both wanted to come to the same place, he was kind enough to delay his parting until I could join him, and we snuck out together."

In spite of the distance between them, she heard his little grunt, which sounded a good deal like disapproval pointed toward Sam for his lack of care and herself for trusting him to see after her. But she didn't really need Sam. A woman of her years, while a bit shy of the number acceptable to be going about without a chaperone, was perfectly capable of protecting herself. Her father had taught her how. "Besides, I always carry a gun in my reticule."

His eyes widened at that. "Do you know how to use it?"

"What sort of ambassador would I be to that portion of the family business if I didn't?"

Her tone indicated she thought he was silly for even asking. He must have accurately read it because the smile he gave her reflected a bit of pride and admiration. "You carry about a pistol, a timepiece, *and* invitations in your reticule. Items I'd have never thought belonged together. I can honestly say, Miss Garrison, you're unlike any other woman of my acquaintance."

Naturally, he'd never met anyone like her. She didn't adhere to the expectations one generally associated with a lady. "You must find me a bit ridiculous."

"Don't assume me to be like those ignorant blighters in New York."

"I would never . . . just what I know of you thus far . . . it's like comparing a goldfish to a shark."

"I do hope I'm not the goldfish."

She laughed. "No. You're not really a shark either." Even if there were times when he seemed dangerous to her heart. "I just couldn't think of anything more opposite of the tiny fish."

"You have the prettiest laugh."

He seemed as surprised by his words as she was. As though each was taken off guard, they both took a sip from their respective glasses. Afterward she dared to confess, "I don't think a gentleman has ever liked anything about me."

"Idiots all, then." He clasped together his hands, resting between his knees, and she wondered if he'd been contemplating reaching for her. "I like the blue of your eyes. I like that I can see a shadow of where your freckles once blossomed."

It took every ounce of restraint she could muster not to slap her hands over her face to hide the remnants of them. "Freckles were the bane of my existence. Especially because I had so many."

"You must have been a favorite of the sun then . . . for it to have kissed you so often."

He at once appeared deadly serious and teasing, as if he wasn't confident regarding how she might take his words and wanted to be prepared to embrace her reaction or shrug it off. In truth, she wasn't quite certain how she should react because she'd never had anyone speak with her so poetically. She felt like she was at the Elysium asking to have someone toss compliments her way, to make her blush, to make her heart sing with gratitude because for a short time she'd feel desired. Finally, she settled on "Are you flirting with me, my lord?"

"Obviously not well if you have to ask."

He sounded a bit disgruntled, as he had when he'd spoken about her falling asleep on him.

"To be quite honest, I've no experience at flirting, either the giving or receiving of it," she admitted.

"If we're being honest then"—he studied her with the intensity of someone searching for a vein of gold—"my flirtation skills are no doubt sorely lacking as I've not used them in a while. But, no, I wasn't flirting, Miss Garrison. Simply speaking the truth."

CHAPTER 12

ROOK was left with the impression that she'd seldom had the truth of her spoken to her—at least not by anyone other than her father. From what he'd observed, her mother found only faults and her brother cared for only his own interests. As for the gents who'd passed through her life . . .

She was a gem so rare that they'd been unable to recognize her true value.

However, he had the uncanny ability to ferret out value, whether in an investment opportunity or a person. It was the reason he had friends for whom he'd lay down his life and knew they'd do the same for him, if it was ever asked of them. The reason when he'd first met Aiden and Finn Trewlove, he'd recognized that they were good men, men he was proud to call brothers. The reason he seldom lost money he'd invested. Even when it had seemed he'd made an error in judgment, with patience his instincts had proven correct.

And so it was that he knew Miss Garrison should be treasured. However, not by him, not by someone who had sworn not to marry, who believed it was best if this particular branch of the family tree withered and died. And that wouldn't happen if it kept sprouting offshoots.

She set her empty glass aside and studied the watch face. "Nearly eleven." She looked up at him, and he could have sworn her features mirrored regret. "I should probably find Sam, so we can return to the hotel now."

"Where are you staying?"

"The Trewlove Hotel."

"Ah, splendid accommodations."

"Have you stayed there?"

"No, I have a place in town."

"Of course you do. I suppose through Aiden you know the Trewloves well."

"I'm beginning to. Across from the hotel is a bookshop owned by Lady Rosemont, within whose garden you engaged in some mischief the other night."

She blushed so red that the remnants of her freckles were nearly obliterated. "A gentleman wouldn't have mentioned that."

"It's one of my favorite memories."

She laughed again, and he wished he knew the secret to keeping her doing just that.

"There you go with the meaningless flirting again."

Not meaningless. He'd meant the words. Their time in the garden was quite possibly his favorite memory. But their time in the nook was a close second. If memories were racehorses, those two encounters would be running neck and neck. But he wasn't going to argue the point with her because he wasn't quite certain how he felt about so many of his thoughts revolving around her.

"My carriage is nearby. I'd be delighted to see you and your brother delivered safely to the hotel."

"That's very kind. We'll accept the offer."

Only they had no luck finding her brother. Not in the library, on the gaming floor, in the dining room—or any number of other rooms, public and private. A fissure of anger rent its way through Rook because Sam Garrison had no doubt gone elsewhere, leaving his sister to fend for herself.

She and he were now standing at the edge of the gaming floor near the doors that led outside.

"It would be entirely inappropriate for me to be in your carriage without Sam. I'll hire a cab."

"You think it's appropriate to be traveling alone this time of night in a hansom cab?"

"More so than traveling with you."

"You've been alone with me in a room, a nook, and a garden. But you're going to draw the line at a carriage?"

"We've no one to ensure we behave."

He wondered if she wanted to misbehave. He most certainly did. But more he wanted to guarantee her safety. What if the driver preyed on solitary women? What if they were accosted by miscreants? If she wouldn't allow him to provide her with transportation, he'd at least follow, although in truth, he wouldn't mind spending a little more time in her company. Hence, the offer to begin with.

"I swear I won't touch you. Have I ever given you reason to doubt I'm a man of my word?"

"No, of course not." She glanced around, trepidation causing her brow to furrow. She took a deep inhale and straightened her shoulders. "We shouldn't be seen leaving together, should we?"

"Don't want to find yourself with another souvenir?"

"Best if I don't. If I create a scandal, who would invest? People need to know we can be trusted to do the right thing, aren't prone to disgrace."

"Fair point. I'll go out first and wait for you by the

side of the building. Give me a couple of minutes and then follow. When you exit through those doors, go to your right."

She nodded, and he wondered if she felt marginally better by not voicing her daring agreement to his questionable proposal. For the benefit of those walking by, he took her hand and pressed a kiss to her fingers. "Thank you, Miss Garrison, for joining me in the library and for a most delightful evening of conversation."

"Thank you, my lord."

Releasing his hold on her, he winked. "I shall wait with bated breath until we once again cross paths."

Her lips twitched, and he envisioned few men—few people—had ever put in the effort to make them react in that manner. Having accomplished that tiny little movement, he felt rather like a holder of magic.

With a lightness to his step, he headed out the door, strode over to the side of the building, and leaned casually against it. He shouldn't feel so triumphant knowing he had her trust. And yet he did. And while there were many who trusted him—offhand, he couldn't recall a single person who didn't—her faith in him seemed like a precious gift. It wasn't something he intended to abuse. He wouldn't touch her in the damned carriage no matter how badly he wanted to.

Something about her calmed the rage within him, the rage that was never far from the surface. For most of his life, he'd fought the stigma of being the Earl of Elverton's son, his heir. Yet with her, he could almost imagine that it didn't matter. She knew his father only by reputation. She'd never had to suffer through him leering at her, making untoward advances, or seeking to convince her no greater honor existed than being his mistress. Apparently, his sire had possessed the ability to be quite charismatic when he wanted and had easily charmed the clothing off ladies. Although Rook suspected Miss Garrison would have seen through the facade, would have taken his father apart ruthlessly, to discover the rot beneath the surface.

Keeping his attention on the entrance to the club, he knew the moment she stepped outside. Straightening from the wall, he didn't quite know what to make of the elation rippling through him at the sight of her. It was more than her hair, eyes, and heart-shaped chin. It was the glow when she was intrigued and exploring something in order to determine how it functioned. While he feared the roulette wheel had ultimately been a disappointment for her, he'd been mesmerized by the anticipation flowing off her as she analyzed its various parts.

She reached him and he offered his arm, grateful when her hand nestled within the crook of his elbow. "My carriage awaits just up here," he told her.

"I like London at night," she quietly.

"Even with the fog rolling in?"

"Especially with the fog rolling in. It gives everything an ethereal quality."

"It can dampen you if you're out in it too long. Fortunately, we won't be."

They reached his vehicle. His footman opened the door, but Rook handed her up and then followed, taking the bench opposite the one she'd chosen. "Trewlove Hotel," he ordered the footman. "The long way."

"Aye, m'lord." The door was slammed shut.

"The long way?" she asked.

"Since you enjoy London at night, I see no need for us to rush." Rook extinguished the light in the lantern, so they could travel in the dark without having to draw the curtains. He didn't want her being clearly seen or identified.

He liked that her jasmine fragrance wafted through the confines and would probably remain long after she was gone. He couldn't quite determine what it was about her that drew his interest. Lust, surely. The manner in which her body fit so perfectly against his. Her height that required he dip his head only a fraction to take possession of her mouth. How quickly her hands took to roaming over him. The feel of her bare fingers against his skin. He couldn't recall any other woman so subtly taking an interest in his skin while he still wore clothes. Most were content to tear them off. But she was an intriguing blend of brazenness mixed with shyness. It sparked his desire while simultaneously calling to his need to protect—even if that meant protecting her from him.

"Does your brother often leave you without escort?" he asked.

"He seldom takes me with him. He probably simply forgot I was there."

He couldn't fathom how anyone could forget she was there. The lights from the street filtered in through the windows, allowing him to view her profile as she watched the passing scenery. He wasn't certain he'd ever found a carriage ride so peaceful.

"Although I do wonder where he got off to," she murmured.

"There are a goodly number of clubs where a gent can find entertainment."

"Club . . . gent . . . entertainment." She swung her gaze to him. "Are you referring to a bordello?"

He loved how this woman could be so forthright, uttering a word that he doubted had passed the lips of any other lady he knew. Although he did regret the shadows that prevented him from determining if she was blushing. "And gaming hells," he clarified.

He saw the flash of her smile. "I imagine I'm closer to the truth. Sam has never liked lying, and he was able to avoid doing so by not finding me to let me know where he was off to."

Her brother should have foregone that one pleasure to ensure his sister ran into no trouble and her reputation was not tarnished. Rook suspected, however, that she wouldn't appreciate his pointing that out, especially as she probably knew the truth of it. "Should anyone like lying?"

"Swindlers and scoundrels, I suspect."

She looked back out the window. "There's the Palace of Westminster. Do you sit in the House of Lords?"

"Not yet. Not until my father passes."

"I cannot imagine having so much responsibility."

What the devil did she think she was carrying on her shoulders if not *so much responsibility*? Was she so accustomed to it that she no longer noticed it, like a splinter that was impossible to remove and eventually became a part of the whole? Or had she simply accepted that caring for her family was her burden to bear? She was the one looking out for her brother and mother. Who looked out for her?

She did. With a pistol in her reticule. Invitations to potential investors. And her father's timepiece that served as a reminder of what she'd lost. Where would she find that love and acceptance again? Was she even aware of what she was truly searching for?

He knew what it was to crave acceptance. His entire life he'd modeled his actions in ways that would result in approval. As a result, he suspected he could be rather boring at times. No secret assignations until her.

Why did he have the sense that with her, he was more his true self than he'd ever been? He wasn't quite certain if he should repel his interest in her or embrace it. Both choices seemed to come with a cost: lose her or lose his respectability.

Suddenly Big Ben bonged the first stroke of eleven. "Can we stop?" she asked.

He immediately banged on the roof, and his coachman brought the horses to a halt. She reached for the door, but Rook beat her to it, leaping out, and then assisting her. Her feet had barely hit the ground before she was hurrying to the edge of the embankment. The Thames separated them from the Palace of Westminster and the Clock Tower, both shrouded in fog. To prevent the dampness from settling on her, he shrugged out of his jacket and draped it over her shoulders. She barely seemed to notice as the bell continued to chime.

"Big Ben sounds so solemn and lonely this time of night," she said nearly on a whisper, as though striving not to wake a sleeping giant. "Perhaps because the streets aren't crowded and there's no din of conversation, laughter, and people going on about their business. It just seems more . . . magnificent . . . than when I've heard it while out during the day."

The streetlamps allowed him to see her more clearly than he'd been able to in the carriage. She looked positively enthralled. He found her beguiling, like an ethereal being who might visit him for only a short while. And he should make the most of whatever time remained to them.

"Do they have people up there ringing the bells?" she asked.

"No, it's mechanized, a complicated series of levers and pulleys that cause the hammer to strike each bell at the appropriate time." A process that would no doubt delight her, and he imagined the inner workings of the Clock Tower strewn out over the street as she disassembled all the various gadgets that came together to create such a masterpiece.

She looked at him as if he'd performed some sort of magic. "Have you seen it?"

"I was given a tour a few years back."

"Oh, I envy you that experience." She turned her attention back to the tower. "How do they illuminate the clock?"

"Gas lighting."

"I assumed as much, but I always like to have confirmation. I constantly angered my tutors and teachers when I asked for proof regarding some of the things they were striving to teach me. What formed the knowledge is usually more interesting than the knowledge itself."

The clock went silent, the final gong seeming to hang on the air with the promise of time continuing, and he wished there was an hour that required a thousand chimes. Whatever was wrong with him to find such peace in this moment? He'd begun to take the ringing of the bells for granted, barely even acknowledged or heard them when he was near enough to do so.

But now he knew he would never again hear them without thinking of her. When he sat in the House of Lords, he would remember her. When he strolled along the embankment and different portions of the hour were heralded with various bells, he would recall how she'd stood there enchanted and enchanting.

"Thank you for halting your carriage. I know you must find me silly for—"

Taking her chin between his thumb and forefinger, he lowered his mouth to hers and tenderly sipped, stealing the words that were the complete opposite of how he found her. Breaking his vow not to touch her. No longer a man of his word, and yet the moment demanded that he not let it pass without making the most of it, without signaling how special she was. He drew back. "Not silly at all."

"How do you label that sort of kiss?" she asked quietly.

"I'm not sure. I've never engaged in one like that before. I do hope you'll forgive my lapse in not keeping my word."

She lifted a slender shoulder. "It was only a small lapse."

"You're extraordinary, Miss Garrison."

"Nora," she said softly, self-consciously.

Strange that they'd shared three passionate kisses, and yet it was this one, as light as a butterfly settling on a rose petal, that had deepened the intimacy between them. "Johnny."

She smiled warmly, and he felt like a hammer had struck his heart with the force required to make Big Ben sing. "I don't know if I've ever known anyone who went by so many different names. Don't you find it confusing?"

"No. The name used identifies who—what—they are to me. Lord Wyeth . . . usually an acquaintance. Rook . . . someone important to me. Johnny . . . someone with a closer association." Someone for whom he'd lay down his life. Although in spite of the Chessmen calling him Rook, he'd lay down his life for them. Until that moment, he hadn't realized he'd do the same for her. But it would merely complicate things between them if he confessed that.

"I've never heard anyone call you Johnny."

"I've never heard anyone call you Nora—so it's an even exchange."

He wasn't quite certain what it was they were exchanging. However, it seemed incredibly significant. A course change that a ship's captain might make when he detected stormy seas ahead and calmer waters elsewhere. "The smaller bells will be ringing soon. Shall we delay our departure until they've chimed the quarter hour?"

"If you don't mind."

"Not at all."

She turned back toward the tower, and he edged closer to her, but didn't touch. For now, within the shadows of the night, it was enough.

As the carriage carried them through London, Leonora was as quiet as Johnny. The sharing of pet names created a bond that she didn't know quite what to do with.

When those quarter-hour bells had finally chimed, as much as she'd wanted to listen to them clamoring through the night air, she'd been more focused on other things. The heat of him that eased into her even though he wasn't touching her. The soughing of his breathing. His stillness. The tension radiating from him, like a tethered creature that wanted to break free of its restraints but forced itself to tamp down its needs in order to receive some reward.

She'd had the wild and absolutely ridiculous thought that perhaps she was the reward. That after delivering such a gentle press of his lips to hers, he'd decided it was to his advantage to keep to his promise of not touching her in order to gain more.

How was it so light a touch could make her chest feel as if it bore the weight of an elephant sitting upon it? She had yet to fully catch her breath.

While she watched the city passing by, she could feel his gaze homed in on her, halfway wished he'd cross over to her bench and give her a right proper kiss. Yet the one he'd gifted her with earlier seemed far more important. He'd given to her something he'd claimed to have never presented to anyone else. The sort of kiss he'd yet to label, that was presently hers and hers alone, that made it so precious, like cupping her hands around a hummingbird, its rapidly flapping wings matching the fluttering of her heart.

"I was wondering," he began, his voice low and soft, signaling the sharing of a secret, "if you might be agreeable to meeting me tomorrow night."

It was a terrible idea, and yet she obviously trusted him enough to be with him alone in his carriage. "You mean . . . clandestinely?"

"Yes. I'd like to take you someplace, show you something."

She swallowed hard. Her breath had left her completely. "Are you going to show me what happens beyond a kiss?" The hushed words still seemed to clang through the carriage as loudly as Big Ben.

She'd had to ask, needed clarification regarding precisely what he was proposing. His perfectly straight, white teeth flashed quickly. "No, you'll have to ask for that. I'd never presume . . ."

She refused to show her disappointment. It would no doubt require an entire bottle of absinthe to work up the courage to ask him to demonstrate how one fucked without fucking. "Then what are you going to show me?"

"I'd rather it be a surprise, but I promise you'll not be disappointed."

She doubted she'd be disappointed in the other either. "I'm not agreeing but if I did, where would you want to meet?"

"There's a mews behind the bookstore I mentioned earlier. I'll be waiting for you there."

"I never know precisely when I can slip away."

"I'll arrive at eight and wait."

"You might be there for hours before I could join you."

"But you will join me? Eventually?"

Had she agreed without realizing she was agreeing? Although if she was honest with herself, from the beginning, she'd known her answer would be yes. Her hesitancy was merely an attempt to give the impression she hadn't fallen under his spell. She couldn't even imagine stopping to listen to the bells with Lord Falstone. He, no doubt, thought as she had earlier, that people in the Tower tugged on ropes, and the poor man would probably be confused by the knowledge that he had it wrong. He didn't seem to even comprehend the notion of a screw being used to push lead out of a pencil. "I'll try." It was the best she could do, all she could promise.

"I can't fathom, Nora, that you fail at anything you *try*."

She was failing right now, having no luck whatsoever in *trying* not to fall for this man.

CHAPTER 13

"Do you have to make that damn clacking noise?"

Keeping her fingers on the keys, Leonora looked over at the door to her bedchamber that she'd left open, to indicate she was ready for the day. Leaning negligently against the jamb, Sam appeared to have been ridden hard and put away wet. Getting out of the chair at the table that supported the writing machine, she quickly crossed the room, grabbed her brother's arm, and dragged him into the room before closing the door.

"You left me last night," she hissed, not bothering to disguise her pique.

Sam collapsed into a chair and held his head in his hands. "Could you be a little quieter with your anger? My head is killing me."

"Because you drank too much?"

"Because I did too much of a lot of things."

She moved closer to the chair opposite his and stood behind it, not to protect herself from him but to shield him from her wrath. "Why did you leave me all alone?"

"You were with Rook. I knew he'd look out for you."

"But he's not family. It was hardly appropriate for me to be with him without you at least being nearby. Why didn't you come find me, take me with you?"

Appearing sheepish, he rubbed his thumb in a small circle on the arm of the chair. "Where I wanted to go wasn't the sort of place a woman should visit."

"Where was that exactly?"

He shifted his gaze to the hearth where no fire burned. "Someplace a woman shouldn't even know about."

"A bordello?"

He jerked his head up. "You shouldn't be aware such a place exists. Much less say the word with such ease."

"I'm put out with you, Sam. You abandoned me. I'd never do that to you. I searched the entire place for you."

"I'm sorry, Nora, but when Lord Lawrence invited me to join him . . . if I'd told you, you'd either want to come or start an inquisition. Just seemed easier to simply leave. I knew you had the resourcefulness to get yourself back here." He grinned like he was proud of her. "And you did."

With Rook's assistance. He had shown her where he'd be waiting for her tonight—if she found the courage to join him. He hadn't said those words, but they'd run through her mind. To risk sneaking out again. To not know exactly what he wanted to share with her. Then he'd escorted her inside the hotel, handing over enough money to the man who stood watch at the door as well as the one behind the desk so they'd both forget he'd ever been there.

"You should have at least bothered to tell me so I wouldn't worry about you."

"I didn't know where to find you."

"I was in the library, quite visible." She almost commented that he should be as resourceful as he expected her to be. But he wasn't, and that was part of the challenge, the reason so much fell to her.

"Were you convincing Rook to invest?"

That's what she should have been doing. Instead, she'd set the business aside in order to enjoy his company without an encumbrance. Rather than share that with Sam, she deflected his question by changing the topic. "As for my *clacking*, I'm creating more invitations for you to take with you later, so you can pass them out to those you've met."

"I probably won't be fit to go out until this evening. Too much booze."

Having woken up feeling miserable after drinking the absinthe, she didn't understand why anyone would overindulge a second time, but Sam seemed to derive some sort of pleasure from it. Perhaps he enjoyed suffering. If so, she'd be happy to oblige him with some scathing retorts.

"I would advise that you exercise a bit more discretion regarding your drinking since the demonstration is almost upon us. Remember what Father taught us?"

"To put everything aside for *his* dream?"

Taken aback by his defensive tone, she edged around the chair and sat. "What do you mean?"

He shifted awkwardly as though the chair was suddenly made of needles. "Nothing."

"Sam, this is the family business, your inheritance. Without it, what would you—" She didn't want to make him feel bad, but what skills did he have? What could he do if he didn't have the business to support him?

He shook his head. "I don't have your knack for designing things."

"And I don't have your knack for talking with people in a way that keeps them interested in what I have to say." She gave a little laugh. "I think most of the gents I've danced with would have nodded off if we'd been sitting on a settee rather than moving over a dance floor."

One corner of his mouth hitched. "I enjoy talking to people."

"I don't." Part of the reason she'd insisted on no talking that first night was because she hadn't wanted the gent who'd come for her to discover exactly how boring she could be. Strange, however, that she found it easier to speak with Rook. He never gave the impression that he found conversation with her mind-numbing. "I always find it awkward. Afterward I spend hours going over what I said and how I might have said it in a more interesting way. Especially when I wake up in the middle of the night. My brain just won't *shut down*. It repeats every bit of conversation I've had for days, for weeks. Sometimes it'll be something I said months ago. Once I've spoken, I can't seem to untether the words."

"It's because you're so smart, Nora. You see things in extraordinary ways, in ways that people like me can't even imagine."

"If I can silence the words, I can't stop the images that are circling about. I'm always trying to fit them together, to make them work." She released a deep breath. "We're a pair, Sam, you and I. The people in the factory love you because you stop and speak with them, and genuinely are interested in what they have to say. It's not that I don't care about them. I'm just not gifted at talking."

"You didn't seem to have any trouble doing so with Rook last night."

Narrowing her eyes, she studied him. "When did you see me talking with him?"

He again shifted uncomfortably in the chair. "I may have glanced in the library before I departed."

"Therefore, you did know where to find me."

He nodded petulantly. "I just wanted to make sure you'd be all right."

"Leaving me alone with a man we barely know?" Even if it was a fellow she trusted implicitly. "You weren't at all concerned with my reputation?"

"You weren't alone. People were about."

She couldn't help herself. She laughed. "Ah, Sam. By the by, I deduced where you'd probably gone and the reason that you left without telling me."

"Of course you did. You're better than anyone else I know at figuring out things."

She sighed. "I'm worried this demonstration won't be a success, Sam. That it won't get us all the investors we require. You should make note of who appears the most interested, so we can meet with them afterward."

He nodded. "The ball portion should provide you with an opportunity to make a case for the gents giving us money. After all, you'll be dancing with them."

She was dreading it. In fact, she was dreading the entire evening: addressing any questions that arose and then chatting with dance partners, striving to be interesting. "It's imperative we ensure they understand what they are investing in and the potential earnings. I've written everything out so you can carry it with you and refer to it if you need to."

"You've probably memorized it all."

Her smile was no doubt a little winsome. "I'm going to pretend I haven't. My mind intimidates people sometimes." Except for Rook. He seemed to accept it. Why else would he have made arrangements for her to explore a roulette wheel? It had pleased her beyond measure that he'd gone to so much trouble for her. She couldn't remember the last time anyone had.

"Will you be going out with me tonight?" he asked quickly, the words following each other at a rapid pace as if he was desperate to change the subject while also hoping that she wouldn't comprehend everything he was saying.

She suspected he had plans that he was hoping she wouldn't witness.

"Not tonight."

He looked somewhat relieved.

And while she knew it was none of her business, she was curious. "Are you returning to the brothel?"

He furrowed his brow. "Probably shouldn't admit it but I thought I might."

"Where are you getting your funding for all these . . . *entertainments* you seem to be enjoying?" They weren't dirt poor, not yet, but neither did they have money for frivolous things. A good portion of what they had, even with investors, would need to go back into the business. They had to provide their share.

He gave a careless shrug. "Sometimes I win at the tables."

He used their money to have fun rather than responsibly allocating it for some of the changes they'd need for the factories. Childishly choosing an immediate reward over a long-term one that might provide him with enough funds to engage in many more enjoyable pursuits. "Do you think it's wise to spend so flippantly?"

"I'm using these excursions to interest fellows in what we're offering."

"Which is my point. They need to know what actions we'll take with what they give us, use it sensibly."

He shoved himself to his feet. "You worry too much. It'll all work out, especially once they see this marvelous machine of yours at work. I need coffee and breakfast. Then I'm off to meet Lord Lawrence at the British Museum to view the Rosetta Stone. Before you chastise me, he's a potential investor so time spent with him won't be wasted. Although I have wondered what you were off doing during the Wolfford ball when your sudden absence prevented you from dancing with him." His gaze was penetrating, and she was left with the impression that he might know exactly what she was doing in that little nook behind the wolf statue. "We all need our escapes, Nora."

As he strode from the room, she was fairly certain he was communicating that she shouldn't begrudge him his escapades. That, somehow, he knew she'd been no saint. She'd had moments when her focus had wandered from their purpose for being here, when she'd gone off course.

She'd do so again tonight. Perhaps she should stay in, but Rook had become rather like an addiction. The more she had of him, the more she wanted of him. Like absinthe. Too much did no one any favors. But the mixture of sweetness and tartness caused even the most stalwart of souls to stray into the oblivion it provided.

When she was with Rook, she didn't have to search for topics of conversation because he took an interest in anything she said. He listened; he asked questions. They carried on an actual discussion, equally contributing. She never felt as if she was spouting a monologue by which someone was pretending to be fascinated—even as she could see the dulling of eyes, the faraway looks.

Rising, she walked over to the writing machine and lovingly traced her fingers over the keys. She imagined skimming them over his skin. Even when they weren't talking, they were communicating. She wanted to explore him inside and out. But she was left with the impression he allowed very few inside . . . he was a fortification.

She had a strong desire to breach the walls in order to prove that she could be to him what he'd become to her: the air she breathed, the sun that warmed, the shelter from storms. With him, she could be her true self without fear of recriminations or mocking. With him, she felt safe.

Therefore, she would slip out late this evening, meet with him, and enjoy whatever he wanted to show her. She would have an escape from worries, cares, and the numerous responsibilities.

And just perhaps, perhaps, tonight she would be able to discern all the intricacies of him that thus far had managed to circumvent satisfying her inquisitiveness.

To REDUCE THE chances of being spotted, Rook knew he should be waiting in the mews, but he wanted to ensure Nora encountered no trouble on her way to meet him. While the streets were mainly deserted of traffic, people were still wandering around, either going to or leaving the nearby pub. Therefore, he was standing with a shoulder pressed against the bookshop wall that faced a side street. From his vantage point, he had a clear view of the hotel—had even seen her brother leaving the establishment earlier. But he, himself, had faded into the shadows so it would take a discerning eye to realize he was even there.

It had pleased him immensely that she'd shared the shortened version of her name with him. Perhaps that was the reason he'd promised to show her something special tonight, spending the better part of the day ensuring he was able to deliver on his promise. If matters hadn't materialized as he'd hoped, he could have provided an alternative, but he doubted any would please her as much as the prize he had worked diligently to secure. Being a lord had gone a long way toward helping his cause. Being able to place an exorbitant amount on palms had gone a lot further. There was definitely an advantage to having spare coins on hand with which to indulge one's whims.

Yet he suspected for her, it would be something she treasured. Even if it wasn't something she could disassemble and study in detail. The anticipation of her pleased reaction was greater than it should be, he knew that. However, its intensity had caused him to stand here for longer than two hours already, growing more eager by the moment for her to arrive.

What the devil was wrong with him that he couldn't go two minutes without thinking of her, of wondering what contraption might have caught her fancy as she went about her day? That afternoon, he'd almost called on her like a besotted suitor, when he was anything but—

He merely enjoyed her company. She'd be leaving soon, and he wanted to make the most of whatever time remained to them.

Because of his positioning, he spied her the moment she reached the two glass doors through which people entered and exited the hotel. Before the well-placed liveried footman had even tugged one open for her, Rook was crossing the street with long strides that were slightly quicker than his usual pace. He refused to consider why it was that he had this overwhelming need to have her presence within his orbit as soon as possible.

When she smiled softly, hesitantly, almost shyly, all the worrisome chatter in his head quieted like the gong of Big Ben when the hammer struck it for the final time to mark the hour. The echo of the ringing remained on the air for a while, but there was an awe to the power that had created it to begin with and, as she'd pointed out last night, a somberness that settled in when the hammer went still.

He realized with a jolt that he was going to miss her rare smiles.

She waited at the edge of the pavement for him to take those last two steps that brought him near enough that he could smell her jasmine fragrance. He offered his arm, and she entwined hers around it, and the satisfaction he experienced was at once fulfilling and troublesome, but he refused to let any doubts deter him from enjoying her. He'd hash out these confounding emotions later.

They were strolling back the way he'd come.

"I've spent a good deal of time today trying to guess what the something is that you want to show me," she said.

"I doubt with even a thousand guesses that you would be correct."

"Is it something I'll be able to tell people about?"

"I'm unsure as to how you'd do it without revealing you hadn't had a chaperone present. I suppose if you can determine how to do that, you could tell anyone you wanted about it. Although I wouldn't bother with Lord Falstone."

Her laugh was as airy as a spring breeze. "I danced with him once. I think I bored him."

"Nonsense. The man is incapable of keeping his attention focused on anything. I once saw him nod off during a derby. And he had a horse racing in it." A slight tightening of her hold on him conveyed that she appreciated his effort to direct the fault away from her. Why any man didn't hang onto her every word was beyond his comprehension.

Once they were in his carriage and trundling through the streets, she asked, "Are you going to tell me where we're headed?"

"It would ruin the surprise." And his enjoyment of watching the delight cross her features when it was finally revealed.

GOOD LORD. SHE could hardly fathom that she was inside the Clock Tower, staring at the three beautiful gear trains that kept everything moving: the hands on the clocks, the quarter bells, and Big Ben itself.

Trudging up the spiral staircase to get here, she must have placed her feet on a thousand steps. She would have climbed a thousand more to obtain this view. On their way here, the guide had explained that every three days he reset the weights used to control the pendulum. Therefore, she was studying the workings of what was probably the largest pendulum clock in the world.

Her father had once given her a cuckoo clock for Christmas. She'd taken it apart with such care, worried that she might stop the carved wooden bird from showing itself and singing its little song. However, she'd successfully put it all back together, but what she was now looking at was far more complicated. Her fingers were opening and closing, itching to have her tools in hand, so she could more thoroughly examine what was before her.

And yet she couldn't help but feel that it would be sacrilegious to disturb even a single cog of this magnificent work of art.

"More interesting than a roulette wheel?" Rook asked, standing nearby.

She should have been completely distracted by the machine that rested before her, but her attention kept wavering, aware of his watchful gaze, almost a physical caress. In her excitement over this gift, several times she'd wanted to embrace him, simply hold him, have him hold her. How well he knew her in order to comprehend exactly how to please her. He understood her, wasn't bothered by her yearning for more information. "I can't even comprehend the brilliance of the man who designed this."

"That would be Edmund Denison, miss," their guide said.

"The scale of it. To have so many different aspects that have to come together perfectly in order for it all to work. No room for error." Slowly, she began walking around it, covering her ears when the quarter bells began ringing. The guide had given them cotton to stuff in their ears, but it barely dimmed the ticking of the clock, the turning of the wheel, the movement of the cogs, the chiming of the bells.

She didn't know how Rook had arranged for this

late-night exploration of the inside of the Clock Tower. She supposed being a lord didn't hurt but also suspected a pouch of coins had exchanged hands. She couldn't help but wonder if any of the coins had been pennies that might eventually be used to slow down the pendulum when it was needed, removed when it was necessary to quicken the pendulum's speed. It seemed like such a whimsical way to keep the clock precise, and yet she'd been reassured that it was the most accurate clock in the world.

"The belfry is above if you'd like to see the bells," the guide said.

The bells were no doubt magnificent, but she could have spent hours right where she was. Still, she nodded. "Yes, thank you."

Not nearly as many steps to climb before she was looking at the four bells surrounding the gigantic Big Ben in the center. It was deafening when the smaller bells struck fifteen minutes before midnight.

When they fell silent, Rook asked, "Would you like to go as far up as we can?"

What I would like, she thought, *is to kiss you in this glorious space*. "I would, yes."

The guide exchanged a look with Rook before handing him the lantern he carried. "I'll wait for you here," he said.

"Very good."

Rook escorted her through the door and back into the passage where spiral stairs awaited them. While she led the way, he followed closely behind, his hand resting against the small of her back. Before long, they were standing in the upper gallery, where a bright light was shining out over the city.

She wandered nearer to one of the apertures and looked out. Tonight's fog was wispy, barely there, and she could easily see the gaslights illuminating the streets. Feeling like she was gazing down on a fairy world, ethereal, not quite real, she became aware of Rook's nearness. He was no longer holding the lantern. It wasn't needed here.

"It's beautiful, isn't it? Magical?" she asked.

"The machinery?" His voice was hushed as if he recognized that up here only the bells were allowed to be loud.

"All of it. How did you arrange all this?"

"You have to know a member of Parliament. Fortunately, I do."

Kingsland, no doubt. She might have laughed, but this didn't seem to be the sort of place where one should. She was also concerned that the sound might ring out, echo over the near-vacated streets, and that someone would look up, see them, and identify them. Even as she was aware they were too high up to be recognized by anyone—not even herself.

Because up here, above the world, she yearned as she never had before for what she knew she was destined to never acquire: a husband who loved her, whom she loved. Children she would adore. A happy home. All the things she'd convinced herself not to reach for because they were beyond her grasp.

Yet this man had known what would please her the most: not flowers or chocolates or an afternoon of sitting on a settee sipping tea.

"I'm sorry you weren't able to disassemble it all," he said, as if reading her thoughts.

"I was able to figure it out for the most part. I'll

analyze it and take it apart in my mind for years to come." And every time she did, she'd remember him.

The bells began to ring out the end of one day, the beginning of another. She stuck her fingers in her ears because the cotton wasn't enough to muffle the loud chimes. His hands came over hers, muting the bongs a fraction more. Because he stood behind her, she couldn't see if he was grimacing, if he was suffering through the sounds that were vibrating through her.

Suddenly she wanted his hands elsewhere.

Turning, she shouted, "Thank you for tonight."

She doubted he'd been able to make out the words, but it didn't matter, because when she rose up on her toes, his mouth was already there, ready and willing, to meet hers.

HE DIDN'T KNOW if he'd ever seen anything more beautiful in his life than the manner in which Nora had glowed when they'd initially stepped into the Clock Tower, and she'd received her first clue regarding what it was he was planning to show her. And as each aspect—the weights, the pendulum, the back of the clocks, and finally the gear trains—was visited, he felt like he was watching the brightness of a gaslight turned up until it rivaled the sun in brilliance.

He'd known she'd appreciate the whole of how it all worked. But it was the intricate mechanics that fascinated her the most. Seeing the end result of the hammers striking the bells would have pleased her, but it was the gears turning until everything was in alignment that called to her clever mind. He wouldn't be surprised to discover that, at some point in the future, she'd create a miniature working version of the Clock Tower.

And at each stop along the way to where they now stood, he'd wanted to touch her, to hold her, to kiss her—to be part of the experience. But at the same time he hadn't wanted to distract her or intrude on her study of all that surrounded her.

Besides, they'd had a witness.

He did have to wonder what his face might have revealed for their guide to allow them to come up here alone.

When she had turned to him, risen up, he'd lowered the drawbridge to welcome her as he never had for any other woman who had passed through his life. He'd never be able to look at the Tower again without thinking of her. Whenever he heard the tolling of midnight, he'd remember her sweet flavor, her eagerness, her boldness. He'd recall the quick flash of disappointment that had raced across her face like lightning before she squared her shoulders, because everything tonight was for looking at, not touching.

Except for him. He was there for touching, as much as she wanted.

She was correct. There was magic to be found here, with her in his arms, his hands cupping her face while striving to protect her ears as the gears, pistons, and pulleys that so fascinated her ticked away the minutes.

Suddenly, the last gong hung on the air, rolling into silence until all he heard were her moans and sighs. Tenderly, reluctantly, he ended the kiss and drew back. "We have someone waiting for us."

"Do you think he'll guess what we've been up to?"

"Does it matter?"

Slowly, she shook her head. He entwined his fingers with hers. "Come on, then. We have a lot of steps to traverse back down to the ground."

"Each one coming up was worth it."

He knew she was no doubt referring to the fact that they'd led her to the various mechanizations she'd seen but found himself hoping she was including the time spent with him.

HIS CARRIAGE HAD been waiting for them. Of course it had. This man seemed to have the ability to command anything he wanted be done. As a viscount, he was formidable. How much more so would he be once he was an earl, once he sat in the House of Lords?

He would need a wife who was always at his side, providing her support, hosting his dinners, balls, soirees, doing what she could to help him secure votes for any laws he wanted to pass. Why was she even bothering to think about the kind of woman he would fancy?

Why was she experiencing sorrow with the realization it wouldn't be her?

Their time together was simply born of . . . well, she wasn't quite sure what it was born of. Perhaps it was driven by lust, a desire to kiss, or a need to explore, sensations that he seemed keen on ensuring she had a chance to experience.

"I hope you didn't take offense at my kissing you earlier," she said.

In spite of the shadows within the conveyance, she saw his smile. "No man is going to take offense at being kissed. It's the animalistic aspect of our natures to mate. How women manage to control their baser instincts is a testament to your gender's inner strength. Besides, you may have noticed that I met you halfway."

"I did note your enthusiasm."

"I'd been dying to kiss you since the pendulum. I don't think you have any idea how a new discovery lights up your face." As though embarrassed by his confession, he looked out the window.

"You gave no hint that's what you wanted."

His attention came back to her. "Last night, I had to promise not to touch you in order to get you into my carriage. I assume I've not been released from that vow."

Now it was her turn to gaze out the window. She wondered precisely what would happen if she released him from it. She remembered that morning at the Elysium when the young maid had assured her that nothing other than a kiss had transpired because she was done up all nice and tight. She supposed she'd arrive at the hotel not quite so done up.

"You'd mentioned there is more that happens on the other side of a kiss—" Although he sat across from her, she was keenly aware of his going still, had the impression he was barely breathing. She forced herself to look in his direction. "How long does it take for it all to transpire?"

He remained quiet as though deciphering the workings of a complicated machine or measuring the weight of his words. "Depends on what 'for it all' entails. Could occupy you for a few minutes. Could require several hours."

His voice had been neutral, no inflection whatsoever. He could have been explaining how to knot a neckcloth.

"Hours?" She hadn't expected it to come out on a

croak, but her mouth had gone dry as she'd tried to envision what hours *would* entail.

"It's not like a machine, where everything has to follow a pattern, nothing varying from the repetition. There's no step one, step two, step three. Rather it's chaotic. Depending on the couple, their desires, their needs. Their passion. It can be slow or frenzied. Quick or . . . take *hours*."

He used that word again, and she wondered if it was his preferred way to go. "It sounds incredibly disordered. I don't know if I'd like that."

"With the right partner, you'd enjoy it. Immensely."

His tone held no doubt, made it difficult to breathe. "You've made no untoward advances."

"I explained the other night that you'd have to ask for more." He leaned toward her. "But know this, Nora. If you ask, I will not refuse you. Once we start down this path, it *will* require hours because I would take my time and savor every minute."

The carriage had suddenly become unbearably hot. Her skin was ablaze. How the hell had this happened? Certainly she was curious but worried that in this matter, curiosity might indeed kill the cat.

The carriage came to a stop, startling her.

"So don't ask lightly," he commanded, before opening the door, leaping out, and then reaching back for her.

He closed his fingers sturdily and securely around hers. As he escorted her toward the hotel, she knew if she gave him leave to do with her what he would, there would be no turning back.

CHAPTER 14

❦

THE following afternoon, Leonora held her breath as two strapping footmen—one on either side—carried the writing machine down the stairs—five interminable flights. She'd climbed so many more the night before. Her pique at the number here was only because she feared they might drop her precious prototype and damage it.

She should find a way to make it lighter, to turn it into something that people could easily carry with them. Or at the very least that one person could effortlessly manage. Following its journey to the ballroom where it would be set up for tomorrow night's demonstration, she became lost in the possibilities. How a less cumbersome machine would increase its appeal. Writers, reporters, and chroniclers could ensure it was always near at hand, ready to be used when they had words to communicate.

All musings fled when she entered the ballroom. Sam was standing near a table resting on a dais. "Ah, good!" he called out, sweeping his arm in the direction needed. "Over here, gentlemen."

She noted that the footmen's brows were damp. Yes, she needed to make adjustments. She also needed to keep weight in mind as she finished designing the tallying machine.

Her mother was ordering servants about as they hung bunting and garland. Arranged an abundance of flowers provided by the gardener who tended the plants in a greenhouse at the back corner of the hotel's gardens. He'd been kind enough to take her on a tour. The walls and ceiling were mostly glass, providing sunlight for the wide variety of flowers he nurtured for the hotel.

She suspected her mother was assisting because she was hoping for the ball portion to be so grand that people would be talking about it for years or it might get a mention in the newspapers.

"What do you think?" Sam asked as he approached her.

Oh, she thought a lot of things—mainly that Papa wasn't here to enjoy the unveiling and to calm her nerves—but knew her brother was referring to the writing machine display. "I feel like it's my child, about to give his first recital. I want it to do so well, and I don't want anyone to laugh at it."

"No one is going to laugh at it."

She wondered if those responsible for the inner workings that ran through the Clock Tower had been uneasy, waiting for Big Ben and the smaller bells to chime. Perhaps worrying at how something might be received was simply part of the process of creativity. With enough investors and the right amount of success, hopefully they'd never have to go through all this effort again.

"We're planning to have that contraption taken away before the ball begins, aren't we?" Mama asked.

Leonora had been so focused on doubts that she hadn't heard her mother approach.

"No," she and Sam said at the same time.

"It's the reason we're here," he continued. "Remember?"

She wanted to hug Sam at that moment, but they'd never been a very demonstrative family.

"It doesn't go with the décor." She wondered how long their mother would carry on so.

"Which is to our advantage," Leonora explained. "It'll serve as a reminder regarding our reason for being here. Hopefully it will entice a few people into wanting to be backers for progress."

"'Backers for progress.' I like that," Sam said. "You should use it in your speech."

"My speech? I thought you were going to present our invention, and I'd field any questions you couldn't answer."

"You should do it because it's not really *ours*. It's *yours*."

She remembered the faraway look in Lord Falstone's eyes as if his entire being had escaped her and gone somewhere else to reside for the space of a dance. He'd not been the only one. While she'd seemed to hold the attention of a few gents, to captivate an entire room into listening to what she had to say was such an overwhelming prospect.

But Sam was correct. He barely understood the machine, had never taken much interest in it except for the role it would play in allowing them not to crash into poverty.

"I should go make some notes regarding what I want to say." Had she known this chore was going to fall to her, she'd have waited to have the writing machine brought down. Certainly, she could use it here, but imagined that pen and paper would serve her better as she was bound to scratch through and rearrange much of what she wanted to say. That little tidbit she wouldn't mention from the dais—that sometimes pen and paper were preferable, depending upon the task.

It WAS LATE by the time she set down the pen, satisfied with her speech.

She got up from the desk and walked to the window. Night had fallen. Mama had retired. Sam had gone out for a little gaming and "other entertainments" he'd told her before leaving, not bothering to invite her to join him nor apologizing for disturbing her. She very much suspected he was going to a brothel.

Why were men allowed their dalliances and not women?

She thought of Rook's offer, the one she would have to ask for. Why shouldn't she ask? It wasn't as though she was ever likely to marry. She wasn't being unfaithful, except perhaps to herself if she didn't embrace this opportunity to experience all her heart longed for.

He wasn't going to take everything. Yet still he'd deliver pleasure. Considering how his kisses made her feel, just thinking of what may be beyond made her tingle in places she didn't even know a woman could tingle.

If all went well tomorrow night, she'd soon be leaving this country, perhaps never to return. Didn't she deserve, once in her life, to put herself first? Her own desires, her own wants, her own needs?

If she was ever going to engage in relations with a man, she wanted to do so with Rook—Johnny. Because she'd fallen for him. Head over heels. She couldn't identify exactly when it had happened. She'd spent hours examining her feelings, striving to take apart all the many minutes when they were together.

With him, she was more herself than she'd ever been with anyone else, including her father. She'd certainly have not told him about the thrust comment. But she could tell Rook anything. He never made her feel judged. As a matter of fact, when she was with him, she was exactly what her mother had ordered her to be: interesting.

He never stared off in the distance as though enduring the minutes until their time together ended. He engaged with her, asked questions, and understood her need to explore, to decipher how things operated. He'd gifted her with the knowledge of how Big Ben and the chimes worked.

She suspected no one else could so well satisfy her curiosity regarding all that could transpire between a couple. For hours.

Her only hesitancy was what if hours weren't enough. What if she yearned for a lifetime?

Although perhaps one memory was better than none at all.

She trusted him to hold her secrets. And she knew a place where a lady's secrets were safely guarded. All she had to do was find the courage to grasp what she'd always feared she was to be denied.

CHAPTER 15

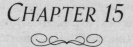

For the next two hours, I will be at the Elysium.
Same chamber as before. Should you wish to
join me.

SITTING behind the desk in his library, Rook knew he should ignore the summons. She was making him do things he'd sworn to never do, was causing him to risk tarnishing his reputation.

He lifted his gaze from the missive to the handsome young man, dressed in evening attire, who'd insisted on delivering it personally to Rook's hand. He recognized him as one of the gentlemen who flitted around Aiden's club like a bee in search of pollen, stopping briefly here and there to give attention to a woman. He wondered if he'd showered his false affections on Nora, rubbed her feet, touched his fingers to her lips while feeding her grapes. He had an urge to get up and punch the man. He didn't want anyone touching or spoiling her, except for himself.

However, he did shove back his chair and stand. "I'll deliver the reply myself."

The blighter didn't seem at all surprised. "Will you

be traveling back with me, sir? Mr. Trewlove thought you might."

He cursed his brother, who had somehow unequivocally discerned the purpose of the message and what it portended. Who would also, no doubt, tease Rook unmercifully because doing Aiden's bidding had, in fact, turned out to be a favor to Rook.

Blast the man for being too perceptive by half.

He could have his own carriage readied, but the time that would take meant leaving her waiting and wanting longer than necessary, perhaps to the point that she would regret sending word to him. Especially as he was fairly certain she wasn't seeking a kiss this time, but wanted to explore what went beyond it.

So he accepted the offer that allowed him to get to her as quickly as possible and tried not to contemplate that he was doing it not so much as a favor to her but to himself. Even if it turned out that all she truly wanted was to sit on the chaise longue and have them stare at each other, at least he'd be in her presence once again.

WAITING, HOPEFULLY NOT in vain, wringing her hands, Leonora paced the small room at the Elysium.

How did one—she couldn't use the word he'd used as it was far too carnal, caused her to feel heated as though she sat in the middle of a fire—get bedded without actually being bedded? Perhaps it was the location. One was chaised or grounded or . . . chaired?

A little over an hour ago, she'd written the missive, her hands shaking. She rather wished she'd prepared the message before she arrived, using the writing machine to tap out the letters, so he wouldn't know how nervous she was. She hadn't signed it—in case it fell into the wrong hands, somehow fell into her mother's to be precise. But it now occurred to her that a man as handsome as he probably received notes like hers all the time, and he might not know exactly whom it was from. If he came, he might be expecting someone else. Would she see disappointment on his face when he realized it was her? Had he not yet shown because he knew it was her or because he didn't?

Obviously arranging clandestine trysts was not her forte. Worrying over them was.

She should leave. Save herself the mortification of waiting for a man who didn't arrive. However, time was needed to deliver the message, read it—he could be a very slow reader—then travel here. It seemed patience wasn't her forte either.

She heard the soft click, the press of the latch on the door. The walls to these rooms were thick, creating a cocoon that prevented sounds from entering or leaving, producing the sense that here one was remarkably alone in the world. Ceasing her pacing, she stared as the portal that would deliver him opened and widened.

Rook stepped inside and closed the door in his wake. He stayed where he was and watched her, his small smile giving the impression that she was precious and required a moment of appreciation. She was remarkably happy that he'd shown up, hadn't abandoned her to her doubts.

"I hope my delay in responding to your missive didn't cause you worry. I had a few matters to tend to first."

She'd never known his hair to be so unruly with curls and wondered if the matter had involved washing up. If so, his hair must have been quite wet when he began the journey here. She was certain he'd taken a razor to his face. This time of night, his jaw should have been shadowed by whiskers. She couldn't have been more delighted that he'd gone to the extra bother if he'd handed her a diamond. "I hope my . . . request didn't inconvenience you."

"Not at all. I was in residence, reading."

"What were you reading?"

"To be honest, I can't remember a word of it because my thoughts continually drifted elsewhere." His gaze took a long, lingering journey over her, from head to toe, leaving her with the conviction that she had been the *elsewhere*. "Does it matter?"

She shook her head. "I've been contemplating your . . . suggestion regarding what couples can do . . . without doing."

Crossing his arms over his chest, he leaned against the door. "Have you?"

Curiosity marked his tone, along with a measure of approval. But no arrogance or conceit. No *How could you have not?* While he appeared completely relaxed, a muscle ticking in his jaw gave away his tension as he awaited her reply.

She nodded. At the moment, it seemed only her head was capable of movement. "I am curious regarding how one cannot lose one's virtue while engaged in the unvirtuous."

A hint of amusement shone in his eyes, and something darker, more compelling, more dangerous. She'd tiptoed up to a line and hovered on the side of safety, and he was considering pulling her across into a place that could lead her to peril. She was a fool to even consider it, to have brought him here when he was so hard to resist. "I could provide you with a recitation but since you confessed to understanding things better when you can take them apart, a demonstration might be best in order to ensure you can examine it in exquisite detail later."

She couldn't imagine that his recitation would bore her—that anything he did would bore her. But she hadn't requested his presence for talk; she'd requested it for action. "Yes, I think you're right that a demonstra—"

He shoved himself away from the door with such swiftness that she barely had time to note it before his arms were locked around her and his mouth was on hers, hungrily devouring, and she was left with the realization that perhaps he wanted this as much as she did. That his relaxed state had been a ruse to ensure she didn't feel pressured into asking for what she might not be fully ready to receive.

But she was ready. She felt as if she'd been waiting for this precise moment her entire life because it seemed the most natural thing in the world to be pressed so firmly against his hard body. She'd also accurately surmised that he'd tidied up before coming to her because his tangy orange-lemon scent was brisk and clean. Not a single whisker abraded her skin.

Pulling back, he smiled at her fondly, and it caused her heart to trip over itself. "No absinthe tonight."

She supposed he'd tasted it before; it had no doubt left a lingering flavor on her tongue. "I didn't want to fall asleep."

His grin grew. "You may afterward—if I do it properly."

Only she didn't want to, didn't want to miss a single moment with him. She glanced over at the clock resting on the mantel. Far too many minutes had already ticked by, leaving them with barely three quarters of an hour. "I suppose we should get to it. We haven't much time left."

"We have all night."

"I reserved the room for only two hours."

He tucked his thumb into the curve of her cheek where it met her mouth. "Thanks to my brother, I have some influence. I've arranged for it to be ours until it isn't needed any longer." He stroked her lower lip. "I'll have you back at the hotel before anyone is stirring."

He'd apparently given a good deal of thought to this encounter. She had as well, but her musings were influenced by books she read, horses and dogs she'd seen rutting, and a general notion of what was involved when two people came together. He, on the other hand, she had little doubt, knew the details, had indulged his fantasies with other women. She would not be jealous of his time with them. Instead, she would view it as giving him the knowledge to make tonight one she'd never forget.

His thumb once more took up residence in that little nook at her mouth he seemed to favor. "We'll go only as far as you're comfortable with—and under no circumstances will I actually be pushing my cock inside you."

Her breath caught and held, almost painfully. Cock. He said that word with such ease, as comfortable with it as she was with *bonnet*. And the image his statement brought to mind—she had little doubt her cheeks were flaming red. What was she to say to that? *Thank you for the reassurance?* He'd already told her that he wouldn't defile her, that they could do all this without leaving any evidence—her loss of virginity—to indicate that they had. Her head barely nodded. Again, it seemed the only part of her that could move.

"All right then. Remember, all you have to say is stop." He moved his hands up, his fingers threading through her hair.

"Stop."

He stilled immediately, his eyes drifting down to hers, a question in his. Concern, not anger or impatience. He simply waited, a heartbeat, two. "Changed your mind?"

"No, just testing that I retain the ability to speak."

"You might lose it after a while. But by the time that happens, you won't want to stop. You'll think you'll die if we do."

"Will you feel the same?"

"I suspect so. But I will stop if you wish it. You are in absolute control. If you're agreeable, I'm simply going to remove your pins. Then your buttons, your laces, your bows."

She dared to flatten her palm against his chest, could feel the hard and heavy thudding of his heart. "Your clothing?"

"Have you ever seen a naked man before?"

Her mouth went dry as she slowly shook her head. "I've seen them shirtless, working." Sweaty, grimy, and yet still somehow beautiful as their muscles strained with their labors.

"Again, I'll go only as far as you're comfortable with."

She wanted to ask if there would be pleasure for him, if he would guide her toward what a man needed, but she didn't want to introduce any expectations she might be unable to fulfill. She wanted to imagine they were both here because of a desire for each other, not simply a longing for the forbidden. She offered him a smile that probably appeared a bit forced. "Carry on, then."

One side of his mouth lifted provocatively. "I like when you order me about."

Her eyes widened at that. "Do you?"

"Mmm. *No names. Just get on with it.* I remember every word you uttered that first night. And every sound you made. I want to hear those sounds again."

He dipped his head and pressed his mouth to her throat, his heated dew coating her skin there. Her eyes closed. She sighed. His tongue created a lazy circle while his fingers returned to her hair. She heard the ping of hairpins hitting the floor and felt the shifting of weight as he began liberating her bound-up strands. Then the tresses were falling around her shoulders and he was groaning. "Glorious."

She'd always hated the shade, a timid sort of red, lacking in the vibrancy that would have made her stand out in a room. Instead, it caused her to become lost in a crowd. Or so she'd always felt, but his admiring it now made her wonder if she'd gotten it wrong. And if so, what else might she have misjudged regarding her worth?

His mouth returned to hers with an urgency, and her thoughts scattered like birds from trees after hearing a rifle report. Her mind focused on the sensations he was skillfully bringing to life with that wonderfully wicked mouth as his fingers went to work on the fastenings of her gown. Not hurriedly but taking the time to leisurely explore each bit of skin that was revealed as the material loosened and parted.

She didn't know if she'd ever experienced anything more sensual than that light, teasing touch that reflected an appreciation for what was being offered. Subtle in a way, and yet so very profound.

When his fingers were finished with the fastenings, he slowly, ever so slowly, as if to prolong the anticipation, eased her bodice down, working her arms free of the shoulders until the silk was draped over her skirt. Her black corset with its red stitching and piping was clearly visible. The risqué undergarment had once been a gift to herself because wearing it made her feel desirable.

Seeing the heat smoldering in his eyes, she couldn't help but believe that it had achieved its ends. While she normally wore a chemise beneath it, tonight she hadn't. She'd wanted the satin against her skin, chafing her nipples. She'd wanted nothing between the upper swells of her breasts and the tightly woven embroidered lace that decorated the corset's curves.

"You're a woman of hidden depths." His voice was low, husky.

She thought his fiery gaze should have made her want to cover herself. Instead, she had an urge to spread her arms wide and announce *It's all yours*. But she wasn't quite as bold as all that. She'd been brought up to give modesty full rein, to entice with only hints of what was available.

He trailed the tip of one finger along the edge of the lace, and a blaze of pure desire scorched through her. He cupped his hands around the outer side of each breast and stroked his thumb over her nipple. It had already pearled but now it hardened into a little pebble. He lowered his mouth and circled his tongue over the peak still covered in silk. She looked down on his bent head, felt the dampness easing through the cloth, her nipple going impossibly tighter. She couldn't prevent the moan as he pushed her breasts together, lifted them, and his mouth closed tightly around that one small still center, his tongue continuing to work not only to drench the cloth but another area he wasn't even touching. That secret, forbidden place between her thighs going wet.

He gave one last lick, one tiny nibble, a tug before pulling back. He reached for the fastener.

"Stop."

He did, with a squeezing shut of his eyes, before opening them to meet her gaze, and she was left with the impression it had pained him to cease his attentions. His breath wasn't quite as steady as it had been a few minutes ago.

"It's not fair for me to be bared thus and you not." His eyes were dark pools of want and desire. They made her bold. "Take off your clothing, down to your waist."

He suddenly appeared feral, untamed. "As you wish."

She'd never known three little words could be filled with such promise.

Without ever taking his direct and almost challenging gaze from her, he shrugged out of his coat and tossed it onto a nearby chair. He unknotted his neckcloth, wadded it up, and threw it in the same direction. It didn't have enough weight to carry it all the way. It merely hit the chair before falling to the floor. The waistcoat was next, landing on top of the coat. He held out his arms. "Would you find no pleasure in divesting me of my shirt?"

She reached and saw, more than felt, the trembling in her fingers. How embarrassing. They were only buttons. He folded his large, steady hands over hers where they hovered in the air, cowardly, not willing to travel those last few inches to gain what she wanted.

He brought her hands up and pressed a kiss to one, then the other, against the backs of her fingers. Nothing salacious, but somehow incredibly reassuring. "My hands shook much worse the first time I unbuttoned a woman's clothing."

She released a startled laugh, then clamped her mouth shut.

The heat in his eyes died to embers, compassion. "It's all right to laugh, to smile. To joke even. Pleasure comes in all forms, Nora."

He carried her hands to the button at his throat before releasing his hold.

Slowly, she pushed the button through its hole and then did what he'd done to her: she circled her finger over that silky flesh. He emitted a low purr that she took unheralded delight in hearing, in knowing she was responsible for creating with just a light touch.

She wanted him less controlled than he was now. His shirt was of fine linen but not so thick that she couldn't see the outline of dark circles beneath it. She covered one with her mouth, running her tongue over the linen, aware of the peak that instantly formed. Releasing a guttural groan, he plowed his hands into her hair, holding her there, not by force but simply by letting her know how very much she reigned over him. Suddenly she didn't want to lick him over the cloth. She wanted to lick his skin.

She returned to the task of granting his buttons freedom, her tempo increasing as more was revealed. She became anxious to see all of him. Perhaps he was anxious as well, to have her touch all of him. Because she'd just moved past his sternum, when he reached back, tugged his shirt over his head, and tossed it aside.

She didn't know where it landed. She didn't care. Because there he was, taut, defined lines, a gorgeous masculine chest that caused her very core to melt. A light sprinkling of hair arrowed down to his trousers, and she wondered if she'd have a chance to follow its path before they were done. Since he'd gotten them this room for the remainder of the night, she could only assume that hours would be needed for all he intended to do to her—with her. She wouldn't be passive. Her father had taught her the importance of partnerships, of giving and receiving equally so all benefited.

"My turn," he said, and hastily unfastened her corset, grabbed it before it could fall to the floor, and flung it aside. It landed somewhere with a resounding and satisfying *thunk*.

Her breasts filled his palms. Gently, he kneaded as though aware that she required a moment to adjust to no longer having them confined. It was always heavenly when the torture device was removed, and she often did her own massaging, but he was so much better at it, seeming to know the perfect amount of pressure to apply. Then he was raining kisses over the soft mounds. She threaded her fingers through his hair, dropped her head back, and moaned, low and throatily, a sound she hardly recognized coming from herself.

When he took her nipple in his mouth and suckled, she released a short keen that echoed her surprise at the pleasure wrought. Oh, yes, not having this experience through linen was definitely more enjoyable. His mouth was so hot, she wouldn't have been surprised to learn it had come from the fires of Hades, and yet it didn't burn. It felt only remarkably good.

He began skillfully loosening more ribbons, ties, and buttons. Not quite as slowly as before. An eagerness marked his actions. She'd always been modest, and yet this seemed the most natural thing in the world, for him to be removing her clothes, piece by piece, kneeling down to drag them along her legs, providing his strong shoulders for her to place a hand on to balance herself as she stepped out of the items. With an impatient arm, he brushed things out of the way. He began removing her shoes.

"No pebble?" There was a teasing in his tone.

That night seemed so long ago. A lifetime. Suddenly she realized what mattered wasn't the length of time that people were together. It was how they filled those minutes or hours, what they shared, how they made it all special. She'd have this. And if it was the only time they were together, she could make it be enough. Because she now had her answer. Once was better than not at all.

"No pebble," she finally responded.

He removed her stockings and lastly her drawers.

She held her breath, studying the part in his hair slowly going beyond her sight as he leaned his head back in order to view all the lines and contours of her body. Finally, his gaze met hers, and the appreciation and marvel reflected in his weakened her knees, caused them to tremble slightly.

"Do you have any idea how lovely you are?"

"You're just saying that because it's expected at moments like this."

A small pleat appeared in his brow. "I never say anything I don't mean. If some man has made you feel you have little to offer in the way of beauty, I'd be obliged to break his jaw so he can't mutter such nonsense again."

He sounded so deadly serious that she almost laughed with the joy of a gentleman defending her like that. "You're the only one to see me thus."

Except for her mother, she supposed, but she'd been a child then. Her maid when she helped her from the bath, but it was always quick and impersonal, and she doubted the woman paid any heed to how she looked.

"'Tis an honor I do not take lightly."

Slowly, so very slowly, as though they had all the time in the world, as if clocks no longer marked the passing of minutes and Big Ben would never again ring, he kissed his way up her body, until he was standing.

Banding his arms around her, he captured her mouth, kissing her deeply and with an urgency signaling he couldn't get enough of her. She loved the sensation of her breasts flattened against the hard planes of his chest. Skin to skin. Because they were nearly the same height—he did have a couple of inches on her—so much of her was able to be against so much of him. It was heavenly.

One of his arms glided down her back and hooked at

her knees. He lifted her, cradling her against that magnificent chest as her arms wound around his shoulders. She broke away from the kiss and studied him.

His brown eyes were twinkling with a touch of merriment, but mostly what she saw was barely leashed desire. "You're going to want to be lying down for what comes next."

BLOODY HELL. NEVER in his life had he been so tempted to break a vow. To shed his trousers, climb on top of her, and have his way with her. Completely. Absolutely.

She wouldn't object. He was rather certain of that because of the heat burning in her eyes, the raw hunger, the intrepid curiosity. But he'd promised her passion without penalty. No deflowering.

He wasn't in the habit of taking what wasn't offered. She trusted him to hold true to his word—that faith was of more value than all the coins in his coffers.

With great care, he set her on the chaise longue, dropped to one knee, and once again took her mouth.

For a novice, she was remarkably adept at exploring his chest, his shoulders, his arms, taking her long, slender fingers on a journey over the skin he'd thus far bared to her. When he'd lowered her skirts and petticoats, he'd almost expected a *stop!* Quickly followed by the command to remove his trousers, but he supposed she wasn't yet comfortable with viewing the whole of a man, of him. Which was all to the good, because it would make it more difficult not to press his currently throbbing cock against her silken flesh. It would also be more of a challenge to hide exactly how desperately he wanted her.

At least with his trousers in place, he could secrete the burgeoning bulge away as long as he kept himself perched on the floor rather than on the longue. But how he yearned to stretch out beside her. Far too many of the women with whom he'd been intimate had been short of stature, leaving much of him untouched when they lay together without curling about each other. But she was tall enough that their lengths, while not a perfect match, would still result in a satisfactory one, when paired. It would be an experience he couldn't recall having before. He enjoyed trying new things.

Hence his lingering attraction to her, surely. She intrigued him, so much of her still a secret to him. But the things he did know . . .

How her breasts filled his palms, seeming to strain for closer contact when he covered them. The dark pink of her areolas. The plump nipples and the way she shuddered when he closed his mouth over one. The tautness of the skin over her ribs, the flatness of her stomach, the lush curve of her arse.

And that auburn-covered mound that beckoned, the sweet valley it hid that he had yet to touch. But he wanted to worship and adore, to listen to her raspy breaths, to take his time. Kneading her breasts. Running his tongue along her collarbones, dipping it in the hollow between, before trailing his mouth up her throat to her ear, outlining the delicate shell, and nibbling on her lobe.

With a low moan, she dug her fingers into his shoulders. At an angle, his chest pressed against hers.

"I want to do something terribly wicked to you," he rasped near her ear.

"What?" The word came out on a rushed breath,

her back arching slightly, her hips turning toward him as though she needed to be closer to him, absorbed by him.

"Just say yes."

The slightest hesitation.

"Have I ever disappointed when showing you something?"

She shook her head before uttering the word that gave him the permission he sought. He slammed his eyes closed. Trust was such a fragile thing and with that one word she'd given it to him wholeheartedly. He'd never felt so victorious, not when he took the king on the chessboard, gathered up the bets made at the card table, or tripled his investments in a year.

"Don't move," he ordered. He considered standing in order to get to where he wanted quicker, but she couldn't possibly miss the bulge in his trousers, and he didn't know if it would give her pause. How much did she know regarding what transpired between a man and a woman? How brave was she?

Very if her latest answer was any indication.

Still, he dropped his arse to the floor and scooted to the open end of the longue where he proceeded to give attention to her feet, ankles, and calves with a sensual massaging, dropping kisses here and there, watching her through hooded eyes: the way she smiled, the bliss that wreathed her face. Gently, he lifted her feet and placed her ankles on his shoulders. Leaning forward, he grabbed her hips and dragged her toward him until her bum hovered at the edge of the cushion and her knees hooked over his shoulders, her legs dangling down his back.

At his actions, she'd gasped, her eyes widening in

surprise, her mouth forming a small O. She studied him. No fear, only curiosity.

"Now to the wicked part," he vowed. He lowered his head, slid his tongue along that valley his cock would never touch, and reveled in the taste of her.

CHAPTER 16

❧❧❧

$\mathcal{O}_F$ all the things she'd imagined happening tonight, having a man's face buried between her thighs had certainly not been one of them. Nor had she expected this slow, meandering journey that made every inch of her skin tingle, that caused her stomach to tighten, her breath to hitch, and her nipples to pucker.

And her hands to traipse over his hair. Her hips to lift of their own accord when she needed additional pressure.

Watching her steadfastly, he moved his hands up to scrape his thumbs over those hardened pearls. She released a raspy breath, laced with a mewling pleading. She couldn't deny that the man certainly knew how to bring about pleasure. He did it in such a way that it seemed the most natural thing in the world, what people were made for.

But more, the manner in which his eyes darkened, the satisfaction she saw glittering within the brown depths, made her think that he enjoyed offering this personal service as much as she did receiving it. Every now and then her moan was greeted with his groan.

She wondered if his body was as tense, if the remarkable sensations cascading through her were also flowing through him. She didn't feel she was alone in what she was experiencing, that the pleasure somehow rolled into him.

Slowly, firmly, one of his hands slid along her torso and joined his mouth to stir to life an intensely compelling sensation that threatened to undo her completely.

"Oh, God!"

Her entire body tightened. Everything was becoming almost unbearable . . . and yet, she didn't want him to cease his ministrations, didn't want to no longer experience the exquisiteness. She might be content to remain here forever, with him swirling his tongue over the remarkably sensitive button. Closing his lips around it, tugging on it, suckling—

She began writhing, searching for something just beyond reach. Cradling his head between her hands, lifting her hips slightly, feeling him increasing the pressure, she thought surely she would die here. The little cries she was making seemed to come from the depths of her soul. She pressed her feet against his strong back, watched his eyes blaze with a command: *Let go!*

She did. Her back arching, her scream echoing around them before she pressed the back of her hand to her mouth to stifle it, shudder after shudder cascading through her like a never-ending waterfall.

Only it did end, fading out, a star shooting across the sky until it was no longer visible. He flattened his tongue against her, held it there, until her body went lax. Moving up slightly, he pressed a kiss to her belly before tenderly, carefully, sliding her legs off the perch of his shoulders. Straightening, he placed his elbows on either side of her and began drawing random squiggles over her skin until her harsh breathing returned to something that resembled normalcy.

She imagined her cheeks were burning a bright red, but she couldn't seem to make herself look away from his heated, satisfied gaze. Her body still felt as though little pinpricks of pleasure were running through it, like when she blew out a candle and a few embers on the wick fought not to be extinguished. Eventually they would wink out.

She supposed at some point her body would return to normal and lose some of its sensitivity but at the moment she thought it would take very little to turn her into a blaze of pleasure again.

Swallowing hard, she dared to ask, "Is there something I should do for you?" The rasp in her voice surprised her.

Slowly, he shook his head. "Tonight was all for you."

Because she'd sent for him, he hadn't come of his own accord or arranged their tryst. Her satisfaction diminished a bit because he hadn't been motivated by an unyielding desire. Then she chastised herself for the silliness because in spite of that, it had been wonderful.

"Scoot back," he commanded, and she obeyed.

He stretched out beside her, brought her in close, and she became aware of the hard press of his cock against her belly. "That touch of disappointment that flashed in your eyes . . . I wanted you to know that I'm raging hard for you."

She ducked her head. He slipped a finger beneath her chin and tilted her face back up until she met his gaze. "But I promised you'd leave here with your virginity intact. If I remove my trousers, you won't."

She offered him a timid smile. After all he'd done,

how could she now be shy? Especially when she hadn't been while all the *doing* was going on. His hair was a mussed fright, some strands sticking up adorably. She'd done that to him. While she had no memory of it, she thought she might have pulled on them in order to get them standing at attention. His shoulders bore the evidence of her clutching him when lost to the throes of passion. Splotchy red marks here and there that she did hope wouldn't bruise. She even noticed a couple of scratches on his chest. He had driven her wild with abandon.

And now here they were, lying on their sides, calmly facing each other as though nothing momentous had transpired, as if he hadn't hoisted her to the summit of pleasure, didn't know the sounds he could wring from her with so little effort. Within his hands, she'd become clay he could mold to his liking.

She trailed a finger down his chest to the waistband at his trousers, incredibly tempted to glide over the cloth. Instead, she moved her finger back up and circled a nipple. "Have you ever been in love?"

She didn't know how she became aware of his going remarkably still. He hadn't been moving, simply holding her. Yet, she was acutely cognizant of a subtle tightening in his body.

"Once," he finally said quietly.

"What happened?"

"My father stole her away."

ROOK SHOVED HIMSELF off the chaise, grabbed the blanket he'd used to cover her that first night, and draped it over her now sitting form, incredibly aware of her penetrating gaze. He strode over to the sideboard. "What do you fancy?"

"An explanation of how that came about."

Without turning, he said, "I meant what would you like to drink?"

"Whatever you're having."

"Scotch."

"That's fine."

After splashing some into two glasses, he handed her one. "Sit back. Get comfortable."

Only one end had cushions against which she could lean. The sides and other end were open. Worked well for fucking but hardly suitable for heartfelt conversation.

"You're going to tell me." Her tone was both question and command. She scooted back and drew the blanket snugly around her shoulders.

"Not much to tell." He sat on the edge of the chaise, gulped down a large swallow of the amber liquid, set the glass on the floor, and pulled her feet onto his lap. Gently, he began kneading her delicate arch.

"How old were you?" she asked.

"Twenty-one. Her name was Rachel. She was the daughter of a man who would eventually become a shipping magnate. One of my first investments. Paid off handsomely."

"Was she the reason you invested?"

She had been. Was that the reason he fought so hard now not to see that a profit could be made with her company, because of his attraction to Nora? His father was in no position to steal her away . . . but she wasn't his, had no interest in marriage, or plans to stay, so what did it matter?

"I invested because I could see the potential for

profit." Not a lie. The prospect for success had been evident, but pleasing Rachel may have borne some influence on his decision.

"I'd been courting her for a few months. My parents were hosting an affair at the country estate. Several days of balls and stag hunting. Mother ensured that Rachel and her family were invited. She knew I intended to ask Rachel for her hand and suggested I do it during the final ball. She would make it very special, with fireworks at the end. And there were fireworks. Just not the ones she'd planned."

He glanced at her, watching him, so still, as though fearing his words might cause her to shatter. "Do you really want the details?" After all this time, recounting the story shouldn't be this painful, and yet each word was like a knife slicing across his heart.

"I loved my father, so very much. He was a good man." She scooted down, her legs bent, her knees pressing against his side. He welcomed the touch of her, the nearness. "I'm baffled by your father's actions. Why would he not want to see you happy?"

"Because he's more of a bastard than any of the by-blows he's responsible for bringing into this world." He shook his head. "I probably didn't help matters. Shortly after I arrived, I boasted about my successes, quite full of myself. I thought there might be a scintilla of pride in him regarding my achievements. But there was none. He never took any satisfaction in my accomplishments, not in school, not in sports. Like a fool, I longed to have his approval."

She cradled her hand against his cheek. "You weren't a fool. Most children yearn for their parents' approval."

"The afternoon before that final ball, a footman

brought me a message, to meet Father at an empty crofter's cottage on the estate, a place we sometimes used when we were hunting. I thought nothing of it. I arrived. Didn't knock. Just walked in. He didn't even bother to roll off her. Just looked over at me with a triumphant gleam in those dark eyes of his."

She wrapped both her hands around his upper arm and squeezed. "Dear Lord, why would he do that?"

"To win, to feel he'd bested me."

"Did she ever explain herself?"

"She came to me later, regretted the hurt she'd caused but confessed she'd lost her head, been lured by his charms. My mother once told me that when he set his mind to it, when he identified a woman he wanted, he could be quite charismatic. I never witnessed that aspect to him, but she must have spoken true because he had so many mistresses. I never understood what any of them saw in him."

"He sounds like a snake charmer, able to make a cobra follow his lead, even when it's not in the snake's best interest, because the snake will be stuffed back into the basket."

"I appreciate the analogy, but I always saw him as more the snake."

Her lips twitched a bit, before she grew somber. "Might not have been the best example. I've never met your father, but I don't like him."

"You'd have never been fooled. You're too wise for that." She'd have taken him apart until she revealed his black heart.

She seemed pleased by his words.

"Still, I was baffled. Her father had yet to make his fortune, but with other investments, I was well on my way to acquiring mine. So whatever she saw in him, it wasn't financial. Anyway, I couldn't forgive her indiscretion."

"As well you shouldn't have."

Her defense of him, the anger in her tone, was a balm. He couldn't imagine her ever being unfaithful.

"I heard Rachel became his mistress for a while. Her father disowned her. I have no idea what eventually became of her." Not that he hadn't often wondered. But he certainly hadn't gone to his sire to ask, because he knew the earl would do his best to humiliate him, to make him pay something—probably coins considering the crumbling nature of his estates and his empty coffers. Or he might require his son to beg. He still saw Rachel's father from time to time, was still a shareholder in his company. But he never spoke of the daughter who'd disappointed him. However, Rook did hope that, when she'd left his father, she'd found a good life elsewhere.

"She's the reason you know about the farewell kiss, and about not realizing that's what it was at the time."

"Very astute." He'd kissed Rachel the morning of that fateful day, when they'd gone on a stroll following breakfast. It had been short, sweet, and innocent, nothing at all like the hungry kisses he shared with Nora. With Rachel, the kisses had been like a light breeze fluttering curtains. With Nora, from the beginning, kissing her had been like a tempest, strong and powerful enough to destroy all in its wake. Then perhaps to build something new and more lasting in its place—but he didn't want to ponder that angle.

"In all these years," she began softly, "you've never met anyone else—"

"A few years later the daughter of an earl caught

my fancy, but she had no interest in being associated
with my family, especially after my father began making untoward advances. He prefers the young and untouched. I threatened him, got him to leave off, but
the damage was done. His reputation for unfaithfulness was well-known by then. She assumed I'd follow in his footsteps beçause it was the example he'd
set for me, growing up. A lack of loyalty, a lack of
commitment. No matter how fiercely I denied being
anything like him, she was unconvinced. I realized
words weren't enough. I had to demonstrate my character with actions."

"That's the reason you were never written up in the
gossip columns . . . until me."

With a shrug, he chuckled darkly. "I have tried to
live a life that was the complete opposite of his."

"Hence no bastards."

"No bastards."

"At balls, it's the cardroom for you, not the dance
floor."

Again, until her. "No sisters, daughters, or mothers taken advantage of. No whispers of clandestine
trysts. No opportunity to be judged as untrustworthy.
I'm considered quite boring, the most lackluster of the
Chessmen."

"But you're not boring or dull."

She stated it vehemently as though he'd insulted
himself by referring to himself as a dullard. "I'm not
bothered by the opposite characterization at all. It is
all to the good."

He was keenly aware of her intense study of him,
and he was left with the impression that she saw him
as cogs, nuts, and bolts and was striving to determine

how they all came together to form him. How they came together to form his thoughts, affect his actions. He suspected if he weren't flesh and blood, she'd have already disassembled him and all the various parts of him would be strewn over the floor. Of a sudden, he had the odd sensation of being not quite put together.

"In striving to be seen as the opposite of him," she said slowly, quietly as though forming her thoughts as she went, "are you not, in some manner, hiding your true self?"

He didn't much like her conclusion. What he showed the world was who he wanted to be, not who he was. Yet had he not, through the years, become the opposite of his father, which then made him his true self?

However, his behavior indicated he was not a man who would meet with a brazen woman in a club designed for wickedness. That he wasn't the sort to bury his face between a woman's thighs. Yet, here he was, where he shouldn't be, doing what he ought not be doing because he wanted her to fall apart into a thousand shards of incredible pleasure. Unable to stop himself—with her, why was he always eager for one more moment, seeking out excuses to spend additional time with her?—he caught strands of her hair, glistening from the candlelight, and tucked them behind her ear. "This is not a conversation designed to lead to seduction."

She gave him an impish smile. "I've already been seduced."

He trailed a finger slowly down her throat, not stopping until he reached the tip of the valley where the upper swells of her breasts met. "Seduction should be an ongoing thing, always there, even when you think it's not."

"Do you seduce every woman in your path, then?"

"Only the interesting ones."

As though taken aback, she jerked her head slightly, her eyes widening. "You find me interesting?"

"Why would I not? You're bold, daring . . ." He eased the blanket down until one breast was exposed and circled his tongue around her areola. ". . . and incredibly delicious."

A tiny laugh escaped her as her fingers plowed into his hair and held him where he was. He took that as a sign to nibble and suck. Her satisfied sigh was soon echoing around him, and he decided another feasting was in order.

SHE'D THOUGHT THEY were done. She hadn't expected more. Hadn't expected him to drag the blanket off her with an almost feral growl of impatience as if he could hardly wait to have her bared before him again. He knew what she looked like now. Shouldn't he be bored with the sight of her?

Yet it seemed he wanted her with a near madness.

She certainly wasn't bored with the sight of his magnificent chest or broad shoulders. Or the way his muscles bunched and flexed as he moved over her, kissing, nipping, licking . . . her breasts, her throat, her shoulders.

Up he went and then down. Over her ribs and past her stomach. He gave attention to her hips, the inside of her thighs. He cupped his hands beneath her bottom and lifted her to his mouth, like she was a goblet of wine—or absinthe—to be savored.

This time, she knew what to expect and released her entire being into his keeping.

How could it be like this again? This madness. This hunger.

She was writhing against him, pressing her hands over every inch of him she could reach, relishing the moans of enjoyment he made, reaffirming this act was not only for her, but for him. He drew almost as much pleasure from it as she did.

Even so, it had to be all lust. Need, desire, want.

But he found her interesting, bold, and daring. She'd never been made to feel any of those things. Was it all just words he uttered for seduction? But he'd done them so earnestly, his eyes clear, meeting hers with honesty.

Perhaps that was the reason that, although she knew she should be exhibiting a measure of modesty and self-consciousness, she wasn't. That she spread her legs farther apart and urged him on. That she felt primal and animalistic. That her cries and keens heightened the sensations.

And why she was suddenly comfortable issuing orders. *There. Softer. Harder. More pressure. That. Do that again.*

When the cataclysm came, she bolted upright and curled around him as best she could, holding him near as pleasure surged through her. Then she dropped back, a lethargic, boneless heap.

He moved up and flicked his thumb over her turgid, sensitive nipple, and she almost cried out from the sensation. "You're so responsive."

"I'm beginning to fear I'm a harlot," she confessed.

His grin was filled with pleasure and a touch of wickedness. "You're a woman who knows what she wants and goes after it. I find that incredibly . . ."

His voice trailed off, and she waited for him to find whatever word he was searching for. Finally, she asked, "Incredibly?"

"Alluring. You're hard to resist. I can't understand how so many men have managed to do it. Resist you, I mean."

He was being kind. She was certain of it. Because in her experience, men had no trouble resisting her. She'd never had to fend off any untoward advances. She'd never had a fellow gaze upon her longingly. She had once done so, gazed at a man longingly, until her mother had chastised her for wearing her heart on her sleeve. No more than fourteen or fifteen years of age, only on the cusp of being interested in boys, she'd begun to realize she probably looked the fool and had shuttered her heart since it seemed she hadn't the means to shutter her gaze, so it didn't reveal what she was thinking. As a result, she suspected her demeanor could sometimes be described as frigid.

But as she'd learned tonight, a man did have the means to thaw her. If he was willing to go to the effort.

Even if that effort was no more than simply lying there, facing her, watching one solitary finger trailing over her side, her hip, and anywhere else it happened to wander. "I should probably get back to the hotel now."

"One more kiss?"

As long as it wasn't a farewell one, she wanted to tell him. But of course, it would be. Eventually. Probably tonight. Because he'd demonstrated what transpired beyond a kiss.

She must have given some indication of agreement because his mouth was suddenly blanketing hers, devouring, one hand gliding slowly down her back, pressing her against his chest, abdomen, hips. One of his thighs slipped between hers and pushed up against her mound, and she very nearly came undone. How could she be so ready again to be sated?

She wound her arms around him, scraping her fingers over his shoulders and down either side of his spine. He groaned low, increasing the pressure at her apex and her back until she thought she might melt into him. Torrid. Sweltering. They generated heat that threatened to ignite them.

This final kiss was bittersweet. She knew there was more, so much more, and she wanted to share it with him. But if she took that step, it would be irreversible. And if it turned out that marriage was the only way to save the business, didn't she owe it to her father, his memory, his legacy, to ensure his dream carried on, even if it did so without him?

Her father had always allowed her to be her true self with him. He'd opened to her the world beyond watercolors, penning letters, reading, and stitchery within which her mother wanted to confine her. He'd introduced her to whiskey, had let her smoke a cheroot, and hadn't been appalled the one time a *damn* had slipped out in his presence.

So when Rook pulled back, she didn't ask for more—in spite of the raw need she saw mirrored in his eyes. She simply pressed a kiss to his chest, scooted down to the edge of longue, rose to her feet, and began to get dressed.

CHAPTER 17

In silence, he helped her put herself back together. It was the least he could do after earlier divesting her of every stitch of clothing she'd been wearing. He mourned losing the sight of each part of her as it was covered. She was so gorgeously lithe, and he was left with the impression that she didn't realize her own beauty. Not only in her features, but in her mind.

Good God, in New York what sort of bores would find her inquisitive mind strange? What type of idiot was intimidated by a woman whose interests extended beyond what was socially acceptable? Darning, arranging flowers, and spending hours at the modiste discussing the latest fashions. He found no fault with any of those endeavors but why be limited to them if a lady wanted to explore beyond them?

He wondered how differently things might have turned out for her if she hadn't begun her life in America, but rather here. The upper echelons in New York apparently didn't accept her family, but then it was highly unlikely that a few years ago, when she was of an age for her coming-out, she'd have been welcomed among the aristocracy.

It was the possibility for investing that allowed them entry now.

People were struggling financially, and not even the aristocracy was immune to the troubles. Nobles were discovering a shifting in their paradigm, a crumbling of their foundation. Floods and blights were ruining harvests. Quicker ships allowed the needed grains to be brought in from elsewhere at a cheaper cost, causing agricultural lands to be left fallow because they were no longer profitable. Tenant farmers were struggling to pay their rents so it was either lower the fees to something they could afford or lose any income completely. And the younger people were migrating to the cities for factory work, leaving behind the land upon which generations of their family had toiled.

Investments had allowed Rook—all the Chess-men—to avoid the pitfalls of reduced income that many peers were experiencing. A goodly number of lords were aware of their successes and wanted to emulate them. Hence the reason that Miss Garrison and her family were allowed into the inner circle now. Because they offered the promise of wealth.

But Rook knew that promises could be broken. And that in the breaking they could harden a heart.

Securing the final button on her frock, he snatched up his shirt from where it had landed on the floor and drew it on, very much aware of her gaze following the path of his fingers as he pushed buttons through holes. Waistcoat, neckcloth, and coat followed. All the while she watched, the set of her features revealing she was mesmerized by his actions, and it occurred to him that she may have never seen the intricacies of a man dressing.

He combed his fingers through his tangled locks before setting his hat in place. He retrieved her pelisse from another chair in the room, draped it over her shoulders, and lifted the hood so her face was partially hidden. "We'll go out a back way."

For a second or two, she held still, appearing startled and hurt, and he realized she might have assumed he was ashamed to be seen with her. After all, she'd been snubbed by tactless gents in New York. "To protect your reputation."

Her chin angled up defiantly. "Of course."

As he was escorting her through a maze of hallways and stairways, she asked, "How do you know of this path?"

"Aiden once took me on a tour of the establishment, during the daylight hours, when no women were about. He's terribly protective of those who come here."

"Most people wouldn't be as accepting of their father's by-blows."

"They are not responsible for the circumstances of their birth."

They reached the back door. A man of small stature slid off a stool. "M'lord."

"Good evening, Eros. You'll let us out, I hope."

"Indeed, guv." He shoved open the door. As Rook walked past, he slipped a coin into the man's palm.

Once they were outside, Nora mused, "God of love? Is that his real name?"

"I doubt it. Aiden has a fascination with mythology, and I suspect he assigns appropriate names to some of his workers."

"There's a fondness in your voice whenever you speak of him."

"I enjoy his company and respect him. Respect all the Trewloves. They did everything necessary to better themselves and succeed in life. Nothing was handed to them." No titles, no properties, no lands. "We'll walk down a ways and find a hansom."

LEONORA ASSUMED THAT hansom drivers were well aware that this time of night a good many ladies who'd visited the Elysium were in need of a ride home because they had no trouble at all locating a cab. She didn't bother to tell Rook that he needn't accompany her, because she knew him well enough to know he would—whether she wished it or not.

However, she was remarkably grateful for a little more time with him, even if they weren't talking. He'd offered his hand to assist her into the carriage and hadn't released his hold, having climbed in so smoothly after her that his movement hadn't necessitated freeing himself from her. Neither wore gloves. His palms sported a slight roughness, like the finest of sandpaper. It was difficult not to recall the soft abrasiveness as his hands traveled over her skin.

The horse clopped along, a steady rhythm that echoed the chant running through her mind. *He's mine. He's not. He's mine. He's not.*

As a child, she'd often tugged the petals off daisies to find answers to the silliest of questions. *He loves me. He loves me not.* Even though she had no idea who the *he* was. She supposed like so many, she simply wanted confirmation she was loved, or would be in the future. When the last petal was a *not*, another daisy was asked to sacrifice its petals in hopes she'd finally receive the answer she'd longed for. Such capriciousness, as though love was simple and easily decided by the fates.

Instead, she was beginning to realize, it was incredibly complex. Not a requirement for matrimony. On the contrary, it was really too flighty a thing upon which to make an important decision that would affect her for the rest of her life. Hadn't her mother drilled that into her enough? Marriage should be dependent upon choosing a partner who would help to ensure her survival and that of her family.

The man beside her certainly had the financial means, but survival meant more than coin. Besides, he'd given no indication that anything between them was more than a moment's passing, a game to be won. Oh, he might dance with her in a ballroom, take her on midnight excursions, but that didn't mean he wanted to marry her. He was her secret, and she was his. These little clandestine assignations were certainly a secret.

Maybe it was their secretive nature that made them so enjoyable, that added an element of excitement because she was doing what she ought not. If she ever did marry, she'd go to her marriage bed without fear and nervousness, knowing almost exactly what to expect. The final bit, the actual joining, the feel of it was an unknown, but she was fairly certain, if tonight was any indication, it was going to be something she craved.

She stared ahead at the horse's rump. "What you did tonight . . . is that always part of it?"

"Not always." His voice was a deep caress in the night, and perhaps because of that it made her brave.

"Have women ever done something similar to you?"

"Yes."

"Are you disappointed I didn't?"

With his other hand, he reached around to press the tips of his fingers to the far side of her face and turned her toward him. "No. The very last thing I wanted was for you to do anything with which you were uncomfortable. It brought me great satisfaction to bring pleasure to you. All the little sounds you make, the manner in which you squirm, the way you move your hands over me as though you want me to never leave . . . I enjoyed every moment."

"I realize it's rather late to be asking, but you won't tell anyone what we've done."

"No." He flashed a grin that was caught by a streetlamp they passed. "This stays just between us."

She fought off the sudden thought that he was holding it secret because he was ashamed to be seen with her. Just once in her life, she wanted a man to whom she wasn't related to want her for her. She hoped the darkness disguised her thoughts, that he couldn't discern how his words hurt. It was silly that they did. She'd sent for him. He'd come. And she'd been glad of it. She would be a fool—a hypocrite—to regret it now.

The hotel came into view. This glorious, miserable night was almost over. How was it possible to reach both the pinnacle of happiness and the depths of misery in one evening, and to bounce repeatedly between the two depending on where her thoughts traveled? She was not one to feel sorry for herself, and yet she wished she hadn't had to send for him. But then she was ever so grateful she had.

The hansom came to a stop, and the doors swung open. Having already instructed the driver that he'd be making two stops, he disembarked and handed her down. "Are you all right?"

She forced a small smile. "Just tired."

He escorted her to the door where a footman stood watch, preparing to open it for her.

"Sleep well, Nora," Rook said quietly.

She suspected she wouldn't sleep at all. Then because she didn't want to watch him walk away, she ducked into the hotel and made her way to their suites. It was so remarkably quiet . . . and dark. She'd left a lamp burning low in her bedchamber, but nowhere else. Gingerly, squinting to make out the shadowy shapes of the furniture, she crept to her room, opened the door, and stepped inside.

"Where have you been? And with whom have you been?"

Jerking her head to the side, she stared at her mother, standing in the corner, her arms folded over her chest, looking very much like a wrathful goddess with her nightdress and wrap flowing around her. Leonora was grateful her window looked out on the gardens at the rear of the hotel and not on the street. She considered lying, but her mother would probably know. She always knew.

"I was at the Elysium. It's a club for ladies."

"I've heard rumors about it. Naughty things go on there. What did you do?"

"I played games." *I won and I lost. At the same time.*

"What sort of games?"

"Cards."

Mama narrowed her eyes. "Why don't I believe you?"

With a sigh, Leonora removed her pelisse and draped it over the foot of the bed. "I don't know."

"If word gets out that you were there—"

"It's an incredibly discreet club. No one talks about who is there. The owner—Aiden Trewlove, by the way, one of the men Sam has approached—will banish anyone who reveals anything about the ladies who frequent his establishment. Trust me, his disapproval is akin to being kicked out of heaven."

Mama stepped forward. "You can't be traipsing about London at all hours of the night. You must be above reproach if you are to gain a husband, if you are to ensure your father's legacy."

Oh, she was good, knew exactly where to stick the knife. "I don't understand why it requires marriage. It requires only an investor."

"A man can be both. As a matter of fact, he will be more committed if he is both. And a woman is better able to control a husband than a stakeholder."

"I don't want a man I can control. I want an equal partner."

Mama scoffed. "There's no such thing. Within a marriage, a woman holds power. Men are simple creatures, easily manipulated because of their animalistic needs. You let them have what they require of you and in exchange they keep you happy. You will marry, Leonora. You will do your duty by this family. No more of these excursions to clubs."

She was so tempted to tell her mother to go to the devil. But her father had placed the woman in her keeping. *They'll depend on you when I'm gone. They haven't your fortitude, your cunning, or your willingness to do what must be done.*

What must be done, she was beginning to fear, was to give up her own dreams for another's.

CHAPTER 18

THE following afternoon, Leonora sat at a small table in the hotel garden sipping tea with the Earl of Camberley. He'd arrived with a bouquet of ten red roses in hand. *You're perfect* was the message that shade and number represented, according to her mother, who'd apparently become an expert on the various ways couples communicated without words in a prim and proper society that did not allow emotions to reign. While Mama explained the message of the flowers as she handed them off to her maid to be placed in a vase, Leonora had been tempted to ask, "What message is a man sending when his face is buried between your thighs?"

But, of course, she hadn't dared because there was no way to explain how she'd even imagined such an act without experiencing it and that would have created an entire host of complications. She'd no doubt find herself locked in her bedchamber as she'd been when she'd taken her father's watch apart. And this time, she wouldn't stretch out on her bed, close her eyes, and think about all the tiny gears she'd uncovered. No, she'd think about how Rook had effectively taken her apart, reduced her to quivering need, and reassembled her into a wanton. Because she wanted him again. Had woken up yearning for the release he could provide.

Sitting across from Camberley, she wondered if he could detect a difference in her since they'd danced at that ball a couple of nights back. Did a woman who had cried out a lover's name in ecstasy carry a different scent than a young girl? It just seemed to her that a man should be able to look at a woman and simply *know* that she wasn't as she'd been before.

Which made her acknowledge that what she'd done was so terribly wrong that even nature didn't want anyone to know she'd done it.

With a watchful eye, her mother sat a short distance away, not even bothering to pretend that she wasn't analyzing each movement made, wasn't striving to determine his purpose and potential.

Lord Camberley was handsome. She couldn't deny him that truth. His lips were a little thinner than she liked. Good Lord, she'd only ever kissed one set of lips, and while they were plumper than his, how did she *know* they were her preference? Shouldn't a lady have an assortment of lips pressed against her own, closing around a nipple, tugging on an earlobe? To determine her favorite by sampling, as one did sweets?

Although perhaps the shape of the lips made no difference whatsoever. Perhaps the difference was due exclusively to the talents of the deliverer. So again, shouldn't a lady have numerous examples from which to choose?

The problem was, there was an elusive aspect to a man, undefinable, that formed an attraction. Because in spite of his fetching features, she couldn't, for the life of her, imagine kissing Lord Camberley. Or even wanting to.

But from the moment Rook had walked through that door the first night at the Elysium, she'd wanted his lips on hers. Not because she'd known that was his purpose in being there. But because the sight of him had caused her heart to skip a beat, her body to grow warm, and she'd felt she was falling, and he alone held the power to stop her descent and send her flying.

With these fanciful thoughts, she was beginning to wonder if the hotel added absinthe to their tea. She was a practical not whimsical sort.

"How do you like England thus far, Miss Garrison?" he asked.

That seemed to be the unoriginal question with which everyone began a conversation. "You seem to have an inordinate number of rules over here."

He chuckled lightly. "I suppose we do."

"Do you always obey them?"

"Not so much in my youth, to be honest, but of late . . . I have found rewards in doing so."

She suspected one of those rewards included not having to deal with an angry Aiden Trewlove. "Have you ever been to the Elysium Club? I believe your brother-by-marriage owns it."

"He does. I haven't. He's not allowed any gentleman of the *ton* inside. It's for ladies only, and he does all he can to protect their reputations."

But he had allowed entry to a lord. One he trusted with his secrets. One she trusted with hers. How had it come about that so quickly she'd known he'd not betray her? "Would you allow your sisters to go there, then?"

He laughed heartily. "To be honest, that's where Selena met Aiden. I encouraged her to go."

Striving not to look too triumphant, she glanced

over at her mother, whose eyes had narrowed into suspicious slits.

"But Aiden Trewlove is not a lord," Mama finally ground out.

Camberley looked taken aback—either by Mama's tone or the fact she'd intruded on their conversation. "No. Son of one, but not one himself."

"I doubt Mrs. Astor would allow him in her ballroom in New York," she continued.

And there it was. The Elysium was not for her daughter. Nothing short of anything that would get her into that famed ballroom was.

"Your father has passed, has he not?" Mama continued and Leonora wished she'd never made eye contact with her, had not introduced her into their conversation.

"He has," Camberley said.

"You'll never rise above the rank of earl, then."

"I will not. You Americans seem to believe that dukes grow on trees over here. They do not." His tone was cutting, and Leonora suspected if he hadn't arrived with flowers to send the message that he had an interest that his voice might have sounded scathing.

"Mama finds no fault with earls," she assured him. "She hasn't quite comprehended how a lord with one title becomes a man with another. Then so many of you have more than one title and your son will have a title—a courtesy I think it's called—she meant no insult. She's simply striving to figure it all out. To be quite honest, I'm rather glad our founding fathers did away with the entire practice of the nobility."

"Well if they hadn't, you ladies wouldn't be coming over here in search of what you can't find over there, would you?"

"I suppose we wouldn't. More tea, my lord?" She smiled as sweetly as possible.

"Thank you, Miss Garrison, but I should take my leave now." He stood, and she followed suit.

"Again, thank you for the lovely roses."

"They were my pleasure. I look forward to tonight's demonstration regarding your writing machine." He leaned forward slightly and said in a low voice as if sharing a secret, "Everyone is talking about it."

That was satisfying news. At least there was interest. It still remained to be determined if there would be investors.

As this wasn't their residence, but simply their hotel, he saw himself out. Leonora lowered herself back to the wrought iron chair, torn between hoping tonight would see them acquire investors and hoping it wouldn't so they'd have an excuse to remain in London a bit longer. She thought she might return often to give reports to the investors. She'd been so keen to leave shortly after they arrived. Now, she'd grown to like the misbehavior she experienced over here.

"Lord Camberley seems like a good prospect," Sam said, as he wandered over and took the seat the earl had vacated. His leg began jostling. She wondered how long he'd been watching them, hidden as he must have been. Or had he just arrived and run into the earl in a hallway? "If you were to marry him, the Trewloves are sure to invest, offer their support."

"The Countess of Camberley," Mama chimed in, as though trying it on for size, even though she'd been more than obnoxious to the earl. "With him, unlike another, say, you're not having to wait to become a countess."

Leonora refrained from snapping that she didn't

give a fig about a man's title. That she was, in fact, in want of a viscount. "Maybe you should marry him."

"Don't think I haven't given it some thought. There are some older lords, widowers, in need of companionship. But marriage is a young woman's game."

"If it's not a game I want to play?"

"Then your selfishness will see us ruined."

Leonora met her mother's furious glare head-on, surprised she didn't feel the slap of her palm against her cheek. "I don't mean to be stubborn. Lord Camberley is incredibly nice, but—"

I can't imagine kissing him. Or having him suck on my breast. Or having his tongue swirling over that sensitive flesh between my thighs.

"—I just don't know that we would suit."

"You make yourself suit. Since the dawn of time, women have made themselves *suit*."

"Did you make yourself suit Papa?"

"We made ourselves suit each other."

"Did you love him?"

Mama looked at Sam, who seemed to be as curious regarding the answer as Leonora. Finally, she sighed. "Eventually I came to care for him very much. And he for me. Because we were good partners together. Like that Darwin conclusion. You adapt in order to survive, flourish, and acquire what you desire most of all. Although your father failed me when it came to giving me my dream of being welcomed into the Astor ballroom."

Leonora had never seen her father as a failure, not even when his latest venture struggled. If he'd had more time, he would have made a success of it. She also couldn't help but believe Mama's dream was as small as a mote of dust. And wasn't reaching dreams more satisfying if one accomplished them, rather than relying on someone else to make them happen? "You don't care about the business at all, do you?"

"I care about it very much. We need an income. But we also deserve a place in Society, here and back in the States. You are our best hope for success there."

She wanted to scream but wasn't going to give her mother the satisfaction of knowing how much she angered her. If Rook was at the demonstration, perhaps she'd slip away with him for a while so she could just *be*. Feel. Without worries or cares. Surrounded by pleasure and appreciation. Valued for herself and not what she could bring to him. Because there was nothing she could offer him that he didn't already have. Rank, power, prestige, wealth. He didn't need to invest in their little company in order to survive.

Perhaps she could convince him to do it simply as a favor. At least then, maybe Sam's nerves would settle. Reaching across, she placed her hand on his knee and pressed down hard enough to cause his leg to go still. "It'll be all right, Sam. No matter what happens, we will survive."

"I wish I had your confidence. I don't want to go back to New York with my tail between my legs. All my friends will laugh at me. They think I'm on a fool's errand as it is. I get tongue-tied when I try to explain what we're doing."

"But you have such a gift for gab."

The smile he gave her made him look like a young boy who'd just been given a puppy. "I like talking with people. Just not about machines and our business."

"If everything goes well this evening, maybe you won't have to for a while."

CHAPTER 19

STANDING within the ballroom of the Trewlove Hotel, Leonora was not nervous. She was terrified. She'd traveled on a small ship across a vast ocean for this very reason—to unveil a piece of machinery that she and her father believed had the potential to change the course of industry, to change lives. It presently rested on a table on a dais and was covered by a large blanket that Sam would remove with a flourish. He did enjoy his theatrics.

Beside it was another table with only pen, inkwell, and paper. For comparison purposes.

Her terror was brought on by the fact that she was not accustomed to speaking before large crowds. When she'd begun the journey, she'd expected to explain their product to four men, probably at the same time, and do what she could to convince them that they should become partners in their enterprise. She had not anticipated that she would be addressing a ballroom crowded with people.

But she could see the advantage of not having all their eggs in one basket. And friendly I've-never-met-a-stranger Sam had invited anyone with whom he'd shared a pint, a gaming table, a meal, or a dance to join them tonight and most, if not all, had taken him up on the offer. She suspected out of curiosity more than an intention to invest. Or perhaps it was the food, drink, and dancing that had drawn them. The Brits did seem to enjoy their evening entertainments.

An orchestra had been set up and was waiting to play. In a corner near the door, a young woman was strumming her fingers over a harp. The harpist was here at the insistence of Mama, who wanted a touch of elegance for this business meeting that would turn into a ball at the stroke of eight. Leonora suspected most of the cajoling would occur then—on the dance floor and with small groups gathered in corners.

"Don't suppose you could sneak me a peek?" Lord Camberley asked.

She'd seen him come into the ballroom and head straight for her. She had yet to catch sight of Rook but was fairly certain his appearance would calm her nerves. Although he'd be distracting in other ways. "That would be hardly fair, and it won't be long now."

"Fairness is important," a familiar voice said, and she swung around to face Rook. Devastatingly handsome and confident. His gaze focused intently on her as though he knew what she looked like without her clothing. But then, of course, he did. She felt her cheeks pinken. Mostly because her fingers itched to slip beneath the hem of his shirt and dance over his firm abdomen, to waltz over his chest.

She could scarcely breathe for the images rushing through her mind.

His tart lemony-orange scent filled her nostrils, making her light-headed. She knew how different he smelled when lost in the throes of passion. He took her gloved hand and pressed a lingering kiss to the back of it. "Miss Garrison."

"My lord."

He looked past her. "Camberley."

Based on the frigid delivery of that single name, she was surprised little chunks of ice didn't fall from his mouth and hit the floor.

"Wyeth. Looking forward to having all your questions answered, I assume. The rumor I've heard is that you and the Chessmen are unlikely to invest."

Her stomach felt as though it had done a somersault.

"We've not decided whether we'll purchase a stake in the company. Hence, the reason we're here this evening. Based on your debt at the Dragons, I suspect you won't be investing."

Camberley grinned. "I appreciate you paying that off, old chap. I had a bit of luck at the tables last night. Who knows what I'll do with my windfall? I'm anxious to hear all about what Mr. Garrison is offering."

Naturally he would credit Sam for being the head of the company, the one seeking investors, the one—

"Perhaps it is Miss Garrison doing the offering," Rook said, his gaze on her and not on Camberley.

"But . . . but . . ." Camberley seemed to be struggling with his thoughts. "But it's a business, man, and men manage businesses."

"I think all the Chessmen would disagree. One is married to a writer, another to an investigator, and the third to a former secretary who no doubt still oversees a preponderance of his affairs. Not to mention her own skill at investing. Having spoken with Miss Garrison on several occasions, I daresay she may know more about the workings of the business than her brother."

"Well . . ." Camberley looked at her as though he'd possibly never seen her before. "Do you?"

She couldn't be disloyal to Sam, even if it meant speaking the truth. He had done his part. This gathering was mainly his doing. Certainly, he'd enticed most of those in attendance into coming. She didn't fool herself into believing they were here because of her. "Sam and I are partners in the enterprise. We each have a role."

"But you'll dedicate yourself to your husband and family once you marry."

"I believe I am fully capable of handling both. Family and business."

His brow furrowed. "A successful business that will provide a livable income for you and yours."

"I should certainly hope so. We're not going into this with the intent of earning meager profits."

He gave her what might have passed for an uncomfortable smile. "I'm not accustomed to a woman talking about profits."

"You'd rather she talked about the various entertainments available at clubs."

"Well, it's certainly more interesting. If you'll excuse me, I think I'm going to get some more champagne. Shall I bring you a glass, Miss Garrison?"

She was striving to keep her wits about her. "No, thank you. I'll have some later."

Following a nod, he walked off.

"You'd be miserable married to him," Rook said.

"I think I'd be miserable married to anyone. Men strive to put women in little corners. I don't properly fit in a corner."

"No, you're too adventuresome. You belong out in the world."

"Adventuresome." She gave him a sideways glance. "Is that another word for naughty or wanton?"

He chuckled low before sobering. "Regrets?"

She shook her head. "No." As a matter of fact, she wanted more. She wanted to go someplace dark with a high vaulted ceiling that would echo her screams of pleasure back to her. She wanted to discover if she could do things to him that would make him scream.

"I do appreciate you explaining to him that women can do more than manage a household."

"Had it recently explained to me, glanced around, and thought, 'By jove, she's right. An extraordinary woman can do anything she sets her mind to.'"

"I believe an ordinary woman can do anything she sets her mind to."

"And that makes her extraordinary."

"Are we having our first argument?"

"I should hope not." He jerked his head toward the stage. "You're going to be the one explaining the machine. That's the reason you declined the champagne."

She gave a little nod. "Sam doesn't truly understand it."

"Is it that complicated?"

"Not really. He simply has no interest in it." Or the business, really. For the first time, she wondered if her obsession with keeping the business going was unfair to him. He hadn't told her exactly what his dream was, but their recent conversation had left her aware that perhaps it had nothing to do with what their father had been trying to build.

A loud clapping caught her attention. Looking to the stage, she hardly recognized Sam. The confidence he projected was so very much unlike him. He liked being up there, liked being the center of attention, and she wondered if he'd been bothered by all the attentiveness and accolades their father had given her. She couldn't recall Papa ever taking Sam somewhere. Mama had doted on him, of course, but perhaps she'd been compensating for a parent who didn't. Maybe that was also why her mother had been so strict with her.

Glancing around, she caught sight of her mother near the stage, her usually harsh features softened by the obvious pride she felt toward her youngest.

"My lords and ladies, welcome." Sam's voice projected throughout the room. "You're here to witness the unveiling of a machine that we believe will change the world of business . . . and perhaps our personal lives as well. Its potential is without limit. Allow me the honor of introducing to you"—grabbing the blanket, he pulled it off with a flourish, somehow making the covering look as though it was flying—"the writing machine!"

ROOK KNEW HE should follow the example of many in the chamber and move nearer to the stage in order to get a better look at what was being offered, but he was unable to tear his gaze from Nora. Her cheeks, her entire face, had taken on a glow that was very similar to what he'd witnessed following each orgasm that ratcheted through her when he'd had his face between her thighs.

What he recognized as mere cold metal gears and levers, she looked upon with wonder and saw something as beautiful as a quiet sunrise, a masterpiece, a work of art. With pride, joy, and happiness rolling off her in waves, she was stunningly beautiful. He wanted nothing more than to be buried inside her, moving within her. To share her joy as closely and intimately as possible.

He'd considered sending her flowers, jewelry, gloves, stockings . . . had even considered calling upon her. But theirs was not a relationship born of courtship. It was born of her curiosity. He wondered how often she might have taken apart and examined the details of what they'd done. As for himself, he'd done it far too many times and been forced to soak in a cold bath until everything shriveled.

He should probably leave, forgo the demonstration. His interest in her was pure lust, and if he couldn't control that . . .

Only he could. He could be polite, cool, diffident.

"And now," Sam continued, "my sister, Leonora, will explain it to you."

"Good luck," Rook said, as she took a step toward the stage.

She gave him a nod, but he could see the nervousness and doubt in her eyes. Because of all those fellows who'd found her odd? Because of a mother who continually berated her, pinched her, and made her feel less than?

"This is your moment, Nora, and you will shine. Don't let anyone dim the brightness of your star."

He wasn't quite certain if what he'd said made any sense. He'd never been one for poetry—spouting it or reading it, because so often it wasn't clear exactly what the poet was trying to convey. Give him a good lengthy novel any day. But the luster of the smile she bestowed upon him hit him in the solar plexus and he was surprised he didn't stagger back from its force.

Then she was stepping on the stage and running her

long slender fingers—as one might over the head of a
favorite child—over what looked to be a rolling pin.
She'd grown pale during her journey from his side to
where she now stood. She wasn't comfortable being
the center of attention, looked as if she might bring
up her accounts. He wanted to shout, "Focus on me!"

Perhaps he did shout it or maybe she simply felt his
wanting to reassure her because her gaze wandered
over the gathering and came to a stop on him. He offered her a warm smile and fought to convey with his
expression that he had faith in her ability to hold this
audience captive.

She gave a little nod, cleared her throat, and ran her
hand over the etched flowers decorating the black iron.

"The writing machine," she said affectionately, "was
an idea dreamed up by our father, who recognized that
a successful business needed a faster way to produce
correspondence. Constantly having to dip a nibbed
pen into an inkwell and drawing precise letters is
time-consuming, especially if you are striving to communicate with a hundred customers. You want it to be
legible—like handbills, printed. So that's the approach
we took here. To tonight's exhibit, many of you received
invitations that were created using this very machine,
because we wanted you to see for yourselves, at your
leisure, how the letters looked on parchment. Much as a
typesetter's. Although they can't be duplicated as a typesetter's work can be, because each page must be created
individually, it does allow for changes to be made so all
documents don't look exactly the same. But ultimately,
it is the uniformity and speed that will propel this machine into a vital business tool. Lady Knightly, as an
author, you've no doubt written thousands of words.

Would you be kind enough to join me at the table here for a demonstration?"

The audience was murmuring as Regina made her way to the stage, but Rook knew that Nora had her audience enthralled. It was her passion. Dear Lord, but the woman did nothing in half measures. Whether it was kissing or striving to sell potential investors on a new invention. No, it wasn't the selling she was passionate about. Or the investors—they were a necessity because of the company's financial straits. It was the machine itself. It was the gears, buttons, levers, and bolts. The way it all came together to make something remarkable. Something she appreciated. Something she . . . loved.

How fortunate a bloke would be to have her devotion directed his way.

He wondered if Camberley had the same thoughts, was noting the strength of her loyalty.

Once Regina was situated, Nora turned back to her rapt audience. "While Lady Knightly with pen and ink writes, 'It was the best of times, it was the worst of times,' I shall tap it out using the keys of the writing machine. Sam, tell us when to begin."

Her brother fairly preened. "Three, two, one, go!"

The machine was not a quiet thing, and Rook wondered if that might get bothersome over time, but there was also a rhythm to the clacking that was comforting, that spoke of something being accomplished.

"Finished!" Nora said.

Regina laughed and set down her pen. "I got as far as, 'It was the best of times, it was.' I daresay I think more than businesses might find a use for this machine. As a matter of fact, is this one for sale?"

"It's only a prototype," Nora said. "But with investors, we would make some changes to our factory so it could produce this machine en masse. Would you like to give it a try?"

"Absolutely."

"If anyone else would like a closer look at how it works, please come nearer to the stage," Sam said. "We're more than happy to let you tap out a message to take with you. We brought lots of paper. Hopefully some of those messages will say, 'Invest.'"

"Well, that was rather impressive," King said, and Rook wondered when he, Knightly, Bishop, and their wives had wandered over.

"I certainly could have used it when I was your secretary," Penelope said. "I think your current secretary might appreciate it."

Knightly furrowed his brow. "But will it sell in sufficient numbers to be a profitable enterprise or will it be considered a novelty? Will it make a difference to the common man or be a toy of the elite?"

"That's the question, isn't it?" Bishop looked toward the stage. "People seem to be taken with it."

They were most definitely curious. Rook knew if he invested, as he was tempted to do, she would return to America, be beyond his immediate reach.

But not tonight. Tonight she was very much near enough to touch. Her luscious mouth, her glorious breasts, her firm bottom. How he yearned to experience them all just once more. Just once more.

He was discovering there were unintended consequences in spending time with Nora. Grinding his teeth down to a nub when Camberley was doting on her. Not that she didn't deserve the praise or the attention. She did. He just hadn't much liked the possessive manner in which the earl had stood beside her conversing with her as though it was his innate right to do so. Or the way that she'd smiled softly at the blighter.

Rook wasn't jealous. He was simply . . . irritated. That someone—Camberley in particular—might eventually know her as well as he did. But at the moment he was winning in that little game because he knew her well enough to know what he suspected no one else did: she'd assembled the writing machine. She understood the intricacies of every lever, every bolt, every rod.

If he spent much more time in her presence, she might try to take him apart, study all the various aspects, strive to understand him, before putting him back together. That thought terrified him.

He was as his surname suggested: a castle. But for her, he wanted to lower the drawbridge.

IT WAS LIKE being surrounded by magpies. All the questions, all the comments, all the interest. And the constant tapping echoing around her as people used the machine to unimaginatively engrave their names on a slip of paper. The gasps, sighs, or giggles that followed.

She wanted to declare the writing machine a triumph but thus far no one had indicated a true desire to invest. It was being met with mixed reviews.

Fascinating.

Too impersonal. You'll get no sense of the writer's personality or character. Everyone's letters will look the same.

Always legible, you mean, she'd wanted to shout.

What if it breaks?

Then you fix it as you would a carriage axle or a rip in your clothing.

The art of penmanship will go by the wayside. Why should a person learn to form letters when a simple tap will produce one?

No more ink on fingers. Wouldn't that be nice?

I like the motion of dipping a pen in an inkwell and applying it to paper. I imagine myself an artist.

You can have both: pen and writing machine. You don't have to kill one to make use of the other.

You could write a letter to someone you admire in secret, and they'd never be able to guess your identity.

Exactly. Our letters would all look the same.

Sam was leaving the fielding of most of the questions to her, especially the ones that involved explaining exactly how it worked. He was comfortable assuring people that if they didn't like having the flowers adorning the sides of the machine, they could have a special one designed with a dog or a cat or nothing at all. And he certainly liked telling the ladies how simple it was to use as though they hadn't the wherewithal to manage something complicated. His comments on that matter irked her. The machine equalized men and women—one wasn't better than the other at using it. It simply provided a faster means for communicating.

However, when the first chords of a violin filled the air—no doubt her mother growing bored and signaling that the dancing portion of the night was to begin—most of the crowd drifted away as if carried out to sea on the tide.

A few stragglers remained to study the machine more thoroughly. King, Knight, and Bishop, along with their wives, wandered over to give it a slow perusal. She wondered where Rook was. It had been reassuring to meet his gaze as he stood in the audience. She'd spent much of her life in solitude or quiet corners examining objects, figuring out the intricacies of them.

But people, she'd never quite come to understand. They were more complicated, and they didn't always work as they were supposed to. They uttered something mean when they should say something kind. They went one way when they should go the other. They didn't all enjoy the same books, or plays, or weather. She loved the rain. Its constant patter against a window was comforting, helped her to think. Sam wanted sunshine and always complained when rain kept him indoors.

But she wanted to understand Rook because she thought he might be the most complicated of all. Or at least her feelings toward him were.

Sam was regaling those who were studying the machine. He didn't need her any longer. He'd become quite adept at avoiding any technical questions.

She required a moment away from the madness of the crush of people who were now dancing, walking about, or partaking of the refreshments. Stepping off the stage, she suddenly found herself facing Lord Camberley.

"That was fascinating," he said. "Do you think it'll bring in a good income?"

Because that's what he wanted, what he needed, the reason he spoke with her and brought her flowers. Not because she was special to him but because in her he saw the potential to refill his coffers. "I hope so."

"Hope is not a strategy."

"It's all I can offer at the moment. I sense a megrim coming on. If you'll excuse me, I just need a moment of quiet."

"Of course. Shall I sign your dance card before you go?"

She didn't know if she'd be returning. "I don't have one at the moment, but I'll sign your name to the last waltz, shall I?"

"Splendid." Then he was edging past her to talk with Sam.

Avoiding eye contact with anyone else, she skirted around people, grateful to reach the doorway. From there, she headed down the hallway to a door that led outside and into the small garden area where she'd earlier that afternoon taken tea with Lord Camberley. When she reached its end, she glanced back over her shoulder. No one was about. No one had followed. Peace and calm rested on the other side of that door. Solitude.

Strange how when she opened the door and stepped out, she was momentarily saddened to realize she would indeed be alone, that she'd been hoping for the companionship of one, of Rook. Perhaps he'd left already, hadn't been impressed with the machine. She wanted to share with him the details of it, every nut, bolt, and screw. She suspected he'd find it most boring—but he wouldn't let on. He'd feign interest and let her speak ad nauseum. She was most true to herself with him. She didn't have to try to be the perfect daughter to her mother or the perfect sister to her brother. She didn't have to work to be the perfect legacy to her father.

When she was with him, all else fell away until it was only the two of them in a little world they created.

Wandering off the terrace, she caught sight of the greenhouse in the distant corner. She headed for it.

Now that the ball was underway, others might decide to make use of the garden and she didn't want to be disturbed. Not yet. She just wanted not to be bothered.

The greenhouse contained a quietness inside, but the music generated by the orchestra hummed along outside, muffled by the glass that allowed moonlight and the glow from the gaslights lining the garden paths to filter in, and she could well imagine nymphs cavorting about in the faint illumination.

And it smelled incredibly wonderful inside. So many flowers resting in little pots on tables, nurtured by the gardener—much in the same way she'd been nurtured by her father. To explore her interests, to blossom into the inquisitive being she was. Which made her so very different from other women. Which made her unmarriageable. Which made her an oddity, not understood. Someone to be laughed at or ridiculed. Someone who would analyze the force of a thrust.

How she wanted to experience that force, that thrust.

She'd been afraid to ask for it when she and Rook were last together. She'd taken all he'd offered but been too timid to declare she wanted a joining. Her father would have been disappointed by her lack of courage. She was disappointed by it. They'd be leaving soon. Did she want to leave England's shores as a virgin?

Did she want a farewell kiss from Rook? Would she even know when their final kiss happened? Perhaps it already had. Perhaps that was the reason he'd disappeared. Because he was done with her.

Hearing the door opening on a hush, the music rushing in and once again muted as the door closed, she slowly turned around. She knew who it was before she saw him. It was the reason she hadn't spun about or felt a moment of panic. Somehow, she'd sensed his presence and she'd known. She'd always know.

"I expected you to stay near your writing machine," he said quietly, "or to be occupied dancing with every gentleman in that room."

"It got a bit overwhelming. I'm not accustomed to that much attention. I wanted everyone's focus on the machine."

As though she was a skittish mare or a deer that would bound away if startled, he took one small and slow step toward her. "You designed it, didn't you?"

The heat swarmed over her face in delight because he knew her well enough to discern that truth about her. For him, she'd always thought the intimacy they'd shared had been only physical, but perhaps like her, maybe he'd discovered that it had encompassed more. Trust, knowledge. If not love, at least a strong fondness or adoration. She would miss him when they left. "Yes. For my father."

"To make him proud?"

Perhaps he didn't know her so well because pride had never played a role in any of her achievements. The accomplishment had always been reward enough. "No. His health had been failing for a while and he'd begun to lose the ability to do things. It was devastating for him. He'd told me that he felt like he was turning into a shadow, just fading away, until eventually he wouldn't be seen at all. He was so robust, so vibrant before he took ill. After a while he couldn't walk without assistance, struggled to feed himself. Then he could no longer grip a pen. He would dictate any correspondence to me. I wanted to return to him the ability to do it on his own. When I told him about my idea and showed him the first few sketches I'd done, the notion of creating something that hadn't existed before seemed to revitalize him. He helped me figure out the more complicated aspects. Then he guided me through creating the various parts and building the machine. When we tested it . . . when he pressed a key and the first letter struck the paper . . . I can't remember him ever looking so satisfied, triumphant, and happy. This project was the last thing we did together."

She didn't know when he'd gotten so close, but his hand was gently cupping her jaw. "And that's the reason it's so important to you that your company survives."

"It's a way to hold onto him, I suppose."

"You'll take no credit for your machine, will you?"

"I know my accomplishments. I don't need accolades."

"Does one of those accomplishments include luring Lord Camberley into falling madly in love with you?"

"I haven't the wiles to do that. Although I like him well enough, I can't imagine . . . misbehaving with him."

"With whom do you imagine misbehaving?"

"You" came out on a soft sigh.

She didn't know if he'd latched his mouth onto hers or if she'd taken hold of his, but now here she was ensconced in a kiss that was different from any that had come before, that stood all on its own. Fiery. Hot. Demanding.

He dragged his mouth along her silken throat, and

she dropped her head back, exposing the long delicate column for further enticement.

She was trembling with needs and desires, very much aware of the animalistic sounds they were both making. His guttural and deep. Hers fainter and of a higher pitch. While every now and then, her mind would intrude with a reminder of exactly where she was—in a glass-walled greenhouse. Being pressed up against him overrode all else. He was all that mattered.

Returning his mouth to hers, he reached down, hooked his arm around her knee, and lifted it to his narrow hip. Instinct had her holding it there when his hand slipped beneath the hem of her skirt and petticoats, wrapped around her ankle, and began sliding up her leg. A tremble cascaded through her, and she tightened her arms around his neck because she was no longer certain she had the wherewithal to continue standing.

But as his hold on her tightened, she realized he wouldn't let her fall, but would provide all the support she required.

ROOK HADN'T COME here with this action in mind, but he certainly wasn't going to push her away when he wanted her with a desperation that far exceeded anything he'd ever known.

He'd been standing in the garden, sipping scotch that he'd gotten Aiden to pilfer for him from the hotel restaurant because this being a Trewlove hotel all the Trewloves were in attendance. After witnessing the demonstration, he'd needed some time alone to consider the merits of an investment because as long as she was in his line of sight, his perception was skewed and the decision whether to invest was taken out of his hands.

He hadn't yet come to a conclusion when he saw her walking toward the greenhouse. He'd known he should let her be, should stay clear of her because where she was concerned, he seemed to have no resistance whatsoever.

A point succinctly proven when her mouth latched onto his and instead of wisely breaking away from the kiss, he committed to it with his entire being. Dear Lord, her father had lost the ability to write a letter and because he was so precious to her, she'd created a machine for him. A machine for which she wouldn't take credit but unselfishly claimed as another's dream.

He couldn't imagine having that much love for a father and almost envied her for it. For being raised by someone who'd instilled that much devotion into her. He rather wanted to erase any memories of his own father.

With her in his arms, they did fade away. No longer had any importance, no longer guided him.

All that mattered was her and this insatiable hunger that made him yearn to possess her and be possessed by her—fully and completely.

He trailed his lips over her bared shoulders. "So lovely," he murmured.

"You make me feel so."

An entire cadre of men over the years should have made her feel so, and yet he was somewhat gratified that in the end the task had fallen to him. That when she left this country, she would be taking memories of their time together with her. Memories of kisses, touches, and slow licks.

He was the first to have ever lifted her skirts. The gentlemanly, compassionate side of him didn't want him to be the last. He didn't wish for her to live alone or in solitude.

Normally he found nothing wrong with solitude. Had sought it out himself.

Perhaps that was part of the reason that he'd crossed the gardens to join her here. Because she'd appeared to be a lonely figure entering the greenhouse. Having entranced a ballroom full of people, many who were most likely here out of curiosity regarding the Americans rather than an interest in their machinery or a desire to invest, she should have been soaking up the compliments.

Instead, she'd been here, alone. Possibly she'd been here waiting for him. Did she know he'd find her, he'd always find her?

Because at that moment, he felt as though they were tethered, that no matter how often they parted, they would always come back together.

But it was no longer enough to simply kiss, touch, and taste.

He should resist. He knew that. He'd known it as he glanced around to make sure no one was about to witness his journey. As he clandestinely made his way here—his smooth unhurried movements not reflecting the wild, rapid pounding of his heart.

The woman occupied his thoughts as no other woman ever had. The jealousy that ratcheted through him when she danced with another man was also novel. Even as he knew she wasn't looking for a true partner, just someone to invest, to help her fulfill her father's dream. He wondered what her dream might be, if she'd ever given any thought to it.

He knew he was on the cusp of emulating his father's unacceptable antics, and yet it seemed that something more than lust was driving him. Certainly he craved the sounds of her cries, his name on a tortured gasp of air, the soft sigh that came after her body had tumbled from the heavens, and the contented smile that warmed her eyes as she looked at him and made him feel as though he had conquered the world.

When he suspected it was she conquering him.

This strong, bold, inventive woman who took things apart, who was dismantling the walls that he'd so carefully erected over the years. To prevent him from being caught in a compromising situation. To ensure the gossips never whispered, "He's just as odious as his father."

In all his years, he'd shown remarkable restraint and held himself to the highest standard. Suddenly he was damned tired of doing so, unable to bear the thought of her leaving England's shores, being so far away that he could never have her.

Not when she was at this very moment squirming with abandon against his aching cock.

His fingers skimmed along the inside of her thigh, down, up, down, up, always going a little higher until finally they slipped inside her drawers and he cupped her intimately. She made a keening sound that could have been a beg, a pleading. *Don't stop. Don't stop.*

One of his fingers parted the folds and slid the length of her.

"You're so wet, so ready for my cock. I'm desperate to be buried inside you. I want to feel the velvet closing around me, to feel you pulsing around me when ecstasy takes over."

She nipped his earlobe and ran her tongue around the swirls of his ear before whispering with a need that made her voice hoarse, her breath shallow, "I want it all, Johnny. I want all of you. I want to know what it is to truly experience everything a man has to offer. I want to actually fuck."

"Christ, Nora." That one scandalous word coming from her was a powerful aphrodisiac. He lost all sense of self. All sense of right and wrong. Or perhaps it was simply that what she asked for seemed so completely right, as though they'd been hurtling toward this moment from the first.

He stepped away from her and swiped his arm across a nearby table, sending an array of assorted orchids crashing to the floor. He'd send funds to replace them on the morrow. Closing his hands on her waist, he lifted her onto the table and took possession of that mouth that somehow managed to own him.

She unbuttoned his trousers, setting him free. Her fingers wrapped around him. "Please," she begged, this woman who should never have to beg for anything.

He eased her back onto the table. Together they were raising her skirts and petticoats, bunching the entire mess at her waist. He tried to draw on his years of restraint, fought to back away, strove to be the responsible man he'd always been—

But she was a temptation such as he'd never known. Impossible to resist.

He pushed himself inside her hot, velvety core, held still, and buried his face against her neck. "You feel so bloody good."

"So do you." She dug her fingers into his bared buttocks, urging him on.

He complied, rocking against her. Why had he ever denied himself such exquisite torment? She was so tight, fitting him like a handsewn glove, perfectly. Once more, he took her mouth because he needed all of her: her taste, her moans, her heat. Her fingers scoring his flesh as they slipped beneath his shirt and up his back.

He was going to let a room so they could do this again, unhampered by clothing. He wanted her on a bed, a soft mattress at her back. He wanted her against a wall, against a window. On a chaise longue. He wanted her in every imaginable position. But for now—

"Well, this is interesting."

She squeaked, her hold on him tightening as though she'd drown if she released him. He'd stilled at her mother's irritating voice. Inwardly he cursed because she was going to get her daughter a damned lord. But more, she was risking bringing shame to her daughter in doing so.

As calmly as he could, striving not to look guilty, he glanced over his shoulder to find not only her mother standing there like a righteous witch but also Nora's brother Sam, Aiden, and Mick Trewlove.

"If we could have a moment of privacy," he said succinctly in a tone that hinted it was not a request but an order.

The three gentlemen stepped out, but the mother

held her ground, crossing her arms over her chest. "I'd be a fool to leave you alone with my daughter."

"No further damage can be done, madam."

Her triumphant smile made him want to throw a potted plant at her.

"Mama, I asked for this," Nora said.

"Of course you did. He seduced you. It's what men do. Then they take advantage. There are consequences. Be quick, girl, in setting yourself to rights. We've a wedding to plan."

Finally, she walked out and the door slapped shut behind her.

Rook helped Nora sit up before pressing his forehead against hers. "I'm so sorry. I should have resisted."

"I'll convince her that we don't have to marry."

He leaned back slightly. In the shadows, he couldn't see the bright blue of her eyes. But they did have to marry. It was the only way to protect her now. "You're not a fool, Nora. Do you truly believe she'll place your wants above hers?"

She released a shuddering breath. "We'll find a way out of this debacle."

"It's not something that can be taken apart, examined, and put back together. It's not a machine. We *will* marry."

CHAPTER 20

❧❧❧❧

$\mathcal{R}$OOK should have known.

Standing within his father's library, pouring himself a glass full of scotch, he fought not to throw the bottle against the wall.

From the moment he was a young man, from the time he learned about sexual gratification, he'd shown remarkable restraint.

Then tonight when she'd widened her legs, he'd slid his fingers across the parted folds to reveal the molten dew that her desire had created for him . . . and he'd surrendered. He'd taken her with wild abandon, and nothing had ever felt so damned good. He'd been mad with lust, with need.

And he'd known that he'd take her again and again—until she stopped him. Having had the whole of her, how could he ever be content with less?

Now he would have her every night. But not by choice. Because of carelessness. Because he'd forgotten himself. Because for those few minutes, he'd been no better than his father, driven by lust. He'd taken what he wanted with no concern for what it would cost her.

He gulped down a goodly amount of scotch. While burning his chest, it failed to burn away the guilt, the shame of what he'd done. He'd always been so bloody sturdy. A castle that couldn't be breached. Immovable. Fortified.

The worst of it was that even now, the remembered feel of her tightly closing around his cock made him grow hard. The manner in which she'd clutched at him, cried out his name. The way she met him, thrust for thrust. Gyrating against him, pulling him under her spell . . . until he'd forgotten himself and who he was.

Now she, who hadn't wanted to marry, was going to be forced to do so. Because of his weak will.

"Johnny?"

The soft voice brought him back from that edge of despair, that edge of need, of temptation.

He turned to his mother. The curiosity etched in the lines of her face turned immediately to worry. "Whatever is amiss, my darling son?"

"I wanted to tell you in person before you read about it in the gossip rags tomorrow. I'm to wed."

Reaching out with one hand, she cradled his face. "Why is it that you don't seem very happy about this change in circumstances, that you look to be a man who is mourning rather than one who is joyous?"

"Because tonight I proved I am my father's son. I gave in to lust with barely a whisper of resistance. And I was caught."

"Who is to be the bride?"

"Miss Garrison. An American. Her family is over here looking for investors. She and I crossed paths and . . ." *I was a fool, unable to resist her charms.* He'd welcomed every opportunity to be near her. Luring her into his company with idiotic things, like telling her a kiss was not yet finished, inviting her to come with him so he could show her something, finding ways to please her inquisitive mind—and in so doing, please himself. While he regretted his behavior, he couldn't seem to regret the time spent with her.

"Pour me a brandy and join me by the fire. I want you to tell me about her."

"There's not much to tell. We were caught in a compromising situation, and I'll not have her ruined because of my untoward behavior."

"Oh, I suspect there's a good deal more to it than that." She patted his cheek. "Brandy. Fire."

Reluctantly, he did as she bade, handing her the snifter before settling into the chair across from her. He'd always wanted her to be proud of him, to be an exemplary son—even before he knew she'd had others before him. She'd suffered through so much embarrassment with her husband, he'd wanted her to suffer through none because of him.

She gave him several minutes to sip on his scotch before she asked, "How did you meet?"

He laughed darkly. "Through Aiden, if you can believe it. Long story. I won't go into it."

An amused twinkle filled her eyes. "By way of his ladies' club, somehow, I should imagine. What is it about her that you fancy?"

Nothing. It was all lust. But that wasn't completely true, and he didn't want his mother believing he was a complete cad. "She's not like other women I've known. Certainly, she's pretty. If you look closely, you can see she had an abundance of freckles when she was younger. She has the most delicate hands. Long, slender fingers. And she uses those fingers to take things apart. Watches, toys, guns. She likes to determine how they work. Then she puts them back together. Inquisitive. Curious . . . Smart. Knows her own mind, knows what she wants." She'd wanted what he'd offered tonight. But he very much doubted she wanted him forever. "She can be a bit commanding in her own way."

His mother smiled. "I think you're strong enough to handle a woman such as that."

He leaned forward, forearms resting on his thighs. "A woman shouldn't be forced into marriage because of an error in judgment."

Watching him steadfastly, she took a sip of brandy. Took a moment. "Can you be happy with her?"

What did happiness in a marriage look like? His parents had certainly not provided an example to emulate. The other Chessmen seemed content enough, always anxious to get back to their wives. Except it wasn't his happiness that concerned him, but hers. Would she be happy living over here away from her factory? "I don't know."

"Then pay her off and be done with it."

Glaring at her, he shot out of his chair and stalked to the fireplace. "I can't do that."

"Why not?"

"Because she'll be mentioned in the gossip rags as well. Not another lord in all of Britain will take her to wife. Her mother will no doubt make her life more hellish than she has already and her brother is bloody useless. She'll have no one to stand beside her. No one to stand up for her. No one to speak out on her behalf. No one to catch and comfort her if this business venture she's poured her hopes and dreams into comes crashing down around her."

He didn't know why his mother sat there looking so triumphant. "Invite her and her family around for tea tomorrow afternoon. I should like to meet them."

After setting her snifter aside, she came to her feet, walked over to him, rose up on her toes, and kissed his cheek. "I know you don't like how this came about, and I know why, but you are nothing at all like your father. Don't give him the power to ruin this marriage for you. Whether you know it or not, you do have a kind regard for the girl. And that's a good deal more than some marriages start with. Think of her as an investment. She'll pay off with time."

"YOU WILL BE living here, my dear," Mama gushed, squeezing Leonora's hand as they walked into the Elvertons' London residence, with Sam and Rook following. "It's so grand. Exactly what I've always wanted."

Leonora tried not to notice how her mother didn't say she'd wanted it for her daughter. No, she'd wanted it for herself. There was ambition and then there was greed. Unfortunately, she was discovering her mother was all greed.

Rook had sent a missive inviting them to tea with his mother. Then he'd sent a carriage for them. He'd been waiting as they disembarked. His face had been an unwavering mask. No smile accompanied his greeting. No wicked glint in his eyes to promise something later. He'd stood there like a formidable castle, the drawbridge up, the moat filled with alligators, ready to devour anyone who tried to cross it.

He hadn't offered his arm but had merely directed

them toward the open doorway where a butler waited to close it once they'd passed through.

"If you'll be so good as to follow me . . . my mother is waiting in the garden," he said now and began to lead the way.

"How many rooms?" Mama asked.

"Close to fifty, I think." His voice held no inflection at all. He might as well be a key on the writing machine, tapping out the letters with no change whatsoever in modulation or tone. Just the steady clack, clack, clacking.

"A ballroom?"

"A grand salon that can certainly be used for entertaining."

"A library?"

"Yes."

"I assume the manor at the earl's family estate is much grander."

"At least four times this size."

Mama gasped. "How wonderful. I can hardly wait to see it."

He escorted them into a bright yellow room. "The countess's drawing room," he said as though reciting from a pamphlet.

"Yellow is a ghastly color for our complexions. I suppose my daughter may redecorate."

"Once my mother no longer resides within these walls, your daughter can do anything she likes with the rooms—except for the library. That will remain my domain."

"Where will your mother live?" Leonora asked.

"After my father passes, I thought to move her

into my London residence. It's somewhat smaller, less upkeep."

"When will that be?" Mama asked.

"Mama!" Leonora chastised.

He stopped beside a door of mullioned windows and rested his hand on the latch. "Unlike this marriage, madam, it's not something you can force into happening."

Quickly opening the door, he stepped out, missing her mother's unladylike snort. Leonora didn't have great hopes for this afternoon's success. But when she walked onto the terrace and set eyes on the woman standing beside the round white-linen-covered table, she felt a slight easing of the tension that had been with her ever since last night's debacle.

The Countess of Elverton came to her son's shoulder. Her brown hair, streaked with silver, also contained strands that looked almost red when the sun caught them just right. Her eyes held a kindness. For all of the dislike Rook had for his father, it was obvious he dearly loved this woman, and Leonora found herself wishing she'd be as fortunate to have his affection turned toward her.

But it was obvious he resented the situation in which he'd been placed, forced to marry her. She'd spent a restless night contemplating returning to New York, but Mama had made it clear that if she didn't go through with this marriage, she'd be on her own. She had used the money she'd saved over the years to keep the factory going, until her savings had dwindled to almost nothing. Who knew how long it might take her to find employment? How was she to survive in the meantime? Where was she to survive?

She'd been caught in a shameful act. Her mother would ensure no one welcomed her. The woman who'd given birth to her held all the cards. Finally, she was getting what she'd always wanted.

"Mother, allow me to introduce Mrs. Garrison, Miss Garrison, and Mr. Garrison."

Leonora was the first to curtsy. "My lady, it's truly an honor."

"Oh, no, my dear. The honor is mine." As Leonora straightened, the woman took her hands. "Marriages don't always come about as we like, but we make the best of it. Johnny speaks very fondly of you."

Leonora jerked her gaze to Rook. He was scowling, and she could just imagine what fond memories he might have. Surely he hadn't shared exactly what he'd done to her.

The countess moved on to her mother, although she didn't bother to take her hands. "Mrs. Garrison, I know we both want what is best for our children."

Leonora heard the steel in her voice and, judging by the way Mama's head reeled back slightly, she did as well. Before Mama could respond, Lady Elverton turned to Sam. "Mr. Garrison, I do hope in time that you will come to think of Johnny as a brother. Now, please, all of you, sit. We'll enjoy tea."

While two footmen moved forward to assist the countess and her mother in sitting, Rook saw to helping Leonora, although he did so without any touch, not even a secretive one. He'd never been so careful not to touch her. Rather than join them at the table, he settled into a nearby chair.

Leonora could sense Mama chomping at the bit. As soon as the countess had seen them all served tea, her mother went straight for what was foremost on her mind. "We want the marriage to happen as soon as possible, before the end of the Season, while people are still in London to attend. I was thinking Westminster."

"St. George's would be more acceptable to the *ton*. Based on the gossip I read in this morning's newspaper, I don't think you want to be upsetting any apple carts. Johnny can obtain a special license and a wedding could take place within the next week or two."

"She and I will both need new gowns."

"I have a seamstress who can see to that. A few extra coins and they can be made quickly. After all, this isn't the first wedding to happen in haste. The Chessmen are known for getting their ladies to the altar at a brisk pace. But we can discuss the details later." She turned her attention to Leonora. "Why do you want to marry my son?"

Did she want to? She didn't want to marry anyone. *Because we got caught. People know I'm a harlot. I need respectability to continue with the business.*

"Mother," Rook ground out.

"My apologies, Miss Garrison. I suppose it was unfair of me to ask. Johnny is the only one who needs to know why you want to marry him. The important thing to remember is that we all change through the passing years. Sometimes we grow together. Sometimes we grow apart. Don't you agree, Mrs. Garrison?"

"What I agree on is that your boy needs to do right by my girl."

"I don't believe he's given any indication that he

doesn't intend to do just that. And hopefully, your daughter will do right by him."

"She'll give him his heir. He needs to give her a wedding that will be written about in the New York papers. We're in this situation because of his inability to control—"

"Mama, I'm as much at fault. I didn't say no."

Rook stood up and held his hand out to her. "Take a walk about the gardens with me while they work out the details for the wedding I'll be paying for."

Even though she heard the bitterness in his voice, she put her hand in his, allowed him to pull her to her feet, and welcomed him escorting her into the gardens, away from her mother because being with him when he no doubt hated her was preferable to being anywhere near her mother when she was so insufferable. She had an insane thought that she'd spend hours out here, and then felt guilty for imagining this residence as her home.

"Wait up," Sam called out. She looked over her shoulder at him. He grinned at her. "You can't leave me to suffer through the bickering."

"My mother does not bicker," Rook said.

"No, but my mother does enough for both of them. Besides, she doesn't think the two of you should be left alone."

"What does it matter now when we're to marry?" Rook asked, and the disdain in his voice was beginning to grate on her nerves.

"Maybe we won't marry," she said tightly.

"We will. I'll not be accused of being a fornicator like my father. I'll not have it said that I take my pleasure and leave the woman to rot."

Her heart was tripping madly over itself. "Do you want to marry?"

His jaw went taut, and a muscle ticked in his cheek. She knew they'd been forced into the situation but considering all that had transpired last night before they'd been discovered, she'd thought surely he didn't completely object to having her as a wife.

"One thing you might not know about the nobility, Miss Garrison, is that we do what we are called upon to do."

She slipped her arm free of his and stepped away from him. "You don't have to marry me if it's so offensive to you."

"Doesn't matter what he wants, Nora. You have to marry him. No other man will marry you now. You're tainted goods."

Rook struck so fast, like a snake she'd once seen going after a rabbit, grabbing Sam by the scruff of his shirt and pulling him up slightly. Rook had such a hold on him that his knuckles were turning white. "You'll not talk to your sister with that sort of disrespect."

"But it's true. You've ruined her chances of marriage to anyone else."

"Don't you think I bloody well know that?" He looked over at her and she saw the resolve and regret in his eyes. "We will marry."

She considered stating clearly and distinctly they would not. But he was the answer to a prayer. He had the means to support the business and couldn't very well not do it when he was part of the family. But it was more than that. She craved the pleasure he could bring her. "Could you possibly not look quite so angry about it?"

He slammed his eyes closed. When he opened them, he flung Sam aside and pointed toward the far side of the garden. "Off with you."

Sam looked at her, a million questions reflected in his eyes. He appeared worried, and she nearly laughed. He thought some harm might come from a walk when he had no reservations about insisting she marry the man. "It's all right, Sam. No more damage can be done."

"Holler if you need me."

As though he was any match at all for Rook. Still, she nodded.

Reluctantly, he walked off.

"He's a little late in offering his protection." Rook didn't sound at all pleased.

"I suppose he never thought I needed it before. That I can take care of myself." Always before last night, she'd been able to do exactly that.

He indicated the path before them but this time he didn't offer his arm. She wasn't certain she would have taken it if he had.

ROOK HATED HOW much he still wanted her. Even now he was tempted to grab her, carry her behind the rose trellis, and kiss her senseless. As a result, he was clutching his hands behind his back to ensure he didn't do something that stupid.

"I didn't plan for us to get caught. I don't know how they knew . . . I should have been stronger. I should have resisted."

She seemed to take the blame for everything: the failing business, her brother's lack of business acumen, her mother's rudeness. He wasn't going to allow her to take the blame for what had transpired between them. "I would have simply pursued all the harder. I wanted you. I still do." Damn his cock.

"You don't sound happy about it."

He chuckled darkly. "This is not how I wanted a marriage to come about." Although he hadn't planned for one to come about at all. "I suspect it's not the courtship you had in mind either."

"Wasn't really a courtship, was it? I simply wanted to experience what I never had before."

Which was how they'd ended up where they were. Because he'd kept offering her new things to explore, to take apart and examine. "I assume your mother and brother will return to America once we're wed."

He could sense her gaze on him, but he kept looking forward because if he turned his attention to her, he was likely to pull her behind that damned rose trellis.

"We didn't obtain any investors last night." He heard the disappointment in her voice. "People were interested in the machine for a while but then they seemed more interested in what had occurred in the greenhouse than on the stage."

"Salacious gossip always takes priority. I doubt it helped matters that your mother was quick to let people know we'd be marrying."

"Therefore, we still need to find investors. When we do, I'll need to return to America for a while because you had the right of it: Sam knows nothing about the details."

He lost his battle not to gaze at her. She appeared to be as miserable as he. "I won't object."

Her laugh was a bit caustic. "I don't think I'm going

to make a very good wife. Because even if you had objected, I would go. I never intended to marry. I didn't want to lose my freedom."

"You won't be my captive, Nora. We'll work things out. All I ask is that we have no more scandal."

ROOK HAD LEFT the ladies with his mother, who would no doubt continue to charm them. Or at least she'd charm Nora. He suspected Mrs. Garrison was not subject to being charmed by anyone. And she certainly didn't seem to be in the habit of providing her own charm.

He'd brought Mr. Garrison to the library to discuss the settlement, which he suspected Nora would have a better handle on. Her brother remained as Keating had informed him that night when King had the family over for dinner—as eager to please as a puppy. Even seemed to have the energy of such a creature, one of his legs jiggling rapidly.

Rook had poured them each a glass a scotch, then taken his seat behind the desk while Garrison dropped into the tall-backed plush leather chair before it. Rook knew he was being obstinate, possibly ungracious. Under any other circumstance he'd have suggested they sit in the cozy area before the fireplace. But Garrison was partly responsible for them being here after all, having caught him in the act of defiling his sister. Although he also acknowledged that the majority of the responsibility fell to him because he couldn't seem to keep his hands or mouth off Nora. Or apparently his cock in his trousers where she was concerned.

He couldn't understand this pull—like the moon on

the tides—that she had on him. It confused, baffled, and irritated him all at once and yet something about it seemed . . . right. And he didn't understand that either. He wondered if she did. If she'd taken apart their relationship until she could make sense of it.

Therefore, he sat there studying her brother, waiting for the pup to come to realize that in this particular chess game the first move was Garrison's to make.

The young man's leg began to jiggle faster, his scotch half consumed. He glanced around and his gaze returned to Rook. "I supposed we should get on with it."

Rook slowly waved his hand over the desk. "Whenever you're ready."

"Right then. The factory." He shook his head. "The business. From the beginning, I decided to divide the entire thing into a hundred shares. I thought to give you twenty-five, in exchange for which, you'd provide the funding needed to carry on with our plans to manufacture and distribute this . . . writing machine."

If Garrison had, in fact, made any of these decisions, Rook would be shocked. Most of the words had come out like a recitation, and he suspected that in fact it was Nora who had determined how to allocate the business. And he imagined she'd done it before they'd ever boarded a ship to come here. She'd have had every minute detail worked out, to avoid any cock-ups.

Rook took a slow sip of scotch before saying, "That's not how marriage settlements work."

Garrison's eyes widened and Rook realized his tone had come out a bit harsh. He'd never enjoyed negotiating with a novice. And he was left with the impression that those in her family were not looking out for Nora's best interests.

Garrison leaned forward, pressing his elbows to his thighs, which at least served the purpose of stopping his leg from bouncing. "I don't understand. I give you something. You give me something."

"I'm giving your sister respectability." He settled back in his chair. "A woman usually comes with a dowry, which is handed over to the future husband as part of an understanding that he will use it to see that the lady is cared for."

"A dowry? Nora doesn't have a dowry. We never expected her to marry."

"Why not?"

"Well . . ." Garrison glanced around as though he might find the answer written on the wallpaper, or lurking in the wainscotting, or nestled in the books. With his brow furrowed, he brought his gaze back to Rook as though he expected him to know the answer and was finding it difficult to believe he was going to have to voice the words aloud. "Well, she's . . . odd, isn't she?"

A wave of anger washed over him and delivered him to the shore of fury. That her brother would describe her thusly was unconscionable. He should have admired her. Garrison knew firsthand who was actually managing the company, who was striving to make it solvent. "How? So?"

The young man must have realized that he was treading on dangerous ground and needed to lighten his steps if he didn't want to fall through whatever support was beneath him and plummet to his doom. "She's not like other women."

"No woman is like any other woman. It's what makes each one unique. The reason for courtship is to judge similarities and differences. If they were all the same, it wouldn't matter who the hell you married. So again, how exactly is she . . . odd?"

Her brother swallowed, lowered his gaze to the edge of the desk for several minutes before finally lifting it. "She doesn't conform to what one expects in a female. She is fascinated by parts that cause things to move. Do you know Mama has to practically hog-tie her to get her to the dressmakers? She has a scant wardrobe and traveled over here with fewer trunks than I did. She finds shopping and fittings a waste of her time." Of course she did. "What lady does that?"

"An interesting one."

His guest looked as if he'd just had a bucket of freezing water tossed on him. He also appeared to be experiencing some guilt at the aspersions he'd made regarding his sister. "I do like her, of course. But I've seen men laugh at her, mock her."

"Then they're idiots and you're an arse for not punching each and every one of them."

"Some are my friends."

"Then you're an even bigger arse for placing a friendship over Nora."

"They weren't being mean—"

"Of course they were. Those who laugh at another's expense or mock them are bullies, not to be tolerated." He knew that well enough because his father had been one.

"She never knew."

But she had. She'd told him so. Perhaps their cruelty had driven her further into isolation, searching for a place where she was in control. Conquering machines provided that sense of being a goddess and powerful. "Of course she knew."

Garrison blanched. Then he jerked up his chin. "You wouldn't marry her if you weren't being forced. We all see how unhappy you are about it."

"I'm not happy for the way it came about, but I assure you that I shall see her well cared for. And that, Mr. Garrison, is what you should be striving to ascertain: if I will be a good husband to her. I don't need her to have a dowry." He gave a curt wave of his hand over the desk as if to brush aside any currency offered. "I have wealth enough. I will not take any shares in your business nor will I invest in it as terms of the marriage." Leaning forward, he placed his forearms on the desk. "Answer me this, Mr. Garrison. How did your mother know to gather a group of people and look in the greenhouse?"

Guilt washing over his features, the young man quickly dropped his gaze to the floor.

"Garrison?" His tone was that of a man who commanded the room, one he used if he sensed anyone striving to swindle him with the lure of a fake investment. He knew it could be both threatening and scary.

Nora's brother finally met his gaze. "Mama saw her go out into the garden so she had me follow her. By the time I got out there, you were walking toward the greenhouse. I peered in . . . and saw the shadows. Since I couldn't find her in the gardens and know she's not comfortable with crowds, that she often seeks someplace where she can be alone for a while . . . and as you'd gone in and I'd seen the way you look at her . . .

like a lean and hungry wolf . . . I assumed her to be the woman in your arms."

"You betrayed her."

"No, I tried to save her from you taking advantage."

"If that was true, you'd have burst through the door and done everything in your power to stop me from making any untoward advances. You wouldn't have gone to get others to serve as witnesses."

"You won't tell Nora, will you?"

He was tempted but she'd experienced enough hurt. "No good would come of it. Now, I will tell you how the terms of this settlement will work. You're going to give half of the business to Nora as a wedding present."

"But she has no money. We'll still have no funds for changing the factory. A few people expressed an interest in investing, but they haven't come through yet. And that won't be enough."

"She'll have money once we wed. As much as she wants from my coffers, to do with as she pleases. But any investors will be purchasing your shares, not hers. She retains the fifty percent. And should I learn differently, if you don't adhere to my demands, you'll discover that being my brother-by-marriage will not spare you from my wrath." He shoved himself to his feet. "I believe we're done here, Mr. Garrison."

"HE SAYS I'M to give you half the company as a wedding gift," Sam said quietly, almost dazedly as if he couldn't quite believe it.

Rook had come onto the terrace and announced, "We've agreed to a settlement." After which, he'd called for his carriage and ushered her along with her family into it.

Now they were on their way back to the hotel, and those were the first words her brother had uttered since they'd begun the journey. Somehow Leonora wasn't surprised that Rook wouldn't take what she and Sam had decided that morning would serve as her dowry.

"Then what are we to give him as the settlement?" she asked.

Sam lifted one shoulder in a careless shrug. "Nothing. He doesn't want anything."

"Therefore, we'll still have the shares so we can have investors."

"Only mine. He demanded we not sell yours."

"He can't order us about when it comes to the business," Mama said. "It belongs to Sam. I'll damned well let him know that."

"He won't like it," Sam said.

"As though I give a fig what he won't like. This marriage will come about on our terms. We're the offended party here. He took advantage of a young, innocent—"

So now, she was *young* and not on the shelf? "He didn't take advantage." How many times was she going to have to say it before they listened and accepted the truth. "I wanted—"

"We won't need investors," Sam interrupted.

Leonora had the feeling she wasn't going to like this. "Why not?"

"Because he says once you're married you can have as much of his money as you want, to do with as you want."

"Ah, that's more like it," Mama said triumphantly. "Well done, Sam."

Although Leonora suspected Sam had, in truth, had very little to do with any of this, a suspicion that was confirmed when he shifted in his seat like a schoolboy who'd gotten caught cheating on an exam.

She turned her attention to the buildings passing by. She didn't want Rook's money. What she wanted more than anything, she suddenly realized, was his love. How were they to ever get to that point, if they were forced into a marriage neither wanted? If it was more to her benefit than his? What was he getting out of it? A wife he'd never wanted. The terms for marriage made it an uneven exchange. To work properly, machines needed to maintain a balance. Like a pendulum. They placed pennies on it to add weight when it needed to be slowed; removed them when it needed to swing faster. Otherwise, the clock wouldn't keep the proper time.

She suspected a marriage worked in much the same way, required a delicate balancing. How could they achieve that if the only thing he was getting was her?

CHAPTER 21

⟋⟍⟍⟋⟍⟋⟍

MUCH later that night, Rook became the Earl of Elverton, a title with no respect, no honor. If he could have avoided taking it, he would have. But no provision in the law allowed a man to turn away from the responsibility thrust upon him at birth.

However, he felt the weight of the obligation to return dignity to the title crushing him.

As he swigged scotch in his mother's favorite room, the one of bright yellow that apparently didn't suit some complexions, he tried to bring forth a pleasant memory of his father, but it seemed for most of his life they'd been adversaries more than anything. The earl had resented any good fortune that befell Rook . . . as though he'd deemed his heir unworthy of even a scintilla of happiness.

He rather feared his father would have taken delight in his son's current predicament. *You see, lad, you're no different than me. You're ruled by your cock.*

Except his cock would be faithful. He'd never stray from his marriage vows.

His mother had stood stoically silent as the earl had been taken away to be prepared for his funeral. Now occupying a nearby settee, she sipped her cognac. "I often thought he'd have been happier if he'd been in-fertile . . . or impotent. I don't know why he became so unlikable over the years. Or perhaps, I simply stopped making excuses for him, saw him as he was rather than how I wished he was."

"For what it's worth, you were in his life the longest so he must have held some affection for you."

Her laugh was caustic. "Yes, well, I think it may have been because I was the least amount of trouble." She held silent for a while before saying, "I assume you'll let Aiden know his father has passed."

"I've already sent word to Aiden and Finn." Al-though he certainly hadn't referred to the man as their father. Rather he'd merely written *The earl has de-parted this world*. He'd rather wished he'd had Nora's writing machine so there would have been more dis-tance between him and the words, to let the uniform letters make them appear less personal.

"It pleases me that you and Aiden have become friends."

They were more than friends. They were brothers in the truest sense of the word. "Surprisingly, for two lads raised apart, we have a lot in common."

For several minutes, only the crackling of the fire on the hearth and the ticking of the clock on the man-tel could be heard. He suspected, like him, she was recalling how Aiden had come back into her life. Ser-endipitously. The earl's evil ways had taken him away and they had returned him.

"A small, private funeral would probably also be best," his mother said.

"No."

Her brow furrowed. "Why not?"

"His bastards should have a chance to—" *Spit on him.* "I don't know who all of his children are. They should have an opportunity to attend, to sit in the area designated for the family. Perhaps even Matthew and Mark will be there." They were her first two children.

She smiled sadly. "I suspect they are long dead. Most are, Johnny." For the first time since he'd arrived after receiving her missive, tears welled in her eyes. "When Aiden was born, I wanted so badly to keep him. I named him Luke. He was the third one to whom I gave birth, and your father had taken the other two away. I begged him to allow me to hold onto him. I'd see to it that he wasn't a bother. But he gave me a choice: continue to live a life of ease in the posh residence he provided or keep my son and live on the streets. I gave over my third son. I often wonder . . . what sort of mother did that make me?"

"A protective one. I'm sure it didn't feel like it at the time, but without the earl's benevolence, how would you have kept Aiden or yourself alive? Even if you'd been allowed to keep him, his life would have been misery, a constant reminder to the earl of what he didn't want. As you're well aware, he had a tendency to permanently rid himself of people he didn't want in his life."

"Like his first wife, who had failed to conceive," she said softly. "At the time, when she died, it never occurred to me he might have been instrumental in bringing about her demise. When he married me, I'd hoped it was out of love, but I suspect it was because I was so fertile, and he needed his heir. Therefore, I got to keep the fourth. You. But the life of ease was never truly easy, even when I was his wife and not his whore."

"Don't use that word," he snapped as the anger roiled through him. "That's not what you were."

"My darling son, your mother was no saint."

"You're a saint to me."

She laughed lightly. "Every mother should be so fortunate to have a son like you."

He took another swallow of scotch. "I'm sorry to have been responsible for bringing more scandal into your life."

"I assume you're referring to your upcoming nuptials."

He nodded.

"People will forget it in time." She waved a hand through the air. "Another scandal will divert their attention away from yours."

"I never wanted to be anything like him."

"You're *not*. You've always been such a comfort to me."

He set his glass aside. "I'm going out for a while, but I'll return to see how you're faring. Will probably stay here tonight." Probably every night after as well.

"Give her my best."

He furrowed his brow. "I'm going to spend time with the Chessmen." Even though they were probably all abed at this late hour.

She smiled softly. "Of course you are, darling."

He *had* planned to rouse his mates from bed and drink himself into oblivion with them at his club, following a toast to all their fathers—the men who had unwittingly and unknowingly been responsible for providing them with a common cause and bringing them all together. Hence, he was a bit surprised when he found himself tapping lightly on a door that led into a suite of rooms on the top floor of the Trewlove Hotel.

The door finally opened a fraction and a wide-eyed maid peered out.

"Will you let Miss Garrison know—without disturbing her mother or brother"—he held out five quid to her—"that . . . her betrothed wishes a word." He couldn't yet force the words *Earl of Elverton* past his lips.

With a snick, she closed the door. A few minutes later, Nora was standing there in her nightclothes, her dressing gown cinched tightly at her waist, her hair plaited and draped over her shoulder. "Your father's died," she said without preamble.

He'd always been so skilled at shielding his emotions. What the devil did his face show? Still, he nodded.

"Wait there." The door again closed, but in a blink, she'd returned, her pelisse draped over her and pulled close around her. She joined him in the hallway.

"Are you still in your nightclothes?"

"I'm adequately covered and there's no one about to see. I'd invite you in, but the last thing you need is for Mama to awaken and begin gloating that her daughter will be marrying an earl. There's a lovely park a short distance from here. It'll offer us a place to talk without being disturbed." She closed her hand around his— hers so warm, his so cold. He didn't understand what was happening to him.

But he didn't object as she led him out of the hotel, across the street, and down another street. The area was well-lit. Mick Trewlove had taken a desolate part of London and turned it into an idyllic spot for the up-and-coming.

After a while, they crossed over to a grassy field dotted with elms. He knew when the sun was out that it was a beautiful expanse of green. When they reached the first tree, she released her hold on him, lowered herself to the ground, and patted the area beside her. He couldn't imagine any other lady of his acquaintance being so unconcerned with the impropriety or the possibility of grass stains. Yet one of the things he liked about her was that she was so incredibly unpretentious.

He dropped down beside her and worked his back against the tree trunk until he found a comfortable position.

"How is your mother taking the loss?"

It pleased him that her first thought revolved around his mother. "She's made of steel, my mother, but I think his going hit her harder than she'd expected." He wondered if Aiden might send that fellow from his club who'd given her attention over to the residence to comfort her.

"Even when we're expecting the death, it still seems to come as a shock when it happens. At least my father's did. I assume you sent word to Aiden."

"Yes, and his brother Finn. As well as the *Times*. They'll no doubt do a special edition."

"You're in mourning now. We'll need to postpone the wedding."

He looked over at her. Most of her was lost to the shadows, except for a faint beam of moonlight and distant streetlamps that illuminated her face. "Your mother won't like it, but we can have a small, quiet ceremony sooner. Close friends, family."

He didn't move when she reached up and combed back strands of his hair that had fallen across his brow. "I'd prefer that actually to the extravagant and attention-getting affair Mama was planning, expecting you to pay for it all."

"I would have. If it's what you wanted." He owed her that for his lapse of control. When she began to move her hand away, he took it and pressed a kiss to the center of her palm. "No honor comes with the title to which you'll be associated."

She brought up her knees, pressed her cheek to them, and studied him. "The holder was dishonorable, not the title."

"Few separate the man from the title." In spite of the aristocracy usually being given a lot of leeway when it came to misguided behavior, his father had pompously flaunted his sins, making them difficult to overlook.

"People know you. They understand you're not him."

He looked up. Clouds of gray blocked out the sight of the stars. He wondered if he'd have many moments like this with her, when desire wasn't rampaging through him, when he experienced contentment in simply being with her. The calmness of her, the quiet. If he were with the Chessmen, they'd be tossing back scotch and recalling all the times his father had been an unconscionable bastard, justifying this lack of feeling he held for the man who had sired him.

"When I was around six, I was racing along the hallways, slate in hand, because I'd just written my father's title without any help from my tutor. I wanted him to see how perfect the letters were. But when I rushed into the library, in my haste, I bumped into a small table upon which some statuette sat. It teetered and toppled onto the floor, and of course broke. My father came to his feet and shouted that I was a damned irritating brat. His anger had me immediately running off to get out of his sight, to hide, rather than show him the prize. That night he woke me from my sleep and told me to dress quickly because we had a chore to tend to. I was so happy to be included, overjoyed that he wanted me with him.

"Soon we were traveling through London, the rain pelting the carriage. I have no memory of the precise time or if I even ever knew it. But I do recall many of the streets being deserted, desolate. We came to a halt in front of a town house. I was ordered to wait. My father disappeared inside and returned several minutes later with a crying babe in his arms. In the doorway stood a weeping woman in a nightdress, keening, 'I beg of you don't take her!'

"But my father leapt into the carriage. The infant bawled the entire journey, her tiny fists flailing. I was too young to comprehend the role of the woman and babe in his life. Mistress and by-blow. Eventually, we stopped in front of a tavern. A crone stepped out of the shadows. The earl handed off the babe and a pouch that jingled from the coins housed within it.

"Then we were off again, dashing through the drenched streets, with the rain pelting the carriage roof in an ominously steady beat. 'Tis easy enough to rid myself of damned irritating brats,' he said."

She gasped in horror. "Dear Lord, but you were his heir. Surely, he wouldn't have given you away."

"As I grew older, I became rather certain it was a bluff, but at the time I didn't fully comprehend the importance of being the heir, of exactly what it meant, and how it quite possibly made me indispensable. What I did understand was the anger in his tone and the threat. Afterward I avoided him the best I could, moving around stealthily, keeping silent, always fearful I'd awaken his wrath, hoping he might forget I even existed. When I couldn't elude him, I would be as still as I could be, quiet. I never sought his attention. I doubt there was a more properly behaved lad in all of Britain."

"Didn't your mother reassure you that you were safe from his threats?"

"I never told her. I was ashamed for her to know I'd displeased him. And I worried if I told her that he might decide to rid himself of her. I grew to hate him. Or I thought it was hate burning through me. Until eventually I realized it was grief. Overwhelming grief because he was not the father I wanted—needed—him to be. I should feel that grief now but after all these years of experiencing it, I am numb to it. I feel rage, though, at all the people he hurt."

She rubbed his shoulder. "I think he hurt you most of all, caused damage."

He started to scoff, to deny her words, but his life rolled before him. It was like looking through a kaleidoscope, watching as the various colors shifted into different images. All the decisions he'd made that had been influenced by his sire. His efforts not to be like him. His desire, his need, to demonstrate he was above reproach, to provide an example of proper behavior.

That example would now include being caught in flagrante delicto with this woman who wasn't deserving of the scandal. Who was being forced to marry him. Without a proper courtship. Without romantic gestures. Without wooing. Just raw lust, barbaric impulses, and an animalistic need to possess.

Yet here he was, coming to her when he had other choices. What the deuce was this pull she had on him? Yet, he didn't truly want to be anywhere else.

"I thought you should know that I'm the sort of man who feels no sorrow at his father's passing."

"I wouldn't expect you to. Everything you've told me about him . . . he was horrid. I'm glad he's gone, that you don't have to carry the weight of him any longer." She shifted until she was facing him, and he was grateful for the absence of the light of day. It was so much easier to confess emotions he'd rather not feel. "You are nothing at all like him."

"Nora, I took you in a bloody greenhouse. Windows all around. Anyone could have seen in. Your brother did. I ruined you for any other man."

Enough illumination existed for him to see her teasing smile. The tightness that had been in his chest since his arrival at her door eased somewhat, that even now she could smile. "Even if we hadn't gotten caught, you'd already ruined me for any other man. From the beginning, you offered me so many things to explore. You never judged my need to understand how things worked . . . whether it was a kiss or a roulette wheel. Let me ask you this. If I had said no last night, would you have stopped?"

"Of course."

"Did I say no?"

"I don't believe I gave you a chance."

"I seem to recall saying I wanted what you were offering. You are not your father. I couldn't—" She stopped, shook her head. "I wouldn't like you as much as I do if you resembled him in any way."

Shifting until she was straddling his hips, she took his face between her hands and pressed her lips to his. No fire, no hunger, and yet he felt as though there had never been a more powerful coming together of their mouths. He wrapped his arms around her, holding her close, wondering how it was that she knew what he needed when he hadn't known. But this quietness, this comforting, was a balm to his soul. *She* was a calming to the years of rage that had been festering within him. How often he'd wished to be the progeny of a better man.

Yet at that moment, with her tender ministrations, he dared to believe that his unprincipled sire was without influence. He was grateful that she'd never known the scapegrace, that she'd never been soiled by his father's attentions. Although the man would have found her to be a formidable player—analyzing him, working him out. Because that was what she did. She was the most powerful piece on the chessboard. His queen.

Drawing away, she sat back and held his gaze. In spite of the shadows. They held no sway over her . . . or him. He realized that even if they were in complete darkness, still they'd find each other. He dared not give a name to all the emotions ratcheting through him. What he did know was that he was grateful she was here with him now.

"I'll be busy arranging the funeral, seeing him interred in the crypt at the family estate. But I should have all these duties behind me by the end of next week. We'll marry then."

"Isn't there an old adage about marrying in haste and repenting at leisure?"

"I shall do all in my power to ensure you don't regret this marriage. But I did wonder if I might trouble you for a favor."

"Do you ever wonder exactly how many of us there are?" Earlier the following afternoon, Rook had sent word to Aiden and Finn to meet him at the Mermaid and Unicorn, a tavern in Whitechapel, that evening.

The two men were studying him now. While Finn was fairer than he or Aiden, Rook could detect shades of his father in the man's features—his jaw, nose, brow.

"By us . . ." Aiden's voice trailed off in question.

"Elverton's children."

"You're Elverton now," Aiden said.

Rook shook his head. "Trust me, it brings me no pride, but still I'm wondering how many children he might have sired. Based on Mother's experiences, he took each of her sons almost immediately after he was born in order to lessen any attachment she might feel toward the infant." He scoffed. "To spare her anguish, he'd claimed, but if he'd truly meant that he'd have never taken them to begin with. However, I assume he did the same with his other children. The two of you were delivered to Ettie Trewlove within six weeks of each other, so it's highly likely he often didn't go even a year between children, especially as he would have multiple mistresses at the same time. I'm not certain when he started this practice. As a young man, presumably. If we factor in the span of his life, we could be looking at close to thirty or forty years of by-blows."

"Surely he took an occasional break from fornicating," Finn said.

Rook shrugged. "Seems unlikely. Sometimes I look at servants or workers and wonder if we're related. Of course, he didn't limit his lovers to commoners." As far as he knew, his sire had never dallied with married women, so he didn't suspect any among the aristocracy of being unknown siblings.

"No, he didn't," Aiden ground out before tossing

back his scotch and refilling his glass with the bottle the serving girl had left for them. He scoffed harshly. "He was giving Selena far too much attention for my liking when she was first widowed."

They all knew now that the earl had hoped to make her his next countess—once he'd rid himself of his current wife.

"Why are you troubled by all this now?" Finn asked. "The man is finally gone, his reign of debauchery over."

It was an idea he'd been considering for a while. "I never thought to ask, but how did you each know he was your sire?"

"He personally delivered both Finn and me to a baby farmer he thought wouldn't properly care for us, expecting us to perish. His coat of arms was on his carriage and Mum made note of it. However, one night when I confronted him, he bragged that he gave most of his paramours the name of the person to whom the babe was to be delivered and a pouch of coins to cover the cost. I think he only saw to it himself if he cared at all for the woman and wanted to spare her any suffering. I can only assume, then, that based on that he did have a perverted sort of fondness for our mum and Finn's."

"I imagine that brought them little consolation."

"If I had to give my child away, I'd tuck a note in the babe's nappy explaining who the father was," Finn said. "Maybe the other mums did the same, if they could write."

"He had standards, our sire," Aiden stated flatly. "Johnny here and me, our mother is the daughter of a baron. Although he seemed to like variety, I don't think he would have gone with an uneducated lass. If the mother was delivering the babe herself, he wasn't there to stop them from providing as much information as they wanted. Some of the women may have even held onto his babe, in spite of the harsh life that would have resulted when he abandoned them." His jaw clenched. "Damn, but he was vile."

Last night, with Nora, Rook had felt that some of that vileness had been washed off him, but still much remained. "Therefore, some, if not all, might know they came from his loins."

"What are you thinking, Johnny?" Finn asked. "Thought we were here to toast his going to hell, but these questions . . ."

"All these children he sired . . . they are our brothers and sisters. If they had been born within the boundaries of his marriage, I would have been responsible for seeing to their care, for ensuring they had an allowance after he passed. I realize some—like the two of you—may have achieved success but for those who may be struggling, I want to use the opportunity of his death to make whatever amends I can. I'm having broadsheets printed and putting an announcement in the newspapers, inviting his by-blows to come to my residence the day following his funeral service to receive financial recompense. I suspect they won't all be able to read, so it is my hope that the two of you, who know the darker parts of London better than I, will help me spread the word."

"What were you considering for recompense?" Finn asked.

"Twenty-five quid a month."

"As you said, you're talking forty years of by-blows. How wealthy are you?"

"Wealthy enough."

The Trewlove brothers exchanged a glance. Rook envied how, having grown up within each other's shadow, they could effectively communicate without using any words. His father, obviously finding no joy in having children, had been willing to risk having only an heir and not a spare. Rook had never known loneliness until Eton. He thought he'd adjusted until it no longer mattered but at times like this, he experienced sharp pangs of feeling isolated, missed having someone who not only knew but understood his very soul. Someone whose soul he'd explored to its very depths. But even as he had those thoughts, images of Nora floated through his mind.

Leaning back, Aiden crossed his arms over his chest. "You do realize that you're likely to have people arrive at your door who are *not* related to us in any manner whatsoever. They'll see your generosity as an opportunity to take advantage, to put coins in their pockets."

"I'm not a fool, Aiden. I'm well aware that in some instances, that will be the case. But if, through this action, I'm able to help even *one* of my true half-siblings who is in need—because there must be some, like you and Finn, who knew he was their father—I will consider it worth the cost."

CHAPTER 22

LEONORA sat in Rook's front parlor serving tea—so much tea—to those who were awaiting an audience with him. The favor he'd asked of her was to serve as hostess at his residence as he met with his father's offspring.

The number was shocking really. At first, they'd trickled in. She hadn't bothered to count, but then they'd begun to arrive in greater numbers, and now every seat was occupied, and some people were standing along the walls. If she had to guess, she'd say close to a dozen people had either already spoken with him or were waiting to. He met with each individually in his library. They'd probably be here all afternoon and possibly into evening.

The butler had been charged with writing the visitors' names in a little notebook before escorting them into the parlor where Leonora greeted them and strove to make them feel at home. A footman escorted out those who had spent time with Rook and then escorted the next in line to the library. And Leonora served them tea.

The guests ranged in ages from the very young, who were with their mothers, to those who looked to be

older than Rook. Some had obviously dressed in fin-
ery for the occasion, as best as they could anyway. She
suspected the majority lived in poverty. Or close to it.

He had told her what a monster his father was, but
now she was seeing the proof of it. She didn't doubt
that those claiming to be his by-blows had in fact
come from his loins because she could see shadows of
Rook in every face. In the jaw, the chin, the nose, or
the eyes. The cheeks, the build.

What must it be like for him to face the reality of
what had been merely rumors? She was grateful and
admired him for sparing his mother a glimpse of the
evidence of her husband's unfaithfulness. She knew
that even if he wasn't happy about how their marriage had come about, Rook would never not honor
his vows.

It seemed wrong that they should both spend the
remainder of their lives paying the price for a lack of
discretion. No, they had been discreet. Except Mama
had been watching her like a hawk. She'd seen an opportunity to have the lord she'd craved as a son-by-
marriage and she'd pounced. Leonora felt like she had
that first night at the Elysium: a man being sent to her
out of obligation, not desire. She didn't want that in a
marriage. While he no longer seemed angry regarding
their circumstance, she would hardly categorize him
as joyful regarding their future together.

She continued to have doubts concerning the path
they were treading. It reminded her of a cog with one
of its protrusions broken or out of alignment, so it
never properly fit with its mate to get the job done.
Always just a little bit off. No steady rhythm.

The butler escorted a woman into the room. She

was petite in stature, with hair raven black, and stunning eyes of emerald green. At her side was a young boy who couldn't have been older than ten. Leonora smiled at her. "Would you care for some tea?"

"Yes, thank you."

As she prepared the tea, Leonora said, "I'm Leonora Garrison, a . . . friend to his lordship." She couldn't quite bring herself to use the identifier of *his betrothed*. She recalled he'd once told her that how people addressed him indicated their place in his life. She was realizing the same applied to how she viewed herself. More friend than future wife.

"Rachel."

Leonora's breath caught and the teacup rattled on the saucer she held with a hand that had suddenly become unsteady. How many Rachels could the earl have taken as mistresses? "Your father's not in shipping, is he?"

The woman's smile was wistful. "The last I heard he was. Could Jack have some lemonade?"

Jack, no doubt a pet name for John. Johnny. Her Johnny who may have been this woman's Johnny.

"Yes, of course." She poured him a glass and offered it to him. He'd not inherited his mother's green eyes. His were as dark as Rook's. His hair was the same shade. And she thought as he got older, his jaw would become more pronounced, stronger, sturdier, and it would look very much like Rook's. "A chair has just been vacated in the back corner."

She watched as the woman moved toward it. She wanted to send her on her way. How dare she come here and remind Rook of one of the worst days, when his heart had been shattered. Her fury had nothing to do with the fact that he had once loved the woman, had planned to propose to her, and follow the gesture with a bonanza of fireworks. Nor did she want the reminder that he neither loved nor had proposed to Leonora.

As though in a trance, she poured tea, heard names called, and watched people leave the room one by one to have their audience with their half brother. If she looked to the doorway, sometimes she'd see the solitary figures strutting past as they headed for the front door and their exit, all seeming far more relaxed and content on their way out than they had on their way in.

Then suddenly, completely unaware of it actually happening, she was alone with Rachel and the boy. No one else had arrived. All the others had been seen to. The butler didn't come call for her. The residence suddenly seemed deathly quiet, the way the air did before a storm hit.

"You're not a servant," Rachel said quietly, her voice sounding as though it came from a great distance, years in fact. A decade perhaps.

"No."

"You're the woman he's going to marry. I saw mention of it in the newspaper. How it came about seemed quite scandalous. He always avoided any sort of scandal. He was always so . . . perfect. Never did anything he ought not."

"Unlike you." Rachel looked as though she'd taken a blow. Leonora shook her head. "My apologies. That was uncalled-for."

"But true. I craved excitement and he was so . . . terribly well-behaved. Staid. Sedate. So mindful of what he shouldn't do. No clandestine trysts in the gardens. No untoward advances. Never touching me where he shouldn't."

"A gentleman, then," Leonora couldn't help but say.

Rachel nodded. "Only I didn't want a gentleman. I wanted to be wild. His father seemed to understand what I craved and was willing to provide it. He did so with a promise that we wouldn't get caught. Of course, we did. The look of betrayal on Johnny's face has haunted me all these years. How could it not? Not his father's perfidy but mine. I knew he wouldn't take me back. He'd always told me I was flawless, like a diamond. But I had imperfections. And he rather likes perfection."

Perfection? Leonora suspected he preferred loyalty. Her gaze wandered over to the boy, who was studying her with large brown eyes, slowly blinking. Her children might favor him. If they had children.

The butler stepped into the room. "Miss Kennedy."

Leonora gave a little start. She stood. "I'll accompany her, thank you."

Knowing she would soon be mistress of this household, the butler gave a quick nod and retreated. Leonora turned to Rachel. She'd risen and her hand was resting protectively on her son's head. "If you'll be kind enough to follow me."

She wanted to usher her right out the front door, worried about the painful memories the woman might stir to life—but then she suspected the people who had visited today had all managed to do that anyway. She assumed Rook would have rather not faced each of the children his father had spawned, would have preferred not to have had confirmed all the vicious rumors that there were so many. These might not be all. Only the ones who had survived, the ones who had seen his broadsheets or read in the newspaper about his willingness to assist them.

"He didn't live here when I knew him," Rachel said softly.

"His mother will soon be taking up residence here."

"I wouldn't have thought he'd want to live where his father had."

She couldn't imagine that Rook would run from his past. Strolling into the library, she saw him standing at the sideboard, pouring himself a scotch. She wondered if he even had a hint as to who would have an audience with him next.

Turning, he smiled at her, his features softening, but when his gaze shifted slightly, she saw him physically bracing himself as he again became the formidable castle that couldn't be breached.

"I'll leave you to speak with your guest," she said, hating that there was a tremble in her voice.

"I'd rather you stayed, if you don't mind."

Only if I can hold you, take away the pain I saw ratchet through you. "Of course."

After tossing back the scotch, he shoved a thick cushioned leather chair closer to his desk, on the side where he would sit, and with his eyes holding hers, indicated it was for her. He stood there, a silent sentinel, until he'd assisted her in sitting. Her lungs felt like mighty bellows, the air she was taking in too hot for comfort, as he moved behind his desk. "Rachel, I hadn't expected you to come here."

The woman he'd once loved, for whom he might still hold feelings, took several tentative steps forward, leading the boy by resting one of her hands lightly on his head of dark curls. "I wanted you to meet your brother . . . Jack."

Leonora's breath rushed out with the force of a

tempest and only then did she realize that she'd been wondering if the boy was Rook's son. Although he'd claimed to have no by-blows, perhaps he simply hadn't known. He was so passionate with her, gave her the impression that he couldn't resist her—but he didn't love her, had never voiced the words. If he could hardly keep his hands or mouth off her, how could he have resisted someone he loved? In spite of the woman's earlier confession that he had done exactly that.

From where she sat, she could see the warmth filling his eyes. He wasn't going to hold the lad's mother's actions against him. "It's an honor to make your acquaintance, Jack. You're quite the handsome fellow. I see a good bit of our father in you."

The boy beamed, then sobered. "I never met him."

"Few of his children did. But that was a failing on his part. You hold no responsibility for it." He leaned forward slightly, his focus on Jack, as though on the verge of imparting a secret. "He wasn't the best of fathers to be honest. However, should he have spent any time in your company, I think he would have thought you remarkable." Straightening, he waved his hand toward the chairs in front of the desk. "Please, you should both sit."

Once they were settled, he dropped into his chair. "I can offer you one hundred pounds a month for Jack's care, which is quadruple what I offered anyone else—child or adult—who was in need."

Leonora fought not to gasp. She'd had no idea he was providing an income for these people. An atrocious amount. Was he going to go bankrupt? How wealthy was he?

"We're going to get right to business, then, are we?" Rachel asked.

"Isn't that the reason you're here?"

"I thought we might visit first. How are you? Glad your father's gone, I suspect."

Leonora found the woman to be cold. Rook's father was also Jack's father. Should she proclaim so little regard for him in front of her son?

"I suspect Jack here is the reason you are no longer with him."

She nodded. "He offered me a choice: keep the babe or keep him. I chose the harder route and left him. It took a while but having grown up around the docks and having an understanding of the various aspects of shipping, I was able to find employment, keeping track of inventory for Mr. Martin Parker. He has several large merchandise stores. I'll never be wealthy, mind you, but I have been able to ensure that my son never went hungry. Do you ever see my father?"

"Occasionally."

"Is he well?"

"He is. And successful."

Tears welled in her eyes. "It's amazing how your life can be destroyed in only a few minutes." She shifted her gaze from Rook to Leonora, and she was left with the sense that this woman was trying to warn her.

In only a few minutes, with a discovery, her own life's path had been diverted. Everything she'd planned, everything she'd hoped for was no more. Instead, it was church bells and a life over here, a life she'd never considered wanting. It seemed wrong that her dreams had to be put aside because her mother wanted to step into a particular ballroom. She was more sympathetic toward Rook's desire to be seen as a man who kept to the moral high ground, but she'd found that when it came to sexual transgressions, men were more easily forgiven than women. Men, especially those of the aristocracy, seldom were tainted because of their passionate natures. That had been the overarching theme of *My Secret Desires*, a book she'd recently read.

"Will you tell him what a fine lad his grandson is?" Rachel asked.

"Perhaps you should."

"He won't give me an audience. I was such a disappointment, you see. But then I suppose I was a disappointment to you as well."

"We're not here to discuss our past. I'm striving to make amends to those the previous earl fathered."

"It's so like you to feel responsible for his actions."

"I don't feel responsible for his actions. I do, however, intend to return some dignity to the title he held that has now come to me. One hundred pounds. If you wish to receive it"—without taking his eyes from her, he reached for a piece of foolscap and moved it to the far end of the desk—"write down where it should be delivered each month."

The woman squeezed her eyes shut and pressed her lips firmly together until they disappeared. Leonora wondered if she was struggling with her pride. Or was it the amount that caused her to hesitate? She gave a barely perceptible nod, opened her eyes, and patted her son's shoulder as though to convey this was for him. Then she leaned forward, dipped pen in inkwell, and began scrawling out the information.

Leonora had never wished so hard that the writing machine wasn't so heavy, was more easily transportable from place to place because she suddenly realized why people thought it impersonal. She didn't want Rook looking at that bit of paper each month and thinking about the woman who had left her clearly identifiable mark upon it. As well as upon his heart.

In all these years, why had he never loved anyone else? Why had he never courted anyone? She was struck with the awful realization that perhaps he was still in love with Rachel.

When she was finished, Rachel placed the tips of her fingers at the bottom of the paper and moved it toward him in a manner that reminded Leonora of tiptoeing through their hotel room, striving not to be caught sneaking out or in late at night. Taking it, Rook placed it on a small stack to his left—no doubt the addresses of everyone he would be paying each month. For his father's transgressions.

He turned his attention to the boy. "I want you to know, Jack, that I recently had the opportunity to become friends with a couple of my other brothers, which makes them yours as well. It's been quite a rewarding experience. I'll introduce them to you if you like."

"Yes, please, sir."

"My lord," Rachel corrected quietly. "You should address him as *my lord*."

Leonora wondered if the woman regretted that she'd lost her opportunity to be his lady.

"We don't need to be so formal, Jack. But know you are welcome to call upon me at any time. Should you require any further assistance, you need only let me know." He shoved himself to his feet and yanked on a nearby cord. "Simpkins will see you out."

Rachel elegantly rose from her chair. "Felicitations on your upcoming nuptials. I do hope you'll be happy."

"I have no reason not to believe I will be."

It wasn't a declaration of love. As a matter of fact, he expressed no emotion at all. He might as well have announced that the sun was an orb. She wished he'd looked at her with something akin to adoration. Instead, he kept his gaze fastened on the woman who had broken his heart, and Leonora was left with the impression that he was seeking to punish himself or Rachel. Perhaps both.

"Simpkins, see Miss Kennedy and her son out."

So focused on the tableau before her, Leonora hadn't seen or heard the butler arrive. But because she was steadfastly watching Rook, she was acutely aware of his tense shoulders visibly relaxing when their guests were no longer visible. He marched over to the sideboard and splashed scotch into two glasses. She'd barely stood when he handed one off to her before taking up vigil at the window and looking out on the gardens. He drank a long swallow of scotch. She indulged in a ladylike sip when she felt anything but ladylike. She wanted to destroy something, couldn't quite understand these feelings—a need to protect, a desire to save—rampaging through her.

Quietly she approached him. "You've had a challenging day."

"Fourteen brothers and nine sisters—not counting Aiden and Finn, of course. I'd always believed—hoped—that the rumors regarding his . . . insatiability were greatly exaggerated. There are no doubt more progenies, those who didn't yet see the handbills or weren't quite comfortable making an appearance today. They may eventually come out of the woodwork. Then there are the ones who perished. Christ, he ensured if they survived, they'd have harsh lives. What a bastard."

"How do you know they are all his? Some could have lied hoping to earn a buck."

His profile was to her, but she saw the corner of his mouth hitch up. "Pound."

He faced her fully and leaned against the edge of the window. He took a sip of his scotch and licked lips she'd gone too long without tasting. "I could see shadows of him in most of them—the eyes, the nose, the chin, the jaw."

Did they have your beautiful mouth? Did they do wicked things with it?

"I suppose it's possible that some weren't," he continued pensively. "I would have thought over the years he'd become more cautious about leaving a trail that led to him, but to be honest, I don't think he cared. Maybe he decided all these children were proof of his prowess. But if they came here today, I couldn't *not* help them, whether they were his or not." Another sip, another lick. "Still, I think most were. Funny thing. I grew up always wanting a sibling."

"Sometimes a sibling can be . . . irritating."

"But I suspect your brother loves you unconditionally. Thank you for being here today. I preferred not to do this at the earl's residence because I didn't want my mother to suffer through how many there were. Or to be reminded of how many she gave up before she was allowed to keep me. Women should not be at the mercy of cruel men."

"Is that the reason you offered Rachel one hundred pounds a month?" She couldn't believe she'd asked.

"So she could take care of herself and her son, if need be? Wouldn't be at anyone's mercy, save yours?"

Other than a slow blink as he studied her, he didn't move, and she was left with the impression he was assessing her, perhaps finding her lacking. She hadn't meant to be so forceful with her questioning.

Finally, he looked back out the window. Dusk was settling in, and it threw shadows over his face. "Perhaps I wanted to boast a little that I had the means. Mostly I was concerned with the lad. He was the youngest who came here today. Eight or nine. The others ranged in age from fifteen to nearly forty. My father left his seed throughout London for a good long while, apparently."

"How do you know the boy isn't yours?"

As it landed on her, his gaze held tenderness, and she wondered if he had surmised that she was plagued with doubts about their future. "Because as I told your mother, I have no bastards."

"But you loved her. Isn't it possible—"

He laid a hand against her cheek, and she wanted to turn her head toward it and press her lips to its center, but she held still, their gazes locked. "Because she and I never went beyond a kiss."

She felt as though all the air had suddenly left her body with relief.

"Because with her," he continued, "I was able to control my baser instincts. Which makes me wonder . . . why it is that I can't seem to keep my hands, my mouth, off you?"

"It must have been hard, though, to see her again."

He shook his head. "I would have thought so as

well. Instead, I was inappropriately distracted, wondering if I removed that black frock from your person if I'd find that black corset hidden beneath it."

SHE RELEASED A little laugh, and Rook wondered when it was that he'd come to love her laughs. He knew that seeing Rachel again, after all these years, should have been like a punch to the gut, but it had taken him a few minutes to even notice her because all his attention had been on Nora when she glided into the room, all lithe and willowy and tall enough that he barely had to bend his head to take her mouth.

And at the sight of her, he'd wanted nothing more than to do as Aiden had suggested that first night: take her in his arms, lean her back a bit, press his lips to hers, and sigh as though he'd never been so entranced.

She mesmerized him at the oddest times—when he should be mourning and bleak. As a matter of fact, he had been desolated as his father's offspring had paraded through. Then she'd come in, bringing with her a breath of fresh air and a ray of sunshine. Nothing seemed unobtainable, nothing seemed gloomy, when she was near.

It was the lad more than Rachel who had distracted him and finally caused him to turn his attention away from Nora. He'd seen too much of himself in Jack. The yearning for approval, the fear that it wouldn't be forthcoming. The embarrassment, the shame. A boy as young as he should experience none of those emotions. He should have a time of carefree living before the responsibilities of life were thrust upon him.

When he'd finally noticed Rachel, the surprise of

her had more to do with the fact that the lad was hers than seeing her again. The years had not been gentle with her, and perhaps that had played a role in the amount he'd settled upon them, so the years to come could be kinder.

What had astonished him the most, however, was that looking at her had stirred to life no sense of *she was once mine*. He tried to recall what it had been like to be in love with her. How easy it had been to walk beside her without thinking about the treasures he'd find beneath her skirts. How often they simply sat beside each other without a need to touch or to slip away unseen for a bit of naughtiness. How she'd had no goals other than marriage. How she'd only ever considered her needs, not those of others. How she hadn't looked at a man struggling to hold a pen and poured all her efforts into finding a way for him to continue to write out his thoughts.

How he'd managed to go five minutes or more without thinking of her.

Whereas the woman standing before him now was constantly on his mind.

"It wouldn't be appropriate," she said quietly.

It took him a few seconds to realize she was referring to the black corset instead of where his thoughts constantly drifted.

"We seem to do quite a bit that's inappropriate," he said. From the beginning with her, he hadn't wanted to behave. He'd been like the ladies who visited the Elysium, seeking something they'd never experienced. It was the reason he'd returned to the club, searching for her, needing to confirm that a lady who sparked such magic in him could truly exist.

"And look at the trouble it's gotten us into."

Was it trouble? At first he'd been angry to have gotten caught in such a flagrant way that had destroyed his reputation for being above reproach. But even when she hadn't been in the library with him today, knowing she was within easy reach in the parlor had brought comfort. And he'd lost track of the number of siblings who had told him that he had a right proper lady welcoming them into his residence. He'd wanted someone greeting them who was kind, generous, and understanding of the awkwardness they might be feeling. Who would put them at ease because she knew what it was to feel as if she didn't quite belong. He wished she'd never been forced to experience any rebuffs, but he was also acutely aware that they no doubt contributed to her empathetic spirit.

"Will you stay for dinner? I can send a carriage for your mother." He wasn't yet ready for her to leave, and when he was finished with this business concerning his father, he'd have her with him every night. He'd depart for the family estate on the morrow, to see his father finally laid to rest.

"She no longer cares if I move about unescorted. I've been compromised. What further damage can be done?"

"The night we were caught, we didn't get a chance to conclude what we'd begun."

Another laugh, easy and airy, that lightened his soul. "That seems to be a habit with us," she said.

"A bed is much more comfortable than a table. I'd be more than pleased to demonstrate . . . so you can add to your repertoire of things to analyze."

His hand still rested against her cheek. She intertwined her fingers with his, holding him in place as she turned her head and pressed a kiss to the center of his palm. It was a simple touching and yet his body reacted as though she'd gone down on her knees. Everything about her was sensual. Little wonder he couldn't resist her.

He lifted her into his arms, grateful she didn't object, but her eyes did widen, more in wonder than in shock. Then she buried her face in the small space where his skin rested against his neckcloth. She swirled her tongue over the sensitive flesh. The pleasure that rippled through him should have caused his steps to stutter. Instead, it energized him as he marched from the room, determined that this time there would be no interruptions. This time, he would take her and shower her in ecstasy.

Because if he'd learned anything at all that afternoon it was that he was damned glad he hadn't married Rachel. He'd thought he'd loved her, but he was no longer certain what his feelings for her had been because she'd stirred nothing to life within him when he'd set eyes upon her again after all these years. And it had little to do with her betrayal and more to do with the woman presently in his arms. He'd have never been unfaithful, which meant he'd have never kissed Nora, much less have enjoyed the taste of her. He'd have never experienced how snugly she enveloped his cock. It was unlikely that he'd have known her laugh, learned of her devotion to her father, or caught a glimpse into the inner workings of her meticulous mind that could envision what others failed to see.

She was an inventor, an explorer, a discoverer. She was interesting in ways that other women he'd met weren't. She didn't pore over the latest fashions, share gossip, or mock those around her. She cared about springs and bolts and cogs.

And he hoped she cared about him, at least to a degree that would provide them with an amicable marriage. She lusted after him, if the nibbling she began on his ear was any indication. He certainly wanted—needed—the sexual satisfaction she could provide.

The escape from his troubles, his burdens.

He'd known meeting with his half-siblings would not be easy. Many were angry or resentful, taking their frustrations out on him, as if he was responsible for their father's actions. But knowing Nora was near, having a moment to think about her between visitors had always helped to restore his equilibrium.

Now he wanted to thank her, even if she didn't realize what a help she'd been, even if she didn't realize how much he'd come to rely on her presence. He'd spent much of his life striving not to be beholden, to not open himself up to hurt—but he needed her in ways he'd never needed anyone. It was a bit terrifying. Yet he wasn't quite ready to escort her back to the hotel.

But to his bedchamber was another matter.

With her licking the swirls of his ear, he strode through the doorway, kicked the door closed behind him, and headed for the bed. No reason to play coy or to pretend they weren't here for any other reason than to scratch the itch that had gone unfulfilled a few nights earlier. Christ, he'd missed her. Crossing her path at balls, sneaking off into nooks and gardens or a scandalous club. Kissing her senseless while she did the same with him.

Before her, he'd always been able to retain control

of his desires. Not once before had he ever taken a risk of being caught—not even with Rachel. He'd never placed her in a situation that could be considered compromising. Resistance had been . . . damned easy, he realized now that he'd become involved with a woman who made it damned hard.

While neither of them might have wanted marriage, they had wanted this. Desperately. To touch with mouth and hands. To explore each other.

Slowly he lowered her feet to the floor and took possession of her sweet mouth. Her sweet mouth that caused so many wicked thoughts to bombard him. He'd never grow tired of her. He knew that with a certainty that astounded him.

LEONORA SHOULD HAVE resisted, should have left. But she understood that they needed to finish what they'd begun, or it would forever plague them. No matter what roads—or seas—they traveled.

They were making plans for a wedding that she wasn't convinced would occur. Shame had driven him to insist they marry. His father's death had burdened him, leaving him no chance to ponder the unpleasant consequences of following this course. Therefore, it was left to her to make the hard choices, to ensure no regrets haunted their future.

But this, the way his luscious mouth moved so provocatively over hers, was not a mistake. It was something she craved, as a rose in the desert did water. It provided sustenance and eventually memories. Of his lips and tongue doing naughty things that felt so incredibly right.

And his hands, his fingers, working to undo lacings, setting buttons free, moving cloth aside. She wondered if he enjoyed her doing the same with his clothing. She supposed so, since he would stop to remove anything that had been liberated. Coat, neckcloth, waistcoat, shirt.

Her fingers were trembling when they moved to the buttons of his trousers. He stilled. His eyes held hers. She watched the movement of his throat as he swallowed. She leaned up and licked his skin. She enjoyed licking him.

With each button she released, his breath became a little more labored, sawing in and out, a runner preparing to sprint. When his cock sprung free of its confines, she wrapped her hands around it. He slammed his eyes closed, his jaw tightened as though he was in pain . . . or perhaps ecstasy. When he opened his eyes, she saw the fire there, the need, the need he'd always kept hidden from her, whether by banking it or becoming lost in the shadows.

She knew a few seconds of remorse for not recognizing what his previous actions might have cost him, how much he'd given to her without asking for anything in return. Until the greenhouse. Until he'd been unable to resist all she offered.

Moving slightly until her breasts were pressed to his chest, she slowly lowered herself to her knees and did to him what he'd once done to her. She licked the most intimate part of him. His groan was as rewarding as listening to all the parts in a factory assembling a weapon or, soon, a writing machine.

Then she took him in, sliding her mouth down the length of him. Growling with a feral intensity, he buried his fingers in her hair. She heard hairpins clicking as they fell around her just before her hair tumbled down. His hands knotted in the loosened strands.

He wasn't keeping her there or holding her captive. Following her movements, he gently massaged her scalp as she massaged him. She could sense the tension in him, as though what he was experiencing was almost too much, was taking him by storm, was consuming him. She understood those sensations. Because of him, because of all he'd been willing to do and show her. He was hers.

Had been hers from the beginning. But even now, the doubts plagued her, because just like in the beginning, he was here out of obligation. He may have sought her out, come to her willingly, in the greenhouse but duty would drive him to the church. A need to prove he was unlike his father would see them wed.

She remembered telling Lord Camberley she would choose happiness over love. Now she was settling for neither.

She shoved all those disturbing thoughts aside so they wouldn't taint what was happening now. She needed the beauty of what transpired between a couple, the glory to be found in sex, because she suspected she might never have this experience again, of being with a man she'd come to love.

She wanted him to look back on this night and realize that with her actions, she'd declared her love for him—even if he was unable to love her. He'd once given away his heart, and she suspected it hadn't yet returned to him. While she believed she could love enough for the two of them, a marriage shouldn't be built on the generosity of one.

The last lingering thoughts drifted away, and she focused on the moment, on him. The silkiness of him against her tongue, the taste of him in her mouth, the steel of him within her hands. The sound of him begging for more with grunts and groans that urged her on. That encouraged her to be a wanton, that ensured she felt no shame in it.

Although he didn't still her movements, his hands came around to cup her face. "It feels so good, Nora, but it's not enough. I've waited too long. I want—need—to be inside you."

Bending over, he placed his hands beneath her elbows and guided her to her feet. He eased back slightly, lifted a foot, grabbed it, hopped to regain his balance, and tugged off his boot. The other quickly followed. His trousers landed in a heap, covering both.

Backing up until her legs hit the bed and her bottom hit the mattress, she studied him. Every line that made up the planes of his stomach and chest. The firmness of his thighs. The glistening of his cock where she had dampened him. She thought she should probably gaze on him abashedly. Instead, she boldly catalogued each part and how they all came together to create such magnificence. Tonight they were hers. He was hers.

After climbing onto the bed, she scrambled back until she was sprawled over it. Reaching down, she parted the folds so he could see that she was more than ready for him. She'd felt the dampness gathering as she'd sucked on him. Bringing him pleasure brought her pleasure.

Now she understood the satisfaction he'd taken in

creating wondrous sensations within her. Giving was as rewarding as taking.

Hunger darkened his eyes as he prowled forward. He placed a knee on the mattress, causing the bed to dip slightly with his weight as he came to hover over her, his arms on either side of her, one thigh nestled between her legs and pressing against her mound. She wanted to mount that thigh and ride it until she was screaming out his name.

Remaining raised up on his arms, he lowered his head, took her mouth, and unleashed the fires of passion and desire. They rushed through her, from head to toe, scoring every inch of her, and suddenly it wasn't enough to have him this close. She needed him closer. Needed the light coating of hair on his chest skimming over her breasts. She wound her arms around him and brought him down.

"I love the feel of you against me," he rasped.

I love the whole of you, inside and out, she wanted to whisper. Every inch, every aspect. There wasn't one part that she could point to and declare: *That is what I love about you.*

Her hands traveled over his broad shoulders, his strong back, his taut buttocks. She squirmed and rocked against him, mewled and moaned. Every aspect of her was on fire, and he alone held the power to put out the flames.

HEATED SILK, BLAZING velvet. There wasn't an inch of her that Rook didn't stroke, caress, lick, or kiss. Every aspect of her was perfection. Every part of her called to him to want more. She was so pliable.

And so demanding as she slowly circled a finger around his mouth and whispered in a sultry voice, "I want this between my thighs."

He gave her a wicked grin. "As you wish."

He scooted down the length of her to do her bidding. He loved the sounds she made. The little squeals. The low moans. The gasps. The *oh gods*. The *there*s.

With a rolling or lifting of her hips, she signaled what she needed from him, and he was only too happy to oblige.

"You're so good at this," she rasped.

Because he'd been determined to never leave his paramours wanting. But giving Nora pleasure was more rewarding than anything he'd ever before experienced.

Then she was pulling on his hair, scraping her nails along his shoulders. Panting and puffing. Her hips and legs were trembling. He skimmed his hands up her torso, cradled her breasts, and stroked his thumbs over her hardened nipples.

"Oh." She grabbed his wrists to hold his hands there.

He continued to fondle those lovely breasts and give attention to the pearling peaks while he plundered the sweet valley between her thighs. She squirmed and writhed. He knew she was close to exploding, could feel the tension, a coiled spring ready to snap free—

Suddenly her back was bowing, and she was calling out his name hoarsely, breathlessly. But he didn't stop with his attentions until she released her hold on his wrists and cradled his head. His gaze met hers. "At least you didn't fall asleep."

She laughed, then quickly sobered. "I want you, Johnny. I want you as I've never wanted."

BEFORE SHE'D GOTTEN on a ship and traveled across an ocean, she couldn't have imagined ever saying those words to any man. But then neither had she been able to imagine being sprawled on a bed—he was right, it was better than a table—with a man nestled between her legs.

His gaze once more smoldering, he eased up the length of her and hovered over her. He lowered his mouth to hers as he lifted his hips and pushed into her with a powerful thrust that she found thrilling.

She'd barely had the opportunity to appreciate their time together before but now they both held still as though they simply needed a minute to enjoy how perfectly they fit. A sprocket that slid effortlessly into its corresponding chainwheel.

He buried his face in the curve of her neck where it met her shoulder and gave her a little love bite. "Christ, you feel so good. So hot. So wet. Velvet, silk, and satin."

Lifting himself up slightly, he held her gaze as he began to rock against her. "Let me know if it hurts. Let me know if it doesn't feel good."

"It feels wonderful. You feel wonderful."

She didn't think the heat in his eyes could grow any hotter, but it did. Reaching down, he bent one of her legs, then the other, and slid in deeper, and she felt as though they'd become two interlocking cogs that were moving in tandem to create pleasure.

And yet at the same time, it seemed wild and frenzied, with nothing at all mechanized about their actions. There were kisses, nibbles, and strokes. Whispered words of encouragement. Guttural groans. Soft sighs, pants.

The sensations he'd created with his mouth between her thighs, he now created with his cock, sliding out and thrusting into her. Strangely, she did take note of the force of each thrust but not in a machine-driven way. Rather as an overall sense of pleasure. He was moving inside her, they were as one.

It was touching and emotional and caused tears to sting the backs of her eyes. This was what it was like to be truly close to someone. She would forever be grateful for this experience.

Then he lifted up to balance himself on his arms and began to pump into her like a piston, steady and sure with a purpose and a goal in mind. The sensations that had been hovering so close to the surface built to a rising crescendo, taking her by storm, carrying her to heights greater than she'd ever achieved before. Locking her arms and legs around him, she rode out the tempest, crying out as her release overwhelmed her.

With a feral growl, he threw his head back and gave a final deep thrust before collapsing on top of her, breathing harsh and heavily. Within her hold, she could feel him beginning to relax, for all the tightness to seep out of him.

She couldn't help it. She smiled with contentment.

"How long will you be gone?" she asked.

They were lounging in bed, still naked, with a tray of cheese, strawberries, buttered bread, and olives between them, each holding a glass of red wine. She didn't know why it seemed more decadent than what they'd been doing earlier.

"Four days. I'll leave in the morning, see Father interred, and then return."

"Will your mother be going with you?"

"No. Perhaps you'd be good enough to look in on her, ensure she's all right. Although I rather suspect she'll spend some time in Aiden's club."

Her eyes widened. "She goes there?"

"Hmm. Apparently, she has a favorite fellow."

"I wonder if it's Julian."

"Who is Julian and what do you know of him?"

"When I woke up that morning after you visited, a maid and I were trying to figure out who you were. She suggested Julian because he was ever so good at kissing. At least that's how she put it."

"Is he?"

"I wouldn't know. He never kissed me."

"How about Camberley? Did he kiss you?"

"Jealous?"

His jaw tensed, but he shook his head. "Yes, damn it. Where did he kiss you?"

"On the mouth."

His frustration was clear, and she didn't know why she was taking such delight in it. Perhaps because she'd never had anyone jealous before.

"I meant where were you?"

She relented. "We never kissed. I couldn't envision it. I just—" *Don't feel for him what I feel for you.* "He's nice enough but he didn't appeal to me in that manner."

He was resting up on one elbow. He shifted his wineglass to that hand and used a solitary finger on the other to trace a circle around her face. "You should have had an opportunity to kiss a dozen men."

"Why not two dozen? Is there an acceptable number that's allowed before a woman is considered a trollop?"

He laughed darkly. "It's probably best not to discuss numbers."

Although, she suspected that for herself it would always be only one.

It was dark by the time he had his carriage readied, and they were journeying through London on their way to the Trewlove Hotel. Leonora had been surprised that Mama hadn't shown up at the door once night fell, but she'd gained what she wanted and her daughter's behavior was no longer her priority.

Although Leonora couldn't imagine she'd be too pleased to see her daughter nestled up against Rook's side, his mouth toying provocatively over hers. He was so very good at kissing, but then he was so very good at anything related to sex. She wondered how many women he might have known intimately, how he'd managed to ensure he had no by-blows. She was struck with an unexpected realization that following what they had done, she could be with child. And she wouldn't mind it.

But at that moment, she was focused on the pleasure rippling through her because of the man who held her. He'd drawn the curtains on the windows as though her reputation needed protecting when she was rather certain that his concern was that of his own.

She wondered what it might take for him to throw caution to the wind and do something scandalous. On the other hand, she supposed he'd done something scandalous with her.

The carriage began to slow, and they pulled apart.

"I'll call on you as soon as I return," he said solemnly.

No *I love you, I'll miss you, I can't wait to return to you.*

"Take care on the journey."

He gave a nod as the carriage stopped and a door opened. He disembarked and then handed her down. Without touching they walked up the steps to the hotel door.

"Thank you for being there today," he said quietly.

"It was my privilege." God, she hated this formality. Was this what it would be like between them except when they were in bed, going at each other like animals? "I'm just sorry your father was the sort of man he was."

"I'm sorry for a lot of things. Good night, Nora."

A footman opened the door. She walked through and strolled to a window. Standing there she watched his solitary figure walking back to his carriage. He didn't glance back to look for her. He simply got into the conveyance.

How was it that passion could reign so fiercely between them, and shortly afterward, she could feel so lonely?

CHAPTER 23

"I_F there is any silver lining to the earl's passing, I suppose it's that you will be a countess from the start," Mama said with a seething undertone in her voice at the breakfast table. "Although I don't see why the wedding must now be small, as though your future husband is ashamed of us."

"Because they are in mourning," Leonora explained for the hundredth time.

"I look hideous in black," Mama said. "I'm not going to wear it. He wasn't my father or husband. I don't see why his death has to ruin things for us. Force us to have a ceremony that is less spectacular. I think the wedding should be delayed until they are out of mourning."

Sam cleared his throat. "We're talking a delay for months, if not a couple of years, aren't we? What if Nora is—" He looked at her, his cheeks turning a red that nearly matched her hair. "What if she's . . . with child?"

The last two words came out on a whisper that was almost inaudible.

Her mother sighed heavily, as if she'd just hoisted up a huge boulder. "I suppose that is a consideration. Although we could wait a few weeks to see."

Leonora chuckled. "A few days ago you were screaming for a marriage made in haste."

"I don't want you denied what you rightfully deserve."

Oh, yes, she was relatively certain it was *her* needs that Mama was worried about. She turned her attention to Sam. "I think we need to redouble our efforts to secure investors."

He looked at her as though she'd announced they should fly to the moon. "But Rook . . . Rook said you can have whatever money you require for the business."

"I don't want to be beholden." More, she didn't want him thinking she was marrying him for his wealth. She thought of all the people who'd come to him yesterday, extending a hand. Her circumstances were vastly different from theirs. She'd had advantages with a loving father who hadn't tossed her aside.

"You won't be beholden," Mama said sternly. "He'll be your husband. It'll be his job to take care of you."

But she wanted to take care of herself.

"Besides, he said I have to give half the company to you," Sam said, "and can sell only my shares."

"Right this minute they are all *your* shares. So we sell some and then whatever remains on my wedding day, we divide equally. We'll take care to ensure that our combined shares give us a majority." And she maintained some independence.

He looked decidedly uncomfortable. "Actually, Nora, I've been thinking of asking Rook for a loan so I can pursue another avenue over here. The factory is so complicated and involves such a tremendous amount of work."

"What about the writing machine?"

"We have pen and ink. Do we really need a . . . machine?"

"How long have you felt this way?"

"For a while."

"We don't even need the factory any longer," Mama said. "You are marrying a man of considerable wealth. He's certain to care for your relations—especially as he seems to be caring for his father's by-blows."

"You're not going to take advantage of his generosity."

"We'll see, my girl. Besides, you'll be a countess. You can't *work*."

Leonora felt as though the rug had been pulled out from under her, only to discover a huge hole to tumble into. She was finally coming to the realization that her brother and mother had never truly embraced the search for investors with any enthusiasm. For them, continuing the business wasn't the true purpose of this visit. The true purpose was to hunt for a husband—not as a possibility but as a final outcome. It was the reason that Sam had secured all the invitations to balls. The reason her mother had insisted on strolls through the park. They didn't care about the company or her father's legacy. They cared about the life of leisure her marriage to a wealthy lord would provide. And its entry into elite circles.

The betrayal felt like a punch to the gut that sucked all the breath from her body.

As though her final words were an edict that would not be disobeyed, her mother rose from the chair. "You will marry or be cast out."

Then she strode from the room, leaving nothing but humiliation and duplicity in her wake.

Leonora turned her attention to Sam. "You do understand what this business means to me. How hard I've worked to see it succeed."

To avoid her gaze, he began spooning sugar into his coffee, and his leg jiggled, hitting the table, causing it to vibrate. "I don't want to manage the business. It's never been *my* dream."

"What is your dream, Sam?"

"I don't know, but it's not that."

Studying him, she wondered if she knew her family at all. "Rook is not a bank, and I'll not have you or our mother taking advantage of his generosity."

She had no plans to take advantage of it either.

"I'm not going to marry him, Sam."

He looked toward the doorway, as if fearing a witch might come charging through to cast a spell on him that would turn him into a toad. He shifted his gaze to her. "But doing so will solve so many of our problems. Mother will get her entry into New York society. I'll have the means to pursue my own interests instead of yours. And he's going to give you the money to do what you will with the factory."

"But he doesn't love me, Sam. He's marrying me because of scandal." To prove to Society—and even more to himself—that he wasn't like his father. "If I leave, the scandal will go with me. If I stay, he and others will always know that he was forced into marrying me. The odd girl who everyone laughs at. I can't do that to him. Not when he's so decent and deserves the sort of woman who can host balls with aplomb and carry on interesting conversations about the weather."

Regret filled his eyes. "I don't want the business, Nora. I think we could get a pretty penny for the land

and the factory. I talked with a couple of men before we left . . . on the off chance that we had no success over here."

He might as well have tossed his hot coffee in her face. Not only because of his lack of faith but because he'd taken action without telling her. "You've spoken to someone about selling it?"

"I needed to know its value so I could accurately assess if it was better to sell or keep."

"It's more valuable long-term. I can prove that, but I need time. I'm still determining how to make the tallying machine work as I envision it. But with it and the writing machine . . ." She trailed off because she could see her brother growing more melancholy with each word she uttered. For him, hanging onto the business was as unpleasant a notion as marrying out of obligation was for her. She couldn't ask him to do it, to follow a path that would never lead to happiness.

"I haven't the means to purchase it from you straightaway. But if I can get investors, will you hold onto it until I *can* purchase it from you? I'll manage it. You'll get a portion of the profits, as will the investors, and I'll have a salary." She needed an income. "Once I've saved enough, I'll buy you out. I should think it would only take a few years. Then you can chase your own dreams." She reached across the table and placed her hand over his. "Please, Sam. You owe me this. You duped me into believing we were on a mission to save the company, while all along you just wanted it to languish. I know I can make it a success."

"I don't think Rook will be happy about you returning to America."

There were a lot of aspects of the plan forming in her mind that Rook wouldn't be happy about, but in the end it would all be for the best. Eventually he'd come to understand that. "I'll handle Rook. Just swear to me that you won't sell the business—Father's dream—to anyone except me."

He nodded, sighed. "Five years, Nora. I can give you that. If it's not profitable by then, we'll sell."

"Thank you." She immediately stood.

"Where are you going?"

To save *her* business. Because even though it had been passed down to Sam, she was the one who loved and cared about it. She was the one who could turn it into the success her father had envisioned. If she could get the backing, and she suspected she knew where she would find it. "I think we've been going about getting investors all wrong, looking to the incorrect people. I believe I know where we should have gone from the beginning."

STANDING WITHIN THE Duchess of Kingsland's parlor, Leonora fought not to recall the night when she'd walked into it and discovered Rook was the gent who'd kissed her. The way her heart had sped up, the horror and the gladness that had fought for dominance within her.

Crisp footfalls, those of someone who was as direct and focused as Leonora, echoed down the hallway. The duchess stepped into the parlor. Leonora curtsied. "Your Grace."

"Oh, please, you must call me Penelope. The Chessmen are a sort of family, and you'll be marrying into it soon enough so we should dispense with any formality."

She didn't see any reason to alert the duchess that she was in the process of changing those plans. Instead, she cleared her throat and lifted her chin. "I wondered if I might meet with your consortium of lady investors."

CHAPTER 24

⌒◦⌒

Elverton Estate

TRYING to see things through Nora's eyes, Rook wandered aimlessly through the estate manor, struck by the notion that life here had never worked properly. The weight of the years clung to it. It had never contained happiness, joy, or laughter. Even now, in spite of its size, it was cloyingly suffocating.

He was grateful Nora wasn't with him. He didn't want to contemplate how this place might oppress her spirit.

But what struck him the most was how damned much he missed her. Ever since he'd arrived, he'd had phantom conversations with her, had contemplated all the history he might share with her, all the various items he would hand over to her to take apart: clocks, music boxes, mechanical toys. The damned instrument he'd discovered in a locked room. At first, he'd believed it to be a torture device until he'd found some etchings that showed how a woman would stand in it, bent over, while a man came at her from behind. He supposed his father had entertained some of his lovers within these walls.

Rook wanted to have the entire building stripped of its contents and scrubbed down.

He didn't want to live here. He wasn't *going* to live

here. He would lock it up and build another dwelling on the far end of the property, one where more pleasant occurrences would happen. Where all his memories would include Nora and not the father he loathed.

During his journey, he'd decided that he would burn down the crofter's cottage. But after he'd seen his father interred, he'd ridden to the cottage . . . and felt nothing upon seeing it. It no longer held any sway over him. The betrayal that had occurred didn't anger him, didn't hurt . . . because now he had something better, he had Nora.

Until he'd stood there, striving to look into the past, he hadn't realized that all he cared about was the future. And that future was Nora.

WHEN HE ARRIVED in London, he didn't immediately call upon his mother or even bother going to his residence. He went straight to the Trewlove Hotel, dashed up the outer steps, and raced up the inner stairs until he reached the Garrisons' suite of rooms. He knocked on the door with an urgency that was overpowering.

He needed her. He wanted her.

When a timid maid opened the door, he strove not to frighten her with his demands. "Lord Wyeth—" He squeezed his eyes shut, took a deep breath, and began again. "Lord Elverton to see Miss Garrison."

"If you'll be good enough to wait, my lord." She closed the door in his face, leaving him standing mute in the hallway.

He considered knocking down the door. Good Lord, he'd never known such need.

Then it opened and her brother gaped as though Rook had risen from the dead.

"I want to see your sister."

He shook his head. "She said she'd told you."

"Told me what precisely?"

"She acquired investors. She's booked passage back to America. She and Mother had a heated argument, as you can well imagine, so Nora left to take the railway to Liverpool. She boards her ship in three days."

SHE HAD TOLD him. He found the letter resting on the desk in his library. She'd used her writing machine to create it, all the flawless letters lined up like good soldiers going into battle.

Dearest Johnny,

Your generosity when it came to the terms of a settlement far exceeded any of our expectations. However, I can't accept them. I need the business to flourish on my terms, through my efforts. Not because of your bounty . . . or charity . . . or guilt.

I know I should have said something the last time we were together. But these are not easy words to speak, especially when looking into your beautiful brown eyes. But I cannot marry you.

Sam focused on finding investors among the aristocracy because like our mother, he believes only the upper echelon are of value and have anything to offer. But it was a world into which I was never truly allowed entry. Until you.

But knowing what it is not to belong, I decided to look elsewhere for funding, and I met with success. I have obtained investors. Women who are referred to as commoners but are anything except common because they're taking actions to better their lives and they know what it is to believe in dreams.

I didn't come to England to find a husband. That was all my mother's doing. I had never considered that marriage was for me. The circumstances under which we would wed seemed . . . wrong. I think eventually the reasons behind our marriage would have poisoned whatever affection we might have held for each other. I couldn't tolerate the possibility. I didn't want to risk destroying the wonderful memories I have of our time together.

You made me feel cherished and that reminiscence will sustain me through the years.

I wish you love and hope your wife will appreciate all your wonderful attributes. Please know this: you are nothing at all like your wretched father. You are kind and generous, with a moral compass that, unlike his, has not broken. No amount of scandal will change that.

Affectionately yours,
Nora

Rook walked to the window and gazed out. The realization hit him that he'd been so worried about being likened to his father that in the end, he'd let his father win.

He'd lived a life that had not truly been his own: until Nora. He'd built crenellated walls around himself—not to keep others out, but to keep himself in. For far too long, he'd lived in a dungeon, pretending contentment, until Nora had brought him into the sunlight.

She'd done it by taking him apart until she reached his heart. It was now and would always remain hers.

Three days. Three days before she left England's shores. It was only a few hours by railway to Liverpool.

He had time, time to assemble a plan that with determination would work with a precision that she couldn't help but admire.

CHAPTER 25

❦

STANDING at the railing of the mighty steamship, Leonora watched as the ribbon of water separating her from land widened. Most of the passengers had been on the deck, waving and cheering, until the ship pulled out of the harbor. Then they'd slowly drifted away, returning to their cabins or to chairs lined up on the deck or to the tearoom. Like her, a few stragglers remained.

She couldn't bring herself to leave. Not as long as England was visible. Because in an odd way she felt as though she was leaving home. Which made no sense whatsoever when she'd been visiting for only a few weeks.

America was her home. It should be calling to her. Yet she wondered if she'd ever be as happy there. She would devote herself to managing the factory and producing so many writing machines that she could export them around the world. They would all bear her father's name: the Walt Garrison writing machine. His name would become synonymous with it until people would just ask, "Have you a Walt Garrison?" or "a WG?"

With each key punched, with each page filled with perfect, legible letters, he would live on. And in that way, she could defeat the cruel condition that had slowly stolen him from her.

Eventually perhaps she would take on a lover because she had learned she had needs. And there was beauty in the coming together of two bodies. She didn't know if it would be as glorious if her heart wasn't involved, but she recognized that it was not on the ship with her. She'd left it behind. It would always be with Johnny. For that was where it belonged.

Light footsteps sounded, and she became aware of someone standing beside her. She wanted to ask the person to leave. She wanted to be completely and absolutely alone as England began fading away, and her chest started to ache, and the salt from the sea caused her eyes to tear up.

She couldn't marry a man who didn't love her. In a relationship, one person's love, no matter how great, was never enough to sustain it. Her father had given her mother everything, and yet she'd never been content. Leonora wanted the joy of being loved.

A lemony-orange fragrance teased her nostrils. Even here, far out to sea, she smelled him. He would always haunt her, no matter the distance—

Only the scent was strong, not a memory.

Slowly, very slowly, she turned her head toward the stranger, who was no stranger at all. Who was watching her and not the land that was barely visible now. Her heart pounded so fiercely against her ribs that she was surprised it didn't knock her over the railing and into the water. "What are you doing here?"

One corner of Rook's mouth curled up ruefully. "Going to America . . . according to the passage I purchased."

"Why?"

"I have some investments to check up on."

"Where?" She seemed incapable all of a sudden to utter more than a single word at a time. He was so beautiful standing there, with the wind tousling his hair and the sun shining around him. America was a large country, and she was certain he had an assortment of investments spread from one end of it to the other.

"New York for the most part, I think. I came into possession of a machine factory."

Her eyes widened. "Not my machine factory."

Damn, Sam. Had he broken his promise to her, had he sold it?

Rook's expression changed to one of deep sadness. "It never was *your* factory. Your father left it in its entirety to your brother."

From the beginning, when the lawyer had read the will, she'd fought not to let it hurt, not to feel as though her father hadn't loved her. "It's what fathers do, isn't it? Leave the business to their sons. Father left me his watch. It was far more personal and precious to me."

"But you poured your heart and soul into the writing machine."

"We have our investors now, and Sam has given me permission to do what I will with the factory—as long it makes a profit." She shook her head. None of this was making any sense. "I don't understand how you have any shares. We sold forty-nine percent of the company. Sam knows it's important that we keep a majority, that we keep fifty-one percent. He wouldn't have sold"—she felt ill—"tell me he didn't sell you any of his portion of the company."

"He's a hard bargainer, your brother. He knows a desperate man when he sees one."

Her hands balled into fists. She wanted to strike him, knock him into the sea, and then return to London to smack Sam. "He promised me he wouldn't. How much did he sell you?"

His curled fingers got to within a hairsbreadth of her cheek before he dropped them to his side. "All of the shares he had left."

She turned her attention back to the sea, to the speck of land that would soon be beyond sight. Just like her factory, moving beyond reach. "If you're as smart as I think you are, you'll hire me to manage your factory."

"Why should I?"

She glared at him. "I know everything there is to know about the writing machine. And what changes need to be made at the factory to make it viable for producing. I expect a handsome salary."

"I won't be hiring you, Miss Garrison." He reached into his coat pocket, pulled out a thin packet, and extended it toward her. "You're the majority shareholder in the company, not I."

As though it could suddenly explode, she stared at the object he was holding. Perhaps it was merely a dream and she wasn't on a ship, but in her bed. Or it was an illusion brought on by inhaling too much salt air. Or maybe it was the result of drinking too much absinthe, and everything that had transpired that first night and beyond was simply one long, continuing hallucination.

She hated that her fingers trembled as she took his offering, loosened the string, and studied the writing that bore her name. But something was wrong . . . because it didn't indicate she was the majority shareholder. No, indeed. She was the only one. "I don't understand. The duchess—"

"She, too, knows a desperate man when she sees one. Her ladies were more than happy to make a tidy profit now instead of waiting what could be months . . . or years."

"Why did you do this?" And why didn't he simply give it to her while they were on land?

"Your father should have left at least half the company—if not all of it—to you," he said quietly. "I merely righted an injustice."

As he was doing with his father's bastards. This man who asked for little, yet gave so much. Who'd captured her heart.

His brow creased slightly. "Why you?" he asked solemnly.

Her body tensed and she scanned his features, striving to determine precisely what he was asking. "What?"

"I'm thirty-one years old, and until you, I'd never taken pleasure by being buried inside a woman. I took pleasure with hands or mouth, striving to discover all the various ways that the flesh could be replete with satisfaction. But with our first kiss"—he shook his head—"no, even before my lips ever touched yours, with your first command—*no names*—all I wanted to do was break the vow I made to never even risk being responsible for the bringing of a bastard into this world."

"I don't understand."

"What don't you understand?"

"Are you telling me . . . you were . . . a virgin?"

He arched a brow and tilted his head. "Until you, yes."

"Because you wanted no bastards."

He nodded. "And that was the only way to guarantee it."

"But you're so skilled when it comes to sexual encounters."

"As I said, I practiced all the numerous ways to find pleasure before the consummation. But what transpired between us in the greenhouse made me realize that I'm not so strong and righteous after all. I am my father's son."

Feeling as though she'd been bludgeoned, she cradled his face. "No, you're not. Not in any manner. I never knew him, but I've seen the results of his existence. And I saw you striving to undo the damage he had done. You're not responsible for his actions, and you are nothing, nothing like him. You're good and kind and—"

"And yet you left me. You gave me a farewell kiss. A farewell fuck to be honest."

"Because we were being forced into marriage and we'd both come to resent it after a while, if we didn't resent it already."

He studied her for a heartbeat, two, as if searching for something important. "When I was twenty-one, I must have told Rachel a thousand times that I loved her. It was so easy to say."

Not wanting to hear about his love for another, she almost strode away, but perhaps listening to his words would make it so she'd at least stop yearning for him.

"I loved her beauty, the way her lashes rested against her cheeks when she closed her eyes. The way she glided so elegantly into a room. The shade of her hair and her eyes. Everything I loved about her was visible. Everything I loved was what I could see and what would change over the years. Well, except for her eyes. However, none of the other things were permanent, and I'm left to wonder if my feelings for her would have remained permanent. But you—"

You were boring or *you aren't pretty at all* or *you . . .* She could imagine all the unflattering words he might say. She would stand here and allow him to batter her with them so her heart would break and no longer be his. She would reassemble the broken shards like she had rebuilt numerous automatons. Once her heart was again whole, she could reclaim it and make it hers.

"You . . . obviously I'm attracted to you. Otherwise, I never would have stepped into the room that first night. But what I love most about you are all the things that aren't visible. Your curiosity. Your clever mind that allows you to take things apart and put them back together. That allows you to envision something that's never existed before. Your kindness. Your strength. Your determination to see something through to the end, even when your family is giving you very little support. Your ability to walk away, to go your own way when you're convinced the path you're on isn't the right one."

He loved something about her. As much joy as that knowledge brought, she knew he could love something about her without actually loving her.

"Those three little words—*I love you*—so easy to say to Rachel, as though they were part of a game, are so hard to say to you. Because my depth of feeling for you is stronger and deeper than anything I've ever experienced before. And it terrifies me. The thought of saying them, only to lose you. But you need to know that I love you as I've never loved anyone before. The words carry a massive amount of weight with them because they are so very important. As they should be. They shouldn't be given lightly. But they should have been given before now. I love you, Nora, and I will love you until I draw my last breath. And that, I now know, was not true of what I felt for Rachel. It is, and will only ever be, true for you. All I want is for you to be happy. And if that means leaving me in order to carry on with your life as you want it to be, then at least leave me with a farewell kiss that I know is farewell."

Her heart was pounding. Tears stung her eyes. Her voice was hoarse as she pushed out the words. "You said you loved me."

"I do. I love you with all that I am, all I will ever be. And there is nothing that will poison my love for you."

"You read my letter."

"Several times. And I desperately want to kiss you right now. I just need to know if it's to be farewell or welcome home."

"It's I love you."

They came together as though they'd been apart for eons, with hunger, need, and gratitude. She hadn't wanted to leave him. It had been the hardest thing she'd ever done. But she'd believed down to her core that she had no choice. That together they'd never find the happiness they deserved.

But now she knew the silliness of that thought. Because happiness was being locked in his arms while his mouth did wicked things to hers. She imagined they were shocking some passengers and she didn't care. What pleased her the most, however, was that he didn't care. That they were being scandalous because couples didn't kiss with such wild abandon where anyone could see them.

He trailed his lips over her neck, causing pinpricks of pleasure to cascade through her. "I've locked up the country estate. I'll keep it maintained for the next generation, but it's not for us. I'll have to be in London when Parliament is in session, but when it's not I'll be in New York with you."

"I was thinking maybe a factory in England would work."

He lifted his head and gave her that devastating grin that the green fairy had fallen in love with that first night. Only now she realized it hadn't been the green fairy at all. It had been her. All along, everything that had transpired had been her.

"I have no doubt you could make it work."

There was another important matter that had to be resolved. "I won't give you bastards."

Sadness briefly touched his eyes before he nodded. "I can ensure that you don't."

By never having what they'd had the last time they were together. By denying her the powerful thrusts that he was so capable of delivering.

"So can I," she told him before pouring all the love she held for him into her smile. "Did you know that a ship captain can marry a couple?"

THAT NIGHT THEY were married on the deck of the ship while a few strangers, an abundance of stars, and a full moon looked on.

Afterward they waltzed over the wooden surface while a violinist performed a series of tunes that echoed out over the water. Leonora thought she quite possibly might never be happier than she was at that moment while her handsome husband held her gaze.

She wore the gown she'd been wearing the night she met him. He was wearing the evening attire that had adorned him when he'd gone down on bended knee and removed her slipper.

Later, they were nestled in his bed, holding each other, husband and wife, lethargic after a frenzied lovemaking followed by a slower one.

Her head rested on his chest, his heartbeat sounding in her ear. He leisurely stroked her back.

"I'll never grow tired of having you enveloping my cock when I push into you," he said quietly.

She still was having a difficult time believing that he'd never enjoyed the full breadth of lovemaking . . . until her. She'd always wanted to be special to someone. With him, she was.

"Johnny," she said softly, not certain if she really wanted him to hear her.

"Hmm?"

"If our time together in the greenhouse had ended differently, if we'd been successful at keeping our little tryst a secret, would you have invested in the company?"

"Yes."

"You have that much faith in the writing machine?"

"I have that much faith in you."

Tears filled her eyes. She eased up until she could hold his gaze. "I love you so much. Even if you'd had no plans to invest, I still would."

Rook studied the face of the woman who meant the world to him. "You'll love me even more after tomorrow."

She tilted her head to the side. "Why is that?"

"I've arranged for you to have a tour of the inner workings of the ship."

She laughed fully and throatily. His Lady of Laughter.

He rolled her over and took her mouth because it was time once again to make her his Lady of Sighs.

EPILOGUE

❦

STANDING on the high platform that was situated out-side her office, Leonora looked down on the activity taking place below her. It very much reminded her of a beehive, so much going on at once, so many people standing at various work stations attending to a single task, so many levers, pistons, switches, and knobs working in tandem to operate the pulley that slowly moved the products along a table that ran the length of the factory, the items becoming more and more what they were meant to be one step at a time.

Very much like people, she couldn't help but think.

With the money Sam had made from the sale of the company to Rook, he'd purchased himself a pub. He'd always loved talking and visiting with people, and his business allowed him to do exactly that as he pulled pints. Seldom was there an empty chair in the place. People lined the walls. She'd never known him to be so relaxed and happy. And he enjoyed the work.

Her mother had decided if Leonora wasn't going to use her title to assist her in getting into the ballrooms she craved, she'd handle the matter herself. She married an aging earl. Became a countess, herself. Made certain everyone knew of her elevated status. But two months after the wedding, her husband died and the title passed to the eldest of his five sons. The old earl hadn't had a chance to change his will to provide for her mother. The new earl bought her a small cottage far from London and offered her a modest allowance—on the condition that she never attended any ball, soiree, recital, or gathering of any kind hosted by a peer. He and his brothers found her too crass, too loud, too rude. "Embarrassing really," the new earl had admitted to Rook at a ball he and Leonora had attended. "Don't know how you put up with her, old chap."

On occasion, Leonora would provide her with passage to New York or bring her to London, but in spite of being a countess, she never received any invitations to elite affairs. Because of her unpleasantness, she was left to suffer the indignity of being ignored.

Unlike Rook's mother, who had risen in esteem because of the years she'd dutifully tended her ailing husband. Having a handsome, young lover at her side who was not averse to occasionally dancing with wall-flowers also garnered her invitations. She'd met him at Aiden's club. Julian had once told her that while he might dance or even continue to flirt with the ladies, his kisses were only for her. Both Rook and Aiden ensured he kept to that promise. No one dared to cross the two brothers.

As arms came around her, she leaned back against her husband's sturdy chest.

"It's so damned loud here," he said near her ear. "Reminds me of the Clock Tower."

"It's the sound of success. Although perhaps I should add bells to chime each time that one of our products is completed."

Orders for the writing machine were increasing yearly—at both the factory in America and the one here. She'd hired an overseer for the one near New York, but she, Rook, and their children crossed the Atlantic occasionally to make sure all ran as well as it should. Her tallying machine had been a triumph. She was currently designing one with a money drawer that would open once a customer's purchases were totaled. She expected it would meet with even more success.

Rook pressed his lips against the side of her neck. "We'll need to leave soon."

Taking one last look at the empire she was building, she nodded. "I'm ready."

It had become an annual tradition that on the day the previous Earl of Elverton had passed, his children and their families would gather in the garden of the residence that was now Leonora and Rook's home—the home where he'd once knocked over a statuette that had led to that awful late-night journey where he'd first realized the horrors his father could inflict.

Over the years, as word had spread that Rook was making atonement for his father's sins, others who claimed to be Elverton's children arrived to receive restitution. A few had alerted Rook that they no longer wanted the money—either out of guilt because they weren't his father's offspring as they'd claimed or because they felt they'd been paid what was owed. Then there were those who took the money offered and used it to better themselves. Leonora had even provided jobs in her factory to some of them.

"I can see the shadow of my late husband in so

many of their faces," Rook's mother, standing beside her, said softly.

She'd begun coming to these affairs a few years earlier, to serve as a hostess and welcome the earl's many by-blows into the fold. Leonora suspected she was also searching for the other two sons the earl had taken from her because she always asked a new arrival for the date when he was delivered to a baby farmer. Not all knew, of course, but occasionally one did.

"Johnny enjoys their company, hearing their tales," Leonora told her. Food, set out on trestle tables, was plentiful. Libations flowed, although she stayed away from absinthe.

"He always wanted siblings," the dowager countess said. "But after he was born, having given birth to four sons, I wasn't quite as firm as I'd once been. It's difficult to get with child when your husband has lost interest in visiting your bed. Although by then, I certainly didn't mourn his absence. I'd come to realize the sort of . . . monster he really was."

"Well, at least he's not here any longer to wreak havoc with lives."

"No, he's not. Neither is he missed. I suspect with Johnny's good deeds, a time will come when people won't even remember much about him."

Rook donated huge amounts to several charities, providing food, shelter, and education to those who lived in the poorer areas of London—the streets where many of his brothers and sisters had grown up.

She watched now as he, with Aiden and Finn at his side, walked toward them. They were all smiling, laughing. This gathering had become a joyous affair as connections were made, challenges were shared, bridges built, and bonds strengthened.

When they reached Leonora, Rook took her hand and bussed a quick kiss over her cheek. Then following Aiden's example, he kissed his mother's cheek before returning to his place near Leonora.

"You have a nice turnout this year," his mother said.

"Thirty." Rook shook his head. "I wonder how many I've missed."

"You can't focus on that," Aiden said. "Look how many you've helped."

One of those raced over and staggered to a stop beside Rook. He ruffled the growing boy's hair. "Hello, young Jack."

"Afternoon, my lord."

"You don't have to call me 'my lord.' You're my brother."

"Mum says I should." Rachel always brought her son, but never stayed to attend the afternoon gathering.

Rook winked. "Well, on this matter, I give you leave to ignore her. How are your lessons going?"

The lad was now at Eton, near enough that Rook visited with him often, was becoming the father the boy had never had.

Jack shrugged. "Well enough, I guess. Had to bloody a nose, though. Someone said something unkind about Mum."

"I bloodied a couple of noses while at Eton as well. Your brothers here didn't attend Eton but I suspect they bloodied a few noses here and there, too."

"We have to stand up for our mums," Aiden said.

Finn cupped his hand around the lad's shoulder. "I'm hungry. How about you?"

"I'm starving."

"Let's get some food, shall we?"

Jack nodded, and they walked away.

"I imagine he's going to teach the lad how to deliver a solid punch," Aiden said, with a grin. "He once terrified people for a living."

"Broke Father's arm one night, as I recall," Rook mused.

"Indeed. Bastard deserved—"

"That's someone who hasn't been here before," their mother said, almost on a hush.

Looking where she was, Leonora saw a tall man, finely dressed, his gaze slowly taking in his surroundings, lingering when it came to them. Just as the countess had said that she could see shadows of her husband in the features of those who were here today, so Leonora could see shadows of Rook in this man. Then with confidence in his step, he was striding toward them.

He came to a stop and nodded at Rook. "My lord."

"You know who I am?"

"I make it my business to know who people are."

"I'm at a disadvantage, sir, as I don't know who you are."

"Inspector Phineas Strange, Scotland Yard." He shook his head. "Apologies. It's how I'm accustomed to introducing myself because I usually arrive places in an official capacity. But not so here." He glanced back toward the gathering. "So all these are our father's bastards, are they?"

"Some are their spouses or children. Why did you not come forward sooner?"

"I wasn't certain I wanted to be associated with

such a vile creature. But then I finally realized I was granting him power over me he hadn't earned."

"You know the Earl of Elverton was your father?"

"All evidence would point to it."

"Care to share that evidence?"

"I was handed off to a baby farmer. That was his preferred method for ridding himself of us, was it not?"

"When?" the countess asked. "When were you handed off?"

He provided the date, and Leonora watched as all the blood seemed to drain from her face.

"I gave birth to a son that morning. I swaddled him in a blue blanket—"

Now it was the inspector who went pale. "With Elverton embroidered in the corner." He reached into the small pocket on his waistcoat, withdrew a scrap of cloth, and held it out. Many of the threads had thinned and broken over time, perhaps from numerous rubbings, but enough remained to make out the word.

The countess pressed fingers to her lips as tears welled in her eyes. "I named you Matthew. You're my firstborn. How you must hate me for letting him take you."

"Madam, I've seen the lengths people are forced to go to in order to survive. I hold no ill will toward you. Fortunately, the woman he paid for my care was benevolent. I also find hate a waste of energy."

The countess released a quiet sob, before reaching out a shaking hand and resting it against his cheek. "For the few hours I held you, I loved you a lifetime's worth."

"How fortunate a lad was I, then."

"I don't suppose I could hug you."

Without a word or any hesitation, he enclosed her in a solid embrace.

"I have three of my boys now." Her voice was thick with tears. "Who would have thought, after all these years . . ."

Leonora and Aiden were introduced.

"I'm another one of his bastards," Aiden said. "The countess is my mother as well."

"I can see the similarities in our features."

Leonora decided she liked the man when Rook told him about the recompense he was willing to pay and Inspector Strange refused the offer. "I've no need of it. Put it to better use elsewhere."

The dowager countess and Aiden took him off to meet his other siblings.

Rook moved closer and circled an arm around her shoulders. "I was hoping one of these days, another of her sons would turn up."

"Do you think the last will?"

"I suspect not all his bastards survived, Nora. And he kept no records of where he took them. Odious man."

With a governess in tow, their two sons and daughter were frolicking over the green, enjoying a ruffling of their hair or a hug from one of their many aunts and uncles.

"We have quite the large family, don't we?" she asked quietly.

"We do, indeed."

"And in a few months, it'll be a bit larger."

He looked down at her and grinned. "Will it, now?"

She nodded. "Around Christmas."

As he took her in his arms, leaned her back just

a little, pressed his lips to hers, and sighed, she was grateful that he was hers.

She became aware of distant cheers and clapping. A few hoots and some laughter. She could sense the number of people looking at them increasing.

Pulling back, he gave her a wicked grin. "They're family. They'll understand."

She furrowed her brow. "Understand what?"

He swept her up into his arms and called out, "Enjoy yourselves. I'm off to show my wife how much I love her."

Laughing, she buried her face into the curve of his neck as he began striding toward the residence. "For a man who once eschewed scandal, you're certainly embracing it now, Johnny."

"Only with you."

AUTHOR'S NOTE

〜〜〜

$\mathcal{B}$EGINNING in the early 1800s—and some claim even earlier—several versions of a typewriter were designed but never went into production. Christopher Sholes and Carlos Glidden are credited with designing what would eventually become recognized as the first commercially successful typewriter. It was patented in 1868.

However, it wasn't until 1873, in an effort to expand their revenue stream, that Remington and Sons entered into an agreement with the Sholes and Glidden company to mass produce the typewriter. The first one became available for sale in 1874.

Therefore, I thought it possible that Nora and her father could design what they believed was the first prototype for a "writing machine."

The typewriter originally met resistance as some felt it was too impersonal. But business owners embraced the typewriter when they realized it was speedier than handwriting. It wasn't until the 1890s that typewriters began being manufactured in Great Britain. Until then they were imported from America. But that's the beauty of literary license and fiction—we can stray a little bit from the truth.

As for the truth about lying and eyes turning purple . . . my mother taught me that when I was quite young. And I did, in fact, close my eyes the few times I fibbed—until I realized I was giving myself away. In later years, we often laughed when sharing that memory.